The Sweet Spot

The Sweet Spot

Anneli Lort

Acknowledgements

I would like to thank my wonderful mother for her constant support and belief in my abilities. She instilled a love of books into me at a very early age and for that I am eternally grateful.

I also want to thank my friends for their unwavering support and encouragement, in particular the amazing Alison Hanmer for her beautiful editing skills, Freda Jackson who was meticulous in her proofreading, and the grammar queen that is Cathy Longhurst. Also Nikky, Emily and Pete who put up with my constant moaning when things weren't going quite so well and held my hand when I needed a confidence boost.

Given the opportunity to produce my own book cover I turned to the best fine artist and illustrator I know, my talented friend Louise Mizen Ferguson. She perfectly captured my vision of Appleton Vale with her stunning creation and I can't thank her enough.

Having worked in public relations for a number of global sports brands throughout my career I had an access-all-areas pass to some of the world's greatest events. Here I saw for myself the tension, drama and emotions that were played out behind the scenes and I was there to witness first-hand what really happened before and afterwards. I used this unique insight to develop an idea that eventually became The Sweet Spot.

I offer my heartfelt thanks to the many elite professional golfers on the European and US PGA Tours that I was fortunate to work and socialise with for over two decades. They unwittingly provided me with enough material, both on and off the golf course, for the entire Appleton Vale series! Thank you also to the managers, Tour officials, agents and the many wonderful journalists I met during the course of my work. Through you all I learnt more about golf than I ever needed or wanted to! A special thank you must go to a golfer who wishes to remain anonymous – trust me, he knows who he is! He expertly guided me around St Andrews, pointing out which shots could make or break even the world's most talented golfers playing in the pressure cooker that is The Open Championship.

Finally, thank you also to Miika Hannila and the team at Next Chapter for taking a chance on me.

For Henry, Woody, Hector and Milo

Prologue

She took a deep breath, closed her eyes and muttered, "Don't screw it up, don't screw it up, for Christ's sake, don't let him screw it up."

The tension was unbearable. All around her, thousands of men, women and children held their breath as they watched him contemplate his next move. They were tightly packed into grandstands, a sea of eager faces anticipating a much- longed-for victory - it was so close they could almost touch it.

On the ground, spectators jostled for position in crowds ten-deep, surging forward time and time again to get a better view of the man poised to deliver long-awaited glory.

The weight of expectation on him was palpable, the air thick with shared desire. Yet he remained oblivious, his concentration unbreakable.

She marvelled at his absolute focus, seemingly devoid of all emotion as he stood on the threshold of greatness.

Every move he made was deliberate, unhurried; he was seeking perfection. To the crowds watching, he was painstakingly slow. She could hardly bear to watch as he made his final preparations, and found herself clutching the arm of an equally enthralled stranger.

He paused and looked into the crowd, his eyes scanning faces, searching for hers. A fleeting look of panic crossed his face when he couldn't find her. She stepped forward, conscious of his need for reassurance at this most crucial moment and, as their eyes locked, she smiled in encouragement.

Moments later, the crowd erupted. Rapturous applause and cries of delight rang out. They were chanting his name, on their feet, friends and strangers, hugging each other in triumph.

She was surrounded by television cameras and photographers, shoving and elbowing each other in their desperation to get closer to her. Unaware of the media frenzy, her eyes were fixed on him. He looked over to where she was standing. They held each other's gaze. For a brief moment in time, it was like no one else on earth existed.

Chapter 1

Olivia swore blue murder as she was nearly taken out by an oncoming battered Ford Fiesta speeding down the middle of the winding country lane. "What do you think you're driving? A bloody Routemaster bus?" she screamed at the passing car, only to be rewarded with the middle finger and a bundle of profanities from its elderly gentleman driver. She shook her head in frustration and pulled off the road into a lay-by overlooking the village of Appleton Vale, her new home.

She was unprepared for the simple beauty of the village nestling in the valley. Of course, it helped that she had arrived on an unusually lovely October day, the sun at its very finest angle, hanging low in a motionless, brilliant-blue sky.

As she breathed in the heavenly countryside air, she briefly recalled the conversation she'd had with her editor, Stella, when she'd asked for a sabbatical.

"Are you completely stark raving mad? You'll hate it in the sticks and I need you here," Stella said, astounded.

"Don't stand in my way," pleaded Olivia. "I've got to get out of London, it's suffocating and I need time and space to sort my head out. I almost died," she reminded her boss.

"And writing a book for a known misogynist is going to help?" was Stella's disbelieving riposte. "I've heard he's got a foul temper."

"Really, you're using that to force my hand?" Olivia shot back. "I'll be fine. Besides, there's no way any man is ever laying a hand on me again, well not the way Saul did."

Olivia winced as she remembered the violent battering she'd received from her ex-boyfriend. She'd spent a week in hospital and several more licking her wounds. During those dark first days, she'd swung so dramatically from one emotion to another that she'd given herself mental whiplash.

But by the time her body had healed and the bruises had faded into obscurity, Olivia had hatched a plan to get her life back on track. Offered the chance to ghostwrite Sebastian Bloom's autobiography, she'd jumped at the chance to do it and leave London at the same time. Hopefully, getting her teeth into a new and all-consuming project would help her forget her recent past.

And now here she was, about to enter the unknown world of quintessential English village life, and she was terrified. She hadn't even seen the cottage she had rented yet, let alone visited the village that would be home for the next twelve months.

She took in a second deep breath of fresh, sweet-smelling, country air and surveyed the scene sweeping down the valley before her. Chocolate-box cottages surrounded a pristine village green. Squinting slightly, she could make out a riverside pub and a moss-covered church with a giant oak tree casting a protective shadow over its tiny graveyard.

Jumping back into the car, she pulled away from the roadside and wound her way down the hill, through the meadows and rolling fields of Appleton Vale, turning into the village and her new life.

Chapter 2

Sebastian slumped, head in hands, on a bench in the far reaches of the locker room, regretting his ill fortune for a second day in a row. After shooting a hideous eighty-six earlier, following an equally shocking eighty-four in the first round, he was contemplating his future as a professional golfer.

Standing over him, a hand reassuringly on his shoulder, was his friend and colleague José de Silva – who'd also had an appalling week of golf in Seville.

"You've got to pull yourself out of this my friend," José said softly. "This path for you is no good, yes?"

Sebastian was in turmoil. His life had unravelled spectacularly over the last two years and he was nearing rock bottom. He'd lost almost everything dear to him through a chain of events for which he blamed himself. Over time, his pain had turned to an anger that threatened to consume him fully.

Unable to temper the rage building inside, he lashed out at José. "Fuck off José," Sebastian snarled.

"Seriously, just fuck off home to your perfect wife and perfect kids and leave me alone."

José didn't flinch, well aware that his friend's tragic loss was the cause of his anger. They'd been living in each other's pockets for almost two decades, firstly as amateur players and then on Tour, and knew each other inside out. They were as close as brothers, and it had been José whom Sebastian had called in the immediate aftermath of the tragedy that had wrecked his life.

"There's a car outside and the plane is waiting. Go home," José said with gentle encouragement. "This has gone on too long, no? You need rest, to find yourself again, my friend."

Sebastian looked up at José, his face contorted with pain. "Find myself?" he snorted. "Fucked if I can do that, wouldn't even know where to start. You saw me out there, I'm a fucking shambles."

"You make it worse for yourself with all the women and the drinking like the fishes. The press loves you, but now they write about sex and not golf, yes?" said his Brazilian friend.

A ghost of a smile crossed Sebastian's tortured face and he looked up. "Drink like a fish José, not fishes." Standing up, he grabbed his gear and stalked towards the exit with José hot on his heels.

Less than forty-five minutes later, after dropping José at the hotel, he climbed on board the plane and was instantly grateful for the sanctuary of the private jet.

"Can I get you anything Mr Bloom?" asked the pretty hostess as soon as he'd taken his seat.

"Scotch please, and you might as well leave the bottle," he replied grimly. He knew drinking himself into oblivion wasn't the answer to his problems, but he craved the temporary respite it gave him from thinking about the role he'd played in his own downfall.

He looked straight through the hostess as she handed him his drink in a gleaming crystal tumbler, not noticing how pretty she was, or her attempts to flirt with him. He swirled the ice around the glass and knocked it back, pouring another almost immediately. Staring out of the window as the sleek jet cut a swathe through the thickening cloud, he tried to turn his dark thoughts to happier ones, to a time when he was truly content.

How has it come to this? Sebastian asked himself as the plane reached its cruising altitude. *Being a selfish, arrogant, stupid prick, that's how.*

Sebastian Bloom came from what country folk might have called *good stock*: a wealthy family, and a sprawling country pile he had inherited at the age of seventeen. The passing of his adored and glorious mother, Sabrina Bloom, two years' previously from breast cancer, had been the catalyst for his father's destructive, grief-stricken drinking. He'd descended a dark road, then climbed back into recovery, searching for his inner self. That's when his father, William, had signed Appleton Manor over to Sebastian and then promptly disappeared off in search of spirituality. Sebastian's younger sister, Georgiana, had taken the death of her mother and the desertion by her father very hard, and he'd done his best to put his own grief aside and care for her.

Privately educated and given every opportunity to excel, Sebastian had known from a young age that golf would be his career. He had grasped it quickly and naturally when his father had first taken him to the local country club at the tender age of three. Encouraged by William, and coached by up-and-coming club professional, Hugh McLauchlin, Sebastian's game developed rapidly. By the age of ten, he was comfortably capturing the scalps of most of the senior club members on a weekly basis.

He was fast-tracked into the West Chesterton County team at the age of twelve and spent the next five years winning every junior competition going, much to the envy of his peers. Single-minded and ambitious, filled with the unerring confidence of a teenager who had lived a secure and idyllic childhood, Sebastian always focused on being the best and playing every shot like it was the one that clinched The Open Championship title.

At seventeen, Sebastian became the youngest amateur golfer ever to play in the Walker Cup, a team competition between Great Britain & Ireland and the USA. He won every one of his matches, his national side clinched the cup for the first time in a decade, and Sebastian was on his way to stardom.

It all seemed so easy then, Sebastian thought as he poured himself another scotch. *How did I get it so wrong?*

Just two years ago he had been at the pinnacle of his career, world number one with three Major titles to his name and countless other tournament wins around the globe. He was the golden boy of British sport, the media loved him, his peers respected and envied him in equal measure, and the public adored him. He had been living a charmed life and he knew it. His game was always linked to his emotions, he played best when he was happy and, up until two years ago, he had always had Ellie by his side... loving him, encouraging him to be the best he could be.

But she's dead, they both are, and I'm finished, he muttered under his breath, as if speaking it aloud would make it more real to him. *How did I get her so wrong?*

Ellie had been the love of his life, or so he had thought. They had met by chance in a swanky new bar in London and he had been immediately captivated by her. She was stunning, with a long, lean, gazelle-like body that fascinated him. The instant they locked eyes he was hooked. The chemistry was undeniable, and within an hour he had abandoned his friends and taken Ellie into the bed in his luxurious waterfront apartment in Chelsea. Fast work, even by his standards, but he was fully consumed by the raw sex appeal that had oozed from her pores like nectar.

It was no secret that Sebastian loved sex: he really loved it. His sexual prowess and list of conquests was renowned on the golf circuit and in the celebrity gossip columns; he had been a playboy, pure and simple. He had a lusty appetite and in Ellie he had met his match. They married within three months and she had taken to her new life with gusto, as an adoring wife and a popular WAG on Tour.

Bursting with happiness, Sebastian began to attack the golf course like a thing possessed, playing both the European and US PGA Tours, achieving success and fame beyond anything he had ever imagined. Just a year after their wedding he claimed his first Major victory at the US Open and the following year at The Masters he won his second with ease, conquering Augusta National, a notoriously difficult course.

During The Masters Tournament the next year, when Sebastian returned to defend his title, Ellie became pregnant. He could pinpoint the day, time and place she had conceived and he thought he was truly blessed, even by his agnostic standards.

Earlier that night they had rowed about her outrageous flirting with his arch-nemesis, US golf star Troy McLoud, at a sponsor's event they had all attended.

"What the fuck do you think you're doing with McLoud?" he snapped at her as soon as they got inside the car taking them back to the house they were renting for the week.

"I don't know what you mean," Ellie replied sweetly.

"Yes, you fucking do. Are you trying to make me jealous?"

"Jealous? No, darling, I'm not. Maybe I'm just making you hot for me?" She unzipped his trousers and slipped her hand inside.

"You little bitch," Sebastian growled, pushing hard against the palm of her caressing hand. "Don't you ever do that again, and most definitely not with him, he's the biggest cock out there and I won't have him anywhere near my wife."

"He may be the biggest cock out there, but yours is by far the biggest one in here and I want it in me," Ellie gave a throaty laugh before bending her head down and taking Sebastian deep inside her mouth.

"Never let it be said that I'm one to deny a woman her pleasure - and it seems her pleasure is to pleasure me," he said, winking at the chauffeur who was watching the whole proceedings through his rear-view mirror.

The ten-minute ride home had been torture for Sebastian, albeit the pleasurable kind, and it was all he could do to stop himself coming in her mouth, right in front of the voyeuristic chauffeur. As soon as they'd got inside the house, Sebastian had pulled Ellie's dress up, ripped off her pants with one hand, bent her over the table in the hall, and had screwed his wife with more lust than he thought even he possessed. The idea of that American bastard McLoud touching his wife had certainly stoked his fire, and had driven him deeper and deeper into Ellie.

That week Sebastian had successfully defended his title, returning home with his second US Masters title and, unbeknown to them both, a pregnant wife.

Right on schedule, nine months later, a perfect baby girl had come into the world and turned their lives upside down. Sebastian was captivated immediately by Elizabeth India Bloom, Ellie less so.

At first Sebastian had thought his wife must have been suffering from post-natal depression, but as time went by, he began to realise that his beautiful, delightful daughter held no delights for her mother.

"She's ruined my body and stolen my husband," Ellie raged when he confronted her about her apathy towards their child.

"Stolen your husband? Don't be so fucking ridiculous. And I can't possibly comment on your body, darling, since you won't let me near you these days. Never thought you'd turn into a frigid bitch," Sebastian shot back his reply with equal venom, immediately hating himself for his reaction when he knew she needed his support now more than ever.

"You're never here, and when you are it's the 'Sebastian and Lizzie show'. I'm so far down your fucking list of priorities these days," Ellie spat. "You love her more than you love me, FACT, and don't bother to try and deny it, you rotten bastard." Ellie was hell bent on getting a reaction out of her husband and knew all the right buttons to press.

Sebastian's temper cranked up to maximum the moment she turned the blame on their daughter and he was unable to stay calm and rational.

"Jesus Christ, you really are a cold-hearted bitch, aren't you? She's your flesh and blood, made out of our love for one another. Of course she's my fucking priority, she should be yours, too, but you're too self-obsessed and shallow to realise it. So you're not travelling around the world in private jets any more, or parading around like Queen Bee with the other WAGs, but look what you've got here. A beautiful daughter, a stunning home and a husband who would walk over hot coals for you. You've never wanted for anything, I've spoilt you rotten and continue to do so. What more do you fucking want from me?"

Ellie rounded on him, eyes blazing with pure hatred, "I want things to go back to how they were before Lizzie, and I want you to myself."

"So you wish we'd never had her?" Sebastian whispered, utterly shocked and appalled. He shook his head disbelievingly, unable to comprehend the ugly words that had come out of her beautiful mouth.

"You're damn right I do. And I wish I'd never met you," Ellie replied in a menacing tone that had rocked Sebastian further.

That had been the start of the end of their marriage.

Sebastian knew they were growing apart, they both did. Yet he couldn't give up his career when he was playing so well, and in his mind Ellie shouldn't have expected him to. Instead of addressing their issues, Sebastian hit the course with renewed single-mindedness, continuing his quest for golfing greatness. But, without Ellie at his side, his game started to stutter and he began, for the first time in his life, to doubt himself.

Having just arrived home after a three-week stint in Asia, Ellie blindsided Sebastian on Christmas Eve, announcing that she was leaving him and taking Lizzie with her.

"You're doing what?" he whispered, stunned.

"I want a divorce Sebastian," Ellie replied, unable to meet his eyes.

"I know we've had problems, but this? Come on Ellie, you're not even giving me a chance here."

"You're never here to give a chance to, you stupid, pathetic man," Ellie sneered. "This is all on you, entirely your fault for not loving me enough and not giving me what I needed to be happy."

"And what exactly is that Ellie? Go on, tell me what it is you need that I'm clearly not capable of giving you," Sebastian challenged her.

"The life I want, the life I deserve," Ellie said, sulkily.

"Which is what? Jet setting, diamonds, publicity?" he couldn't believe what he was hearing. His tone softened, "Don't you think you're being bit unreasonable, darling? I had no idea you were this unhappy, but if you give me a chance I'll make it up to you."

"It's too late, you've changed. What happened to the fun, sexy, extravagant man I married? You promised me the earth," Ellie pouted. Sebastian moved towards her. He wanted to take her in his arms and magic away her pain, to tell her she was everything to him, that he had enough room in his heart to love both her and their daughter equally. She backed away from his outstretched arms and shook her head defiantly.

"It's over Sebastian, I don't love you anymore," she looked at him with pity.

"You think you can live without all of this?" He threw his arms expansively around the enormous hallway of his ancestral home, filled with fabulous antiques and art.

"I won't have to, soon I'll have more than you'll ever be able to give me." Ellie's eyes glinted with greed.

"If you think you can screw me in court then you've another thing coming, darling," Sebastian said in a cold, low voice, his anguish and shock suddenly turning into bitterness and rage. "And if you think you're setting one foot out of that door with my daughter in tow then you're seriously mistaken."

"Why would I need your money when I've found a man with much more, in fact a vast amount more, than you have?" she replied, smiling triumphantly.

"You've met someone else?" he said, disbelievingly.

"Yes."

"Who?" Sebastian's heart shattered into a million pieces. It was dawning on him that this was more than just an argument they'd fix in the bedroom, as they had done so many times in the past.

Ellie looked sheepish and blushed as she replied, "Troy."

"McLoud? You're just fucking with my head, you wouldn't dare," he roared.

"You just watch me. He's a better man than you'll ever be," Ellie screamed. "And he's dynamite in the sack!" she threw at him for good measure.

Reeling, blind with rage, Sebastian rounded on her and in a moment of madness lashed out, slapping her across the face and pinning her against the wall as he ranted furiously. When he finished, he stood, shell-shocked, as his wife dragged his darling Lizzie out to the car. Unable to muster a response, to summon the will to beg her to stay, Sebastian simply watched as they walked out of his life forever.

He wasn't aware of the moment he dropped to the floor and for how long he had been sitting there, his misery engulfing his entire being, but it had turned dark outside by the time there was a knock on the door.

"It's Christmas fucking Eve, just piss off whoever you are," Sebastian shouted from his place on the floor.

"Mr Bloom, please open the door, it's the police."

Sebastian stood up, opened the door and gestured for the two officers to come inside.

"What's so important that you're disturbing me on Christmas Eve?"

"Sir, perhaps you'd like to take a seat," the older of the two policemen, unflustered by Sebastian's tone, urged him gently.

"I'm fine standing," Sebastian replied.

"I'm sorry, sir, there's no easy way to say this. There's been an accident. Both Mrs Bloom and your daughter were killed instantly when an HGV hit them on the Fiddlebury road."

Upon hearing those words, Sebastian's world crumbled at his feet and he was plunged into a hole so dark and disturbing he'd been unable to find even a tiny chink of light: there was no escape.

For the two years after he lost his wife and daughter, Sebastian was alone. Still heartbroken and wracked with guilt at driving his family to their deaths, the future looked cold and dark and unforgiving. He had watched his father's life follow a now-chillingly familiar pattern - somewhere inside he couldn't help feeling resigned to history repeating itself.

The season was almost over, and Sebastian couldn't wait. For the first time in his golfing life all he wanted to do was throw his clubs in the back of the garage and forget about things, take some time out to re-evaluate his life and reassess his game. He needed help, with his game at least, and now he wasn't afraid to admit it. It was time to go back to basics.

But before that, he faced baring his soul to a journalist who he'd been told was 'keen' to ghostwrite his autobiography. She was due to start next week, and was apparently taking it so seriously that she'd upped sticks from London and moved to Appleton Vale for the next year. *More fool her*, thought Sebastian, with a grimace. It was the last thing he needed, but he had no choice. Sebastian was never one to back out of a commitment. Hidden somewhere deep beneath the gloom, he still had a sense of honour, and a deal was a deal. He would just have to suck it up.

Chapter 3

Boris! *Heel!*" shouted a panting Dee Dee Bains. It was too late. Boris the Jack Russell terrorist had taken off after the rabbit that was now running for its little life, and Dee Dee was struggling to catch up. Well, she was in her sixties, although she would never admit that to anyone. She had lived in Appleton Vale for the past twenty-five years with her partner, Jane Coombes, running the local tearooms, spreading gossip and hosting the weekly book club. Shunning the WI in nearby Fiddlebury - "too old" - Dee Dee and Jane lived for village life, their neighbours, long walks in the hills with their surrogate child, Boris, and of course, each other.

Dee Dee, pausing for breath, looked up to the brow of the hill where she spotted the lean, striking form of a young woman taking in the scenery next to a dark grey car. *Could she be our new resident?* she pondered, wondering what the girl's story could be. Everyone who came to Appleton Vale had a tale to tell, and Dee

Dee saw it as her neighbourly duty to root it out of each and every villager. She turned on her heel and started for the path back to the village, pausing to inform the missing Boris that he would be left to fend for himself unless he came back *right now*. Perhaps she would pop into the Riverside Inn later to see if anyone had met the new girl.

As 'new girl' Olivia turned left past the village green at the bidding of her satnav, Tom Feltham, owner of the Riverside Inn and Bistro, was overseeing a delivery from the local brewery. He and his wife Susie took pride in sourcing and serving as much local produce as possible, which attracted punters from far and wide. Tom, being a natural host, strode over to where Olivia had parked up and introduced himself.

"You must be our new neighbour." he said cheerily. "I'm Tom Feltham. I own the pub with my wife, Susie. We were wondering when you were going to turn up." Tall and lean, Tom had floppy, mouse-coloured hair that kept falling into his eyes. His face was soft and had kindness etched into it, along with a permanent but genuine smile.

Olivia paused before offering her hand to greet Tom. How much did the locals know about her already? She had heard village life could be intrusive. "Hi, I'm Olivia," she smiled. "Pleased to meet you. The estate agent said you would have the keys for the cottage for me to pick up?"

"Indeed I do," he smiled and nodded his head towards the pub. "Why don't you come and meet Susie and have a drink while I get them? You must be parched after your journey."

"That would be great," said Olivia, but as she started to follow Tom into the pub, a muffled *woof* reminded her that Hector, her gorgeous, goofy golden retriever, was still wedged in the car, surrounded by various items of luggage and boxes that Olivia had brought from London.

Outwardly, Hector had the appearance of the perfectly-trained dog, with his lazily wagging tail, goofy smile and gentle nature. However, as Olivia opened the door he bounded out and made a bee-line for Tom, jumping up and sending him flying, narrowly missing the open hatch of the pub's cellar.

"Hector, NO," she shouted too late, and rushed over to where Tom was lying on the ground. "Are you ok? I'm so sorry, he doesn't have an off button. He's possibly the worst-trained dog in the world," said Olivia, with the practiced, disarming smile she had used so often to make amends for Hector's boisterous behaviour. "Does your pub welcome ASBO dogs, as well as their owners?"

Tom laughed, picked himself up and dusted himself down, "Of course! Come on then, Susie will be delighted you're here, she does love a new face in the village."

It was the end of the lunchtime rush and the pub was emptying as people went about the rest of their day, many to return later for a swift half before going home for dinner. Olivia breathed in the heady mixture of delicious scents wafting from the restaurant, and the slow burning wood from the logs hissing away in the inglenook fireplace that dominated the room. In front of her lay an immaculate mahogany bar, and beyond that a cosy but stylish restaurant. Oak beams and uneven creaking floorboards added to the charm, and the atmosphere was warm and welcoming.

A series of delicate, exquisitely detailed watercolours adorned the walls. "By our resident famous artist, Charles Harkley," Tom said, nodding at the paintings. "You'll see his work dotted all around the village. Ah, here's Susie now. Susie, Olivia."

"Olivia," Susie cried, pulling her into a bear hug. "Welcome to Appleton Vale! You're going to love it here, everyone does."

Olivia smiled. She usually liked to take time to get to know people, but something about Susie, aided possibly by the very large glass of red wine that had been thrust into her hand, made her feel like she had come home and all her troubles would be swept away.

Susie was as short as Tom was tall, and they looked an odd couple. An elfin crop of brown hair framed her oval face, accentuating her huge grey eyes. Her cheeks were full and rosy, and she too had a smile that seemed to be an enduring fixture.

Turning to Tom, Susie said, "Darling, can you call Mandy and see if she would come in later? I could really do with a night off."

"Your wish is my command," Tom replied, doffing an imaginary cap as he pulled out his mobile phone.

"We work round the clock so we really cherish the nights we get off together," explained a blushing Susie. "And we're trying for a baby," she whispered to Olivia.

At that moment, the door crashed open, hitting the coat stand behind it. A draught of autumn air and wood-smoke hit Olivia, and she looked around to see the very man she was here to work with, Sebastian Bloom, six feet and two inches of perfection. He was broad-shouldered with thick dark hair, cut short; his olive-skinned, angular face was breathtakingly chiselled, with a defiant chin. Dressed casually in what she recognised as an ultra-stylish, ultra-expensive Damian de Landre tweed jacket and jeans, he commanded the room before he set foot in it.

They hadn't met before, even though she'd spent time at some of the more prestigious golf tournaments interviewing his peers. She knew he was good-looking, but close up he was mesmerising. Sebastian had the rare condition of Heterochromia, which had gifted him one smoldering brown eye and one exotic dark green eye under long, thick lashes. For the first time in her working life, and with all the fabulously famous sporting stars she had met, she went a little weak at the knees. *Pull yourself together, Carmichael,* said the little voice of reason in her head. *This is purely professional.*

Sebastian strode across the saloon towards her, stopping briefly to kiss Susie and exchange greetings with Tom. "You must be Olivia?" He offered his hand and Olivia, somewhat nervous, extended hers towards him.

"Yes, that's me, guilty as charged," she grinned and noticed a ghost of a smile cross his face.

"Welcome to Appleton Vale. I trust you've settled in already. I'd like to start work as soon as possible if that's ok with you? Tomorrow morning around nine o'clock?"

It was more of a demand than a suggestion. Olivia immediately switched into work mode, her professionalism at the very top of her list of attributes when it came to dealing with superstars and their egos.

"Tomorrow's Saturday, not strictly a working day," she replied carefully, matching her words with a smile so as not to appear rude.

"Does that make a difference?" Sebastian replied. "Feel free to bring the dog if you want to." He stooped down and acknowledged Hector's presence with a loving chin scratch and then he was gone, leaving Olivia smarting in his wake, but unable to stop herself from sneaking an admiring look as he walked away.

She swung back round to the bar and looked at Susie, whose embarrassment was evident. "Who the hell does he think he is?" she demanded through gritted teeth. "I know he's had had a rough time of it lately but that was just downright rude. I haven't even set foot inside the cottage, let alone had a chance to settle in."

Susie, flustered, leant over the bar and thrust an envelope into Olivia's hand. "He's a wonderful man, take my word for it." She was becoming an expert in explaining away Sebastian's boorish behaviour. "These are the keys to Brook Cottage. Get yourself sorted, and tend to Sebastian in your own time. His bark is worse than his bite, and I'm pretty sure you can stand up for yourself. Don't judge him on what you've read and what your journalist friends have told you, he really is smashing when he's on form," she added with a smile. "Now, off you go. Pop in later and I'll have something delicious ready for your supper; you can't cook on your first night."

"I thought you were having a night between the sheets with Tom?" Olivia raised an eyebrow and smiled.

"He can wait. Besides, it's only supper," Susie smiled warmly. "So I'll see you later?"

Olivia smiled, nodded her agreement and pulled on her jacket to brave the unseasonably cold wind outside. She didn't have far to go as Brook cottage was just fifty yards down the road from the pub. *Convenient*, she thought, *when writer's block sets in, of course.*

With Hector trailing behind, clearly annoyed at being asked to leave the warmth of the pub and the possibility of the odd chip making its way down to floor level, Olivia paused outside the cottage, already delighted with what she saw. Nestled behind a white picket fence was a beautifully proportioned, flint-built cottage, quaint and quirky with slanting window frames, a crooked chimney and the remnants of what had been a full-blooming wisteria crawling across the honeyed stone face.

She pushed through the gate. Sliding the heavy iron key into the front door, she paused, excited at what she might find inside.

Olivia hadn't been that bothered when she initially took on an agent to find her something to rent in the area, she just wanted to get out of London fast. Terry Gullan, the agent, had called and told her that he had found a real gem. "This type of property just doesn't come up in Appleton Vale... *ever*," he'd enthused. So, on the word of a man she had never met, and an estate agent at that, Olivia had signed herself up for a year, renting a house she had never seen.

With trepidation, she opened the door and stepped inside, but she was pleasantly surprised to be hit with a wall of warmth: someone had been in and turned on the heating. The light was fading outside; the long winter night starting to set in. Olivia flicked on the light switch by the door, and gasped at the picture-perfect scene before her. The house couldn't have been more 'her' if she had designed it herself. Brook Cottage looked quaint and chintzy from the outside, but inside it was all mod cons and understated elegance which somehow blended seamlessly with the character of the property.

Oak-beamed ceilings set off the smooth, original flagstones on the floors, and an inglenook fireplace in the centre of the lounge added yet more character. Walking into the kitchen she found a note fastened to the fridge door with a magnet:

Welcome to Appleton Vale. I hope you don't mind me taking the liberty of popping in to get the place ready for you, there's a little something in the fridge to celebrate your new home. I clean for you on Tuesdays but am sure we'll meet in the village before that. Sincerely, Pat Cowan.

She moved from room to room, turning on the pretty lamps and drawing the heavy, lined curtains. Heading up the creaking stairs, she turned the corner at the top and poked her head in the first door, the master suite, and she gasped at how pretty it was. A huge wooden bed stood in the centre of the room, covered with a thick goosedown duvet adorned with pink and white rosebud bedding. Matching bedside tables and a pink velvet chaise longue completed the furnishings and a small wood-burning stove was ready to light. Two further doors in the bedroom housed a dressing room and an en-suite bathroom that had come straight out of a Ralph Lauren catalogue.

After exploring upstairs, Olivia went in search of Hector. She could hear him shuffling round under the bushes at the back of the cottage. Opening the stable door from the kitchen, she set off down the little path that led, to her delight, to a tiny waterside terrace with what, in summer, would be a rose-covered pergola.

Olivia hugged herself, partially to keep out the cold wind, but also because for the first time in almost a year she felt content.

A sudden bleep from her mobile brought her back to reality and she pulled it out of her pocket to find a text from Sebastian.

So are we on for tomorrow?

Smarting again at his abruptness but resolving to remain professional, Olivia tapped her reply,

Hi Sebastian, if it's OK with you I'd prefer to start on Monday as per our

contract. I could do with a little time to settle in to your wonderful village and find my feet. I'll see you bright and early on Monday morning, have a fabulous weekend. Olivia Carmichael.

She re-read the text, not wanting to give Sebastian any reason to be offended and, satisfied she had hit the right tone, pressed send.

"I think we've landed a tricky one here," she said to Hector, who rolled onto his back and covered his eyes with his paws.

Chapter 4

Olivia had had a succession of pallid, pimpled, and slightly awkward boyfriends in her teenage years, most with a loping presence and ruffled long hair calculated to underline their cool, art-school wannabe credentials. As she looked back now, she could no longer remember much about any of them, but what she did recall was the revolting aroma of stale rollups and unwashed denim that were de rigueur in the 1990s.

After having completed her English Literature degree at Durham University, Olivia had returned to Hertfordshire clutching a First and had walked straight into a job on the local newspaper. Thanks to hard work and an injection of good luck in the form of a local kid called Tom Illingworth - who's career she had championed and now a star striker at Manchester United - she'd been offered a job on the sports desk at *The Times*, where she had met Saul Bianchi.

It had only been Saul's second day at the newspaper when they had collided. Olivia had been running all over the building looking for her boss to sign off additional expenses for an *At home with David and Victoria Beckham* feature that had been dangerously close to deadline. Stepping out of the lift, eyes firmly on his mobile, Saul had walked straight into her, knocking her flat on her back.

"Shit, sorry," she stammered, clambering to her feet. "I'm so bloody clumsy, are you ok?" *'Holy shit, you're gorgeous'* she had muttered under her breath.

Saul grinned a slightly crooked smile, and offered a gracious, "No problem, I'm Saul, the news desk newbie." He shrugged his shoulders and carried on with his day, and Olivia wanted to die. The first hot man she had met in a very long time and she had practically dropped on her knees in front of him.

She hadn't had to wait long to see Saul again. The next day, he sauntered over to her desk and asked her out to lunch.

"Hey, recovered from your fall yesterday?" he joked. "Join me for lunch." It was a command, not a request.

"Err, OK," Olivia stuttered, completely floored by his confidence and arrogance.

"There's a great little Italian I know close by, let's go." He grabbed her hand, pulled her up from her desk and walked briskly towards the lift.

"I like you Olivia," Saul said in a sexy, low voice. "And don't look so surprised. Dave on the picture desk filled me in, I know all your dirty secrets," he continued with a glint in his eye.

I'm going to fucking kill Dave, Olivia thought briefly *or perhaps not... Christ he's so hot.*

The restaurant had been dark, cramped and lively, and they'd had a wonderful meal. Within four months Olivia had deserted her disapproving best friend and flat-mate, Emily Delevigne, and moved into Saul's loft in trendy Clerkenwell.

The first two years had been wonderful. Saul scooped a few big stories and was quickly promoted and Olivia had begun to gain a reputation as the go-to writer for sports lifestyle features. The money had been good, their social life had been crazy and the sex had been outstanding. They had been happy until Saul knowingly misquoted a prominent politician, landing the MP in hot water, the newspaper with a libel suit, and Saul out of work.

Unable to secure another job in journalism, very quickly his social drinking had turned into a bottle of vodka a day and his once flash-in-the-pan temper had begun to surface more frequently. He started staying out on the odd night here and there, and when Olivia had become suspicious and questioned him, he quickly turned on her, making her feel guilty for questioning his loyalty.

Emily had been enraged.

"Just fucking leave the bastard, Liv," she ranted down the phone line. "You've turned into a weepy, pathetic bag of nerves, just tell him to take a walk, and come back to the flat."

Laughing through her tears, Olivia sniffed and replied, "Don't hold back, tell me how you really feel."

"I've made no bones about not liking him. He's an arrogant tosser and you can do way better."

"It's complicated," Olivia sighed. "But you're right, it's over."

"Yeah, yeah, yeah," said Emily. Olivia could imagine her rolling her eyes in frustration. "Shit, is that the time? I've got a sodding meeting with some wanky investment bankers. I'll call you later. If you're serious then get packing. Love you."

Emily had rung off and Olivia had begun the task of packing up her life, anxious to go before Saul had the opportunity to return.

Her suitcase was sitting by the door and she had been about to leave with Hector in hand when Saul had stumbled out of the lift.

"Where the fuck d'you think you're going," he slurred, reeking of vodka.

"What does it look like?" Olivia was wary; she'd seen his temper flare one too many times recently. "I'm leaving, please don't try to stop me."

"Like fuck you are, and you can leave the fucking dog too," Saul's eyes burned with rage.

Olivia attempted to squeeze through the gap he had left in the doorway.

"Not so fast, bitch," Saul sneered, and strong-armed her back into the flat, slamming the door on Hector who began frantically pawing and howling in fear for his mistress.

"What the hell are you doing? Get your fucking hands off me," Olivia shrieked.

The first blow from the back of his hand across her face had been so completely unexpected that Olivia had hardly felt it. She tried to run but Saul hauled her back. A series of punches split her lip, fractured her jawbone and broke three ribs, lacerating her spleen. Slumped on the floor, she readied herself for the next blow, but it didn't materialise. She looked up to see Saul weaving out of the flat, vodka bottle in hand. She allowed herself a moment of pity, and offered a reassuring moan to Hector who had glued himself to her battered body as soon as the door had opened. Then she crawled across the room, agonisingly slowly and in tremendous pain, and reached for her mobile to call an ambulance.

It had taken the police just under an hour to pick up Saul and arrest him for GBH. It took even less time for the doctors to assess Olivia and rush her into surgery to repair her spleen. In the following weeks, as Saul was charged and incarcerated at Her Majesty's pleasure, Olivia's inner strength had shown signs of returning, and her wounds had slowly healed.

When she had received the call offering her the Sebastian Bloom book project, she had jumped at the chance of getting away from London and everything that reminded her of Saul.

Emily had been less than impressed with her decision to leave.

"You're running away."

"Yes, I am," Olivia replied, honestly.

"I should have come over that night, I blame myself," Emily, anguished, took her hand and whispered. "You know how sorry I am, right?"

"Christ Em, it's hardly your fault. Even I didn't know he was capable of this," she said, indicating her fading bruises. "I need a clean break, time away to get my shit together. It's a great opportunity and its come at the right time. And I'm only a couple of hours away, it's not as though I'm leaving the country."

The very next day she accepted the job as Sebastian Bloom's official biographer. A week later she ushered Hector into the car and drove to Appleton Vale, hopeful that she could fully recover her broken heart and her once-indestructible spirit.

Chapter 5

Sebastian nosed the Bentley between the forbidding wrought-iron electric gates that shielded the ultra-exclusive Riverside Golf and Country Club from the rest of the world. Hearing the satisfying crunch of gravel under the car's huge tyres, he accelerated up the drive towards the clubhouse. The club crest, a golden eagle, had been fashioned into the gates and the raised flowerbeds either side of the entrance were studded with immaculate topiary.

Moving up the driveway, giant oaks nodding on either side, Sebastian spotted his long-term coach Hugh McLauchlin and head greenkeeper Jim Wellington deep in conversation as they examined a patch of the impossibly green fairway beneath them. Hugh waved as the Bentley surged past, indicating that he would be along shortly.

Even though he had promised himself some time off the course, Sebastian knew that he had to work on his game. *What else do I have left*, he thought.

Reaching the end of the driveway, the Riverside clubhouse came into view. Built in 1726, The Riverside Estate had housed a former prime minister, been used as a weekend retreat by royalty and hosted several knights of the realm before finding its current form as one of England's most exclusive sporting clubs.

"Morning Sebastian, been a while," joked Clive from his sentry box at the entrance to the club, raising the barrier for Sebastian's car.

"Clive," Sebastian nodded his greeting. "I think you'll be seeing a lot more of me from now on." He smiled weakly and sped off towards the car park.

He swung the car into its designated space, a brass plate reading: *Sebastian Bloom, Touring Professional.* He snorted; *nothing I've done in the past two years has been anywhere near professional.*

He hadn't even drawn the Bentley's key from the ignition when a frantic tapping at the window invaded the quiet cabin, announcing the unwelcome arrival of Club captain Harry Bellamy, also the Conservative MP for Fiddlebury, Appleton Vale and nearby Bears Bridge. Harry was a large, overbearing man in his late fifties with thinning grey hair and piggy, watery blue eyes – bloodshot from one too many evenings in the clubhouse bar. Formerly a bigshot in the City, Bellamy and his equally imperious wife Shelly had moved to Appleton Vale in search of a safe seat from which he could launch a parliamentary career.

"What-ho, Sebastian," Bellamy boomed crossly, leaning into the car as Sebastian opened the door. "We need to talk urgently old boy, about your dip... in both form *and* reputation. You're attached to this golf club and as such have an obligation to behave in whatever we decide is an acceptable manner."

Sebastian groaned inwardly. He loathed the man and was incapable of keeping his temper in check around him, even before Ellie and Lizzie had died. He rolled his eyes and swung his feet out onto the gravel and, as he pulled himself languidly up to every inch of his six foot two frame, he towered over the captain, who now shifted from foot to foot, quivering with indignation.

"Look, Bellamy, I don't give a shit what you or the rest of the club committee thinks," he retorted. "Call the dogs off and let me practice in peace."

"Now, you listen here," Bellamy puffed, a puce flush spreading quickly through the folds of his jowls as he hopped ridiculously from side to side. "We've supported you since you turned pro, and many a blind eye has been turned to your antics over the years. But enough is enough. Your recent behaviour has been inexcusable, and all you appear to be doing is bringing shame to the good name of Riverside GCC. Turn this around boy, and fast, or we'll be having another conversation that won't end so well."

At that, Harry turned and stomped off in the direction of the clubhouse. *No doubt in search of another few fingers of malt*, thought Sebastian.

Sebastian leaned back against the car, exhaling. On reflection, he didn't really care if the club dropped him as its touring pro. After all, it meant that he wouldn't have to be nice to the god-awful lady members who fluttered around him at every opportunity, dripping in diamonds, wearing stifling perfume and strutting silicone, and all without a single interesting thing to say between them.

God, he hated this side of golf. Whatever happened to him just getting out there and enjoying the beautiful game?

Reaching for his clubs and slinging the heavy bag easily over his shoulder, Sebastian headed for the practice range in search of Hugh. *If anyone can help me get my game back on track, it has to be him.*

Chapter 6

Olivia woke with a start and it took a few moments for her to work out where she was. *Ah yes, Appleton Vale, Sebastian Bloom, no Saul, new life*, she mused.

Hector stirred, grunted and cast his open eye towards Olivia to see if it really was time to get up yet. Still dark outside, inside the cottage was warm and quiet. Olivia sighed with momentary satisfaction. Maybe this place really would be her healing Mecca.

She moved towards the window, pulled open the curtains and greeted the rising dawn, the sun heavy and dark orange, hanging low over the hills that ringed the village. A sprinkling of unusually early frost glistened in the dimming glow of the Victorian streetlamps dotted around the green. Soon, it would be light and there was the promise of a glorious day. *Perfect for having a nosey round the village*, she thought.

Ten minutes later she stepped out of the shower and studied her reflection in the mirror, a little upset to see that she looked tired and drawn. After applying minimal make up, Olivia pulled on some skinny jeans, picked out a warm cashmere sweater and dressed with purpose. She was going to drag Hector round the meadows, whether he liked it or not.

It was crisp underfoot as she stepped outside, sending a shiver across her back. Zipping her coat up tightly, Olivia called Hector and set off across the green towards the rolling fields beyond. The village was silent, the polar opposite of London, and she loved it. Lights glowed here and there from behind the curtains of houses dotted around the green. Appleton Vale was slowly waking up to what was going to be a splendid day.

"Come away from that window at once, Dee Dee Bains," called a disapproving voice from the next room. "I know you're looking out for the new girl. By all accounts, she's a real gem...and a looker, too."

Jane Combes was Dee Dee's long-term partner, the more sensible and sensitive of the pair. In her mid-sixties, Jane was tall and had what Dee Dee always referred to as 'fantastic' legs. Her long, coarse black hair, pinned up into a bun as always, told of hidden grey beneath. Contrastingly, Dee Dee was short and plump with fading blonde hair and rosy cheeks.

"Why are you so fascinated with our new neighbour...Olivia, I think her name is?" asked Jane, to a still curtain-twitching Dee Dee.

"Why aren't *you* interested, more importantly?" said Dee Dee. "She's here to take the lid off the whole Sebastian story, isn't she...and I, for one, don't approve of tittle-tattle and lies being in the public domain like that. We should be supporting the poor man. He's been through the mill."

Dee Dee had always had a soft spot for Sebastian – she had known him when he was just a hopeful boy with so much ahead of him. He had handled his mother's death and father's disappearance with dignity, and supported his sister throughout the whole ordeal, too. The Ellie saga was another matter entirely, and he had taken that less than stoically, but that had just made her want to protect him all the more.

"Dee Dee, you know Sebastian is a grown man, don't you? He can take care of himself," Jane replied with a conciliatory smile. "Let's just wait and see what happens. Hopefully, your latest stalking victim will pop in for a coffee, so we can pass judgment after meeting her, and not before."

With a final glance, stepping away from the curtains, Dee Dee padded through the lounge: a riotous bohemian mismatch of chintz, ephemera and carefully chosen antiques, and made her way downstairs to prepare for the day ahead.

If Dee Dee and Jane's flat was all-out furniture war, the tearoom was a picture of understated decorative harmony. With duck-egg blue walls and white woodwork, and shutters framing the windows, the tables, chairs and other fixtures and fittings were shabby-chic, rather than country kitchen...and more shabby than chic...but that only added to the charm of the place. 1950s retro-style posters that advertised long-since forgotten food and drink brands adorned the walls, and there was an airy feel to the place that made it seem much bigger than it actually was; although as Dee Dee would constantly remind Jane, on a busy day you could hardly swing a cat in there.

Saturdays were busy at the tearooms. The cakes were legendary, drawing a steady mix of tourists, passers-by and locals as the day wore on. Dee Dee and Jane had never got round to mentioning to Bert, the local baker, their satisfactory and highly profitable partnership with his wife Tessa Butters. Bert believed baking was for bread and nothing else. He had no idea that his wife was in cahoots with the ladies and had even complimented them many times on their delicious, light and tasty French Fancies, much to their secret amusement.

Dee Dee heard a tap on the back door. "It's open," she shouted.

Tessa, arms full of plastic containers of varying sizes, pushed the door open with her knee and stumbled inside the kitchen.

"Can't be too long, need to get back to help Bert with the morning orders," she puffed. "It's a good job he plays golf most afternoons, or I'd never get away with our little arrangement."

Dee Dee carefully relieved Tessa of the most precarious boxes. "What's on the menu today, then? Ooh that looks delectable."

"Carrot cake, a selection of muffins, Battenberg…who doesn't like a Battenberg?… and today's special is tiramisu", said Tessa, planting the remaining boxes on the stainless-steel counter. "I thought I'd do a pecan pie for Monday's special, if that's ok with you?"

"Sounds delightful, darling. Now, off with you before Bert sends out the search party."

Tessa bade her farewell and Dee Dee switched to tearoom mode, methodically going about her day.

Chapter 7

The October wind still stinging her now-rosy cheeks, Olivia took a deep breath of countryside air and delighted in her surroundings. Having grown up in a market town and then moving first to Durham and then London, she had never really appreciated how charming and peaceful the real countryside could be. It really was rural bliss.

Making the turn back to the village, Hector bounded alongside her, stopping every now and then for a satisfyingly long sniff. They had been out for a good hour and a half, and all Olivia could think about was coffee and breakfast.

Depositing Hector at home, content with his own doggy breakfast, Olivia grabbed her purse and made for the café she had seen on her way into the village yesterday. The bell above the door tinkled as she stepped into the warmth, and she looked around seeing she was the first customer of the day. There was a scuffling noise and a raised voice, then another from behind the kitchen door, through which Dee Dee burst into view.

"Welcome to Appleton Vale, my dear," she said, flushing slightly. "Why, you really *are* a pretty young thing. Take a seat and I'll be right over, I'm Dee Dee and that's Jane you can hear grumbling at me from the kitchen."

"Ah, thanks," said Olivia smiling warmly. "Could I order a coffee please... strong, black, no sugar?" Nodding rapidly, Dee Dee whirled off, returning thirty seconds later with a steaming mug.

"You look like you need that. It's cold out there this morning, although I do love to shake the cobwebs out of my hair on days like these. Now tell me all about yourself." Dee Dee sat down opposite her and began firing questions, and Olivia concluded that breakfast might take some time.

Almost an hour later, Olivia extracted herself from the tearoom, having politely refused a second, even more generous helping of eggs and bacon from an unrelentingly keen Dee Dee. She was exhausted from the flood of questions, but all things considered, her hosts had been perfectly charming.

Somewhere, in amongst all of the questions, Olivia had managed to wheedle Dee Dee's own story out of her and she had found it delightful.

Dee Dee and Jane had met by chance when they had both signed up for a singles' painting holiday in Italy, expecting to find creative enlightenment, but instead finding each other.

Jane had recently come out of a relationship with a left-wing, politically motivated teacher called Clare, for whom Jane had fallen over a shared pot of weak and insipid tea at a Labour Party convention in Bournemouth. They were happy until Clare attended a TUC convention and had never returned, running off with a headmaster from an all-girls' school in Rochdale.

Jane had always been keen on painting and had found the delightful-looking holiday advertised in the back of Woman's Own whilst waiting at the doctor's. She had booked it the same day and a month later found herself on Capri, paintbrush in hand, and that's where she found Dee Dee.

Reaching the ripe old age of forty and never having had a serious relationship of any kind, Dee Dee Bains had resigned herself to being alone. She had grown up in Bears Bridge, a village about seven miles west of Appleton Vale, and having had several boyfriends, had never felt a burning desire for any of them. Dee Dee was in denial about her feelings towards women for many, many years, knowing her parents, staunch Catholics, would not have tolerated such an arrangement.

Meeting Jane had changed her life forever. Dee Dee had joined the Italy trip because she was lonely - she didn't have a creative bone in her body. She had been spellbound by Jane the moment she had laid eyes on her across a crowded airport baggage hall, and had been delighted and excited in equal measures when they had both checked in for the same holiday. Jane had been incredibly friendly from the start, and Dee Dee found herself wanting to spend every moment of every day in her company. Jane, having sensed that Dee Dee had been wrestling with her feelings, had suggested a sunset walk along the beach where she urged her to 'come out' and be proud.

"How did you know?" Dee Dee gasped.

Jane took her hands: "My darling girl, your innocence is your downfall, it's written all over your face." Reaching up and stroking her cheek she continued, "You beguile me. I know it's only been a few short days but I'm completely charmed by your gentleness. Could I kiss you, or is it too soon?"

Dee Dee had gone weak at the knees, her heart beating in time to the waves crashing against the shore, not far from where they were standing. Without hesitation, she nodded and steadied herself for her first kiss with a woman. A small part of her had been hoping that she might hate it and be repulsed, but when Jane's lips had met hers, all her doubts faded away in an instant.

That night, Jane had taken Dee Dee's virginity with a heady combination of tenderness and desire, and they had spent the next ten days together, inseparable and falling deeply in love.

Just a few short weeks after they had come back from Capri, Dee Dee moved into Jane's flat in Pimlico. She had become an outcast to her own family but no matter how hard she tried, Dee Dee not been able to settle in the city, desperately missing the vast open spaces and sweet-smelling air of West Chesterton county. When she had finally got up the courage to discuss it with Jane, Dee Dee had been both surprised and delighted when Jane said she would happily live anywhere, as long as they were together.

Dee Dee had wanted to go home but knew Bears Bridge was out of the question. She had always loved Appleton Vale and suggested to Jane that they try their luck there, also hoping that the proximity to her family might encourage a reconciliation. Unfortunately, the welcome that they received in Appleton Vale hadn't been as they'd expected. They were viewed with a combination of disgust and curiosity from the more established families and older villagers, and it had taken a monumental effort on their parts and, what Dee Dee had called 'Operation Charm Offensive', to get their neighbours on side.

Twenty-five years on and they were viewed as the very heart and soul of Appleton Vale, and were no longer the 'only gays in the village', since Devon Murphy and Patrick Strand had taken up residence several years earlier.

As Olivia headed home, she heard a powerful clatter of hooves thundering up behind her. She turned and came face to face with an enormous chestnut gelding, frothing at the bit and covered in sweat. Snorting and swishing his tail with a wild look in his eye, he seemed in a state of cat-like readiness, poised to turn and run at any given moment.

The rider, seemingly undisturbed by her steed's agitated behaviour, announced herself as Lucinda

Walton-Smythe and proceeded to strike up a conversation with Olivia.

"And you are?" she demanded, looking down her long pointed nose at Olivia.

Olivia discreetly gave Lucinda the once-over and decided immediately that she was the kind of person that gave a bad name to country folk. She was overbearing, and quite frankly rude. Not a great first impression.

Lucinda was squeezed into a pair of overly tight and unflatteringly high-waisted, cream breeches that did nothing to disguise her cellulite, or her proportions. Combined with the alarmingly long nose, and small, flinty grey eyes, Olivia concluded she had few redeeming features, personally or physically.

"I'm Olivia Carmichael," she replied. "And what's your name?' Olivia's attention was focused on the horse rather than his rider.

"This brute is Cassius. He's bad tempered, difficult and needs taking in hand. One of my liveries."

Olivia smiled inwardly, thinking that horse and rider were well suited to each other. A keen horsewoman herself, Olivia wasn't fearful of Cassius' restlessness and stepped forward to give him a scratch on his neck.

"He's lovely, despite the snorting," she laughed.

Ignoring her efforts at making light conversation, Lucinda launched into an attack. "I suppose you're the one writing the book about Sebastian?"

"Yes, guilty as charged. I must have done something bad in a previous life to end up with this gig."

The joke was met with silence. Olivia was forced to consider that, in addition to her other shortcomings, Lucinda had absolutely no sense of humour. This wasn't someone she would be going out of her way to spend any time with.

"Sebastian isn't as bad as you media types make out, you know. Careful how you tread, my girl, or things could get tricky for you around here."

Taken aback by her tone, Olivia fought the urge to respond in kind, instead holding her tongue and answering as sweetly as she could bear through gritted teeth. "I'd be committing career suicide if wrote a pack of lies, and it's my job to make sure that his story is told in an engaging and sympathetic manner...you needn't worry."

Lucinda snorted and the barbed comment washed right over her rhino-thick skin.

"My husband Godfrey and I own the Whiteside Estate. You must call by some time."

"Yes, well, thank you for the invitation, Lucinda," Olivia replied politely.

Before Olivia had finished her sentence, Lucinda had stabbed her spurs into Cassius' ribs and they were clattering off into the late morning.

Chapter 8

Monday morning, and Olivia was already dreading her first day on the job, the first time she would sit down with Sebastian and begin writing his story.

Having spent most of the weekend unpacking and settling into the cottage, Olivia was happy with her progress. Aside from taking Hector out, dinner in the pub with Susie and Tom, and her visit to the tea-rooms, she hadn't ventured into the village. The locals would have to wait another few days to confirm their pre-formed opinions of her.

Olivia dressed in the skinny black jeans she knew made her legs look endless, teamed with biker boots and a chunky cashmere sweater. She tied her long, glossy, blonde hair back in a jaunty ponytail, and kept her makeup simple and natural, applying just enough mascara and eyeliner to make her vivid jade green eyes sparkle. She ignored the niggling voice in her head asking why she was making such an effort to look effortlessly beautiful when she was going to work for such an unlikeable man.

It was only a short distance to the manor, but Olivia took the car as the rain showed no sign of letting up. The dark clouds that had gathered around the village and across the valley suited her mood today.

Passing the stone pillars that marked the entrance to the Bloom estate, she looked down the sweeping, tree-lined driveway, and took in the beauty of the land around her. Clearly it was tended with much love and, to her untrained eye, there wasn't a blade of grass out of place. To her immediate left, post-and-rail paddocks contained horses and sheep, and further beyond lay open land. To Olivia's right was manicured parkland, studded with ageing trees, slowly shedding their crisp, autumnal leaves for another year.

Even through the driving rain, Olivia saw it was a breathtakingly beautiful estate, and as she rounded the corner the Manor came into view.

An overwhelming sense of history poured from the building. It was vast but not foreboding, impressive but somehow not overwhelming. Olivia closed her eyes for a moment and tried to imagine what this great house had seen through its 400-year existence. She made a mental note to ask Sebastian to fill her in on the history of the manor: she wanted to soak it up and be a part of it.

She pulled the car up alongside Sebastian's Bentley and dashed through the rain, up the steps, to the sanctuary of the covered entrance. The brass knocker was the size of her head, and Olivia had a job to get it working due to its sheer weight. After two booming knocks, she heard footsteps coming towards her and the door swung open.

"Hello, my dear, you must be Olivia, welcome to Appleton Manor," said a comely woman with incredible warmth. "I'm the Bloom's housekeeper, Hattie Banbridge. Let's get you out of the rain."

"It's a pleasure to meet you, Hattie," Olivia smiled warmly, glancing quickly at her surroundings. "Wow, this is amazing."

Olivia stepped through the doorway into the entrance hall, cathedral-like in its size and serenity. Stairs swept down from both sides adjoining a central staircase that dominated the back of the hall, and hanging high above, a vast centerpiece chandelier cast shards of light all around, even on this dark autumnal day.

"It's a family home," said Hattie. "We don't stand on ceremony and we like to have as calm and relaxing an environment as possible."

Just as Olivia was about to respond, there was a crash from another room followed by shouting. She could hear every word and could only assume it was Sebastian and his sister, going at it like a pair of terriers.

Hattie took Olivia buy the elbow and steered her towards the kitchen, away from ground zero and the argument that was still raging.

"Well it's usually calm and relaxing here, honestly," Hattie said, with an embarrassed smile.

"Oh God, don't worry, it's fine. I'll pretend I didn't hear anything", Olivia was equally embarrassed that she had wandered into the battle of the Blooms.

"I shouldn't tell you this, but he isn't in the best of moods and Georgiana, bless her, has a habit of pushing all the wrong buttons," Hattie confided. "The combination of the two of them like that is always explosive. Now, take a seat there and tell me what I can get you to drink while we wait for this to blow over."

"Coffee please. Maybe I should just make a quiet exit and come back tomorrow?" Olivia winced as another crash came from the far reaches of the house, followed by another outburst of expletives.

"Sebastian won't be happy if he knows you've been here and not seen him. Please, stay for a drink and I'll see what the commotion is about." Hattie placed a steaming mug of coffee in front of her and shuffled out of the kitchen to broker peace.

Olivia felt awkward and intrusive, as though she shouldn't be there witnessing this most intimate of family moments. Restless, wanting to be somewhere else, she got up and wandered to the window overlooking the back of the manor. Here she got a better view of the lake that ran alongside the vast expanse of lawn, which in turn was set against a backdrop of thick woodland. The tree cover in the distance gave structure to the landscape, and only the raindrops spattering against the windowpane dulled the otherwise stunning vista.

Hearing heavy footsteps approaching, Olivia turned and tried her best not to look as embarrassed as she was feeling. He had to know that she'd heard the row, it had been loud enough to shake the very foundations of the centuries-old manor house.

"This isn't a good time. I thought you'd have had the common sense to work that out when you arrived," Sebastian told Olivia in a voice that was quiet but unnervingly menacing.

Shocked at his rudeness Olivia just stood and said nothing.

"Just leave, Ms Carmichael. Come back tomorrow…and for God's sake don't regale the entire village with tales of your visit. We like to keep our family business private."

Olivia was grateful for the escape route she was given. She grabbed her bag and almost ran out of the house, trying to retain some air of dignity and nonchalance about Sebastian's treatment of her.

It was only when she was at the edge of the estate and heading towards the village that the anger set in. *How rude. What gives him the right to talk to me like that?*

Anger made her drive like a woman possessed, and one who had been fighting for her space on London roads for years. She screamed through the village, almost taking out old Mrs Banks who was slowly and painfully negotiating the route from the tea-rooms to the duck pond.

Pulling up outside the house, she was just getting out of the car, muttering obscenities under her breath, when she saw Susie.

"Bloody hell, you nearly killed old Mrs Banks just then. Who's rattled your cage?" she was a little shocked. "Actually, you don't need tell me, first day of work with Sebastian?" She rolled her eyes and gave Olivia a sympathetic look.

"Well, seeing as it's only half past ten I think we can safely say that it's not gone well," Olivia replied with a grimace. "I'm not sure this is going to work out."

"I'm not going to ask what happened, it's none of my business, and I don't think you're the kind of person to break someone's trust. Not that I know you yet of course, but I do intend for us to be great friends. Now, why don't you come in for a drink and we can get to know each other a bit better, seeing as you have a free day and all?"

Olivia laughed, "Christ it's a bit early for the hard stuff, Susie."

"Actually, we do the best coffee in the village, just don't tell Dee Dee and Jane I said that. I hear you've already met them both. Lovely, aren't they?"

"I thought I might not get out of there alive," Olivia joked.

"They're an Appleton Vale institution, along with Marjorie Rose who is the postmistress, but I don't think you'll have met her yet. Marjorie's away on a Saga coach holiday."

"Sounds thrilling," laughed Olivia. "Now tell me, do you serve pastries with that special coffee or do I have to risk life and limb at the tea-rooms to get a mid-morning snack?"

Giggling conspiratorially Susie linked arms with Olivia and walked towards the pub.

Chapter 9

The rain had given way to a clear and bright morning when Olivia set off for Appleton Manor the next day. She decided to take Sebastian up on his offer of letting Hector accompany her - and she needed the back up. He trotted alongside her quite contentedly, completely unaware that he could be sniffing his way into a war zone.

"Olivia, good morning," trilled Dee Dee from the doorway of the tearoom as she walked past. "Off to see Sebastian?"

"Err, yes, off to work anyway," she replied with a smile. "At least it's stopped raining: the river was quite high last night."

"Oh, no need to worry about that, it's never flooded the village, although it came close a few years ago down in Bears Bridge. Would you like to take some cake up to the manor?"

"That's a lovely idea, what's good?"

Dee Dee laughed, "It's all delicious, my dear, but Sebastian has a bit of a sweet tooth so I'd recommend the Pecan Pie."

"He does?" Olivia was surprised. "And here's me thinking his body's a temple."

Dee Dee raised her eyebrows and giggled.

Olivia quickly corrected herself, realizing how that had sounded. "No, not like that," she said, embarrassed.

"He's a very attractive man, even I can see that and I've only got eyes for my Jane," Dee Dee giggled. "You'd make a handsome couple. You're like a breath of fresh air my dear, just what he needs," she continued, encouragingly.

"Have you been talking to Susie?" Olivia raised an eyebrow. "I think she's got it in her head that we'd be great together which is ridiculous. I don't know him at all, and he's not exactly made a good impression on me yet."

Seeing Dee Dee's face drop she started backtracking, "Look, I think it's lovely that you all seem to love and protect Sebastian: that must count for something. I'm just not really interested in meeting anyone right now, that's all."

Touching her arm gently, seeing that she'd overstepped the mark, Dee Dee said, "Ignore me dear, I have a tendency to get a little ahead of myself, can't keep my nose out. Let me get you that pie."

Ten minutes later, Olivia arrived at the manor and braced herself for her first real meeting with Sebastian. "Help me, Hec," she whispered to the dog at her side, and patted his head.

This time, Sebastian greeted her at the front door and was brimming with uncharacteristic warmth that threw Olivia off guard for a moment. She had not been expecting an easy meeting after yesterday.

"Good to see you Olivia, and you too Hector," bending down, Sebastian gave Hector a scratch under his chin, which was received enthusiastically.

"Traitor," Olivia muttered in Hector's direction.

"What was that?" Sebastian hadn't quite heard her.

"Oh, nothing," Olivia squeaked.

"I thought we could do this in my study, we won't be disturbed in there."

The thought of not being disturbed was quite disturbing to Olivia. "That's a daunting thought", she muttered, again under her breath.

As they were making their way across the hall an enormous, sleek, blue-coated Great Dane came lolloping towards them, making a beeline for Hector.

"This is Ace," said Sebastian, smiling lovingly at his dog.

"He's gorgeous," Olivia bent down and fondled his ears.

"He's a big baby, scared of his own shadow," joked Sebastian. "Wouldn't be without him though," he said affectionately.

Hector and Ace were conducting the usual doggy greeting process and, after a few sniffs and tail wags, decided they were friends and bounded off into the rain to chase leaves together.

"I've asked Hattie to bring us some coffee and croissants, I trust that meets with your approval?"

God he's so proper, Olivia thought.

Sebastian's study was located in the east wing and Olivia was surprised at what she found, expecting it to be all harsh lines and cold draughts. Instead, she discovered floor to ceiling French doors, beautiful oak bookcases containing many first editions and classics, and a huge inglenook fireplace that dominated the room, with flames already licking generously across the crackling logs.

A sumptuous dark brown leather sofa faced the fire, looking comfortable and inviting, and in the corner was an exquisite antique desk. The shelves behind the desk were filled with replica trophies from his many victories, heartbreakingly interspersed with silver-framed photographs of his daughter Lizzie.

Olivia noticed a child's painting, framed, and taking pride of place on the mantel, and a battered teddy bear next to it, both clearly having belonged to Sebastian's daughter.

"This is perfect," she breathed. "I love it."

"Well, that's one thing we have in common," he rewarded her with the first genuine smile he'd given since they'd first met. "This is my favourite room in the house, I can relax in here."

"Yes, I can see that. I could easily write in here," she said dreamily.

"Bloody good job really," Sebastian laughed, and motioned for her to sit on the sofa.

Shit, you really are gorgeous, Olivia thought as Sebastian flashed her another megawatt smile, and she felt a tiny flutter deep inside the pit of her stomach. Realising she was blushing, she quickly looked away, hoping Sebastian wasn't a mind reader.

"Not disturbing you two, am I?" puffed Hattie as she pushed her way through the heavy oak door, holding a tray full of delicious-smelling coffee and croissants dripping with butter, accompanied by a pot of homemade strawberry jam. "Best get tucked into this little lot before it goes cold. Call me if you need anything. Lunch will be at one o'clock."

"Thanks Hatts, you're a gem. What would we do without you?" Sebastian rushed to relieve her of the tray and set it down on the table in front of the fire.

So that's at least one redeeming quality, thought Olivia, sensing genuine warmth between them.

Sebastian eased himself onto the sofa beside her and poured the steaming coffee into two huge mugs.

"Right Ms Carmichael, where do we start? Steer me in the right direction from the get-go," he flashed her another disarming smile.

"I find it is usually appropriate to start from the beginning," Olivia joked lightly. "Start with the earliest memories you have of your childhood, what it was like growing up somewhere like this, tell me about your parents, stuff like that."

Sebastian laughed and settled back into the deep filled velvet cushions and began to talk.

The next thing she knew, the Grandfather clock in the hall outside Sebastian's study was chiming, indicating that it was two o'clock. She had been completely engrossed in their work, fascinated by what she was being told, and time had flown.

"I'm starving, can we take a break please?" she asked Sebastian, leaning forward and pressing the pause button on her mobile phone's voice-recording app.

She got up, walked over to the window, and looked out across the lake and sighed, "It's so beautiful here, Sebastian. It's tranquil and inspiring."

"Tranquil?" Sebastian scoffed. "It wasn't so tranquil yesterday when you arrived was it?"

Olivia hadn't wanted to bring up the subject of yesterday's fight in fear of what he would say, and she was relieved that he had mentioned it.

"Is Georgiana ok today? She sounded very, er, upset," Olivia didn't want to intrude.

"She's fine, she's always fine, just a cheeky little madam who loves to push my buttons. She knows exactly how to wind me up and I'm afraid I fall for it every time." Sebastian softened when he talked about his sister.

"She was so young when our mother died, and then Dad pushed off, so I became the father figure. I guess it stands to reason that she pushes the boundaries," he rolled his eyes. "She's a good kid though."

"I'm looking forward to getting to know her," Olivia said. "Where is she today?"

"Gone hunting, she'll be out all day but I'm sure you'll meet her tomorrow. Now, about that lunch."

Olivia followed Sebastian back down the corridor and through into the kitchen.

"Thought you two weren't ever coming out of there, I didn't want to disturb you," said Hattie, dishing up a casserole and motioning for them to sit down at the battered pine table.

"Smells delicious as always, Hatts," Sebastian grinned and Hattie beamed with pleasure.

Olivia was hungry, "Mmmm, that looks amazing, Dee Dee told me you're a fantastic cook."

"Ah, bless her. Now tuck in before it goes cold, there's either mashed potato or soda bread, take your pick."

The speed at which Olivia devoured her lunch amused Sebastian, who'd been watching her intently all morning.

He studied her thinking, *she's gorgeous, clever as a fox and oh so sexy, wouldn't mind seeing that body melt under me.*

Olivia looked up and caught Sebastian watching her. Her heart skipped an involuntary beat and she silently cursed herself for being so attracted to him.

Hattie, who had been quietly watching the silent exchanges between the two of them, felt a tiny surge of hope ignite within her. *'She'll be good for him,* she thought and smiled inwardly.

Keen to get some fresh air before settling back to work, Olivia asked Sebastian to show her some of the estate.

"I'd love a tour. Show me your kingdom," she joked.

Sebastian scraped his chair back over the flag-stones and jumped up with gusto.

"Ok, let's go," he said, looking delighted that Olivia had shown interest in his home.

During their brisk walk around the lake Sebastian gave Olivia a brief rundown on the history of the manor and spoke in depth, and with some pride, about his ancestors. His enthusiasm for his home was infectious and Olivia found herself wanting to see more.

"Perhaps you'd give me one?" She suggested to Sebastian.

"I beg your pardon?" he grinned.

"A guided tour!" she was mortified. "You know what I meant."

Sebastian laughed, "Yes I do. Shall we get back inside and crack on?"

Later that night, as she was typing up her notes from their first session, Olivia felt they had made good progress, although she was confused by Sebastian who was turning out to be a bundle of contradictions. She found herself aching to understand him better. Today he had been funny, irreverent and passionate, making it an enjoyable experience for them both.

I don't know why I was worried, she thought. *This isn't going to be half as bad as I thought it would be.*

Chapter 10

Just a week later, Olivia was cursing herself for thinking that spending this much time with Sebastian
would be easy. His mood swings were starting to take
a toll, and she found herself walking on eggshells,
never knowing what frame of mind he would be in
from one day to the next. It was exhausting.

Her only saving grace was her burgeoning friendship with Georgiana, who was always pleased to see
her.

"Morning Liv," Georgiana called, bounding down
the stairs two at a time into the hallway as Olivia
arrived.

"Hey Georgie," she smiled as she closed the heavy
front door behind her. "What's the mood in camp?"

"Changeable," she sighed. "He was crashing
around most of the night looking for God knows
what, he's a bit mumpy this morning."

"Mumpy?" Olivia asked.

"Yeah, you know, moody and grumpy: mumpy," Georgiana giggled. "That's what Mum used to call Dad when he was sulking."

"I like that," Olivia laughed. "You look lovely, by the way. Who's the lucky man?

"And why would you think it's for a man?" she winked and twirled around, showing off her outfit.

"Well, isn't it?"

"Yes, but don't tell grumpy-pants, he never approves of any boys I bring home, so I don't bring them home. I'm fairly certain he thinks I'm still a virgin," Georgiana rolled her eyes. "I'm almost twenty for fuck's sake, he was banging everything going at that age."

Olivia was surprised at how much the thought of Sebastian screwing around upset her. *What's wrong with me*, she thought. *I don't even like the man, let alone fancy him.*

"You like him, don't you?" Georgiana blurted out.

"Your brother is an unusual man," she replied tactfully. "Stop bloody meddling and tell me what's going on with you."

Fifteen minutes later, after Georgiana had filled Olivia in on her latest beau, Max Morgan, who was taking her for a day out in Cirencester, she made her way down the corridor to Sebastian's study in trepidation.

"Coffee?" Sebastian had his back to her as she walked in the room, and she didn't have to see his face to know that today was another dark one for him, she was beginning to read the signs.

"Good morning, yes please, that'd be lovely."

She took the proffered mug gratefully and made her way over to the sofa.

"Sebastian, I'd like to have a quick review of how you think things are going before you go to China on Sunday."

"How do you feel it's going?" he'd moved over to the window and was distracted by Ace and Hector, chasing each other around the garden.

"Well if I'm honest, I'm struggling to make anything work right now. I need you to give me a more personal insight into your life. I can get the golf stuff anywhere." She sat nervously, awaiting his response.

"Warts and all," he muttered, turning towards her, and, for a fleeting moment, Olivia registered real grief on his stricken, but still beautiful face.

Oh you poor man, she thought, suddenly feeling overwhelmed with the need to take him in her arms.

She took a deep breath. "Well, we've not really touched on Ellie." She cringed as she said her name and didn't dare look him in the eye.

He turned back to the window and stood in silence for a moment, although, to Olivia, it felt like an age. She hardly dared to breathe.

"I find it hard to talk about my family, Olivia. Such a lot of death and destruction, and disappearances, if you count William." He tried to make a joke about his errant father but it rang hollow. "I'll do my best to be more open, although I can't promise anything."

And breathe, Olivia was relieved she hadn't overstepped the mark.

"Can we do something else today?" he pleaded.

"Of course," Olivia smiled. "You're the boss, what did you have in mind?"

"I'd like to give you a *personal* tour of the estate, if that's ok?"

The way he emphasised 'personal' made Olivia blush and she stammered her reply. "That would be lovely, thank you."

Sebastian grinned, pleased with her enthusiasm for his home. "Let's go then, grab your coat."

He strode towards the French doors and led her out into the garden.

"I thought we could start at the outer reaches of the estate, beyond the woodland you can see over there," Sebastian pointed across the lake to a vast open space on the edge of the forest. "And then make our way back, finishing up at the glasshouses, always a show-stopper."

Olivia could only nod in agreement. For the first time, she felt she was seeing the real Sebastian Bloom, the man who was, according to his friends and neighbours, a truly wonderful human being.

Damn it, not only is he sexy as hell but he's also pretty bloody charming, Olivia thought as her heart started pounding against her chest and her knees weakened. *Get a grip*, her inner voice of reason screamed at her.

Chapter 11

Reclining in his first-class seat, Sebastian glanced at his watch and sighed with exasperation - there were still seven more hours in the air before they reached Shanghai.

He hated being stuck on a plane with only his thoughts for company. He liked to keep active, it kept his mind from wandering into dangerous territory, but today all he could think about was Olivia.

She challenged him on everything. It was frustrating and tiresome but he relished it in some warped fashion. She was also beautiful and incredibly sexy, made all the more attractive by her lack of ego. She really didn't have any idea of how stunning she was, which made her all the more beguiling. He'd gone very quickly from dreading their time together to being eager as a schoolboy, and he felt himself spinning out of control.

After what had happened with Ellie he no longer trusted himself, nor anyone else. Every time he felt a surge of emotion, or more to the point desire, for Olivia he tried to bury it, but she had started to invade his dreams as well as his every waking thought. She made him feel alive again, and he could breathe when he was with her.

He looked out of the tiny airplane window and thought back to a few days ago when he had taken her on a tour of the estate.

"Jump in," Sebastian opened the door of the ancient Land Rover for her and then they were off, bouncing across paddocks, stopping now and then to open gates or usher a wayward sheep back into its field.

Right at the far end of the estate a team of specialists were undertaking restoration work on a pair of 18th century farm cottages. Sebastian stopped the car and led Olivia over to the site to get a closer look.

"They'll be finished in the spring, bit of a building site now so it's not safe to take you in there. Another time," he promised.

He had a quick word with the foreman and, satisfied with his response, ushered Olivia back into the car and continued on to the ancient stable block that was anything but ancient, in terms of its state of the art facilities.

"I had the yard and schools restored as a project for Georgiana to get involved in," Sebastian said proudly. "She adores horses and she's a cracking little rider, I'm hoping she'll turn it into a business when she's ready."

"It's perfect," Olivia replied, dreamily.

"You can come and spend some time here with Georgiana if you like, when I'm not breathing down your neck."

"Right now, I wouldn't mind one bit if you were breathing down my neck," Olivia muttered under her breath. Looking up she was relieved he hadn't heard her as he drove on.

"Ready for the showpiece?" Sebastian's eyes danced with anticipation of her reaction.

As they rounded the corner, a magnificent pair of 19th century glass houses came into view. The weak sunshine bounced off the glass, reflecting a myriad of colours intensely rich against the backdrop of the autumnal sky.

"They represent a remarkable confluence of opposites in architecture and technology," Sebastian informed her.

"A remarkable what of what?" Olivia teased.

Sebastian smiled and continued, "They were ground-breaking in their day, come and have a look," He steered her through the vast iron framed door and into a veritable paradise.

Olivia gasped, "Oh Sebastian, it's beautiful."

"We've got over a hundred different types of exotic plant species in here, and Hattie grows enough fruit and veg to feed the five thousand next door."

"It's like being in another world." Olivia began walking around, softly fingering leaves, and bending to take in the scent of the flora surrounding her.

"Sebastian, come over here," Olivia called from across the room. "You didn't tell me you had turtles stashed away in here."

He could see her kneeling down by the oasis that Georgiana had created for her pet turtles.

He pointed them out. "This one's Queen Boadicea and the other one's Joan of Arc, or it could be the other way round, I'm not entirely sure."

Olivia burst out laughing.

"Georgiana's keen on strong, historical women, she was very insistent on the names at the time," Sebastian explained.

"That's hilarious." She turned away from the turtles to continue the tour and tripped over a terracotta pot. Tumbling forward, she was destined for a bath with Boadicea and Joan before Sebastian's lightning-quick reactions intervened.

"Woah, steady on," he grabbed her, pulling her towards his chest, gently wrapping his arms around her, holding her close and nuzzling the top of her head.

Olivia squeaked, "No, please don't, I can't." She pulled away from Sebastian as if his touch had scalded her. "I'm sorry, I wasn't expecting that, you confuse me," she admitted. But as she looked into his eyes she saw the shutters to his soul come crashing down once more.

"Can I get you anything to drink Mr Bloom?" asked the polite stewardess, interrupting his thoughts and dragging him back to the present.

Sebastian wanted nothing more than a stiff scotch, but he knew the drinking had to stop if he was going to get things back on track.

"No, thank you. Please can you make sure I'm not disturbed for the rest of the flight."

He pressed the button that reclined his seat flat and shut his eyes, hoping to get some much-needed sleep - it had been hard to come by lately.

Chapter 12

As Sebastian struggled with both his game and the oppressive humidity in China, the stunning, shimmering browns, golds and reds of the autumnal landscape around Appleton Vale slowly turned to winter. Trees and branches swirled in the bitter winds, shedding their leaves in an unrehearsed dance and the temperature plummeted.

It was a bright Saturday morning and the village was a hive of activity. Taking up her usual position at the window, Dee Dee spotted a removals van passing the tearoom.

"Oh Jane, look, that must be Peter and the children. Did you get Tessa to make the cake for them? I want to drop it round to welcome them home."

Jane smiled fondly at Dee Dee. "I'm so glad they've decided to come back here after everything that happened with poor Sarah. The cake's on top of the fridge, it looks delightful."

"Lovely, I'll pop over in an hour or so, they'll need a tea break by then."

"My love, you have such a big and beautiful heart, but just give them a little time to settle in, don't go running over there immediately being all nosy, you've no idea how Peter will react."

"I'm not nosy." Dee Dee was indignant.

Jane laughed, "That's not what I was saying my dear. You're a wonderful woman with a lot of love to give. I'm the lucky one, I have you all to myself."

As Dee Dee shuffled off to make a start on breakfast, Jane heard the tinkle of the door chime behind her and turned to find Andrea Hartley, general manager of nearby Church Farm Food Barn.

"Hello duckie, to what do we owe the pleasure? We don't usually see you in here this early."

"Bloody hell that bacon smells divine Jane, it's making my mouth water."

"Do you want a bap to take away?" Jane loved nothing more than to see her customers enjoying their food.

"Christ no!" replied Andrea, laughing. "The diet's going well, I've lost three pounds this week, don't tempt me."

"I know how that feels darling. Dee Dee and I were really quite svelte back in the day," Jane said contentedly.

Andrea laughed, but felt a pang of insecurity and sucked in her wobbly bits before continuing.

"Malcolm wants some cakes for Lilith and Lucifer. They're staying for the next two weeks, I'm dreading it," Andrea said, rolling her eyes.

Malcolm and Maud Crailley owned Church Farm on the outskirts of the village. They had two grown children and a host of unruly grandchildren, two of which, twins, were particularly demonic.

"You can't call them that," Jane shrieked with laughter.

"Why not? They're the twins from hell, spawn of the devil. Last time they stayed they wrecked my beautiful autumn window displays and terrorised the cows. I may end up in the funny farm after this."

"I'm sure it'll be fine. How much damage can two six-year-olds inflict?" Jane tried to reassure her.

"You'd be surprised", Andrea replied. "Oh, I meant to ask, do you know who's moving into Blossom Hill? I walked past yesterday and it was a hive of activity. It's been empty for as long as I've been here, and that's cracking on four years."

"Peter Jenner and his kids, such a sad story really," Jane said in a sombre voice. "Peter's a local but hasn't been around for a few years now. To cut a long story short, his wife Sarah was diagnosed with vascular dementia not long after Teddy, their second child, was born."

Andrea gasped with disbelief, "Oh my God, she can't have been very old?"

"Thirty-four, it's virtually unheard of." Jane lowered her voice as another customer entered the shop. "It came on so quickly. She started forgetting little things and it took ages for a proper diagno-sis, by which time she'd gone downhill. Peter was devastated, rightly so".

"That's unimaginable," said Andrea. "Where is she now?"

"In a lovely nursing home just the other side of Bears Bridge, been there a few years now. Don't look shocked, what was he supposed to do? He had two babies to think about."

"No, I didn't mean that," Andrea replied. "It's shocking, what an awful thing to happen, and the children, it's heartbreaking. Why do you think he's moving back now?"

"My dear, you'll learn over time that people always come back to Appleton Vale," Jane patted her arm and smiled. "Peter was born and raised here and his parents and sister are still here. He had a happy life here once and can again. I hope so, he's such a lovely man."

Andrea mulled over what she had just been told and thought how desperately sad the situation was for the husband. She couldn't imagine what he had been through.

"Hopefully they'll be happy here," she said. "I'll take the lemon drizzle, the whole thing, one of those tea loaves and six chocolate cupcakes. Actually, make that seven, there's just no point denying myself my only pleasure in life."

Nodding her approval, Jane said," I'll stick in on Malcolm's bill."

"Thanks, must dash, I'm meeting Maud to plan the Christmas displays," said Andrea with a grimace. "And you know how painful that's going to be, she just goes on and on and on."

She left in a hurry, closing the door behind her with such ferocity that old Mrs Banks, sitting at the table tucked into the corner by the entrance, jumped out of her skin and fell face first into her iced bun.

Chapter 13

"Are we there yet," came the voices from the back seat for the umpteenth time, followed by a torrent of giggles.

"Yes," said Peter, wearily. It had been a trying journey.

"Really," Evie breathed, suddenly taking interest.

"Yes, really. Do you remember it?" Peter asked gently.

"A bit," she replied.

"Can't see, Daddy, can't see," Teddy squealed, straining to get a look out of the window.

"It's ok Ted, we're here now," Peter reassured his son.

Peter turned the car into the driveway and took a deep breath. It had been four years since they had left.

"Well here goes nothing," he muttered.

"It's so pretty," exclaimed Evie.

"Can't see Daddy, let me out," Teddy cried.

Evie helped Teddy out of his car seat and they ran towards the house. Peter followed, somewhat less enthusiastically. *Christ, I hope I'm doing the right thing by coming back here*, he thought.

The front door swung open. "Darlings," Janice Jenner threw her arms open to greet her grandchildren. "Haven't you grown?"

"Gam Gam." Teddy launched himself at his grandmother.

"Peter, darling, you look shattered," Janice said, giving him a hug. "Let's get you inside. I've had a good clean and made the beds, and your Dad's out at the supermarket. God only knows what he'll come back with but it'll do you for a few days till you're settled."

"Thanks Mum," Peter was grateful. "It's strange being back, so full of memories."

"Good memories darling, they're the ones you have to remember. You were happy here," Janice said gently.

"I don't know if it's the right move but it's time we put down some roots," Peter replied. "And we need you. The kids should be around family, I can't do it all on my own, God knows I've tried."

"Well we're all delighted," Janice said, unable to contain her joy. "This is your home darling, you belong here. Now, where have my grandchildren disappeared to?"

They found Evie and Teddy tearing around the garden, exploring their new surroundings.

"Daddy it's so big," Evie shouted excitedly.

"Daddy, want tree house," Teddy cried, pointing to a big oak tree.

"Can we have a dog now?" Evie begged. "We've got room and you said when we had room we could."

"Maud Crailley's lab just had puppies," Janice offered.

"Don't encourage them Mum. I'd like to settle in first, then I'll think about it."

"Puppies, really?" Evie was excited. "Oh Dad, you promised. Can we go and see them?"

"It'll be so good for them, Peter," said Janice. "Every child should grow up with a dog. I'll pop in and see Maud on my way home, let her know you're interested. They won't be ready to leave for another six weeks anyway, that's plenty of time to get yourselves sorted."

"Is there any point in me trying to stop you Mum?" sighed Peter.

"Oh, don't be so churlish darling. Oh look, here's your father."

James Jenner, laden with shopping bags, greeted his son warmly. "Good to see you, old boy. How was the trip?"

"Hi Dad, yeah, it was fine. Think I'm a bit overwhelmed being back here if I'm honest."

"Grampy!" Evie and Teddy shouted with glee, racing to get to him first.

James beamed, "Hello you two rascals."

"We're getting a puppy Grampy," said Evie.

"Are you now? How splendid," James replied.

"See what you've started Mum," complained Peter.

"Oh hush, let's get the kettle on and I'll fill you in on the latest news," said Janice. "Jim darling, did you remember milk?"

"I'm not a complete idiot, dear," James chuckled. "There's also tea, coffee and juice for the kids. Oh, and I bumped into Dee Dee on my way back, headed her off at the pass. Didn't think you'd be ready for visitors yet. She sent this," he said, handing a white cake box to his wife.

"Oh, that's so thoughtful, it's just like Dee Dee and Jane," exclaimed Janice.

A few minutes later, cake and coffee in hand, Janice filled Peter in on the happenings of Appleton Vale.

"The Jarvis's moved to Wales a couple of years ago, Carrie and Seamus O'Donnell live next door now, lovely couple," Janice told Peter.

"Devon and Patrick, you remember them, don't you? Well they live opposite now, bought it from old Mrs Banks, it was in a right state when they moved in by all accounts. Beautiful now though, gays really do have such good taste," she said, dreamily.

"Mum!"

"What? Can't I even call them gay now?"

James guffawed.

"Oh, and I bumped into Michael Pratt in Bears Bridge the other day, he said to give him a call to arrange a drink. You two were so close at school, you should call him."

"Give it a rest Mum, I've only been back five minutes," Peter pleaded with her.

"Ok darling, baby steps," she said gently.

"How's Sebastian?" Peter asked. They'd been close as children.

"Bloody fool," James puffed. "Can't keep it in his pants and permanently pissed. Shame, such a waste, all that talent."

"Not without good reason Dad," Peter said. "He's had a shitty time too."

"Language Peter," Janice tutted.

"I'm joking Mum," he replied.

"At least you didn't hit the bottle like Sebastian," said Janice, a little smugly.

"Bloody fool," James muttered.

"The poor sod had it splattered across every newspaper in the world, how'd you think that would feel? It's not like he did anything wrong, is it?" Peter was sympathetic for his old friend.

"Chaps at the club aren't impressed, thinking of dumping him, bad for their image," said James.

"That's bloody typical. Kick a man while he's down, why don't they?" Peter exclaimed.

A shriek came from upstairs.

"Dad...daaaaadddd....daddy, there's a spider in the bath," cried Evie.

"I'll go," said James, and headed towards the stairs yelling "Grampy to the rescue."

"So, what else can I tell you?" Janice continued. "Oh, Church Farm now has a fantastic shop, they call it a food barn, I ask you! Lovely lady who runs it for Maud, Andrea Hartley. You'll meet her soon I'm sure. Oh, and there's a girl who's moved here from London to ghost write Sebastian's autobiography, it's all very exciting."

"Sounds riveting," Peter rolled his eyes.

Janice ignored him. "Tom and Susie, you know, from the pub. Well, they've shipped in a fancy French chef and now you can't get a table for love nor money, it's all townies," she crinkled her nose.

"Christ Mum, you're such a snob."

"I AM NOT," Janice was indignant. "I just liked it more when Appleton Vale was a secret. They've gone and put it on the map and we're being invaded by foodies."

Peter sighed, "Whatever you say. Look, do you mind if you and Dad bugger off home now? I appreciate you being here to welcome us but I need a bit of time to adjust and get the kids settled in".

"Yes, yes of course darling. James, we're going," she called up the stairs.

"We've only just got here, woman," James called back, gruffly.

"Peter needs to get on, we can see them later, come on," Janice urged him to hurry.

Turning back to Peter she said, "You'll come over for family lunch tomorrow won't you darling? It's about time Evie and Teddy got to know their cousins."

"Yes Mum, of course. Thanks for everything, it's great to know you're just around the corner," he bent to kiss her cheek. "See you tomorrow. Bye Dad."

As Peter closed the door behind them he thought, *well here goes nothing.*

Chapter 14

It was November fifth and up at Church Farm a huge fire was blazing, Guy Fawkes was burning and a succession of fireworks exploded into the cold night sky.

Susie had insisted Olivia come to the village bonfire night to get to know some of the other residents, and they were having fun.

"Glad I dragged you out?" Susie ribbed Olivia, handing her another glass of wine.

"It's great, they know how to put on a good show, that's for sure," Olivia was impressed. "Must've spent a fortune on it."

"The Crailley's son-in-law, Steve Saint, is a pyrotechnics expert, always away on film sets blowing things up," Susie told her. "He gets the fireworks at a huge discount and the village committee funds the rest."

"Shame they didn't stomp up the cash to get better wine," Olivia winced as she took a sip. "It's like bloody vinegar".

"Crap, isn't it?" Susie laughed. "Barnard's incredibly upset that he wasn't put in charge of the booze".

Barnard LeFeuvre was the Michelin-starred French chef responsible for putting Riverside Inn on the map.

Olivia felt a tap on her shoulder. "Excuse me. You're Olivia?"

"Hi, yes," Olivia smiled.

"I'm Pat Cowan, your cleaner."

"Oh hi," Olivia replied, "Thanks for getting the house in order before I arrived. Sorry I keep missing you, I've been up at the manor most days."

"Hairy isn't he," said Pat.

"Sebastian?" Olivia and Susie exchanged glances, trying not to laugh.

"The dog. He leaves hair everywhere".

"Oh, Hector, yes, sorry about that," Olivia tried to hold back the laughter and failed miserably when she caught Susie's eye.

As they giggled like a pair of school girls, Pat looked at them both quizzically, turned on her heels and wandered off.

"Told you she was odd," Susie grinned.

"I really thought she meant Sebastian for a moment," Olivia wiped her tears and took another gulp of wine. "God, this really is bad."

"Let's sneak back to the pub and grab a couple of decent bottles, we won't be missed, for a while at least," said Susie.

They didn't make it back to the party and Tom found them a little worse for wear on his return to the pub.

"Oh, so this is where you two disappeared to," he said. "How much have you had to drink?" he laughed.

"Juss the one bottle," Susie slurred.

"Each," Olivia added.

"I hope it was the good stuff or you're going to feel crap in the morning," said Tom.

"Feel a bit shit now," Susie was green.

"Right, bed, now," Tom said firmly. "I'll see you home Olivia,"

"Don't be silly, it's fifty yards door to door, I'm fine," she replied and slipped her coat on.

"Ok, 'night then, and drink some water before you go to sleep." Tom was insistent.

"Yes sir," Olivia said with a mock salute and stumbled off home.

She woke the next morning with a head full of cotton wool and a raging thirst. "I'm never drinking again", she muttered. Hector looked up at her and rolled his eyes.

Gently easing herself out of bed, Olivia quickly downed the forgotten glass of water and went for a shower.

An hour later, after several strong coffees, she ventured out to Church Farm Food Barn.

She had just walked through the heavy glass doors when she saw Andrea Hartley heading her way. The diminutive, bubbly redhead was a riot of curls and curves - Olivia had liked her very much when they had met the previous evening.

"Morning," Andrea trilled. "You look a little jaded, heavy night?"

"Just a bit," Olivia laughed. "Susie and I demolished a couple of bottles of wine after the bonfire party, I feel terrible".

"Oh dear," Andrea was sympathetic.

"All self-inflicted, I've no one else to blame," said Olivia. "I'm crap at drinking, don't know why I bother when I feel like this."

Andrea laughed. "I've got a delivery coming in now, but if there's anything you need that you can't find just ask one of the staff. Let's meet up for a drink soon, maybe the pub quiz? We need some brains on our team."

"Sounds great, maybe just an orange juice though" Olivia replied with a smile. *I think I'm starting to like it here*, she thought.

On the short journey home, car laden with shopping, Olivia passed the parish church of St Saviours' and pulled the car in to take a quick look. A giant oak tree, said to be at least four hundred years old and rumored to have magical properties, dominated the churchyard, casting a protective shadow over its resting souls.

"Good morning," a gentle voice came from behind her.

Olivia turned around to find a pale, wiry man with twinkling eyes and a dog collar.

"Hi," she replied.

"Olivia, isn't it?" he asked. "I'm Kevin Flett, Kev the Rev."

"Kev the Rev?" Olivia laughed.

"That's what they call me. Welcome to the village, will we be seeing you in church?" he enquired.

"Er, no, I don't think so," Olivia replied. "I'm a non-believer I'm afraid."

"Ah well, we all have our crosses to bear. What brings you to God's humble abode today?"

"This," Olivia touched the tree.

"Magnificent, isn't it?" said Kev, with pride. "Some of the carvings date back hundreds of years, all couples from the village who married here, a tradition of sorts."

"Yes, that's what Dee Dee told me," she said, slowly moving around the vast trunk, gently touching each carving as she read the inscriptions.

Sensing she was lost in thought, Kev said, "I'll leave you to it my dear. The door's always open if you change your mind, God doesn't hold grudges."

"Nice to meet you," she said before turning her attention back to the tree.

Eventually she found what she had been looking for. There it was, etched deeply into the wood, "S & E Forever Bloom".

She felt a pang of jealousy and muttered, "For God's sake, pull yourself together, how can you be jealous of a dead woman?"

Momentarily, Sebastian filled her head. She missed him. *Don't fall for him, DON'T fall for him,* she said to herself, and tried to shake it off.

Chapter 15

It had not been a successful trip for Sebastian. Playing far from his best, he missed the cut in Shanghai which put him out of the final stages of the tournament. So he had time to kill before moving on to Malaysia, and although he knew he should be trying to right the wrongs in his game, he just couldn't focus.

Another missed cut in Kuala Lumpur, coupled with a hefty fine from the Tour committee for smashing up his wedge in frustration during competition, and he was at breaking point.

He picked up the phone and dialled his personal assistant, Poppy Jones, assigned to him by his manager.

"Poppy. Sebastian," he said curtly. "I'm going home, get me on the next flight."

"Oh hi, Sebastian," Poppy purred. "Does Richie know you're leaving?"

"I sent him a text," he replied.

"Is anything wrong?"

"Just get me on the next flight, text me the details."

"Yes of course Sebastian, anything for you."

Five minutes later the text came through and Sebastian was on his way to the airport. A little over an hour after that, he was strapped into his first-class seat and on his way home.

Sebastian's arrival back in Appleton Vale a week early threw everyone into turmoil.

"What are you doing home?" Georgiana shouted as she flew down the stairs to greet him.

"I live here," he snapped.

Ignoring his tone, she threw her arms around him. "We've missed you.

"You too," he said, softening somewhat. "I'm going to my study; can you ask Hattie to bring me some coffee?"

"Come and have breakfast," Georgiana pleaded.

"Not hungry."

"Oh. OK," Georgiana replied in a small voice. "Perhaps you'll feel like it later?"

"Let's have a quiet family meal tonight," he said gently, realising he had been unkind.

Georgiana beamed. "That's a great idea, I'll tell Hatts." She skipped off towards the kitchen, leaving Sebastian and his black mood in the hallway.

His mobile rang just as he walked into the study.

"What the fuck do you think you're doing?" His manager Richie's voice boomed down the line. "You don't just leave when you've got a sponsor's invite, Sebastian. Do you have any idea how hard I had to work to get you into that tournament?" He was furious.

"I don't want to talk about it right now," Sebastian sighed.

"I'm coming down there tomorrow," Richie said firmly.

"Why bother? I'm a fucking wreck," Sebastian was morose.

"Stop feeling sorry for yourself, you asshole. Don't give me that bullshit. You forget how well I know you." Richie was exasperated. "I'll be there in the morning".

"Fine," Sebastian grunted and hung up the phone.

Then a text came through. He saw it was from Olivia and his stomach lurched.

'Hi Sebastian. Georgiana just told me you're home a week early.

When do you want to start work? Olivia x'

He punched in his reply, short and to the point.

'You can come over after lunch. Be good to see you. SB.'

I want to see her. I've missed her, he thought.

Olivia arrived at the manor at one thirty and headed straight for Sebastian's study. She shrugged off her jacket and threw her bag on a chair, and was just about to go in search of him when she heard a commotion from beyond the windows.

"You useless piece of shit," Sebastian shouted at the axe he was holding. He was taking his frustrations out on a pile of logs in the courtyard behind the kitchen. Ace was chewing off-shoots and keeping his head down, while Sebastian ranted on.

Olivia held back and silently watched him. *Shit he looks angry*, she thought. *Double shit, he's got no shirt on.* She let out an involuntary gasp, admiring the way his muscles rippled with every stroke of the axe.

Sebastian paused, sensing he was being watched, and turned and waved at Olivia. She opened the French doors and wandered out towards him.

"Hey. Shall we get to work?" he said wearily, offering her a weak smile.

"Hey," Olivia returned his smile warily. "You sure you want to do this? You only got back this morning, aren't you tired?"

"I need to do something," Sebastian replied, looking lost.

"Why don't you go to the club, see Hugh?" Olivia urged gently.

"Been talking to Georgiana, have you?" he snapped. "I'll decide what I'm doing and when I'm doing it, thank you."

"Oh," Olivia cringed. "It was just a suggestion, of course we'll work, if that's what you want?"

Sebastian sighed, "Sorry, I don't mean to snap your head off, perhaps we shouldn't work today."

"OK, I've got plenty to be getting on with anyway."

Sebastian turned away and picked up the axe, signalling to Olivia that their conversation was over.

Calling Hector, who looked most upset about leaving his friend and the pile of wood they had been chewing, she turned back towards the house.

She ran into Georgiana on her way out.

"Your brother is a nightmare to work with," she was frustrated.

"Tell me something I don't know," Georgiana replied with a grin. "Look Liv," she said softly. "He's complicated. I wish you'd known him before, he was funny and kind and really easy-going".

"I'm finding that hard to believe," Olivia fished inside her bag for her car keys. "All I hear is how wonderful he is. Am I missing something?"

"He's been much better since you arrived," Georgiana told her. "I even heard him singing in the shower before he went to China and he hasn't done that for years. Out of tune, but singing nonetheless."

"We've hardly touched the surface with the book and I'm exhausted," Olivia said, disheartened.

"No! Don't give up on him, please Liv," Georgiana begged. "He needs you, he likes you."

"Well he's got a funny way of showing it".

"Just give him a chance, please?" Georgiana implored. "What happened anyway?"

"I suggested he went to see Hugh."

"Oh, right. Well someone had to and he wasn't listening to me. Maybe he'll do it now you've pushed him." Georgiana was hopeful.

"Why on earth would he do it because of me?" asked Olivia, bemused.

"He likes you, a gentle nudge in the right direction from the right person may do it," Georgiana explained.

"That's not me," Olivia stated.

"I think it could be," Georgiana replied with a wink. "Gotta go, the farrier is coming, I swear that bloody horse gets more new shoes than I do." She disappeared into the kitchen leaving Olivia in the hallway, still looking for her car keys.

Realising she must have left them in Sebastian's study, she wandered down the corridor and in through the open door.

"There you are," she said to the keys sitting on the wooden mantle above the colossal fireplace. She picked them up and walked over to the window, unable to resist sneaking a last peek at Sebastian labouring over the wood before she left.

"Oh," she gasped. He was sitting on the cobblestones leaning against the wall, with his arms around Ace, sobbing uncontrollably. She had a desperate yearning to go to him, to take him in her arms and wipe away his tears.

"You see." Hattie's voice made her jump. "It breaks my heart," she sniffed and pulled a tissue out of her apron pocket.

"I had no idea." Olivia turned away from the window, feeling like she was intruding into his privacy. "I should go." She was embarrassed.

"He's having more good days than bad since you arrived," Hattie said pointedly.

"I know how he feels," Olivia muttered.

Hattie smiled, "Maybe you can help each other. Georgie told me about your ex-boyfriend, I hope you don't mind me bringing it up."

Olivia looked at Hattie's anxious face and replied, gently, "Of course not."

"Broken hearts and broken bones, they all mend," Hattie said, knowingly, and shuffled off down the corridor, leaving Olivia rooted to the spot, unable to take her eyes off Sebastian.

Chapter 16

The next morning Sebastian's agent, Richie Rogers, arrived at Appleton Manor in his flashy, yellow Lamborghini and immediately launched into an attack on his client.

"Are you kidding me? Walking out of the tournament like that! Do you know how much damage this has done? You couldn't even be bothered to feign an injury to save face, could you?" fumed Richie.

"Yeah, I know. Sorry. Don't know what came over me. I just needed to be at home," Sebastian offered his explanation wearily.

"You're a fucking idiot," Richie replied. "We've got sponsor trouble big time. Oyster Bay's dropping you and we're perilously close to losing Damien de Landre. As you're fully aware, we've only been able to hold onto them both for this long as you had the sympathy vote, but now it's old and tired and they want out. Be thankful that PowerSports has a history of standing by its former and fallen stars."

Sebastian had been with Oyster Bay, a luxury watch brand, since he had turned professional, and had also enjoyed a long-term contract with the French fashion label Damien de Landre. PowerSports was a global sportswear and equipment giant that had signed him up as soon as he had relinquished his amateur status, and had helped make him one of the most-recognised golfers on the planet. If they dropped him it would be over.

"Shit, this is all I fucking need right now. What do I have to do to make it right?" he asked Richie.

"I think it's too late for that. We just have to make sure we hang onto PowerSports or you're totally fucked. No one wants you right now Sebastian, that's the truth. I'm sorry to be so blunt."

"Christ Richie, I'm a mess. I'm getting grief from every bloody angle, including my own sister. She's ganging up with Olivia. They want me to see Hugh, go back to basics. I know I need to but I'm such a stubborn bastard that it's taken me this long to admit it."

"But you've admitted it now, to me at least, and that's a good first step mate," said Richie. "We go back a long way. I only have your best interests at heart, you know that. You put me in this job because you know I'm not one of those corporate fuckers you hate so much, so trust me. See Hugh, listen to Georgiana, do the work now and it will pay off, I promise you."

"Thanks Rich. I don't know what I'd have done without you all these years."

Sebastian choked back the tears and it almost broke Richie's heart. He badly wanted his friend to get back on track.

"Yeah, the feeling's entirely mutual my friend. Now are you going to give me a sodding drink or what?"

"Coffee?"

"Thank Christ for that, thought you were going to crack open the scotch," Richie was relieved.

"I'm off the booze. At least that's something, right?"

"I'll say so, you're a lousy drunk," Richie laughed.

He followed Sebastian into the kitchen.

"Richie, how lovely to see you. Breakfast?" Hattie greeted him warmly.

Richie walked over and kissed her on the cheek "Looking as stunning as ever, Hattie," he replied.

Hattie chuckled, "You know how to make an old woman happy, now sit down and tell me what you want. Eggs? Bacon sandwich? Pancakes?"

"Christ, are you trying to finish me off," Richie laughed. "Got any fruit?"

"Of course. Sebastian?" said Hattie.

"Just coffee please. Don't look at me like that, I'm not hungry, I'll get something later. Where's Georgie?"

"Up at the yard with the vet, I think she fancies him," Hattie chuckled.

Sebastian scowled, "Over my dead body. She's too young to be dating."

"That's rich, coming from you," Richie spluttered through a sip of steaming coffee.

"Sebastian, she's nineteen. Of course she's interested in boys. You can't keep her under lock and key," said Hattie gently.

"Besides, she's a stunner, they'll be flocking to the manor in their droves before you know it," Richie offered, somewhat unhelpfully.

Glaring at him, Sebastian replied, "I'm not having some spotty, hormone-addled youth getting his hands on my sister. She's not going to make the same mistakes I did, not if I can help it."

"If you interfere she'll just push back harder, you know how stubborn she is," said Hattie.

"Runs in the family," muttered Richie. Sebastian shot him a withering look.

"Worry about it when there's something to worry about; she's quite capable of making her own decisions. You've got bigger fish to fry," Richie continued.

Sebastian sighed, "Best get on with it then. What's the plan?"

"Charm offensive, to PowerSports at least. I'll set up a meeting in London as soon as; just make sure you turn up. It's your last chance, don't let me down," Richie pleaded.

An hour later, after a series of calls and a double serving of humble pie, Sebastian was feeling a little better. Richie had arranged a meeting with Power-Sports on Friday, and he was determined to get them back on side.

Seeing Richie off, he was grateful, "Thanks for coming mate, and for your unerring faith in me. I'll turn it around, I know I can."

"You'd better," Richie beamed at him, and got into the car. "See you Friday."

"I'll be there."

Back in the office, a few hours after his meeting with Sebastian, Richie put the phone down, leaned back in his chair and looked around his corner office on the top floor of the glass-domed Global Sports & Entertainment Inc. (GSE) headquarters.

The walls were covered with framed photographs of Sebastian winning tournaments around the world as well as replica trophies, pin flags from his Major victories and countless other items of memorabilia that most golf nuts would kill to get their hands on.

How has it come to this, when did I take my eye off the ball?

Richie recalled the day they met, almost fifteen years ago, when he had been playing, rather badly, in a corporate golf day. He had hooked his tee shot into the car park and straight through the windscreen of the club captain's Rolls Royce, where he found Sebastian assessing the damage with a look of glee.

"I'd get myself a lawyer if I were you pal, the captain's a mean bastard and this is his pride and joy." Sebastian patted the car, laughing.

"I *am* a lawyer," he grinned. "And you're Sebastian Bloom, *the* next big thing in golf. Richie Rogers." He extended his hand to Sebastian.

Sebastian had charmed the captain on Richie's behalf and that had been the start of their friendship. Richie had been a corporate lawyer for five years and hated it, but meeting Sebastian changed the course of his career forever.

Six months after that first, fortuitous meeting, Sebastian became the youngest player ever to be picked for the Walker Cup team, an amateur golf tournament held between Great Britain and Ireland, and the USA. He played some stunning golf and helped secure an historic victory for the team. There had been talk of him turning professional after the tournament, and it had been Richie he had turned to for advice.

"You're the one with the brains, I need advice."

"I can certainly look over the contracts for you, no problem," Richie offered.

"That's not what I meant. I want you to represent me, be my manager," Sebastian said.

"Me? Why? What the fuck do I know about golf?" Richie laughed.

"I trust you, and I've got no one else," Sebastian didn't want to make career defining decisions without someone representing his interests. "I just want to play golf."

In the end, they'd come to a mutually beneficial compromise. Sebastian would sign with GSE Inc, and Richie would be his manager, working directly for the company. That had been the condition of Sebastian signing his contract and it had been one of the best decisions he had ever made. What Richie didn't know about the golf business he would learn from his peers, and what he didn't know about Sebastian Bloom wasn't worth knowing. It was a match made in heaven.

The last two years, since Ellie and Lizzie had died, had been terrible. He had to fight fires on a global scale to get Sebastian out of some sticky situations, using his considerable power to put a lid on scandalous events that could have sunk his client many times over.

There had been a host of kiss-and-tell stories plastered across the media, a few true, the majority fabricated, and a sex tape that Sebastian neither knew nor cared about. Then there was the heavy drinking, black moods and his deliberate efforts to piss off just about everyone he knew. Richie knew his friend was grieving and leaving him to get through it on his own had been the wrong decision - he should have done more to help him.

If this is rock bottom, then there's only one way to go from here.

He picked up the phone and started the seemingly impossible task of getting Sebastian back on track. He could only do so much though; the rest was up to his client, both on and off the golf course.

Chapter 17

Sebastian skulked into Riverside Golf and Country Club very early the next morning. Georgiana, Richie and, to some extent, Olivia, had backed him into a corner and he knew they were right to get him back on the golf course. In an emotional call the previous evening to Hugh McLauchlin, his coach and mentor, he apologised for his actions over the past few years and they had arranged to meet the very next day.

It was bitterly cold and frosty, and still dark when he arrived, *much like my mood*, he mused. He got to the driving range just as the floodlights burst into action, almost blinding him in the process, and Hugh appeared.

"Morning Sebastian, ready to start?"

"I'm here, aren't I?" he said wearily.

"I think you have forgotten how long I've known you Sebastian. Your bad manners don't rattle me. We're here to work and get you back to winning ways, that's all."

"Shit, I'm sorry," Sebastian sighed. "I don't know where to start, I can't focus."

"So we go back to basics. And don't worry, I have a plan. It's not so much your game as your state of mind, it's always been like that, even when you were a nipper. From this moment on you're going to stop blaming everyone else and admit you're the problem. Got that?"

"Yes, Sir!" Sebastian gave Hugh a mock salute, picked up his Tour bag and walked over to his reserved spot on the range, where he began his warm-up, while Hugh dispensed balls in to several buckets from the machine behind him.

"Tell me Sebastian. Do you want to win again?" enquired Hugh.

"What kind of bloody question is that? Of course I do. No matter how shit I feel or what else is going on, I don't want to end my career as the once-best golfer in the world who had a meltdown and lost his game."

"Good. Now we've established that, we just need to get your confidence back in your game and your self-belief restored to where it was before Ellie."

Sebastian cringed at the sound of her name.

Shaking the dark thoughts out of his head, and with renewed determination, he grabbed his wedge and began pounding balls down the range.

Olivia arrived up at the manor later that morning to find a much-changed Sebastian. Gone was the doom and gloom of the past week, instead he was much brighter, almost enthusiastic.

Thrusting a large mug of coffee in her hand, he started babbling on about his session with Hugh and Olivia breathed a sigh of relief. How long this good mood would last for was anyone's guess, but for now she would take it.

"I've been a complete shit, taking things out on you, forgive me?" he asked Olivia. "I hit rock bottom, but on the positive side, the only way is up," he joked.

Olivia smiled "Well I'm glad to hear it. I've got to deliver four more chapters next week."

"Let's get to it then. We can't have you getting told off now can we?" His eyes twinkled as they met hers and she felt her stomach lurch again. She couldn't help thinking that a kaleidoscope of butterflies had set up home in there, twisting and turning whenever Sebastian was around.

Firmly ensconced in Sebastian's study twenty minutes later, Olivia was finding it impossible to concentrate. She had started the day's questioning with his womanising early years, and Sebastian, for once, wasn't holding back.

"Sex was on tap. There were groupies at every tournament and it was easy to bed them, sometimes more than one at a time."

Olivia raised her eyebrows.

"Let me tell you about the night in Marbella," he grinned. "It involved four well-known golfers, myself included, six cocktail waitresses and a drag queen named Krystal."

Olivia almost spat her drink out. Laughing, she replied, "Poor Krystal, I don't think we need the details".

He's enjoying this, seeing me squirm. Bastard!

He left the study to replenish the coffee pot and Olivia had a few moments to compose herself.

"Get it together," she muttered, just as Sebastian returned.

"What was that?" he asked.

"Nothing," Olivia scrambled back to the sofa to continue their session.

"I want to hear a bit about you Olivia," Sebastian said softly edging closer to her. "You know all about me and I know nothing about you".

Alarm bells started going off in Olivia's head. *Oh crap, it's not just me. He's flirting. What do I do? WHAT DO I DO?*

Stuttering, she replied, "I'm not being paid to talk about me, Sebastian."

"What difference does that make? I want to know, no arguments".

"What do you want to know?" she almost whispered, her heart banging in her chest.

Leaning in towards her, Sebastian gently brushed a tendril of hair away from Olivia's face, a gesture so innocent yet so intimate she gave an involuntary gasp and felt a rush of lust course through her body.

"What happened to make you so wary of men, of me?"

"Has Georgiana not told you?" she was surprised.

"No. It seems there are some things she's capable of keeping to herself," he grinned. "Olivia, look at me," he urged gently. "Tell me".

"Let's just say my last boyfriend didn't just break my heart, there were a few bones and a lacerated spleen involved too. But I'm over it," she was defiant.

"Oh God, no, how could anyone do that to you?" he pulled her into his arms, holding her tightly, kissing her head.

"Sebastian, don't," she whispered.

"I have to," he replied gruffly, taking her face in his hands and bending to kiss her.

Tentative at first, she melted into his arms, responding to his mouth and allowing his tongue to probe softly against hers.

Olivia lost herself in his kiss, sensing that his desire matched her own, and at that moment she knew that she would allow him to devour her body and soul.

"You're so beautiful, Liv," he whispered in her ear. "I want to take you to bed".

At that moment, there was a knock at the door. Springing apart, they just about managed to regain some composure before Hattie came bustling in carrying a package for Sebastian.

Mortified that she had given in so easily to Sebastian, and for being caught at it by Hattie, Olivia mumbled something about needing the lavatory and bolted out of the room.

"Didn't interrupt something important, did I?" Hattie asked with a glint in her eye.

"Work, that's all," he replied, face poker straight, giving nothing away.

"Yes, that's exactly what it looked like. Be kind to her Sebastian, she's the real deal."

"I'm starting to realise that. I know I'm no good for her but I can't help it, she makes me feel alive again. Is that wrong?" He trusted Hattie's opinion.

"Of course it isn't. You deserve some happiness, if she can give you that, then you must at least try," urged Hattie. "Don't rush her and stop taking your moods out on her, listen to this wise old woman."

Down the hallway, in the cloakroom, Olivia was admonishing herself for the monumental mistake she had just made. *What the hell was I thinking? I'm supposed to be a professional.* That was exactly the point, she hadn't been thinking. She had allowed her heart, or more like her sexual frustrations, to rule her head.

Turning on the cold tap, she splashed some water on her face and took a long hard look in the mirror. *He's no good for you, he can't give you what you want.*

Forcing herself to leave the sanctuary of the bathroom, she headed back to the study where she found Sebastian, smirk and all, awaiting her return.

"I'm sorry, that should never have happened. It wasn't very professional and I don't know what came over me." She could hardly bring herself to look at him.

"What came over you was me, Olivia," replied Sebastian rather too harshly. "Don't apologise, it was

I who was out of line and it won't happen again. Perhaps we should finish for the day."

Olivia had never felt so small and insignificant; it was all she could do to hold it together as she grabbed her bag and scuttled out of the room.

You could have handled that better, you stupid cow. Oh God, what have I done?

She didn't understand him and she had never felt more bewildered.

Chapter 18

"Susan Feltham room one please," crackled the voice over the intercom.

Putting down the ancient, dog-eared copy of Woman's Weekly that she had been thumbing through in the waiting room; Susie got up and made her way down the corridor.

Dr Elliot was a kind, softly spoken man who immediately put Susie at ease.

"How can I help you today Mrs Feltham?"

"I feel a bit silly for coming here as I can't really tell you what's wrong," Susie admitted. "I'm fairly certain it's nothing that a good holiday wouldn't sort out."

"Why don't you tell me what's been going on. I know you have an incredibly busy life and the pub can't be easy, all those long hours."

"It's hard work, that's for sure, but we wouldn't have it any other way. I'm just a bit burnt out. I haven't felt well for a while."

"Any symptoms to speak of?" asked Dr. Elliot.

"A bit light-headed and nauseous and I'm exhausted all the time."

"Ok, let's have a look at you. Pop your coat off and I'll give you the once-over." He pressed a button on his desk and the practice nurse joined them almost immediately.

"I'm sure there's nothing wrong. My husband was the one who wanted me to come here, he's such a worrier," Susie babbled, nervously.

A few minutes later, satisfied that all the basic tests he had done were normal he said, "Susan, if I may call you that?"

"Susie, only my mother calls me Susan."

"OK Susie, I need a urine sample," he handed her a white stick.

Susie was confused, "What's this?"

"What does it look like?" Dr. Elliot smiled. "I've glanced over your records and see that you were trying for a baby at one point. Both you and your husband had the fertility tests and it was deemed that there was no reason you couldn't get pregnant. Do you think it's possible that that could explain your symptoms? When was your last period?"

Susie started counting back and realised that it had been a few months since her last one. They had been so busy that she hadn't given it a second thought.

Slowly a smile crept across her face. "Do you really think I could be pregnant?"

"Well why don't we find out right now?" He pointed her in the direction of the bathroom.

Scuttling off to the toilet, Susie quickly bolted the door behind her and stood silently for a moment staring in the mirror.

Could this be it, could we really be this lucky?

She couldn't get her trousers undone quickly enough. Peeing on the stick, she put it to one side and washed her trembling hands. Two minutes felt like an eternity.

"Five, four, three, two, one," she counted out loud, looking at her watch. And there it was, she could hardly believe her eyes. Positive. A big fat positive. How could she not have known?

Unable to contain her joy she let out a huge whoop and hurled herself back into Dr Elliot's office.

"I take it from the joyful noise I heard out there, and by the look on your face, not to mention the pregnancy test you're waving under my nose, that there's a baby Feltham on the way," he said.

"How did you guess?" Susie laughed. "This feels like a miracle, we've been trying for years, I'd re-signed myself to not having a child, and we were even considering adoption."

"That's often the way in circumstances such as yours. No real reason you can't have a baby and then bang, just when you give up, it happens."

Half an hour later, armed with information on midwives, scans and a follow-up appointment in the diary, Susie rushed home. She couldn't wait to tell Tom, he was going to be over the moon.

Tom was beaming. He had the biggest smile plastered across his face all day and it showed no sign of disappearing. His wife wasn't ill; she was having their baby, a tiny little miracle they had wanted for a very long time.

"What?" he asked in disbelief.

"A baby, we're having a baby darling." Susie was jumping for joy.

"How? When?"

"I think you know how," Susie laughed. "And as for when, I'm already three month's gone so we can tell everyone straight away. You'll never be able to keep your trap shut anyway. I can't wait to tell Olivia, she'll be so pleased for us."

A little while later she found Olivia in the post office, "I've been bursting to tell you our news. I'm pregnant, isn't that just the best thing you've ever heard?"

"Oh Susie, that's amazing," Olivia exclaimed, hugging her friend. "When did you find out, when's it due, what does Tom think?"

"Tom's over the moon, naturally, we both are. We were at the point where we didn't think it would happen after trying for so many years. I'm three months gone and I didn't even know. Thought I was just a bit run down, didn't even register that I'd been missing periods. Can you imagine it? I'm trying not to think about the alcohol I've drunk though."

"I'm so happy for you both; hopefully I'll still be around when he or she pops out."

"Did someone say baby?" came a squeak from behind the counter.

Marjorie Rose was the timid, mouse-like post mistress whose ear for gossip almost rivalled Dee Dee's. She had just returned to Appleton Vale after an exciting Saga holiday in Budapest.

"Oh Susie," she breathed. "I'd hate you to think I was eavesdropping but that's such wonderful news. I've been standing here all morning wishing I was back in Hungary, delighting in the beauty of the Esztergom Basilica, and now you've cheered me up immensely."

"Thanks, Marjorie," Susie tinkled. "Hopefully you'll be around when the baby arrives or do you have another Saga trip in the offing?"

"You know me, can't resist a European mini-break and there really are some lovely people on each trip. It's so much fun." Her squeaky voice was going up an octave a minute as she chirped on and on about the cultural differences between Budapest and Seville, where she had been on her previous holiday.

"Sorry to butt in Marjorie, but I really must get off, I'm on a deadline. Susie, didn't you say you wanted a lift up to the farm shop?" Olivia elbowed Susie, looking for her agreement.

Reading Olivia's mind, Susie replied, "Yes please, chef has run out of shallots and swears blind he can't use a normal onion in the Coquille St Jacques."

Olivia, suppressing a laugh, gently steered Susie out of the post office.

"Bye, Marjorie," she shouted over her shoulder.

"Good bye dear girls. Do pop in again soon, I'll have my Budapest photos back from the shop in a few days and you really must see them."

Giggling, Olivia and Susie walked arm in arm across the village green.

"That was quick thinking; we could have been in there all afternoon. I'll have to hide out in the flat for an hour just in case she comes into the pub."

"Go and put your feet up for an hour anyway, you've got precious cargo on board now," Olivia smiled warmly. "I predict Tom won't let you lift a finger till that baby's born, and probably afterwards too. Make the most of it."

"He's going to drive me crazy, I know it. You should've seen his face when I told him; I thought he was going to burst with pride."

"You're a lucky woman," Olivia said. "Now go and hide before Marjorie sees you."

Olivia watched with envy as Susie walked back into the pub and fell into Tom's arms, so obviously in love and brimming with happiness.

That's what I want.

Chapter 19

Peter was beginning to feel claustrophobic. His mother and sister had been camped out on his doorstep ever since he had moved back to Appleton Vale, and it was driving him mad.

He broached the subject just a few days after their big family get-together.

"I need space Mum. You're suffocating me and the kids."

Janice was indignant. "We are not, you said you needed help."

"We do, I do, just not twenty-four hours a day." He took her hand. "It's all I can do to hold it together, knowing she's just down the road and being too bloody chicken to go and see her. I don't need you on my case all the time."

"Darling," Janice said gently. "Sarah doesn't know you, she doesn't remember anything of you and the children, or the life you had together. I know you feel guilty but her going into the home was the best thing for everyone. You had to put Evie and Teddy first.

Peter held his head in shame.

"For what it's worth, your father and I believe you did the right thing, and Sarah's parents do too. They were so upset the last time they visited, I think they finally understood why you did what you did," Janice continued.

"But to lie to my children, that's unforgiveable." Peter was distraught.

"Yes, well you know how I feel about that," Janice tutted. "But you can put that right. They'll forgive you when they understand what it all means."

"I hope so Mum, I couldn't bear to lose them as well, due to my own stupidity."

Just being back in the house that Sarah had loved so much was painful. She was in every room; everywhere he looked he could see her.

He remembered the day they were handed the keys for Blossom Hill - he and Sarah had run around each room squealing with joy that it was all theirs. That seemed like a lifetime ago now.

She had become ill quickly, and the once vivacious woman, brimming with life, began to disappear before his eyes. Vascular dementia was a cruel, debilitating and heartbreaking disease.

Sarah now lived in Meadowbrook Nursing Home in the neighbouring village of Bears Bridge. Housed in a beautiful Georgian mansion, it offered the best care that money could buy - Sarah had barely existed there ever since.

At first he had been visiting daily but, as the weeks and months went on, her memory deteriorated at an astonishingly fast rate. She became confused easily, which would then turn to anger and frustration, and the doctors had told him he was doing more harm than good by visiting so regularly.

Heartbroken, destroyed and demented with grief, he was unable to come to terms with what had happened to his beloved wife. Her mind had been so cruelly snatched away from her at such a young age, and life would never be the same again for any of them. Unable to bear being so close to her, it was too much for Peter, so he had packed up his family and left Appleton Vale.

He had been in constant touch with the care home over the years but had not had the guts to face her, or the inevitable heartbreak, he would feel again. He was wracked with guilt and ashamed of himself for leaving her.

"I'm going to see her tomorrow," Peter told his mother.

"Do you want me to come with you?"

"Thanks, but I need to do this on my own. Will you be able to pick the kids up from school?"

"Yes of course, but are you sure. Dad can come if you'd rather."

"Really, I'm fine," he reassured his mother.

It's time to face my demons.

Chapter 20

"If someone doesn't stop those devil children from wrecking this shop I won't be responsible for my actions," Andrea screamed at no one in particular, not noticing members of staff ducking out of her way at every turn. Even the giggling duo of Chloe and Lauren, who worked on the tills, was strangely muted. They knew their boss had a temper to match her fiery red hair, although any outburst with her was normally justified and was usually over as quickly as it had begun.

She was at her wits end after having her employer's grandchildren dumped on her all morning, and now they were wrecking her carefully arranged window displays and running wild on the shop floor, upsetting customers and almost knocking poor old Mrs Banks clean off her feet at the Deli counter.

Luke and Lilly Crailley were the six-year-old twins of Malcolm and Maud's son Martin, and his wife Sophie. They were regularly left in the care of their grandparents at the drop of a hat. If their parents were aware that they had spawned the devil's children, they certainly didn't let on.

Just as Andrea was contemplating her resignation, Olivia wandered in through the glass entrance doors.

"God, am I glad to see you." Andrea gave a huge sigh of relief.

"Why what's up?" Olivia cringed as she heard a loud crash behind her followed by a squeal of high-pitched voices and footsteps running into the distance. "Actually, I don't need to ask. I take it the evil twins are in residence again?"

"Christ, I've just about had enough. Don't get me wrong, I like kids, but these two are vile. It's no wonder Martin and Sophie dump them at every opportunity," she was seething.

"Take a breath," Olivia put a soothing arm around her shoulder. "How about we go for a bite to eat in the pub tonight and drown our sorrows?"

"What are you drinking to forget then?" Andrea joked.

"You really don't want to know," she laughed in return. "How about we meet at seven? I'll book a table in the bar just in case it gets busy later."

"Sounds perfect. Although if you get a call you don't recognise on your mobile later make sure you answer it. You may have to bail me out for murder."

The sound of shattering glass echoed across the barn and Andrea's face turned white.

"What the hell have they gone and done now?" she was murderous. "Sorry Olivia, I've got to sort this out, see you tonight."

She scuttled off across the shop while simultaneously punching the number of Malcolm Crailley into her mobile phone.

After ranting for ten minutes down the phone line to her boss, Andrea was on her hands and knees carefully sweeping up the broken glass.

"I'm going to kill those little buggers," she muttered over and over again. "Mark my words."

Despite her employers' demonic grandchildren, Andrea Hartley enjoyed her job. She had arrived in Appleton Vale four years previously, having seen an advertisement in the back of Country Life magazine for a 'highly experienced and professional general manager' to run the, soon-to-be-opened, Church Farm Food Barn.

She was both professional and highly experienced, and had won over Malcolm and Maud immediately with her engaging nature and sense of humour. They offered her the job on the spot and she took it, upping sticks from her life in Norfolk and moving to the village within a week.

Getting the food barn off the ground had been a challenge, but one that she had relished, getting involved in every aspect from pricing to PR. She had scoured the county for homemade and home grown produce with the aim of creating a sustainable business. The majority of meat, vegetables and fruit came from the Crailley's farm and the many grow tunnels

they had erected. Baked goods came from Butter's bakery in the village, and all the drinks on offer were locally made or from breweries in the region.

She had found, and nurtured, a small but loyal team of workers who labored harmoniously and were a joy to work with. Customers often remarked on the cheeriness of the staff, and were highly impressed with their knowledge on each and every item that was stocked. Four years on and business was booming - the county was filled with wealthy residents who remained seemingly untouched by the recession.

Andrea had a good life in Appleton Vale, delighting in her tiny cottage on the village green. She had made it into a truly comfortable home for her and Cleopatra, her tabby cat.

Inside it was cosy and warm, with muted tones on the walls, and stripped wooden floorboards. A battered leather sofa dominated the sitting room, and all around the house were bookcases stuffed with an eclectic mix of romantic, crime and historical fiction, as well as a host of encyclopaedias and well-thumbed copies of Country Life, Farmers Weekly and Hello magazines.

Her bedroom was in stark contrast to the rest of the house, with its bright pink feature wall, whitewashed floor and queen-sized bed, complete with an overhanging canopy. At the small, leaded windows hung billowing swathes of organza, embroidered with tiny shimmering crystals that sparkled in the morning sun, and either side of the bed lay

luxurious sheepskin rugs. She had injected passion into the room hoping that, one day, she would be sharing her life with a wonderful man.

Andrea had been desperately unlucky in love but still held out hope: the eternal optimist.

No one's going to come knocking on the door anytime soon. I've got to get out there and meet someone.

Hearing the giggles and squeals coming from the entrance to the shop, Andrea's heart momentarily stopped beating. *Please God no, what have they wrecked now?*

She rose to her feet, walked past the Deli counter and came face to face with Peter, Evie and Teddy Jenner, who all seemed to be in great spirits and making the most of the beautiful day.

"Hello! I'm Andrea, general manager here at Church Farm Food Barn," she offered her hand to Peter in greeting. "Feel free to browse and ask any questions, we're here to help."

Smiling broadly, Peter shook her hand, "Peter Jenner, and these little bundles of joy are Evie and Teddy. This place is great; it was only being built when we moved away. I never imagined it would look like this."

"I'll take that as a compliment," Andrea grinned, giving him the sly once over. She knew the tragic story of his wife, and how it had ripped his heart apart, and she felt a wave of sympathy for him.

"How are you settling back into the village?" she politely enquired.

"The kids have taken to their new surroundings like ducks to water and love being around family. My parents still live locally, just out past the Whiteside Estate, and my sister and her family are in Bears Bridge."

She noticed he had not indicated how he was feeling about being back.

Why would he? He doesn't know me and he's hardly likely to pour his heart over cooked hams and paté.

They chatted for a while longer, with Peter remarking on all the changes that had taken place in the village since he had left. Thinking she had taken up too much of his time, Andrea excused herself and left him to shop in peace.

As he walked away, Andrea could not help but notice how good looking he was.

Charming, good looking and lovely kids. That's the trifector. The first nice man I meet in forever and he's completely off limits.

Chapter 21

Olivia could not remember ever being this sociable, even during her time in London. In the run-up to Christmas it seemed like half the village was throwing some sort of soirée, and she had been strong-armed by Susie and Andrea into attending all of them.

The first invitation she had accepted was from the vile Lucinda and Godfrey Walton-Smythe who owned the Whiteside Estate. She had agreed to attend the '*Christmas carols and cocktails*' party more out of curiosity than desire, and was pleasantly surprised when it turned out to be a jolly occasion, with superb outside catering and the Fiddlebury gospel choir in fine voice.

Last night, on Christmas Eve, she had been at the vicarage where Kev the Rev, after one tipple too many, had led his guests in a raucous conga around the village green. Fortunately for Olivia, she had been in the lavatory at the time the conga was instigated and had managed to avoid it. She had doubled over with laughter at the sight of Susie and Andrea attempting to prop up old Mrs Banks, who had clearly had several more swigs of cherry brandy than she was going to let on.

The next morning there were a few sore heads and a very muddy conga track around the green, much to the irritation of the village committee members who had just submitted their entry to 'Britain's Blooming Marvellous'.

"Woof." Hector jumped on the bed. "Woof".

"Ok, ok," Olivia croaked, feeling a little jaded. "Merry Christmas big man." She ruffled Hector's ears and climbed gingerly out of bed.

Her parents had wanted her to go home for Christmas but she had decided to stay in her little cottage and work. She couldn't face it, as it was their turn to host all the relatives. Instead, she had happily accepted Susie's invitation to Christmas day lunch at the pub.

Shivering as her feet hit cold floorboards, she cursed the central heating in the cottage for being as temperamental as Sebastian, and quickly pulled on some warm clothes to take Hector for a walk.

She made her way downstairs and into the utility room, where she gave the boiler an almighty kick before pulling on her boots, coat and gloves. Opening the door, she stepped out into a gust of biting wind that took her breath away. There wasn't a cloud in the pale blue sky and the winter sun was barely rising across the horizon. The little family of robins who had nested in one of the trees was up and about, pecking through the frost for worms and looking expectantly at her to serve up their breakfast, as she had been doing since the day she moved in.

"Holy crap, it's cold," she said to Hector. "Let's get going."

She set off towards the vale with purpose, planning to climb right to the top, with Hector trotting companionably alongside her.

Sebastian woke on Christmas Day with a raging hangover from the vast quantities of single malt that he had downed the previous night in search of oblivion. He had turned down the invitation to the church knees-up in favour of another night in, alone with his misery, and he had fallen spectacularly off the wagon.

He had been making progress at the practice range. It was slow and painful, but going back to basics was starting to reap rewards. Hugh had him at the club at six o'clock every morning, pounding balls under the frosted floodlights, working on his swing.

They had the same conversation daily.

"It's not working."

"Give it time," Hugh replied. "It's only been a few weeks."

"How long's it going to take?"

"As long as you need," sighed Hugh. It was getting boring.

"Look what happened to Faldo," Hugh continued. "He went through two major swing changes in his career and he's still Britain's best ever golfer - six

Major's, Sebastian, six. You've got three so there's some way to go, but you're a better player than him, naturally talented, you can easily beat him."

For the first time in his career Sebastian was actually listening and taking advice. He was implementing the changes slowly, with an intelligence that showed he understood the mechanics of what Hugh was asking him to do.

Olivia invaded his thoughts night and day, and it was disturbing him. He wanted to take her to bed so badly and at the same time wanted to laugh with her and passionately argue his point when they disagreed on a subject. She infuriated him and excited him in equal measure... it was intensely frustrating.

"Get you mind back on the job, Sebastian," Hugh snapped his fingers in his face and brought him out of his Olivia-induced haze.

"You need to focus until you get it right. Now, take the wedge and give me some yardage drills. You're not leaving until you've hit every target ten times in a row, so get to it."

"Bloody task-master," Sebastian muttered under his breath, thinking Hugh was out of earshot.

"Task-master I may be, but you forget I've known you most of your life and I know what it takes to get you to the top, and that's where we're heading."

He deposited another bucket of balls at Sebastian's feet and went into the office to make some coffee.

Sebastian allowed his mind to drift into dangerous territory. Just for a moment he thought about Ellie and how much she had loved Christmas. She had always made it so special, and when Lizzie had come along it had been even more magical.

After they had died, Christmas had never been the same again.

Scrabbling around for some paracetamol, he stumbled out of bed and stubbed his toe on the antique wooden boards.

"Fuck, fuck, fuck," he shouted miserably.

He quickly showered and pulled on his usual white t-shirt, Damian de Landre cashmere V-neck and designer jeans, and made his way downstairs. Delicious smells of Christmas wafted in his direction from the kitchen and, as he descended the sweeping staircase, he stopped briefly to admire the handsome Norwegian pine that dominated the hallway.

It had been beautifully decorated, Hattie and Georgiana weaving their own special blend of Christmas magic. There were tiny white lights twinkling amongst the exquisite antique decorations that had been in the family for years and a battered fairy balancing precariously on the very top - Georgiana had made it for their mother when she was still in prep school. He wished he could find it in himself to at least try and enjoy the day.

He was drawn to the mouth-watering smells coming from the kitchen, and Georgiana threw herself into his arms as he entered.

"Merry Christmas Sebastian," she exclaimed excitedly.

"Merry Christmas, princess," Sebastian replied. "And to you too, Hattie. Something smells great. I'm starving, what can you knock up for breakfast?"

"Give me half an hour and I'll bring something through," she said. "Why don't you go and relax?"

"Think I'll take Ace out for a walk, blow away the cobwebs," he replied.

He grabbed a warm coat and some old leather boots that had seen better days and made his way down the drive and out across the village.

"Fancy walking to the top of the vale, Ace?" he asked his faithful dog.

"Woof!" Ace barked his agreement and loped off ahead of his master, sniffing every blade of grass he passed.

Chapter 22

Olivia was gasping for breath when she reached the top of the vale, and it took her a few seconds to register that she was not the only one out for an early Christmas morning walk. She instantly recognised the man with his back to her, sitting on the bench, taking in the view.

"Merry Christmas, Sebastian," she said, hesitantly.

He had been in a world of his own and hadn't heard her approach.

He jumped at the sound of her voice, stood up, hastily wiped his eyes, and gave her a weak smile. "And to you, Olivia."

"Are you ok?" she asked tentatively, in fear of poking the bear.

"I used to love Christmas, but now," he gulped and was unable finish his sentence.

Olivia moved towards him, the sheer wretchedness of his pain was evident.

Sebastian shook his head, "No," he held his hands up, stopping her in her tracks. "I don't want your pity, I'm sorry enough for myself."

Olivia gulped and was lost for words. All she wanted to do was hold him, make him feel safe, but instead she felt she ought to walk away and give him space.

She looked around for Hector, who had inconveniently vanished into the undergrowth with Ace. *Damn you dog, just when I need a quick getaway.*

Standing there like a spare part, she fiddled with her scarf and looked anywhere, other than at Sebastian.

"Aren't you going to say something?" A ghost of a smile flickered across his face. "It's not like you to be lost for words."

"Err, I'm not exactly on top form today, I've got a rotten hangover. I blame Susie, and Andrea, and myself," she grinned, thankful the moment of awkwardness had passed.

"I'm sorry." Sebastian looked woeful. "Forgive me. Christmas is a difficult time and I had a skin-full last night too. I feel like shit if truth be told."

"Thought you were on the wagon?"

"I was. I just happened to go over a few bumps and fell off. I'm paying for it now," he said sheepishly.

"I'm a terrible drunk. Good job we weren't together last night, it would have been carnage," Olivia laughed.

"God, if only," Sebastian muttered under his breath.

"What?" she asked.

"Nothing," he smirked.

"You think I'm a little hostile, don't you?" she said.

Sebastian looked perplexed. "We've been getting on well, I thought," he said.

"Getting on my nerves more like," she muttered.

"I heard that," Sebastian laughed. "So what is it that you find so irritating about me, Ms Carmichael?"

"Do you really want to know?"

"By all means," Sebastian teased.

She took a deep breath. "You have this impenetrable wall around you, you're always on the defensive, and you can be so unbelievably rude sometimes, and that's just for starters." Olivia pointed her chin defiantly, she was on a roll.

She glanced at Sebastian, hoping she hadn't overstepped the mark; he was her boss after all. "You don't see how good your life is, you push everyone away and you don't give a toss about your career, which is disappointing to say the least. I didn't peg you for a quitter."

"You forgot misogynist." Sebastian grinned. "Feel better now?"

"Yes, lots," Olivia was relieved.

"Water off a duck's back, nothing I haven't heard before," he said honestly.

"I'm sorry, I shouldn't have said all of that, I didn't mean it," said Olivia.

"Yes you did. Well, most of it, and you're bang on the money, and I'm a complete bastard." Sebastian reached out and stroked her cheek. "But being with you makes me want to be less of one."

Olivia's heart skipped a beat.

"What?" she squeaked.

Sebastian was now standing so close to her their faces were just millimeters apart.

"You make me want to be a better person, Livy," he whispered.

"Oh," she gulped, averting her eyes in case they betrayed her feelings for him.

"Olivia, look at me," he urged her gently.

At that very moment, Hector and Ace came bounding out of the bushes and launched themselves at Sebastian, knocking him flat on his back.

"Ouch, you little buggers. That's hardly a nice thing to do at Christmas."

Olivia suppressed a giggle and offered her hand to help him up but, instead, Sebastian grabbed her wrist and pulled her down on top of him.

"What are you doing?" Her voice was shaking; she was in danger of losing control.

Her breathing was short and shallow as she tried to disentangle herself, but the force of his hands on the small of her back kept her firmly in place.

"Livy?" he whispered, as if asking for her permission.

She hesitated and Sebastian seized on her moment of indecision, gently placing both hands around her face, drawing it to meet his. He kissed her, tentatively at first, as if he were testing the water, and she found herself unable to resist. She melted into his arms and allowed herself to be consumed by her own desire.

Through the thick layers of her winter clothing Olivia could feel every muscle in his honed body rippling under her, his desire amplified by an erection that was straining against the buttons of his jeans.

"You have no idea what you do to me," Sebastian whispered. "I can't see clearly when I'm with you."

Olivia moaned and Sebastian, encouraged by her obvious, reciprocal desire for him, unbuttoned her jacket and slid his hands under several layers of clothing, expertly unhooking the clasp of her bra one-handed. He gasped as her full, olive-skinned breasts tumbled into his hands and she writhed in pleasure under his touch.

"Sebastian, stop," Olivia whispered.

"I don't really think you want me to, do you?" he murmured in her ear, gently tugging at her nipples and kissing her neck.

"We can't," Olivia said weakly, gasping with pleasure.

"Oh yes we can. Don't fight it; you want me as much as I want you. Your body's telling me that, even if your gorgeous little mouth isn't."

"I can't, we can't, what about the book?" she scrabbled for excuses.

"Fuck the book," Sebastian replied gruffly, his mouth finding hers again, silencing any further objections.

Olivia was lost as he ran his hands down over her jeans-clad bottom and gently nudged her legs apart with his own, moving his palm firmly against her groin. She pressed herself against him, inviting him to continue his exploration, and Sebastian obliged. He took a breast in each hand and his mouth claimed her nipples, giving equally attention to both.

"You're so beautiful, so sexy, Christ, I want you Olivia," Sebastian's voice was choked with emotion. "Let's get out of here." He maneuvered himself so they were both sitting up and kissed her again.

"You seem lost for words?" he laughed.

"Mmmm" she couldn't speak.

Getting to his feet, he helped her up and took her hand in his.

"Your house is closer." His voice was charged with lust. "I'd have you anywhere I could, but frostbite's a bit too much of a risk don't you think?"

"I'm not cold," replied Olivia.

"No, you're damn hot," he grinned.

Their walk down to the village took longer than it should; it was interspersed with sweet, lingering kisses, each one more passionate than the last. Oblivious to the world around them, they stumbled across the village green without taking their eyes off each other, and finally reached Olivia's cottage.

"Keys?" Sebastian asked.

"Here," Olivia thrust them into his hand, her own shaking too much to open the door.

"Get your gorgeous arse inside, now," he growled sexily.

Slamming the door behind them, Sebastian pushed Olivia against the wall in the hallway and ran his hands over her still clothed body.

"Too many clothes," he muttered.

"Take them off then," Olivia said shyly.

"Ah, found our voice again, have we?" he laughed and began to peel off the layers that stood between him and her bare flesh.

Olivia, desire overcoming her fear, began to explore Sebastian's body. Undoing his belt and unbuttoning his jeans, she slipped her hand inside and gasped when she felt his erection growing further under her touch.

"Christ that feels good," Sebastian moaned. "Tell me what you want Olivia."

"You," she whispered.

"Yes, that's patently obvious," he smiled. "But what do you want?"

"I want you to fuck me," she said honestly, a little embarrassed.

"Fuck you eh? Not make love to you?" He pulled her jeans and pants down so they were round her ankles, and slipped two fingers gently on to her clitoris.

"I need it Sebastian, don't make me beg." She gasped again as he stroked her, gently rubbing the nub between his finger and thumb.

"Sure you don't want to take it slowly?"

"No!" she cried, feeling her orgasm building.

"Nothing wrong with a little begging, but since you asked so nicely…" he swiftly freed his cock from the confines of his Calvin Klein's and lifted her up against the wall.

Olivia was impatient to feel him inside her.

"Please, Sebastian," she begged.

"Your wish is my command, darling," he whispered in her ear.

He entered her, slowly at first, and then quickened the pace and ferocity as she responded to him.

"Oh, you like that do you?" Sebastian murmured in her ear as she quietly moaned. "Let go Olivia, don't fight me."

She had never felt anything this intense before, not even with Saul, and she had thought the bountiful sex they enjoyed during their relationship had been off the scale.

Olivia closed her eyes and let the intense, pleasurable sensation of feeling Sebastian inside her take her towards her orgasm.

"Come, my darling, come for me." he thrust in and out, deeper each time. "That feels incredible, I can't hold back much longer."

Olivia cried out as she climaxed and Sebastian swiftly followed with his own.

Still locked together, basking in sexual bliss, they were interrupted by a screech of tyres and the sound of an almighty collision from just outside the cottage.

There was a knock at the door. "Olivia, are you in, darling?" came the voice from the other side.

"Shit, shit, shit!" Olivia scrabbled to get dressed while Sebastian smirked at her.

"Don't answer it."

Bang, bang, bang. The knocking was more insistent this time.

"I have to," she hissed. "You heard that noise, it could have been anything. Hurry up and get dressed properly."

"Fine." Sebastian was irritated at being interrupted.

Smoothing her hair down, desperately trying to not look like a wanton slut, Olivia moved to open the door and came face to face with Devon Murphy, the local vet, and his husband Patrick.

"Your car's a write-off," said Devon.

"And we found these two rogues digging up the village green," said Patrick as Hector and Ace barged past them, running muddy paws through the hallway.

"What?" Olivia looked past him towards the village green where she had parked her car.

"Old Mrs Banks seems to have had one too many. Came round the green like she was in the bloody Monaco Grand Prix, lost control and totalled your car," Patrick explained, looking worried.

"Oh shit, is she ok?" Olivia was concerned.

"Tom's taken her to the pub for a stiff brandy, probably the last thing she needs if you ask me."

Seeing Sebastian appear behind Olivia, Devon and Patrick exchanged glances and smirked in unison.

Olivia looked at Sebastian and saw panic in his face. It was as though he had seen a ghost, and he was rooted to the spot, trembling.

Patrick didn't register Sebastian's obvious distress. "Nothing you can do about the car today, darling, so you may as well carry on with whatever it is you were doing," he winked. "Devon darling, let's leave these two love birds to it, see you later."

They linked arms and wandered home, leaving Olivia and Sebastian standing in the hallway looking at each other. The moment was gone. Sebastian bent down and picked up the coat he had so hastily discarded in the throes of passion.

"Are you leaving?" Olivia was surprised.

"I'm sorry. I can't," he whispered, anguished. "I have to go. Merry Christmas, Olivia," he leant in and kissed her cheek, and then he was gone, leaving her dumbfounded.

Chapter 23

Sebastian could not get out of the cottage fast enough. He practically mowed Olivia down on his way out, and went stumbling home through the village.

Many of his friends and neighbours were out of their houses, wrapped up in winter warmers - some wearing ridiculous festive jumpers and reindeer antlers on their heads - enjoying the bright and frosty winter morning. Squeals of excitement from children rang all around him, but he didn't hear them, nor did he acknowledge the Christmas greetings that were being shouted in his direction.

All he could see was Ellie and his darling Lizzie, and the mangled wreck they had died in. Seeing Olivia's crumpled car had triggered the memory he had been trying so hard to bury. He had insisted on seeing what remained of his wife's car after the accident, and had forever wished he had not. It had haunted his dreams ever since.

Hattie and Georgiana were in the kitchen as he limped through the back door.

"What's happened?" Seeing his face, Georgiana was concerned.

"Nothing," Sebastian was almost inaudible. "Leave me alone."

He rushed through the kitchen and sought refuge in his study, leaving Hattie and Georgiana stunned. Slumping down on the sofa, he reached for a glass and the half-drunk bottle of scotch left over from the previous night.

"He only went out for a bloody walk," Georgiana moaned, after Sebastian had left the room. "How could anything have happened in that time, and on Christmas Day?"

"I've no idea, but he looked sad, not angry," Hattie replied gently. "It's a bad time of year for him."

"It's hard for all of us, we lost them too." She sniffed and looked around for a tissue. "There's been too much tragedy in this family."

Hattie enveloped her in a motherly hug, "There, there darling, it'll get better. Time's a great healer, and then there's Olivia."

Georgiana sniffed and wiped her nose on a tea towel. "He'll just push her away because he's scared of getting hurt again. I can see how much he's into her, and she likes him too, it's obvious."

"Obvious to you and me, but not to them," she wiped away Georgiana's tears. "He's falling in love with Olivia, that's for sure, but I'm not entirely convinced either of them is ready for a new relationship just yet."

Party poppers and streamers were exploding across the pub, and the sound of Slade's 'Merry Christmas Everybody' was blaring from the speakers in all four corners of the bar. It seemed that the majority of Appleton Vale's residents were crammed inside, toasting each other's good health, and singing along raucously to Tom's 'Now That's What I call Christmas' playlist.

The fire was crackling and the atmosphere was one of fun and frivolity. Tom and Susie were fantastic hosts, welcoming every customer with genuine warmth, interested to hear their news. Attentive, always smiling, the affection they had for their regulars was evident.

From the hundreds of sparkling fairy lights, to the handmade paper chains and the beautifully decorated tree in the corner of the bar, Tom and Susie had gone all out for Christmas, and their obvious love of the festive season was infectious.

But Olivia had spent the last two hours lurching from anger to despair and back again.

How did I let that happen? Why did he leave? Oh God, oh God, oh God.

She could not sit at home and let it eat her up, it was Christmas Day and she didn't want to be alone. Knowing spirits would be high in the pub, she grabbed her coat and headed out, leaving Hector happily investigating the contents of his doggy stocking.

Tom thrust a glass of piping hot mulled wine into her hands as soon as she walked through the door.

"Happy Christmas, Olivia," he slurred merrily, and gave her a kiss on the cheek.

"And to you too," she smiled, shrugging off her thoughts of Sebastian. *I'm not going to let him ruin my day.*

Susie, reveling in her pregnancy, was high on life and chatting merrily to all in sundry as she made her way up and down the bar. She spotted Olivia and waved her over.

"Merry Christmas, Liv," she shouted over the noise. "You still coming for lunch?"

"Try and stop me," Olivia laughed. "You look amazing; this whole baby thing really suits you."

"Aww thanks, Tom thinks so too," she winked and broke out into a fit of giggles. "Let me just serve a few more and then I'll get Tom to take over and I can have a break, been rushed off our feet."

"Come and find me when you're done," Olivia replied and walked off across the bar towards Dee Dee and Jane who'd been desperately trying to get her attention.

"Darling," Dee Dee exclaimed and enveloped her in a bear hug. "We heard what happened earlier, your car's a disaster by all accounts. Are you ok?"

"It's just a car," Olivia shrugged her shoulders.

"Devon said old Mrs Banks was lucky to escape unscathed. She's a bloody nuisance," Jane shook her head.

"Apparently, she'd been drinking," Dee Dee interjected.

"That's just hearsay, you're such a gossip dear," Jane said to Dee Dee.

Dee Dee ignored her and turned back to Olivia. "He also said Sebastian was with you, on Christmas Day no less. And?"

Olivia went pale. "God no, don't be ridiculous," she spluttered. "He just popped in to wish me a merry Christmas."

"With or without festive cheer? Don't look at me like that Jane, you know how he's been, I was just wondering, that's all."

"I think you've questioned the poor girl enough, don't you? Oh look, Marjorie's over there."

Dee Dee stuck her tongue out when Jane's back was turned and Olivia laughed, "I love you two, you're so well-suited."

"Thank you darling. I know another couple that would be well-suited, too," she patted Olivia's arm, smiled warmly and followed Jane over to where Marjorie was sitting.

The noise levels were deafening thanks to Devon and Patrick who had commandeered Tom's iPod, and were leading a merry band of revellers in an out-of-tune rendition of Cliff Richard's 'Mistletoe and Wine.'

"Let's go upstairs," Susie was at her side. "Can't hear myself think with this din."

She ushered Olivia round the back of the bar and through the door that led to the flat above.

"Do you want another drink?" she asked Olivia. "I'd bloody love one, but Tom won't let me touch a drop."

"Yes please, whatever's lying around."

"Oh, that bad, is it? What's happened?" She poured Olivia a large gin and tonic.

"Sebastian," Olivia replied, rolling her eyes, trying to make light of her pain.

"Come on." Susie motioned for her to sit down. "Tell me."

"I slept with him," Olivia said in a small voice, head hanging in shame. "Well not slept exactly, there wasn't even a bed involved."

"Holy crap. How? When? What was he like?" Susie was astounded.

"What was he like? God, Susie, here I am, feeling completely mortified and all you can do is ask if how he was in the sack?" Olivia laughed.

"Well, was he any good? You never really know with men as gorgeous as that."

"Yes."

"Yes? That's it? Come on, spill the details."

"I bumped into him on my walk earlier and it just happened, I don't know how."

"What? This morning? Wow." Susie's eyes nearly popped out of her head.

"It was wow, properly wow. I just can't believe I did it. I promised myself I'd keep it professional and now look at me. What am I going to do?"

"Where is he now?"

"Ran off after old Mrs Banks totalled my car," said Olivia, obviously upset. "It was like he completely shut down. One minute he couldn't get enough of me, and the next he was gone. I feel horrible."

"Oh Liv, I'm sorry. I think I might know why he ran away, though."

"Because he got what he wanted," Olivia said sharply.

"No, because his wife and child died in a car crash on Christmas Eve. It probably brought back all those awful memories for him. Knowing Sebastian the way I do, he'll be feeling just as bad as you. He's a big softie inside; his emotions often get the better of him."

"Oh shit, I should have put two and two together, I'm so dense," Olivia repented. "Do you think he's ok?"

"He'll be fine; he's improved so much since you've been around. I'd give him some space and let him come to you."

Olivia sighed, picked up her drink and downed it in one. "Right, I'm going to have a good day and forget about him altogether. What do you need me to do?"

"Nothing, it's all done. Tom was like a demon possessed last night, he didn't want me doing too much today. I think he thinks I'm going to break or something."

"He's a great husband, you're lucky Susie."

"And he reminds me of it every day," she laughed.

A couple of hours later they sat down to a sumptuous feast of roast turkey with all the trimmings, and a constant flow of wine from Tom's private cellar.

Olivia had allowed the gin to work its magic and was finally having fun. Devon and Patrick had been last minute invites as they had been too pissed to cook for themselves, and Andrea from the farm shop had also gratefully accepted the offer of joining them.

"It would've just been me and Cleopatra at home with a Church Farm ready meal for one, and a bottle of wine to drown my loneliness," she joked with Olivia.

They ate far too much and drank copious amounts of wine and, when it came to the end of the night, Olivia hugged Susie and thanked her effusively.

"You rescued me today. I could easily have locked myself away and wallowed in my misery, thanks for making it so great."

Susie returned her hug. "Don't worry about Sebastian, what will be will be."

Devon and Patrick escorted Olivia and Andrea home before stumbling and swaying down the road to their own house, launching into yet another chorus of Slade's greatest hit. "And here it is, Merry Christmas, everybody's having fun…"

Over on Blossom Hill, Peter was enjoying Christmas day for the first time since Sarah had become ill. Surrounded by family, Teddy and Evie were in their element and he had been able to sit back and relax instead of trying to do everything himself.

Both of the children had received shiny new bikes from Santa, and had been playing outside on the street all morning. Teddy's had stabilisers so he was able to whizz around with his older sister and cousins without feeling left out.

Peter allowed his mind to wander to Sarah while he watched their children joyfully embrace Christmas.

That was my fault; I should've tried harder to make it more special for them.

He had mustered up the courage to visit his wife the day after they arrived back in Appleton Vale and it had been the second hardest thing he had ever done, the first being when he had put her in the home.

Peter had been greeted by the nursing home's general manager, Dickie Farrell, who updated him on Sarah's worsening condition.

"I'm afraid to say that she's not fighting the infection well at all, gone to her chest, doctor says it'll probably turn into pneumonia before long," he said in a grim voice. "Her heart's a little weak too, mainly due to the drug regime we've got her on. I'm sorry to be so blunt Mr Jenner, but in cases like this, we know what the end game is, it's just a matter of time."

"Will she recognise me, even a little bit?" he asked shakily.

"Highly unlikely," Dickie replied. "She's not been lucid at all for a few months now. We did have glimmers, as you know, but I'm afraid she's gone completely."

"Can I see her?"

"Of course, but try not to push her to remember anything, we find it doesn't help any of our dementia patients, just adds to the confusion, and, of course, it leaves loved ones very upset. I'll let Dr Scott know you're here and you can see him on your way out, he'll be able to answer any medical questions you may have. Follow me."

Peter followed Dickie down the corridor towards Sarah's room. The home was the best money could buy, both he and Sarah's parents had seen to that, and the patients lived in suites that were individually decorated and filled with familiar pieces of furniture, photographs and other important keepsakes. The facilities were top-notch and the care was first class.

He approached the doorway with apprehension. Sensing his fear, Dickie patted his shoulder, "Dear boy, you did the right thing, don't for a moment think you could have cared for her yourself. Go on, in you go."

What Peter saw shocked him to the core. His beautiful wife had been replaced with a fragile, confused woman, and it broke his heart all over again. He had spent ten agonising minutes trying to engage her in conversation before Dr Scott arrived and rescued him.

"Mr Jenner, do you have any questions I can answer for you?"

"No, thank you. I need to get back to my kids," Peter said, barely holding it together.

He ran out of the home and by the time he had reached his car he was sobbing uncontrollably.

Hearing Teddy's voice shouting at him, Peter was jolted back to the present.

"Daddy, daddy, daddy."

"Yes, Teddy?"

"Take wheels off," he said, pointing to the stabilisers.

"I'm not sure you're ready for that just yet, my boy," Peter laughed and ruffled his son's hair. "Maybe tomorrow when we've got more time. Gam Gam's been cooking all morning for us, so why don't we go and see if we can be of assistance?"

"Ok," Teddy pouted. "Can I have chocolate?"

"After lunch, I promise."

Lunch was a jolly and slightly chaotic affair. As well as Teddy and Evie, Peter's sister had four children of her own, and her husband's parents were also invited. Janice outdid herself, as if she had been waiting for Peter to come home before unleashing her Cordon Bleu training.

After lunch, the adults collapsed in front of the television to watch the Queen's Speech, and the kids were running riot outside, playing with an array of new toys and causing general mayhem.

"Help me clear the table darling," his mother called from the dining room.

Peter collected some of the dirty plates and followed his mother into the kitchen.

"That was a superb meal, Mum, I've missed that. Wasn't it great to see the kids so happy?"

"Yes," Janice smiled at him. "And it's great to see you a little more relaxed today too. I wish I could take away your pain my darling but I promise you, it will get better, just give it time."

"It's been four years Mum, how much more time is it supposed to take?"

"Look darling, I hate to say it, but as long as Sarah's alive it's going to be a struggle for you, so you have to find a way to get on with your life. She wouldn't have wanted this for you; she would want you and the children to be happy."

"I know Mum, I'm trying to adjust but I feel so guilty, living a life when hers has gone."

Janice walked over to her son and hugged him. "You're a wonderful man. I'm so proud of you; your father is too, even if he doesn't tell you. The job you've done with those darling children is nothing short of remarkable, especially given the circumstances."

"I've lied to them Mum, how's that remarkable?"

"You did what you thought was best at the time."

"I was wrong. How am I going to tell them?"

Chapter 24

Christmas up at the manor had been a wash-out. Sebastian had locked himself in his study for the remainder of the day, leaving Georgiana and Hattie to celebrate by themselves, much to their dismay.

"Come on Sebastian, it's bloody Christmas Day," Georgiana shouted through the door to her brother's study, banging her fists on it with frustration. "Hattie's slaved over the cooker to make us a delicious lunch and you're wallowing in self-pity."

She was met with a wall of silence and gave up.

"He's not coming out any time soon," she sighed at Hattie. "Looks like it's just you and me. Not that I mind," she said quickly as Hattie's face fell.

"I'll make sure there's some cold cuts and salad before I go to Timothy's later, so he won't starve," Hattie replied, busying herself at the fridge.

"I think he'll drown before he starves, given the amount of scotch he's drunk the last two days." Georgiana was flippant. "What time are you off?"

"I'll stay for the Queen's Speech and go after that. And I'll be back by lunchtime tomorrow. I don't think I can stomach my brother's wife longer than that," Hattie grimaced.

"Is she still a total bitch then?"

"Well I might put it slightly more eloquently than that, but yes and my nephews are sadly the same. Must be in the blood."

Georgiana jumped up and gave her a hug, "Not your blood Hattie, you're the least bitchy person I know. Come on then, let's eat, I'm starving."

Boxing Day dawned and Sebastian was seriously regretting finding solace in the bottom of a bottle. He couldn't even sit up without wanting to be sick and was aching all over from spending the night slumped on the sofa in his study.

She'll never forgive me, why would she, I just fucked her and left.

He leant over the table to pour himself another whiskey and found the bottle was empty.

Ouch, no wonder I feel like shit.

He gingerly made his way from his study towards the kitchen and found Georgiana making coffee.

"Make mine a strong one," he said weakly.

She spun around. "Oh, decided to show your face then?"

"Georgie, please don't," Sebastian pleaded.

"You promised you would be better this Christmas but it's still the same old story. It's all about Sebastian, you self-centered bastard. You ruined it for us."

"Don't be a bitch, it doesn't suit you." Sebastian's eyes darkened.

"Fuck off Sebastian, you were a wanker yesterday, and I don't know what you did to Olivia but she's gone."

"Gone? What do you mean gone?" His face went from green to white.

"I got a text earlier saying she was going away for New Year and that she would see me when she got back. You must have done something because she was all set to spend New Year's Eve with me, and now she's made other plans."

"We had a little run-in yesterday." Sebastian played it down.

"I might have known it was your fault. She's so perfect for you, and all you do is make her life a misery. She would have been long gone if it wasn't for your bloody book," Georgiana replied pointedly.

"Everything's my fault," Sebastian said and walked off.

So she's run away, can't bear to be around me. She regrets it. Was I disappointing? But why did it feel so right?

He picked up his phone and dialled Olivia, but it went straight to voicemail, so he hung up. What he had to say couldn't be left on an answerphone message. He was brutally ashamed of how he had behaved and needed to make it up to her.

I need help. I want to move on but I'm stuck in the past.

He resolved to discuss it with Hugh the next day and take his advice on board, whether it was what he wanted to hear or not.

Chapter 25

"Ladies and gentlemen," the Captain's voice came over the intercom. "Welcome to Abu Dhabi. The local time is five o'clock in the morning and it's another beautiful day, with the temperature rising to a glorious eighty degrees. I'd like to take this opportunity to thank you for flying British Airways, and wish you all a safe onward journey."

Olivia was dreading this trip. It was the first event in the Middle East swing, a series of three tournaments in the United Arab Emirates with big prize money, and even bigger world ranking points. Sebastian needed a good showing here to convince himself, and his loyal sponsors, that he was making progress, and she was obliged to shadow him at several key events to better understand his life on Tour.

After everything that had happened at Christmas and the awkward meetings since, the thought of being stuck with him in the desert, in the heat, was one she didn't relish.

Sebastian had flown out privately with VIP-Jets at the weekend and taken Hugh with him. He had been working tirelessly on his game since Christmas, but still wasn't sure he could get through the changes Hugh had made to his swing, and win again. Olivia could have flown with him but had opted to join him later, limiting her time in his company.

Their first meeting after the Christmas Day fiasco had been fraught with tension and neither said what they had wanted to say. Instead, they both brushed it under the carpet, hoping it would go away.

She was riddled with embarrassment and Sebastian, mistaking her discomfort for disinterest, had pulled down his emotional shutters and stuck a padlock on for good measure.

Fast-tracked through immigration, Olivia had her bags and was in a chauffeur-driven limo before she could even say UAE.

"Here for the golf, madam?" the chauffeur was politely making conversation.

"Yes, how did you know?" Olivia replied leaning back against the plush leather of the car Sebastian had sent to pick her up from the airport.

"Only golfers are staying at Emirates Palace this week."

"Oh, right," said Olivia. "Yes, I'm a guest of one of the players."

"May I ask who, madam?"

"Sebastian Bloom," she sighed and looked out of the window.

"I know of him madam. He used to be good player, yes?"

Ouch, Sebastian wouldn't like to hear that.

"I think he's just lost a bit of form." Olivia was diplomatic.

Sensing she didn't want to talk, the chauffeur put on some classical music and sped off towards the seven-star Emirates Palace.

Arriving at the hotel thirty minutes later, she was whisked away to her suite where she was introduced to her personal butler, Abdul.

"Ms Carmichael, what a pleasure to have you staying with us this week. May I show you around your suite?"

Olivia was exhausted and wanted to be left alone, but she responded warmly to Abdul, not wanting to offend him.

"It's lovely to meet you Abdul. Yes please, I'd love a tour."

Abdul beamed and began his well-rehearsed introduction to the Emirates Palace.

"This, madam, is the guest bedroom with its own en-suite and dressing area," Abdul opened a door that revealed a room big enough to fit the entire two floors of Brook Cottage.

"And this is your living room," Abdul continued. Olivia had stopped listening to him, taken in by the sheer opulence of each room. The décor, furnishings and technology were the very best that money could buy, and she could now understand why everyone raved about this hotel.

Finally, Abdul showed her the main bedroom, throwing open the double doors and beckoning her to follow him.

He was still beaming at her. "Well? Do you like madam?"

"I do, very much," Olivia lied. It wasn't to her taste at all, and she hated sleeping in an overly large bedroom, but the bed looked like a cloud floating in heaven and she eyed it longingly.

"I will leave you now to sleep, madam. Please press this button at any time of day or night and I will be immediately at your service." He handed her a small device that looked much like a pager.

"Thank you, Abdul."

"No, thank you madam, and sleep well. Please advise when you're ready for breakfast." He bowed his head and backed out of the room, closing the doors behind him.

Five minutes later, Olivia climbed into bed, sank into a sea of pillows and a deep, dreamless sleep.

Chapter 26

Sebastian's courtesy car pulled up outside the iconic 'Falcon' clubhouse of the Abu Dhabi Golf Club early on Monday morning, just as the sun was rising over the desert.

He climbed out, followed by Hugh, and walked up the steps towards the revolving doors and the entrance to the club.

"Good morning Mr Bloom," said the doorman, ushering him inside.

Sebastian acknowledged him with a nod and headed towards the locker room where Aiden, his long-term caddy, was meeting him.

"Hugh," he called behind him. "Meet me on the range in ten."

"Sure," Hugh replied as Sebastian disappeared behind the wooden door.

He was alone; he had got the jump on everyone, and was relieved he could start his season in relative peace.

"Hey boss, how's it hanging?"

Aiden Leary was a short and stocky Irish man with a shock of red hair and face full of freckles. He was just a couple of years younger than Sebastian, they had been a solid team for more than a decade and he was loyal to the core.

"Aiden, good to see you. How was Christmas?"

"Ah, it was deadly. Mam and Dad invited the whole fecking family, it was chaos," Aiden laughed.

"Sounds infinitely better than mine," Sebastian replied, as he changed into his golf shoes and stashed his valuables in his assigned locker.

Aiden knew better than to push him and quickly changed the subject. "Right boss, new season, let's do it." He picked up Sebastian's tour bag and marched off towards the practice range.

A few minutes later Sebastian was doing drills – exercises that improve the game - with Hugh watching from behind. Every now and then Hugh stepped in and adjusted Sebastian's stance or pointed out where he was going wrong, and they pored over the numbers that Hugh's Trackman device delivered on ball flight, speed and trajectory.

"It's good, it's coming together," Hugh reassured him. "Keep working and stay focused, that's the key."

After an hour on the range, Sebastian went out for a practice round with one of the new kids on the block, a young Irish lad called Eamon O'Connor who was playing his first season on Tour. Sebastian was surprised at how much he enjoyed his company.

He was bright and engaging and a really solid player who wanted to learn and improve.

"Aiden said I should ask you for tips about the course, seeing as it's my first time here and all," said Eamon on the second green.

"Did he now?" Sebastian raised an eyebrow, grinned and launched into a hole-by-hole instruction manual for his young colleague.

The course was an oasis of tranquillity carved out of the desert, forming a tough but fair challenge to the best golfers in the world. Lush fairways and fast greens weaved through undulating terrain that featured pockets of palms, shrubs and several spectacular saltwater lakes. Sebastian pointed out the areas to avoid and the correct line to take to the various flag placements on the greens for the holes - and found that imparting his vast knowledge to a youngster eager to learn was very satisfying.

By the time they reached the turn, they were getting on brilliantly and Sebastian enjoyed the last nine holes immensely. As he relaxed and chatted with Eamon, he found that his game improved and he was sinking more putts.

"Thanks Eamon," he said, shaking his hand after the final putt dropped. "I enjoyed that, if you want to go out again just let me know."

"Sure, that was a great craic, appreciate your help," Eamon grinned. "To be honest, some of the lads said it would be hell playing with you but it's been quite the opposite, thanks a million." He headed back to the locker room with a skip in his step.

He'll do well; perhaps I can mentor him.

Sebastian was surprised at himself for letting his guard down - he wasn't on Tour to make friends. He had actively avoided becoming close to any of his fellow Tour professionals, with the exception of José de Silva who was more like a brother to him.

Checking his watch, he realised he was running a little late and headed towards the clubhouse to meet Olivia for lunch. He didn't want to keep her waiting. Before the incident at Christmas he would have been excited to see her, reveling in her company, but now it was awkward and he didn't relish the prospect of spending a week skirting around their issues.

He thought back to the conversation he had had about her with Hugh a few days previously.

"Focus Sebastian," Hugh growled at him as he smashed balls down the range at the Riverside Club. "Abu Dhabi is next week, you need to be ready."

"Christ Hugh, I'm trying," Sebastian was weary. "She's on my mind day and night."

"Olivia?"

"Who else?"

"I've known you since you were a boy and I've never seen you struggle to focus, no matter what else was going on in your life. Find a way to shut it out, and fast. How are you going to play when she's watching you if you can't even practice without your cock taking over your brain." Hugh was unforgiving.

"It's got nothing to do with my cock," Sebastian replied angrily. "She's different, not just someone I want to fuck."

"Do you want to win again?"

Sebastian nodded, "Of course I do, why else do you think I'm letting you boss me around?"

"Then I suggest you make an appointment to see Anthony Daniels and get a handle on it."

"Bloody shrinks," Sebastian muttered.

"He knows what he's talking about, look what he did for Ernie Els," said Hugh.

"Do you really think it might help?" Sebastian asked, looking at Hugh for reassurance.

"Worth a go, don't you think? I'll call him when we've finished here."

Hugh made the appointment almost immediately, and Sebastian was due to meet with Anthony back at the hotel after he had finished at the course for the day.

On his way up to the clubhouse he was accosted by the producer of European Tour Weekly, a TV show broadcast by Sky Sports during the golf season.

Peppy Grainger had been at the helm of the show for a number of years and was a real force of nature. She could hold her own with the boys on Tour, and she did a brilliant job of producing the show. Fun and vivacious, she was Amazonian in stature and wore revealing outfits that accentuated her huge breasts and curvy figure.

"Sebastian, hi, how are you, great to see you." She leaned in and planted a smacker on his lips, engulfing him with an overpowering dose of Estée Lauder's Beautiful.

"Peppy; looking sublime as always," he grinned, genuinely pleased to see her. "How was your ski trip? I heard you'd been busted shagging your instructor in broad daylight on the nursery slopes shouting something like 'oh, yes that's it big boy, make me come?" He laughed.

"You know me, got to get it where I can." Laughing she pulled out her clipboard and started flicking through some production notes.

"We haven't done anything with you on the show for ages and we want you on."

"Really?" He was surprised.

"Yes, why not? Look Sebastian, you were someone once, and personally I think you'll be up there again when you get your shit together. The public still loves you, despite all the bad headlines."

"I'm not sure anyone still loves me, Pep," he replied.

"Don't be ridiculous," she said. "So, will you do a sit-down with me and talk about your hopes for this season, and spill the beans on what you've been up to recently?"

"Seeing as it's you Pep, I'll do an interview, but my personal life is completely off-limits. One question from you about that and the interview will end immediately."

"Ok, ok, no need to be so bloody dramatic about it. How's three o'clock?"

"Fine for me. I'll be on the putting green by then, so come and find me."

"Thanks Sebastian, you're a real trooper, see you later."

And then she was off, chasing the previous week's winner on the practice range, with the cameraman and the sound guy trailing in her wake.

Making his way up to the clubhouse Sebastian was stopped several times by autograph hunters and kids wanting selfies. It gave him a little boost.

I'm still worth something.

He climbed the stone steps that led up to the back of the clubhouse, and spotted Olivia sitting at a table near the far end of the terrace, seemingly engrossed in conversation with David Duncan, the golf correspondent for The Times and a colleague of hers.

He wasn't a fan of David Duncan, and the feeling was entirely mutual. Sebastian made no bones about trying to hide his disdain for the man when he reached the table.

"I'm sure you two can catch up later," he glared at David.

Ignoring Sebastian, David stood up and bent to kiss Olivia on the cheek.

"Let's have dinner this week, Liv," he said as he walked away.

"That wasn't very nice of you Sebastian," she frowned as he sat down in David's recently vacated seat.

"He's a wanker. Don't know why you'd give him the time of day."

"Yes, I know what he's like, but I have to work with him and I'd rather keep the status quo intact."

"Ok, ok, I get it. I won't get you into trouble, scout's honour," he held up three fingers and grinned. "How was your flight?"

"It was good. Thanks for the upgrade, first class, very swish," she laughed.

"You deserve the best." He was serious.

"Shame my budget doesn't stretch that far, but thank you." She was embarrassed.

"And what do you think of the hotel?"

Olivia rolled her eyes, "It's a bit..."

"Ostentatious?" Sebastian butted in.

"Yes, for want of a better word," she laughed. "I can't see it being your cup of tea either."

"You know it isn't, but the Sheikh insists on us staying there, and we wouldn't want to offend the ruler of these fine lands," he winked.

They were interrupted as a waitress approached their table.

"Sir, Madam," she nodded her head and beamed at them in turn. "What may I get you?"

"I'll have the Caesar salad please, and a sparkling water, ice, no lemon. Thank you." Olivia smiled at the waitress.

Sebastian didn't even glance at the menu. Instead, he shot a dazzling smile at the waitress. "Would it be possible to ask Chef to magic me up a Mezze platter? Just tell him Sebastian Bloom requested it."

She giggled, reacting to his charm as so many other women did. "Of course, Mr Bloom, no problem, Mr

Bloom. Chef will be happy to do this for you, Mr Bloom." She backed away from the table and Olivia laughed.

"Do you even realise the effect you have on women?"

Sebastian was amused. "I'm aware. But I'm only interested in the effect I have on you, Olivia."

She gulped, and quickly changed the subject. "What's the plan this week then?" She rummaged around in her bag, pretending to look for something, while she composed herself.

"Sponsors dinner tonight, José and his wife Angelica will be there too. Tomorrow Richie's arriving and we'll see him in the evening, he mentioned something about Pirelli tyre testing at the circuit, if you fancy that? Wednesday is the Pro-Am, and you'll be my partner at the dinner afterwards."

Before she could respond, he was swallowed up in a whirlwind of Chanel No 5, and a flurry of kisses on each cheek.

"Chérie, it's so good to see you, it's been too long," chirped the stunningly beautiful French wife of Sebastian's best friend.

"Angelica, you're looking as gorgeous as ever." Sebastian jumped up and threw his arms around her.

Angelica was the epitôme of French chic - petite, beautifully dressed and enchanting. She had amazing bone structure; her luscious brunette hair was loose and fell in waves down her back.

"Ah Sebastian you're too kind, chérie," she laughed and turned to Olivia. "So, you must be Olivia?"

"Yes, sorry, how rude of me." Sebastian turned to Olivia. "This is the utterly delightful Olivia Carmichael."

Olivia's cheeks flushed. Sebastian was being completely charming. She rose to her feet and extended her hand to Angelica. "Lovely to meet you."

"Enchanté. I hope we can be the best of friends."

"Sebastian only has great things to say about you and José, so it's nice to finally put a face to a name."

"He's too kind," she laughed. "But seeing as he's godfather to all four of my babies he has to be nice, non?"

Sebastian smiled, "And how are my God-fearing charges?"

"Fantastique, they can't wait to see you." She looked at her watch and gasped. "Is that the time? Must go. See you tonight." She blew them both a kiss and dashed off across the restaurant.

"Wow," said Olivia.

"Amazing, isn't she?" Sebastian grinned, and she felt a pang of jealousy.

"She seems lovely."

"She is. José's one lucky man. Do you think I could be that lucky, Olivia?" he gave her a smouldering look, and her heart skipped several beats.

She was dumbstruck, but miraculously saved by the club's general manager, Abd Al Alim, who hurried over to their table once he realised Sebastian was there.

"Mr Bloom, please do excuse my interruption, I just wanted to welcome you back. It is very good to see you."

"You too. May I introduce Olivia Carmichael? She works for The Times, award winning writer." He was showing her off.

Abd Al Amin took her hand and bowed. "A pleasure to make your acquaintance Ms Carmichael. I am Abd Al Amin, general manager. Is this your first visit to Abu Dhabi?"

Olivia smiled, "No, I've been several times, always with work, sadly. I interviewed Lewis Hamilton at the grand prix last year."

"That is very good, very good. Now I will leave you to enjoy your lunch." He bowed and swept away as their food arrived.

Olivia sat back down and looked quizzically at Sebastian. "Are you feeling ok?"

He smirked, "Never better, why?"

"You're being, erm, incredibly nice."

He laughed. "Nice? I hate that word, so non-descriptive. Surely you, the writer, can come up with something better?"

She blushed. "Not right now I can't, no. Better eat our lunch before it goes cold." She was desperate to change the subject, cursing herself silently for bringing it up.

"Cold? He chuckled. "You ordered a salad."

Chapter 27

Olivia took a last look in the mirror and, pleased with her reflection, and with her flowing Jenny Packham dress that was the same jade green as her eyes, she swept out of her room to meet Sebastian and his sponsors for dinner.

He made her squirm all through lunch, much to his own amusement, with his double-entendres and sultry eyes boring into hers, and she had been more than relieved when he left to do his interview with Peppy Grainger.

On her way down to the lobby, she bumped into Angelica and José.

"Olivia! Très chic." Angelica kissed her on both cheeks and smiled her approval. "English women don't always dress well but you, I like it very much."

"Thank you, that's a lovely thing to say. Versace?"

"This old thing?" Angelica pulled at the sleeve of her dress and laughed.

José, stepped forward. "Hmm, so you're the one," he grinned and kissed her hand.

"The one what?" Olivia laughed.

"He talks about you often, you're as beautiful as he says," José winked.

Angelica giggled, "Your Brazilian charm works only with me, my love."

José smiled at his wife. "I'm a happy man. The watch is clicking, no? Sebastian will be waiting." He pressed the button to call the lift.

"The clock's ticking," Olivia grinned.

"That's what I said," José was confused, and Angelica laughed.

"He does that a lot. Sebastian loves it, he calls it a slip of the de Silva tongue," Angelica patted her husband's arm affectionately.

They stepped into the lift and were whisked effortlessly down to the lobby, where the famous Le Vendôme Brasserie was situated. They had arranged to meet Sebastian in the bar, and he was waiting when they arrived.

Olivia let out a gasp when she saw him.

"He's very handsome, non?" Angelica whispered.

"Err, no. I mean yes. Yes, of course he is." Olivia was flustered, and Angelica giggled.

"Angie, beautiful as always," Sebastian kissed her on both cheeks, and turned to José and pulled him into a hug. "Great to see you mate."

"You too my old friend," José returned the hug. "We'll talk on the course tomorrow, no? Now, I need a big drink." He signalled for the waiter to come over.

"Champagne?"

"What else is there, chérie?" said Angelica, rather too seriously. "Is that ok, Olivia?"

"Yes, lovely, thank you." She could feel Sebastian's eyes appraising her, and couldn't look at him. It was such an intense sensation that she found herself fidgeting in her four-inch Louboutin's. He took a step towards her.

"Olivia." He brushed her cheek with his lips, and she felt the fire ignite inside her.

"Sebastian." She forced herself to look at him. "Nice suit," was all she could think of to say.

Sebastian chuckled, and whispered in her ear, "You're beautiful."

Olivia was dumbfounded, a feeling she was becoming all-too-familiar with where Sebastian was concerned. This version of Sebastian Bloom she had only seen a handful of times, but it was the one she found impossible to resist.

She gratefully took the champagne that José was offering, and almost downed it in one gulp. Out of the corner of her eye she could see Sebastian watching her, and it was unnerving.

"I think you and I need to have a talk, non?" Angelica whispered to Olivia when Sebastian and José were out of earshot. "I'm French, I know what l'amour looks like."

"Then you know more than I do," Olivia sighed, and drained the contents of her glass.

Sebastian looked at his watch. "We'd better go, can't leave the bastards waiting, I'm on thin ice as it is."

They left the bar and were walking across the lobby, towards the restaurant, when Sebastian stopped in his tracks and his face contorted.

"Well, well, well, Sebastian Bloom, the has-been," a crass American voice carried the length of the lobby.

Olivia spun round to find Sebastian's nemesis, Troy McLoud, striding towards them.

"Making up the numbers this week, Bloom?" Troy goaded Sebastian, and Olivia noticed his jaw and fists clenching. She knew that there was no love lost between the two, but she had no idea that it had escalated to this level.

"Who's the little lady?" Troy's southern drawl turned its attention to Olivia, and he moved to introduce himself to her. Before he had taken a step, Sebastian blocked his way.

"Fuck off McLoud." He grabbed Olivia's hand and started to walk away, with the de Silvas quickly following.

"That all you gotta say to me, Bloom?" Troy shouted after him.

Sebastian's hand tightened around Olivia's, and he ignored the jibes that continued to fly at his back as they walked into Le Vendôme.

Only when they were seated did he let go of Olivia's hand.

"What was that about?" she asked gently.

"Nothing. I don't want to discuss that man, ever," Sebastian was furious. "Scotch please, large," he said to a passing waiter.

Olivia's heart sank. *He was fine a minute ago. Damn Troy McLoud.*

Sebastian downed the scotch as soon as it was put in front of him, and appeared to compose himself.

"Sorry," he said quietly, so only Olivia could hear him. "Can't stand that fucker."

"Well let's not think about him again then." She touched his hand to reassure him and felt the, now familiar, jolt of electricity course through her. She quickly changed the subject. "Anything I need to know about these gentlemen before they arrive?"

"Johnny Grey and Roger Gould, co-owners of Glow-Pro, the energy giants. Pair of complete tossers, arrogant ones at that. Can't play golf for toffee, and just love having José and me in their back pockets to show off to their friends."

"Oh," Olivia laughed. "It's going to be a fun night then."

"It would be, if it were just the two of us," Sebastian muttered under his breath.

"I heard that," said Olivia.

"Good," said Sebastian.

Angelica had been quietly watching the exchange between Sebastian and Olivia and nudged José.

"See, what did I tell you?" she whispered.

"You're always right my love, I prefer to you." He kissed her hand.

"Defer," she smiled.

"That's what I said," José replied.

The Glow-Pro duo arrived at that moment, and Sebastian and José quickly switched to business mode.

Angelica whispered to Olivia: "They pay huge money; it's a big contract for both of them so we have to be nice. They're horrible men, let's disappear after dinner and leave them to talk business. You can tell me all about Sebastian then." She winked and slid along the banquette to make room for the sponsors.

The buffet at Le Vendôme was legendary. Sebastian had told Olivia that she couldn't go to Abu Dhabi without sampling it and she had been looking forward to it for weeks.

Once the wine had been ordered the party left the table, plates in hand, to explore the vast array of gourmet food that was on offer. Olivia was spoilt for choice; there were delicacies from every corner of the world, cooked to perfection with the best ingredients - and by some of the best chefs in the world. She stood in the middle of the opulent restaurant, looking perplexed.

"See, I told you," Sebastian whispered from behind, making her jump. "Too much choice, it's impossible to know what to go for, try a bit of everything."

"I'll pop out of this dress if I do that," Olivia laughed.

"Now that's something I wouldn't mind seeing." Sebastian flashed Olivia a boyish grin and her knees almost gave way. She could forgive him anything when he was in this mood.

Angelica was on her fourth circuit of the room and finally lost her willpower, returning to the table with an array of delicious looking deserts and petit fours. "I can't help it," she cried. "Sweet tooth."

Almost as soon as they sat down to eat, the Glow-Pro duo took over the conversation, and proceeded to bore them all senseless for the next hour. Sebastian and José were engaged in a serious discussion about a new pipeline that Glow-Pro was negotiating with Russia, leaving Olivia and Angelica rolling their eyes and giggling every time one of the men said, 'deep drilling'. They had both had a little too much champagne, and were finding everything hilarious.

José leant over and whispered in Angelica's ear, "Darling, why don't you go, it's a bore for you, no? And you should have fun with your new friend."

They didn't need asking twice, and left the table in double-quick fashion. Olivia looked back at Sebastian and registered the disappointment in his face. She quickly pulled out her mobile and sent him a text.

I'm only going to the bar, don't look so annoyed x.

She only had to wait a few seconds for his reply.

I'm annoyed because I like having you next to me. Don't go to bed until we've finished here, there are things to be said.

Her heart skipped a beat. *There are things to be said indeed,* she thought.

She linked arms with Angelica and walked through the bar, out onto the terrace that overlooked the beach. It was a balmy night, eerily still, with a gentle breeze that wafted over them with every crashing wave.

"Wow that was boring," Angelica thrust a glass of Laurent Perrier Rosé into Olivia's hand. "So chérie, tell me about Sebastian?"

"There's not much to tell," Olivia lied.

"I don't believe that for one moment. Are you lovers?"

"No!"

"But something has happened, yes?"

"We slept together on Christmas Day," Olivia was embarrassed. "I don't know why I'm telling you this, I hardly know you." She laughed nervously.

"He's different with you, more intense. I didn't see this with Ellie,"

"Oh, really?" Olivia felt a stab of envy whenever anyone mentioned Sebastian's dead wife.

"Yes really. He can't keep his eyes off you, it's adorable." She reached for the bottle of Laurent Perrier and refilled both of their glasses. Leaning back in her chair, she looked at Olivia.

"I want to know the whole story, from the beginning, all of it. If I'm to be your confidante then I need details, lots of details!"

Olivia laughed, and began to recount the goings on between her and Sebastian since she had arrived in Appleton Vale, back in October.

Chapter 28

"Old Mother Hubbard went to the cupboard," Evie and Teddy chorused, giggling.

"Yeah, yeah, very funny. I'll go shopping after I've dropped you two scoundrels at school," Peter laughed. "Teddy, stop feeding Woody and eat your toast. Evie, can you find his shoes, please?"

"I can only find one." Evie ran back into the kitchen dangling a solitary shoe, which was stolen by Woody in seconds, much to the delight of Teddy who was giggling uncontrollably.

"We haven't got time for this, we'll be late. Find something to put on your feet, NOW," said Peter, his frustration growing by the second.

Five minutes later he bundled them into the car and set off to school.

"I'm not entirely sure your teacher is going to be happy with your choice of footwear," he said to Teddy as they pulled up at school.

Teddy looked down at his feet and giggled, "Spi-derman!" He was wearing his superhero slippers.

"Bye, Daddy." Evie kissed him and ran off to join her friends in the playground.

"Have a lovely day, darling," he called after her. "Now young man, let's get you to class." He deposited Teddy into the care of his teacher and made his way to Church Farm Food Barn.

He arrived just as Bert Butters was unloading his van. The smell of freshly-baked bread wafted in his direction, making his mouth water.

"Morning, Peter," Bert shouted over to him.

"Hi!" Peter waved and made his way towards the entrance, grabbing a trolley on his way past. It was early and he was the only customer in the shop.

"I'll be with you in a moment," came a voice from the stock room behind the deli counter, and a few seconds later Andrea popped her head around the door.

"Oh, hi," she smiled warmly at Peter.

"Hey, how are you?" He was pleased to see her.

"Great, thanks. Nice to have Christmas out of the way though, it was frantic. How are things with you?"

"Apart from forgetting to feed my children?" he laughed. "I'm good thanks."

"How are the kids settling in at school?"

"Ted loves it. Evie took a bit of time to make friends but she's doing well now. We've moved around a bit in the last few years and it's been hardest on her I think. A bit of stability is exactly what she needs."

"I wish someone would stabilise the evil twins," she muttered under her breath.

"Sorry?" said Peter.

"Oh nothing, just gearing myself up for a day with Malcolm and Maud's grandkids, they're truly horrible," she laughed. "Anyway, best get on. Bert's just arrived with the bread so if you're after some it'll be out in a few minutes. Lovely to see you." She rushed off across the shop.

Peter was paying for his goods when he saw Andrea again, standing across the shop, chatting merrily to another customer. He stood and watched for a few seconds and decided he liked the way she laughed.

She met him at the door on the way out.

"Did we have everything you wanted?" she asked Peter.

"Yes thanks. It's great here. I'll never need to go anywhere else."

"That's the general idea," Andrea laughed. "It was great to see you Peter, I won't keep you any longer, enjoy your day."

She was gone in a flash, before he had even had a chance to say goodbye.

Peter arrived home at exactly the same time his mother was pulling up outside the house.

"Darling, glad I caught you. How about making your old mum a nice cup of tea? Earl Grey if you have it somewhere in all those bags?"

"Let me get this lot inside and see what I can dig out, can't promise it'll be posh tea though."

"Oh, anything will do, really. Hello darling," Janice patted Woody on her way through the front door. "Down, GET DOWN, what have I told you? Paws on floors." Turning to her son she said: "Instil discipline while he's young, Peter. Don't let him form bad habits; no one likes a badly-behaved dog."

"God Mum, he's still a baby, give him a chance. The kids love him and he's great company when they're at school. It was a good decision getting him."

"I told you so." Janice was pleased.

Peter unpacked the food while Janice put the kettle on, and found the teabags that had been languishing on a shelf at the back of the pantry.

"Do you know the woman who runs Church Farm shop," Peter asked his mother.

"Andrea? She's lovely. Bit overweight and her hair's shocking, but very pleasant all the same. Why?"

"No reason. She's friendly, very welcoming."

"By all accounts she's done wonders with the shop. The Crailley's think she walks on water. I think she's single."

"That's not what I asked," Peter was angry. "I'm not interested in meeting anyone else, I have a wife."

"Darling, you know I didn't mean that, I was just saying."

"Well, don't."

"I'm your mother; it's my prerogative to worry about you. I just want you to be happy. You're still young darling, you can find someone else."

Peter slammed his mug down on the kitchen table. "How many bloody times do I have to tell you? I'm not interested. Do you need me to spell it out? Just go Mum; I don't need to listen to you banging on."

Janice saw the torment in her son's face and realised her mistake. "I'm sorry darling. I'll leave you alone."

Peter broke down the moment his mother left the house.

Chapter 29

When Sebastian and José finally extracted themselves from the Glow-Pro duo, they found Olivia and Angelica on the terrace in fits of giggles.

"How much have you had to drink?" Sebastian asked.

"Only two, chérie." Angelica winked and fell about laughing again. "Bottles, not glasses, naturally."

"And the rest," he rolled his eyes.

"S'ok, not like we're drunk or anything." Olivia slurred. "I need the bathroom." She got up from the table, wobbled on her four-inch heels, and fell straight into Sebastian's arms.

"I think you've had enough. Time for bed."

"Bed, yeah, great idea," Olivia grinned and began to totter off across the terrace, towards the hotel lobby.

"You take her, no?" José said to Sebastian.

"What do you think I'm doing? She's not in any fit state to do anything. Why did you let her drink so much, Angie?" Sebastian was annoyed, but didn't wait around for an explanation.

He caught up with Olivia by the lift, jabbing the wall with her finger in an attempt to find the call button.

"Sebastian," she cried gleefully when he approached. "Let's go dancing."

He grabbed her elbow and guided her into the lift.

"Ow, that hurts," Olivia snatched her arm away from him and slumped against the wall.

"You're a mess, look at you," he turned her around to face the mirror.

"Stop it, you're being mean," Olivia shrugged his arms off her shoulders and pushed him away. "Always so mean," she muttered.

"Mean?" Sebastian looked puzzled.

The lift came to a stop at the ninth floor.

"Where's your key?"

"Bag." She pointed to the floor.

Sebastian rummaged around for the key card, and proceeded to manhandle her all the way back to her suite. He opened the door and waited whilst she kicked off her shoes and stumbled towards the bathroom.

"You're the most frustrating woman I've ever met", he shouted across the room.

"Yeah, well, right back at cha, 'part from the woman bit."

"I had plans for us tonight." Sebastian was disappointed.

"Should have said." Olivia was leaning against the bathroom door, one eye closed, trying to focus on him.

"I didn't think I had to." He was at a loss what to do.

"You're drunk. Go to bed. We'll talk in the morning."

The second he closed the door she ran into the bathroom, only just making it to the lavatory in time to throw up.

The shrill of the phone beside her bed woke Olivia with a start. Her head felt like it was stuffed with cotton wool, and everything was out of focus.

"Hello," she whispered.

"Bonjour Olivia,' it was Angelica, sounding incredibly perky. "'How are you feeling chérie?"

"Like shit" Olivia croaked. "What happened last night? Everything's a bit fuzzy."

"I think we had too much to drink, Sebastian wasn't happy. What happened when you left?"

"I've no idea," Olivia groaned. "I just remember him dragging me down the corridor, and then it's a complete blank."

"Meet me for breakfast and we'll piece it together. José and Sebastian left for the course already so it's just us. How does half an hour sound?"

"Not sure I'm up to eating but ok, see you downstairs."

Olivia's stomach was churning at the thought of breakfast, *or is it because of Sebastian?*

Chapter 30

"FOCUS," Hugh shouted at Sebastian. "Your head's not in it."

"Sorry," he muttered, and continued bashing balls down the range. He had been quiet and brooding all morning, and Hugh was frustrated.

"It's as though we take two steps forward and one back. Why did you fly me out here?"

"I need you," Sebastian replied weakly.

"Then concentrate."

Sebastian paused and looked up and down the range at his fellow professionals working on their game. Guys were chatting and joking with each other, agents were pressing the flesh with sponsors and manufacturers; photographers and film crews were ever- present, and the general public clamoured to get a better view of the world's best golfers.

"I'll be better on the course. What's the time?"

"Nine forty-five," Hugh replied looking at his watch.

Sebastian turned to his caddy. "Aiden, grab me a banana and let's get out of here."

"Sure boss. Want me to tell José?" Aiden replied.

"Yes please. On the tee in ten." He turned to Hugh, "You coming?"

"I'll walk the first nine and see how you're going. Is Olivia coming?"

"How would I know? She got hammered with Angelica last night so I doubt she'll be out any time soon." He was still smarting from his plans going awry.

"No need to bite my head off. She's really under your skin, isn't she?"

"It's not up for discussion, I thought you wanted me to focus, so don't bring it up." Sebastian shut him down. "Let's go." He marched off the range towards the first tee.

Hugh held back momentarily. "Aiden, keep an eye on his focus. I'm only going to walk nine with you; I want you to tell me what he's like without me around for the rest, ok?"

"Sure. We're out with José so he'll be grand," Aiden replied, picked up Sebastian's bag and followed him off the range.

Olivia was mortified. She knew she couldn't tolerate more than a few glasses of wine, and was paying for it now. Angelica was treating her with kid gloves and she found it was nice to be looked after for once.

"Thanks, Angelica," Olivia said as they arrived at the golf course. "I'd have still been languishing in bed feeling sorry for myself if you hadn't dragged me out."

"Pas de problème, chérie," she said, giving her a small hug. "We've all done it. So, how are you going to handle Sebastian?"

"I'm so embarrassed, I really didn't need him to see me like that, just when we were getting on so well."

"If anyone should understand it's him. He's spent the last two years drunk, and then he met you," Angelica smiled.

"Christ, I feel like crap." Olivia was suffering. "Remind me not to do that again."

"They'll be on the course now, let's go and find them. José likes me to follow him for a few holes each day, he says it relaxes him."

Olivia slipped her sunglasses on and linked arms with her new friend.

"Don't leave me, please," she begged. "I can't face him on my own."

Angelica laughed, "Fear not chérie, I'll protect you."

"He's twice the size of you," Olivia laughed weakly, following Angelica out into the blazing sunshine.

They caught up with them on the twelfth hole and, although she was sure Sebastian had seen her give him an embarrassed wave, he didn't acknowledge her presence.

"Uh oh," said Angelica. "He's in a mood".

"Oh God, I can't bear it," Olivia cringed. "I don't even know what I did to upset him."

"Take no notice chérie, this is how he is."

"Easier said than done," Olivia grimaced.

The rest of the day was a struggle. Olivia hid out in the media centre, pretending to work, and eventually surrendered to her hangover by scuttling back to the hotel to sleep.

That evening she plastered on a brave face and went to meet Richie, who had arranged a private trip to Yas Marina Circuit to watch Pirelli testing tyres. Olivia joined Richie, José and Angelica in the lobby, still feeling sheepish about last night.

"He's not coming," Richie was annoyed.

"Sebastian?" asked José.

"Who else? That'll piss the sponsors off even more; he knows he's got to get them back on side. I give up," said Richie.

Olivia didn't know whether she felt more relieved or disappointed. She had endured a day of anguish, wondering what had gone on between them, and wanted to have it out with Sebastian but she didn't feel strong enough.

"Well that won't stop us enjoying ourselves, will it?" she said brightly, forcing herself to be upbeat.

By Wednesday morning Sebastian's mood had gone from bad to worse. He was avoiding Olivia, ashamed at how he had reacted to her being drunk, and it hurt him to realise that she was keeping out of his way as well.

He stayed in his room sulking while the rest of the group went out with Richie on Tuesday night, and hated that he was, yet again, feeling so dark and twisted. He had endured a sleepless night, and played so badly in the Pro-Am that his amateur partners, who had paid a princely sum for the privilege of playing with a three-time Major champion, were left feeling short-changed.

After the Pro-Am, and as a past winner of the tournament, he was obliged to do a press conference for the headline sponsor.

He sat on the stage, fielding mundane questions from the world's media, when Troy McLoud, who was due in immediately after Sebastian, burst into the room larger than life, his Hollywood smile glinting in the glare of the flash photography that followed.

The press pack crackled with anticipation. Bloom versus McLoud was a fight they would pay good money to see.

"Come on, Bloom," he drawled. "Can't be much to talk about with the state of your game, I'm surprised anyone's remotely interested in anything you gotta to say. You're finished."

In a flash, Sebastian was off the stage, lunging towards Troy, his fists clenched, ready to pack a punch. Richie jumped up, just as quickly, and managed to manhandle him out of the media centre before he could get close enough to inflict any damage on his enemy.

"What the fuck is wrong with you? I thought we'd talked about this," he snarled at Sebastian.

"That fucker is everywhere. Why can't he just stay out of my way?" Sebastian was seething.

"Get over it. Ignore him. Be the bigger man. How many more times do I have to tell you?" Richie was losing his temper.

"How can you expect me to act like nothing happened? You know damn well what he did. I'll never forgive him."

"I'm not asking you to forgive him, I'm asking you to ignore him. You've been in a shitty mood all day. If you can't behave and focus while Olivia is here then send her home. This is your job Sebastian, stop fucking around, stop thinking with your dick, and get on with it."

"I suggest you watch your step, you're forgetting who the client is," Sebastian was furious.

"I've known you long enough to say it how it is. Don't be a prick, I'm on your side mate." Richie softened, and looked at his friend who was clearly in torment.

"Send her home," Sebastian said, and walked off.

Chapter 31

"Cabin Crew, seats for landing." The Captain voiced his final instruction over the intercom to his crew as he prepared to land at Heathrow.

Olivia breathed a sigh of relief. It had been a truly awful twenty-four hours since she had messed up any chance of being with Sebastian, and she couldn't wait to get back to the sanctuary of her little cottage, and Hector.

She was part angry and part embarrassed at being sent home like a naughty child, but also desperately unhappy at how things had been left with Sebastian. She could not work out what she had done that had been so terrible, and they hadn't spoken at all since he had left her in a drunken stupor that night.

Her one saving grace in Abu Dhabi had been Angelica. Olivia had enjoyed her company very much, and they had become close in the short time they had spent together.

Angelica had been tremendously helpful with all things Tour-related, and had filled in the gaps of Olivia's golf knowledge with a level of expertise that surprised her. She had opened Olivia's eyes to the circus that was the PGA European Tour, and given her a good insight into Sebastian's day job.

She had explained: "So, we arrive on Mondays most weeks depending on where we're coming from, and then there's two days' practice as you know. The top-ranked players and past winners play in the pro-am and attend the dinner on Wednesday night, and then it's four tournament days. Players who miss the cut, where the field is halved on Friday afternoon, will fly home, and the rest stay and fight it out. Then we move on to a new country and start all over again. It's not as glamorous as it sounds, believe me."

Olivia learnt that it was a merry-go-round of madness, and that even the strongest of relationships struggled to survive life on Tour. The wives who opted to stay at home with their children were in danger of their marriages ending in divorce, or choosing to put up with a serial adulterer. There was temptation at every twist and turn of the golf course, with groupies and PR executives, desperate to bag themselves a rich man, willingly offering up their pert, nubile bodies at any given opportunity.

"It's disgusting," Angelica said. "These women don't care who they hurt, and they think the guys will fall in love with them. Fools." She gave a hollow laugh.

"But not you and José," Olivia stated.

"Ah, but I'm a lucky girl, and I don't let him out of my sight. Why else do you think I'm here every week? I trust him, I just don't trust them."

"What a nightmare - the girls I mean." Olivia wasn't all that surprised. She had been around professional sportsmen for years, and had both seen and heard a lot of torrid tales.

"It's the same every week. I'm so glad I've got the children with me or I'd die of boredom," Angelica admitted to Olivia. "I adore my husband, but he has no idea how hard it is, following him all over the world with four children, a tutor and a nanny."

"You make it look easy," Olivia laughed. Angelica had introduced her to many interesting and helpful people over the few days she had been there, so her time in the Middle East hadn't been completely wasted.

As the wheels touched down at Heathrow, Olivia made a conscious decision to shrug off her disappointment and concentrate on the book. Sebastian was away for the next three weeks so she had room to breathe.

Out of sight out of mind, she said to herself over and over again.

A delirious Hector greeted her when she stopped off at the pub to collect him, and she was so very happy to see him, burying her head in his fur, and cuddling him to within an inch of his life.

"Christ, I can't tell you how glad I am to be home. Thanks for looking after him Susie, was he ok?" she said.

"Yes, he was fine. He's so easy, and greedy," Susie laughed. "What's up? You look frazzled."

"Do you really need to ask?"

"Oh God, what's he done now?"

"How long have you got?" Olivia gave her a weak smile and followed her back into the warmth of the pub.

Chapter 32

"Woof," Hector barked. "Woof, woof, woof."

Olivia looked up from her laptop and saw the postman walking down the path towards the front door. She leapt into action and retrieved the mail just before Hector skidded up behind her, hoping to catch and destroy. She had lost count of the number of letters he had shredded, and it had become a daily battle of wills.

She flicked through the pile of junk mail and gasped as she came across a card, addressed with the almost unintelligible scrawl that belonged to Sebastian.

They had had no contact for a week, not even a text or email, both of which had been daily occurrences before Abu Dhabi.

Her hands trembled as she opened it. On the front of the card there was a goofy-looking golden retriever, and on the inside it read...

Olivia,

Yet again I have to ask for your forgiveness. I'm a complicated man but trying to be less so, for you.

I'm sorry.

Sebastian.

She looked at the postmark on the envelope. It was sent the day she had been banished from the desert.

"Oh thank God", she muttered.

She grabbed her mobile and texted Sebastian.

Apology accepted.

She pressed send and jumped when it rang a few seconds later.

"Thank you." Sebastian's voice was gruff.

"Hey," Olivia said gently.

"I'm sorry," he said.

"I know."

"I miss you," he sounded shaky.

"You sent me home."

"I'm sorry." His voice was so quiet Olivia strained to hear him.

"So you said," she replied.

"Don't be angry, please. I fucked up, I won't do it again."

"Yes, you will, it's who you are. It's a good job I'm tough enough to handle it."

"Ok, maybe I will. Guess I'm going to get really good at saying sorry," he chuckled in relief.

"There's always room for improvement," she joked. "How did you play today?"

"Actually, not too badly." Sebastian had regained his composure. "A couple of birdies and one double bogey that wiped them out, but at least I got round in par, best I've done for a while."

They chatted for a while longer before Sebastian had to rush off to dinner with his sponsor, fashion magnate Damian de Landre.

Olivia smiled as she put her mobile down and looked over at Hector, who was busy shredding the envelope her card had arrived in.

"It's ok, big man," she said fondly. "I've still got a job so you won't go hungry."

"Woof," he replied, tossing soggy bits of paper in the air.

Chapter 33

"I insist you go out tonight darling," Janice called across the kitchen as she prepared supper for Evie and Teddy. "They have that great little pub quiz going on and I'm sure you'd be welcome to join one of the local teams. In fact, I was talking to Devon and Patrick the other day and they said for you to come along."

"For Christ's sake Mum, when have I ever been to a pub quiz?"

Janice shook her head: "Language, Peter."

"Look, if it shuts you up I'll pop out for a quiet pint later if you'll stay with the kids."

"No need to be rude .... Of course I'll stay. Go and have fun."

He oversaw Teddy's bath time and checked Evie had finished her homework before making the short walk down Blossom Hill towards the pub.

On entering, Peter had to fight his way through the throng of quizzers that had come from far and wide, attracted by the generous prizes on offer. Susie spotted him waiting at the end of the bar and shouted above the noise: "Peter, great to see you, what'll it be?"

"Just a pint please, Susie. Wow, it's busy in here tonight."

"Quiz night, always busy on a Tuesday, plus we've a full restaurant so we're fit to burst. Not that I'm complaining." She smiled and handed him his pint. "Fancy joining in? I'm sure there's a few teams that'd be delighted to have a Cambridge graduate on their side."

"It's not really my thing," Peter replied. "I just popped in for a quick one really, to get Mum off my back. She's looking after the kids."

"Nonsense, a pub quiz is everyone's thing. Patrick was asking after you earlier, I think he's been speaking to your mother," Susie laughed.

Feeling a hand on his shoulder he turned to find Patrick beaming at him.

"Peter, you've made it, how wonderful. I've been meaning to pop over to the house but it's been frantic - we're in rehearsal, you know."

"Er, no I didn't know. What's the play?"

"Othello, but it's a disaster darling, Desdemona's up the duff".

Peter laughed. "Oh dear, how about the understudy, can't she step in?"

"She's a he. We're a little short on women. Now are you joining our merry band of brothers or not? We've got to declare the team before kick-off," said Patrick.

"It's not football, Patrick," Susie giggled. "Tom just likes everything to be above board, no latecomers, and strictly no mobile phones."

"Come on then, grab your pint and follow me," Patrick dragged Peter across the pub and deposited him on the banquette next to Andrea.

"Hi Peter," she squeaked her pleasure at seeing him.

"Hey." He smiled warmly at her and whispered, "This is mad!"

"What?" she asked.

"It's packed, and it's so loud."

"Quiz night, it's always like this. It's so much fun, you'll enjoy it, I promise," Andrea reassured him.

"Peter, I think you know everyone apart from Dr James Elliot and Olivia, although she's in danger of being a late comer."

Peter reached over the table and shook James's hand. "Nice to meet you," he smiled.

There was a spontaneous round of applause, and a few cheers, as Tom took to the microphone to start the hotly-anticipated quiz.

"Welcome one, welcome all," he said. "The count-down has progressed, anyone not at their table in precisely one minute will be unable to take part, and I want all mobiles handed in to the bar, no exceptions." He looked pointedly over at Dee Dee's table and a ripple of laughter followed.

"How dare you, "Dee Dee called across the pub, looking a little embarrassed. "You know full well I was waiting for an important call."

"So you said, my lovely," Tom laughed and looked at his watch. "Right, that's thirty seconds now."

Olivia ran into the pub just as the countdown had reached five, and quickly squeezed onto the end of the banquette next to Peter and Andrea.

"You're cutting it a bit fine darling," Patrick looked at his watch.

"Lost track of time, sorry, I was writing," she explained and turned to Peter.

"Hi, I'm Olivia, and you're the Cambridge graduate. No pressure then," she joked.

"Three, two, one," Tom shouted. "Ok folks, let's kick this off with an easy one. "A phlebotomist extracts what from the human body?"

Patrick automatically assumed his role as leader. "Doc, this one's for you," he said.

"Blood," he replied with authority. "If I don't know that then I'd be a really poor doctor," he laughed.

"Lower your voice," Patrick looked furtively around at the other tables.

Devon laughed. "Stop taking it so seriously, it's just a quiz."

"You won't be saying that when the Bears Bridge Boffins wipe the floor with us again. I'm sick of the triple Bs making us look stupid," he said rather too sharply.

Tom's voice crackled over the microphone again: "What is the longest river in England, that runs through England only?"

"Ooh I know that," Dee Dee squealed.

"No, you don't," Jane replied, patting her arm. "You just think you do, darling."

Tom continued: "Who had a 90's hit with the song 'Bump n grind'?"

Andrea banged her glass on the table and whispered excitedly, "R Kelly. Definitely. I love that song." She giggled.

Peter laughed, "I'd never have taken you for an R Kelly fan."

"I've got really rotten taste in music if I'm honest."

"We like what we like," he smiled.

Tom fired off another ten questions that got progressively harder, before signalling a fifteen-minute lavatory and bar break.

"I want all those sheets handed in immediately. You'll get new ones for round two," Tom said.

Peter drained his pint and stood up. "Who needs a refill? Andrea?"

"White wine please, whatever's open, thanks Peter."

"I'll have another glass of red please, the Shiraz if possible," said Olivia.

"Yes, I'll have the Shiraz too, and Devon will have another pint if he ever gets back from the lav," said Patrick.

"I'm driving, so just a Coke for me please," said James.

Peter returned from the bar just as Tom was beginning round two.

"Which song did Bruce Springsteen win an Oscar for?"

They all turned to Andrea.

"What?" she asked. "Like I'm the music expert now?"

"You're our best hope darling." Patrick reached over and squeezed her hand encouragingly.

"Well, I think it's the Streets of Philadelphia, but don't shoot me if I'm wrong." Andrea crossed her fingers, hoping she was correct.

"Yes! That's the one, couldn't think of the name. Tom Hanks was in the film, wasn't he? Well done you!" Peter grinned and chinked his glass against Andrea's.

"Which current Premier League and England football superstar started his career at Letchworth AFC?" Tom's voice boomed over the mic.

"Tommy Illingworth," Olivia whispered with authority.

"Are you sure?" Patrick asked.

The rest of the team looked at Patrick and laughed.

"I think Olivia's more knowledgeable on sport than all the teams put together," Andrea giggled.

"Oh, yes, of course," Patrick chuckled. "I'll never doubt you again, darling."

"I've been known to be wrong on occasion," Olivia laughed. "But seeing as Tommy was my first major interview, it's kind of stuck with me."

"*What was the name of the civil rights leader who Dorothy Parker left the bulk of her estate to?*" Tom continued.

"*Where do camels store water?*"

"*What was the name of the dog that orbited earth in Sputnik 2?*"

"*How many feet are in a fathom?*"

The questions were coming hard and fast, and the temperature in the pub was rising. Other teams were engaged in heated discussions, and the triple Bs were hurling insults at each other from their table across the room.

Peter was enjoying himself and was pleased he had managed to answer some of the harder questions.

"Can't say I had the best education," Andrea told him. "I hated school, I went to the local comp and it was a hotbed of thugs and drugs."

"You knew R Kelly," Peter said gently. "And look at you now, running a highly successful business and contributing tremendously to the village. I'm impressed."

Andrea blushed. "Oh, I don't know about that, but thank you. Now I think it's my round." She squeezed past Peter and accidentally brushed her chest against his hand. His stomach lurched and he felt a pull in his groin, but almost immediately his lust was replaced with disgust and a horrible feeling of betrayal.

In sickness and in health, till death do us part, he said over and over again in his head.

Patrick, misreading Peter's face said: "Don't look so crestfallen, darling. It's only a quiz, and we've never won before so there's no expectations whatsoever."

"Only a quiz?" Devon spluttered. "Try telling that to yourself, Pat."

"I'm not the only one who takes it seriously you know," Patrick pouted. "That lot from Bears Bridge swoop in here every week and always win, maybe it's fixed."

"And that's why I love you," Devon smiled, leaning over and kissing him. "Your unwavering commitment to the dramatic arts is commendable."

Olivia, Peter and James burst out laughing.

"What's so funny?" Andrea struggled back to the table, sloshing drinks around on a tray.

"Pat's decided the triple Bs are either cheating or have somehow managed to bribe Tom. Of course, it has nothing to do with the fact that they're just better at this than we are," Devon explained.

"Oh, that old chestnut. Change the record Patrick, we can't have people thinking we're sore losers," Andrea joked.

"We are, aren't we?" said Olivia, desperately trying to keep a straight face.

"NO, WE ARE NOT," Patrick was peeved. "Nothing wrong with being competitive. It would just be nice to see them off at least once in my lifetime."

"I think we just missed two questions," said James, suppressing laughter.

"Damn, look what you've all done. Bang goes our chance of toppling the triple Bs now," Devon said. "Any chance of repeating the last two questions Tom?" he shouted.

"You snooze, you lose, my friend," laughed Tom. "You know the rules."

Devon groaned. "Only too well."

"We've never won though, we're usually dead last," she laughed. "Hopefully we can change that now you're on board."

"Christ, don't rely on me. I'm not sure I'll be able to do this regularly, what with the kids and all."

"Olivia drops in and out as she's away quite a bit with Sebastian, so you don't need to feel like you have to be here all the time. Just whenever you fancy it and can get a babysitter."

"I'd like that," said Peter. "It's nice to mix with adults for a change. I love my kids to death, but the conversation isn't all that scintillating."

"You really do have to try harder darlings," Patrick said as he arrived back at the table with their 'one for the road'. "We were a decent team before, but now we've got Peter there's no excuse. Can we all do a little prep before next week?"

Devon groaned: "For the love of God, it's a bit of fun Pat."

"I wouldn't mind getting my hands on a few of those vouchers," said Andrea.

"Well then, do some homework darling. All of you." Patrick was deadly serious.

"Yes sir." They stood up, mock saluted him and fell about laughing.

Seeing his face fall, Devon put his arm around Patrick's shoulder. "Let's go home, you know we're just messing with you."

"Home, yes, good idea," Patrick picked up his coat. "Good night darlings, can't wait to do it all again next week. Are you here Olivia?"

"I most certainly am. Sebastian's away for another two weeks so I'm around," she replied.

"Peter?" he asked.

"If I can get a babysitter then yes, I'll be here. I really enjoyed it," he smiled. "Speaking of which, I'd better get back before Mum thinks I've done a bunk. Night everyone, and thanks for making me feel so welcome."

"Drink up please, ladies and gentlemen," Susie shouted across the pub.

Peter quickly finished his pint and made his way toward the door, giving his team one last wave before disappearing into the night.

"He's lovely," Andrea said dreamily.

"Isn't he," replied Patrick, equally as dreamily.

"Hey, you're a married man. Definitely time to get you home," Devon linked his arm through Patrick's. "Night Andrea, Olivia." He kissed them both. "Good to see you, Doc."

"Can I offer either of you a lift?" James asked Andrea and Olivia.

"Thanks, but I think we're both just about capable of walking the fifty or so yards home," Olivia laughed.

"Speak for yourself." Andrea wobbled as she stood up.

"I'll walk you back, come on," said Olivia. "Bye James, see you next week." She grabbed her coat and guided a tipsy Andrea across the pub. "See you tomorrow, Susie," she shouted as they left.

Peter paused at the end of Blossom Hill and looked back towards the pub. He saw his new friends leaving and smiled.

That was fun. Andrea's lovely.

Chapter 34

"Christ, Sebastian, just grow a pair and go and see her, tell her how you feel." Georgiana stood in the doorway of his study with her hands on her hips. "You've been dancing round each other for months? Do you like her or not?"

"Of course I do." He looked up from his laptop and scowled at her.

"Well do something about it then," his sister replied. "If you don't then someone else will. She's perfect for you. To be fair, she's pretty perfect for anyone - don't be surprised if you wake up one day and find you've lost her."

"She's not easy to read, I think I make her nervous." He shrugged his shoulders.

"She was beaten to within an inch of her life. Is it any wonder she's wary? And with your mood swings, I don't blame her."

"It's complicated," he said.

"Life's complicated," Georgiana sighed. "Doesn't mean you have to hide away and deny yourself some happiness."

"I don't deserve to be happy."

"You weren't driving the car that killed them, you didn't cheat or lie, that was Ellie."

Sebastian cringed at the sound of her name. "Don't talk about her like that."

"Sebastian, it's time to move on, let it go. Don't you want that?"

"Yes, of course I do. I'm trying, just don't push me."

"Try harder. No time like the present." Georgiana grabbed his coat and shoved him towards the door.

"What? Now?"

"Yes, now," she grinned. "And don't come back till you've convinced her that you're in love with her."

"I'm not!" Sebastian spluttered.

"Yes, you keep telling yourself that," Georgiana smirked and skipped away.

Sebastian stood for a moment and mulled over what Georgiana had said.

She's right, I'm being a complete and utter prick.

There was a knock on the door, and Olivia wearily pushed back her chair and went to answer it, somewhat annoyed that she had been interrupted just when she had overcome her temporary writer's block. Hector scrabbled up off the wooden floor and took off down the hallway, sliding into the big oak frame door with his full body weight, barking and wagging his tail madly.

"Not exactly subtle are you, Hec?" Olivia grabbed his collar and hauled him away from the door.

"What are you doing here?" she gasped.

Saul her ex-boyfriend was standing, larger than life, in front of her. Hector planted himself between them and growled, sensing Olivia's fear.

Saul bent to pat Hector and almost had his hand taken off. "Christ, when did he get so bloody vicious?"

"Around the time you beat me and left me for dead," she retorted, wincing as she recalled the pain he had inflicted. "What the fuck are you doing here? When did you get out of jail? How did you find me?"

"I saw photos of you and the golfer in the papers, and when I realised you'd left London, it seemed obvious that you'd come here. Can I come in?"

"No, you bloody well can't. You've got a fucking nerve. I've got nothing to say to you." She was shaking.

"Please Liv, hear me out. I'm not here to cause trouble, only to apologise. I've had a long time to think about what I did and how I treated you, and I need to make amends."

Olivia looked over Saul's shoulder and saw Dee Dee making a beeline for her across the village green.

"That's the last thing I need. You'd better come in, I don't want my business all over the village." She stepped inside and ushered Saul into the living room, whilst stooping to picking up the baseball bat she had hidden under the hall table for security.

"Jesus!" Saul's eyes widened when he clocked Olivia's weapon of choice. "Although I can't say I blame you. How are you?"

"How the hell do you think I am?" She was trying desperately to keep calm. "Because of you I left my home, friends, job and my self-esteem in London. Because of you I spent weeks in hospital, and months recuperating. But other than that I'm great, thanks for asking." She was astounded at his nerve.

"Oh God, Liv, I'm so damn sorry." Shame-faced, he took a step towards her.

"Don't fucking touch me," she screamed, and wielded the bat in front of his face.

Saul held his hands up and backed off. "Ok, ok, don't worry, I'm not going to hurt you."

"Damn right you're not," she spat. "When did you get out?"

"Two weeks ago. Terrible place, full of the scum of the earth."

"Well, you should've fitted right in then." Her voice was shaking, along with the rest of her.

Brook Cottage was supposed to be her sanctuary. She came here to escape the physical and mental pain he had inflicted on her, and now he had taken that from her. She shook her head, as if waking from a nightmare, and galvanised herself into action. She took a really hard look at him, and found that she felt nothing, nothing at all.

"Well, you're here now, so say your piece and get out." She rested the baseball bat against the fireplace, but still within reach, should she require it.

"I've driven a long way to see you Liv - the least you can do is offer me a drink."

"I didn't ask you to." She was indignant. "I don't have anything to give you and, quite frankly, if I did it'd be laced with arsenic."

"Still as feisty as ever then," he grinned.

"Yeah, well, that's the only thing you didn't manage to knock out of me." She was calm now, in control of her emotions again.

"You can't imagine the pain I've been in, knowing what I did to you," he said, contrite.

"You left me for dead," she whispered.

He shook his head in dismay: "And for that I will never forgive myself. I have no excuse, not one you'd believe at any rate - I just snapped."

"I don't care. I don't want excuses. I don't want anything from you ever again." She had further regained her composure. "You changed me, I'm not the same person I used to be."

"I can see that. You seem harder, somehow."

"Well, I can thank you for that," She stared at him, and still she felt nothing, not even fear. He seemed small, insignificant even.

"I didn't come to argue," he said softly. "Won't you just hear me out?"

"No. Just go please, now." She pointed at the door, gesturing for him to leave, and was shocked when he dropped to his knees in front of her and grabbed her hand.

She snatched it away from him. "Get off, get up and get out."

222

Saul stayed on his knees and looked up at Olivia, full of remorse.

"I'm so sorry. I loved you, I never meant to hurt you. Please Liv, I need you to forgive me," he begged. "I can't leave without your forgiveness."

"Yes, you bloody well can because you're not getting it, and you're not staying here." She was incensed. "Did you really think you could turn up on my doorstep, unannounced, and that I'd welcome you with open arms?" She waited for a response that didn't come, so she seized the opportunity to let rip. "You're more of a self-centred, sadistic, selfish bastard than I thought. I've got the worst taste in men, I should be ashamed of myself."

"Please Liv," he pleaded. "I need closure so I can move on."

"All I'm hearing is YOU'RE sorry, YOU'RE in pain, YOU need forgiveness. Well you didn't think about any of that whilst you were beating the living shit out of me. Get up Saul, NOW."

Saul rose to his feet and turned to leave. "I can see this was a mistake. I'm truly sorry Liv, even if you don't believe me."

"Close the door on your way out, and don't contact me again, ever," she said, with as much force as she could muster.

Olivia watched Saul leave and slumped to the floor, tears spilling down her cheeks, and that's where she stayed until night fell, with Hector's head in her lap.

Sebastian had been wrestling with himself all the way from the manor to the village.

Can I make her happy? Can I be the man she needs me to be? What if she doesn't feel the same?

"Right, this is it. Take a deep breath and jump, you silly sod," he muttered.

Picking up speed he strode past the tearooms, prompting an ever- watchful Dee Dee to scuttle to the open door and find out where he was going with such purpose.

Sebastian strode passed the pub, turned into Olivia's gateway and stopped dead in his tracks. There, through the window, he saw a man on his knees, holding Olivia's hand, and she was blinking back tears. Looking at her, standing there, so beautiful and serene, his heart contracted.

You're too late.

Unable to bear the pain of yet another loss, he turned and walked away.

From across the green, Dee Dee saw the anguish on his face and immediately knew it had something to do with Olivia's visitor.

"Oh, you poor, poor man," she whispered and promptly headed for the kitchen to update Jane.

Sebastian walked home in a daze.

That must be Saul. After all the terrible things he did, how could she want to be with him?

He crashed through the front door, pushing past Georgiana and sending her whippet Lady into a ter-rified spin, and headed into his study, slamming the door behind him.

"That clearly didn't go well," Georgiana whispered to a trembling Lady. She knew better than to try to talk to him when he was in this kind of mood, so she picked the dog up in her arms and headed towards the heavenly aroma that was coming from the kitchen.

Hattie was deeply engrossed in the latest bonk-buster novel, but quickly threw in to a drawer when she spotted Georgiana hovering by the doorway.

"You don't have to hide your girl porn from me, Hatts," Georgiana laughed, plonking herself and Lady down on a seat at the battered old pine table.

"It's not porn, you naughty girl." Hattie was embarrassed. "Now, do you want some cake and a nice cup of Earl Grey?"

"Oh, go on then, you've twisted my arm. Can Lady have some tea too, with a little milk to cool it down?"

"You spoil that dog."

"I'm all she has."

Regarding the pair, Hattie thought how alike they were.

"So what was all the banging about just now?" Hattie asked as she poured the tea.

"Sebastian," sighed Georgiana. "I kind of cajoled him into declaring his love for Olivia and I don't think it went all that well. He was in a very black mood when he got back."

"I told you not to interfere."

"I know, but they're so right for each other, and I can't bear for him to lose this chance to be happy." She loved her big brother, despite his moods.

"Darling, you have to let him find his own way. You've both been through so much and I'd hate for him to get hurt again, but it's his life to make or break, just like it's yours to do with what you want."

Taking a knife from the block, Hattie sliced into the sumptuous chocolate cake she had made earlier, and handed a plate over to Georgiana."

"Oh my God, this is amazing. Bet it's got thousands of calories in it."

"You need fattening up, there's nothing of you."

Georgiana laughed: "I'm not a bloody Christmas turkey."

"No one could ever accuse you of being a turkey, you're a beautiful young woman, I'm so proud of you." Hattie sniffed and rummaged in her pocket for a tissue.

"Aww, don't cry," Georgiana jumped up from the table and threw herself into Hattie's arms. "You raised me, well, you and Sebastian, but he's no role model, so you should be proud of yourself if anything."

"If your mother could see you now. You're a lot like her you know?"

"I don't know if that's a blessing or a curse. If you saw the way Dad looked at me you'd think he'd hated her."

"You couldn't be more wrong, darling. He and your mother were deeply in love. The kind of love I hope you both find."

Georgiana shrugged her shoulders. "He didn't love her enough to stay around and raise the children he had with her, did he?"

Hattie took her hand. "He loves you, he just doesn't know how to show you."

"Don't give me that crap," said Georgiana. "Why are you sticking up for him? I've seen the man a handful of times in the last ten years and that's only because Sebastian forced it."

Georgiana sat back down at the table and helped herself to another slice of cake.

"Look what you've done now." She jabbed her fork in Hattie's direction. "There's no way I'll get into my new breeches."

"You're the one who mentioned your father," Hattie retorted. "Where is he anyway?"

"The last I heard, he was running some kind of cultish yoga retreat in Bali. Seriously!"

"Who's doing what in Bali?" Sebastian's voice made them both jump.

"Dad, yoga, cult," Georgiana replied. "You ok?"

"Fine," he replied curtly, and sat down on a chair next to his sister.

"No, you're not. What happened?" Georgiana probed for details.

He sighed. "I don't really want to talk about it."

"Have some cake then." She grinned and slid her plate over to Sebastian.

"What? No Spanish inquisition?"

"It's your life, you've got to live it your way, isn't that right Hatts?"

Hattie nodded in agreement. "But you know we're always here if you do want to talk."

"I don't. What I do want to talk about is what your next move is Georgie."

"Meaning what, exactly?" she replied.

"Meaning that, exactly. So what is it? University? Job? Modelling?"

"Modelling?" Georgiana burst out laughing. "What planet are you on? Besides the fact that I'm no beauty, I'm about a foot too small to make the big time."

"You're very beautiful, just like Mum." Sebastian smiled at the memory of his wonderful mother.

"And we're full circle,' Georgiana laughed again.

"What?" Sebastian looked confused.

"That's what Hattie and I were talking about before you came in."

"Oh right. So?"

"So?" Georgie shot back.

"Stop being obtuse. What do you want to do with your life? I won't let you sit around here wasting it."

Georgiana sat up straight and put on her serious face. "Horses. I want to open the yard."

"And about bloody time." Sebastian smiled. He was relieved. He had invested a lot of money into bringing the estate's equestrian facilities up-to-date in the hope that she would want to run it as a business one day.

"Well, now that's settled, let's have some more tea and cake and discuss plans," said Hattie, clearly delighted that Georgiana was going to be a permanent fixture at Appleton Manor.

Georgiana turned back to Sebastian. "So?"

"So what?" he sighed, knowing what she was going to say.

"Olivia?"

"Leave it, Georgiana, I mean it." He gave her a withering look that stopped her dead in her tracks.

"Ok, fine." She rolled her eyes and stretched across the table for the cake. "Best have another slice then," she grinned.

Chapter 35

As Sebastian's courtesy car turned into Magnolia Drive, he opened the window and breathed in the fresh, azalea-scented air. He loved it here, his two champion's Green Jackets were testament to that.

The hallowed grounds at Augusta National Golf Club were a masterpiece and envied worldwide for their impeccable conditioning. Lush, manicured fairways, dotted with white bunkers and velvety greens, stood in contrast to a riotous explosion of azaleas and dogwood, all set amid a stunning backdrop of Georgia pines.

Sebastian drank it all in and felt a ripple of excitement run through his veins. Pulling up outside the white colonial-style clubhouse, he knew that he wanted to make it count this week more than ever.

Unwavering in its homage to tradition, and taking it upon themselves to zealously safe-guard the integrity of the game, the members at Augusta National were an elite bunch. Entry was only gained through an exclusive invitation, or by claiming the champion's Green Jacket at the first Major of the year.

The Green Jacket had been awarded to champions since 1949, and custom dictated that the victor must return his jacket to the Club exactly one year after his win, and there it would remain in the champions' locker room, only to be worn when in situ.

"Good to see you back Sebastian," drawled Bob Tisdale, the chairman of Augusta. "I gotta say, it's nice to have some of you old guys back in the field this year."

"I'm thirty-five Bob," Sebastian replied. The Chairman's Southern charm had clearly taken a day off. "And I was here last year, never missed one."

"Yeah, yeah, right. You gonna play in the Par three?"

"Your crowd-pleasing, family-friendly, let-my-child-be-my-caddy-showcase? Yeah, sure Bob, I'll fit right in." Sebastian's attempt at a joke went right over Bob's head.

Bob Tisdale had ascended to his Augusta National throne only two years previously, an appointment that had sent ripples of laughter throughout the golfing community. Universally known for putting his foot in it, he had managed to offend pretty much everyone who walked into his golf club.

Finally realising his mistake, Bob stepped forward, somewhat embarrassed, and slapped Sebastian on the back, "Gotta go, Jack's just arrived. Great seeing ya."

Sebastian turned around and saw Jack Nicklaus, whom he considered to be the best golfer that ever graced the fairways, affectionately nicknamed the Golden Bear, pull up outside the clubhouse.

"Saved by the bear," Sebastian muttered.

Bob dashed off towards the entrance without a second glance at Sebastian.

Continuing down the corridor, Sebastian looked at the walls that were adorned with scores of beautifully-framed, Green Jacket 'moments', and was pleased to see that both his victories were still on display.

I've not completely hit rock bottom, then.

Reaching the door of the Champion's locker room, he paused and took a breath. There was so much history inside its four walls that it always took him a moment to remember that he was a part of it.

In the centre of the room, a Green Jacket was displayed in a glass cabinet alongside a replica of the Masters trophy. Gleaming, solid wood lockers stood to attention, bearing the names of the best golfers in the world.

All legends in their own rights - Sam Snead, Ben Hogan, Arnold Palmer, Nick Faldo, Seve Ballesteros, Tiger Woods and the best of the best, Jack Nicklaus – they had all shared the same compact but beautifully-decorated room, year after year, and Sebastian almost burst with pride every time he opened the locker that he shared with the great Gary Player.

As he had the room to himself, he took the opportunity to sit quietly for a moment before the madness and excitement of Augusta swept him away.

His mind immediately drifted to Olivia - not that she was ever far from his thoughts. His heart had been crushed by what he had seen through her window that day, and he had completely shut down emotionally ever since. He had been professional and courteous but had avoided the elephant in the room. If Olivia had been aware of the distance he had put between them, she had not let on. What he could not understand was why she had not said anything about getting back together with Saul. She had been upbeat, laughing and joking, and more relaxed than he had ever seen her.

"Snap out of it Bloom," he muttered, shaking his head as he stood up. Checking his watch, he realised he was cutting it fine to meet Aiden on the range.

"Hey there, how you doin' Seb?" Jack Nicklaus drawled from the doorway.

Sebastian grinned and turned to greet his old friend. Stepping forward to shake his hand, he was surprised when Jack pulled him into a bear hug and slapped him on the back.

"Been watchin' your progress these past months, gotta say it's about time man," Jack grinned.

"Thanks Jack, means a lot coming from you. How's Barbara?"

"She's great, here this week with the family. Come on over to the house one night, we've not seen you much the past few years."

"Yeah, well I've not exactly been the best company or, quite frankly, of sane mind most of the time." Sebastian laughed.

Jack placed his hand on Sebastian's shoulder. "Look, son, you've had some real bad times, but you're still here. That's gotta mean somethin', right?"

"Well when you put it like that," Sebastian smiled. Glancing at his watch again he said, "Sorry Jack, I'm due on the range in five. Tell Barbara I'll come on Thursday, if that's ok with you both?"

"Sure, you know where we are. I'll see ya at the dinner tomorrow night."

"Looking forward to it." He left Jack to have his own five minutes of privileged contemplation in the coolest locker room in golf.

On his way to the practice ground, he was greeted by several past-champions before he noticed Eddie Franklin from the BBC, making a beeline for him.

He still had not forgiven Eddie for breaking the story of his misdemeanor with the slutty Hawthorne twins. Everyone had been with the Hawthorne twins, Sasha and Cleo, they were Tour groupies and easy lays. Sebastian felt he had been singled out and had made a point of ignoring Franklin ever since.

"Sebastian," Eddie yelled in his direction.

"Fuck off Franklin," he snapped, leaving him agog.

The crowd burst into applause when Sebastian entered the practice range, and he beamed his appreciation. He could always rely on a thoroughly biased audience at Augusta. They loved a tragedy, and they loved him - not as much as home grown hero, Troy McLoud, but almost.

"Top of the morning to you, boss," Aiden greeted him with a cheeky grin.

"Why are you always more Irish in America?" Sebastian joked.

"The ladies love it, to be sure they do," Aiden replied.

"So it would seem," Sebastian motioned to the group of all-American girls that had gathered behind the barriers at the edge of the range, pointing and giggling in Aiden's direction.

"Let's get to work, shall we?"

Chapter 36

There was a mist hanging in the air early on Tuesday morning when Sebastian set off on his practice round. He liked getting out at dawn during the Majors so he could concentrate on his course management, and work with Aiden on yardages and reading the greens before it got too busy.

Aiden was on the far side of the range, waiting for his boss, and was decked out in the white overalls, Masters hat and white trainers that all of the caddies were required to wear, another Augusta National tradition.

They had been together for eleven years, through the glory and the pain, and Sebastian trusted Aiden with his life. Despite his happy-go-lucky, laid back attitude, he was steady, reliable and a pretty good golfer, and his reading of a course was second to none. Sebastian knew he was lucky to have him, and even luckier that he had stood shoulder to shoulder with him over the past two years.

He did not care what Aiden got up to, or who he spent his nights with, just as long as he was on time, prepared, and didn't make mistakes. There had been so many incidents over the years where caddies had made silly and unnecessary blunders that had catastrophic consequences for all concerned.

Only last year, Frenchman Claude Besson had received a two-stroke penalty on the first hole of The Open Championship for having fifteen clubs in the bag, when only fourteen were allowed. His erstwhile caddy had forgotten to take out the extra wedge they had been working with prior to tee off, and it had caused uproar of gigantic proportions.

An hour later, Sebastian finished his warm-up and made his way to the first tee to meet up with his playing partner, the Argentinean, Diego Estabor.

"Hola Sebastian, cómo estás?" Diego greeted him warmly.

"Saludos Diego. Todavía fingiendo que no hablan Inglés?"

Diego laughed raucously and threw his arm around Sebastian's shoulder. "My friend, I speak good English, I just don't want to."

Sebastian laughed. "Shall we get this show on the road then?"

"Si me amigo. Care for a small wager?"

"$10 a hole? Yeah, why not."

Diego teed up his ball, dug out his driver, and launched his ball down the fairway, and they were off. For the next four hours, Sebastian was thoroughly entertained, so much so, he stopped over-thinking his game and played well, going round in a credible one under par.

He called Hugh when he returned to his rental property later that day.

"Well?" Hugh asked.

"Yeah, not bad. Steady, but nothing spectacular," Sebastian gave him a hole by hole run-down for the next ten minutes, listening intently to the advice Hugh offered in return.

"You're nearly there, Sebastian. Your swing is solid, you're sharp, all that's left to sort out is your damn head. It's the only thing holding you back."

"I'm working on it," he sighed.

"Work harder, work faster." Hugh was relentless.

"Ok. Look, I'll call tomorrow around the same time. I'm out with José in the morning."

"I want you to work on blocking your emotions tomorrow. Make like you're the only one on the course. No golfers, caddies, spectators. Just you and the course," Hugh urged his pupil.

"I'll do my best," Sebastian said, and hung up the phone.

His second practice round had gone as well as the previous days, and Sebastian had managed to do what had been asked of him, much to the annoyance of José.

"Eh, bastardo," he shouted over to Sebastian on the second green. "Why you no speak?"

"Don't take it personally. I'm working on my poor mental health, whatever the fuck that means," Sebastian grinned apologetically.

"Ees it working?" José asked.

Sebastian shrugged his shoulders: "Damned if I know".

His head was bursting by the time they had reached the 18th. He could not get Olivia out of his mind and was struggling to switch off.

"Christ, I'd kill for a drink," he said to José as they shook hands and walked off the green.

"No, no, my friend. You're better without it, trust me." José gently steered him towards the locker room. "Come back with me, we relax, Angie's there."

"Thanks mate, but I've got a massage booked and want to speak to Hugh again. And then there's the dinner tonight."

The Champions' Dinner was another tradition, held on Tuesday evening, and was exclusively for past winners and privileged board members of the Club.

The honour of hosting the dinner fell to the previous year's winner, and it had become the norm for the carte de jour to be made up of dishes popular in the victor's native country.

From haggis to paella, cheeseburgers and barbeques, to sushi and everything in between, the elite bunch of Green Jacket owners had seen and eaten it all. Sebastian had ordered traditional roast beef, with Yorkshire pudding and all the trimmings after his first win, and had plumped for fish and chips when he claimed his second title.

At precisely seven o'clock, Sebastian's courtesy car pulled up outside the clubhouse and he stepped out into an explosion of flash bulbs from the waiting media. It was a special night and he enjoyed being part of a very exclusive club that was exceptionally hard to get into. But he no longer loved the media attention that came with his success and, more recently, his failures.

He was thankful when Jack Nicklaus's car pulled up behind his, and the waiting press hounds averted their attentions to the greatest golfer on earth.

"Thanks Jack," he grinned as he hurried into the main entrance and made his way to the private dining room. Half an hour later, he had relaxed in the esteemed company and was enjoying listening to Gary Player and Jack recounting some of the epic duels they had fought over the decades.

At dinner, he had Jack to his right and the German Hans Hass, who had won his one and only Major at Augusta back in the early eighties, on his left.

"What zee fuck is this," Hans stabbed his knife at the plate that had been placed in front of him.

Sebastian laughed and handed him the table menu.

"Elk? I vill never understand zees traditions," he said, shaking his head in disgust.

"I have one word for you Hans... sauerkraut. Thank Christ it was before my time," Sebastian joked.

"Ya, ya, but Elk? Let us hope for a European winner zis year, ya?"

"Couldn't agree more," Sebastian grinned. "And this," he inspected the Elk, "Is nothing short of revolting."

Later that evening, back at the rental house, Sebastian picked up the phone to call Olivia, and quickly put it down again. He desperately wanted to speak to her, he missed her, and had an overwhelming need to hear her voice.

What's the point? She'll be with him anyway.

Chapter 37

"Christ, you look knackered," Richie said when he met Sebastian for breakfast the next morning.

"Didn't sleep a wink. I've ordered coffee already," Sebastian replied. "Are you eating?"

"Yeah, I'm famished." Richie glanced at the menu and quickly chose pancakes and bacon. "When in Rome," he joked when Sebastian raised his eyebrow.

"Thought you were supposed to be on a health kick?"

"Yeah, yeah, whatever." Richie grinned and pulled some papers from his briefcase. "You'd better be your most charming today, these guys are really fucking important, and I've worked my arse off to get them here to meet you."

Richie was referring to some potential new sponsors from Tokyo who were mad about golf and keen to get a foothold in the sport.

"Apps and games eh? You'd think they'd want a younger model, someone to appeal to the kids." Sebastian was feeling every bit his age, and then some, after his sleepless night.

"Technology. They're the fastest growing tech company on the Nikkei and are planning IPO here next year. You don't have to know about games or apps, and you don't have to care all that much, though it'd help if you did. You need this, they're your next cash cow." Richie's eyes glinted greedily.

"Feeling the pinch, are we?" Sebastian grinned.

"You've made me a lot of money over the years, and I'm grateful, but I've also got a wife who spends it quicker than I can earn it. I'm relying on you to replenish my bank balance," he laughed.

"Well, Georgiana's finally decided she wants to open the stables as a livery business, so I'm going to need a cash injection myself. You'd better fill me in so I know what I'm talking about."

They enjoyed a leisurely breakfast on the balcony of the clubhouse before meeting with Akio and Hiro Iwakura, the Japanese brothers who had created their technology empire from an app they had developed as teenagers. Their company, Gijutsu, was fast becoming a global leader in technical innovations and app development, and they were making a move into sports.

Sebastian had arranged for the Iwakura brothers to join him and Richie in a private lounge in the clubhouse, knowing that entry to the legendary venue would impress them from the off.

Two hours later, they emerged smiling and the deal had been done.

"Mr Broom, we're happy to do business with you. We see you in Tokyo," said Hiro Iwakura.

"Please call me Sebastian, Mr Broom is too much." Sebastian was struggling to keep a straight face.

Richie escorted them out of the clubhouse and returned to find Sebastian chuckling.

"Broom! Priceless."

Richie slapped him on the back in congratulations. "That was a job well done Mr Broom. We're back in business."

"Only if I perform on the course," Sebastian replied grimly.

"Make sure you do then," said Richie. "It's in your hands now. The performance bonuses are incredible, and you know you'll be treated like royalty when you go out there?"

"Yes, that's the bit I'm looking forward to," Sebastian grinned. "Are we done now?"

Richie despaired at Sebastian's lack of enthusiasm when it came to the business side of the game.

"Yes, go on," he sighed. "That's the boring stuff out of the way. What time do you want to meet for dinner?"

Sebastian checked his watch, "I'm going to practice now, so I'll be finished around four o'clock. I need to talk to Hugh and go over some stuff with Aiden as well, so come over to the house at seven o'clock and we'll take it from there."

Several hours later, as Sebastian was finishing up his practice round with José, he heard the crowd roar in delight as their hero, Troy McLoud, won the par three contest with Justin Timberlake as his caddy.

"Christ, I loathe that man," Sebastian muttered.

"It's ok my friend," said José. "No man has ever won the par three and also won the jacket. It's the fate, no?"

Sebastian grinned. "You're right, fuck him, he's not worth it. He hasn't got the game to win here anyway."

He was wrong.

José was leading going into the final round on Sunday and Sebastian could not have been more pleased for him. He deserved to win a Major more than anyone else on Tour, and had been dubbed 'the nearly' man by the media, much to his annoyance, for way too long.

Unfortunately for José, Troy McLoud was breathing down his neck and, with just one Major title to his name, he was hell-bent on surpassing Sebastian's three.

In the end, he it had not taken much for Troy to overhaul José's lead. Sebastian's buddy had imploded at the famous Amen Corner, dumping two tee shots into the legendary Rae's Creek, and destroyed any hopes he had of winning. Troy took advantage of José's collapse and strode on to claim his first Green Jacket, much to the delight of the American hosts and spectators, and to the disgust of Sebastian.

Having never really been in with a chance of winning after a poor final round, Sebastian was satisfied with his performance over the four days of play. A top ten finish was better than he could have hoped for a few months ago, and a flame of desire for the game had reignited within him. He was burning to be back at the top, winning every title and accolade that was within his grasp.

Buoyed by his performance at the Masters, and encouraged by a jubilant Richie, Sebastian headed straight off to Valencia for the Open de España.

Chapter 38

"I can't believe what I'm seeing, this is the Sebastian Bloom of old!" Eddie Franklin's commentary boomed through the television set.

Olivia, Georgiana and Hattie were gathered in the drawing room at the Manor, glued to the final round of the Open de España with their hearts racing. Sebastian had played fantastically well over the four days, and had been the overnight leader going into the final round.

"That was an audacious shot from the deep rough, the ball must have been buried in that fluffy stuff and he still hit it stone dead," Eddie roared.

"Does that ridiculous man have to shout all the time?" asked Hattie. "It's rather putting me off."

"I think it adds to the excitement." Georgiana, overjoyed at what she was witnessing on the TV, was on the edge of her seat.

"Two putts to win," she squeaked, hardly able to watch. "He can't mess this up now."

Olivia was silently praying that he wouldn't let this one slip away.

"This is a tricky putt, downhill, a little left to right, and he needs to get the speed just right or it could keep on running and end up in the drink." Eddie's voice went up another decibel.

"This is the shot that could signal the return of Sebastian Bloom. Class is permanent, form is temporary. Is he really back?"

They watched in silence as he addressed the ball and sent it on its way, with the lightest of touches. It was a pure strike, moving slightly left to right as Eddie had predicted, and as it dropped in the middle of the cup, Sebastian looked nothing short of relieved.

The drawing room erupted and Georgiana started jumping up and down on the sofa. "Oh my God, he did it. He really fucking did it," she cried.

Hattie collapsed into an armchair and was sobbing openly.

Olivia was speechless. She continued to watch as Sebastian and Aiden high-fived and hugged on the 18th green, thanked their playing partners and walk off to the scorer's hut to sign his card. She could see the delight on Sebastian's handsome face as the cameraman zoomed in, and then he disappeared from view.

She jumped as her mobile started to ring, and seeing Sebastian's name flashing up on the display like huge neon lights on a Broadway opening night, she answered it breathlessly.

"Oh my God, Sebastian, that was incredible. Congratulations. I'm so happy for you." She was jubilant. Before she could utter another word, Georgiana snatched the phone from her hands.

She listened as Georgiana fired questions at him, tinkling with laughter at his responses, and then he spoke to Hattie who continued to sob throughout their brief conversation.

Olivia wanted to talk to him again but he was dragged away for the presentation. As they watched him accept the trophy, and listened intently to his media interviews, a tingling sensation spread through her body.

He called me first. I was the one he wanted to talk to before anyone else.

In Valencia, Sebastian was being slapped on the back and congratulated by his fellow golfers.

"You see my friend," said José as he threw his arms around Sebastian. "You just had to have the faith. Let's go celebrate."

"Thanks José, but I just want to get home. I need to get home."

He rushed through his press conference and was on board his jet an hour later, on his way back to Appleton Manor. He couldn't think of anywhere else he would rather be.

Settling back in his seat, Sebastian closed his eyes and fell into a deep sleep for the duration of the flight. He was exhausted, mentally and physically. He had dug deep to win, deeper than he had done in a long time, but it had paid off and he was on his way back to the top.

Chapter 39

The day of the village fête dawned bright and clear, with dew on the ground and the smell of apple blossom in the air. Early May had brought with it an abundance of warm sunshine and an explosion of vibrant colours throughout Appleton Vale. The fields and meadows were lush and green, and flowers in every garden, window box and driveway were bursting in bloom.

Church Farm, the venue for the fête, had been a hive of activity since the crack of dawn, and Malcolm Crailley had been commanding his troops with military precision.

The twenty-acre field had been transformed into a magical setting. Pony rides, face painting, a Ferris wheel, a helter-skelter and an old-fashioned Punch and Judy show were just some of the attractions. Later in the afternoon, traditional games of egg and spoon, the sack race and three-legged race would take place, and were renowned for bringing much hilarity to the proceedings. The main attraction was the hotly contested tug-of-war competition at the end of the day.

Olivia and Susie strolled the half a mile or so up to Church Farm, soaking up the early summer sunshine along the way. Susie was chatting about the impending arrival of the baby and filling Olivia in on her birthing plan, which was something Olivia really didn't care to know too much about. She was listening to Susie with one ear and smiling in all the right places, but her mind was firmly fixed on Sebastian's triumphant return from Spain.

He had burst into the Manor, jubilant and giddy from his win, and had been greeted by an ecstatic Georgiana, a still-sobbing Hattie and a howling, tail wagging, Ace.

"I'm so damn proud of you." Georgiana threw herself into his arms the moment he walked through the door.

"Thanks Sis," he grinned and looked over at Hattie. "Are you still crying?"

She blew her nose on her apron. "I knew you'd do it."

Sebastian turned to Olivia. "So, Ms Carmichael, what say you?" He desperately wanted to bask in her approval.

"Not bad," she laughed. "Not too bad at all."

Olivia had failed to make it home that night, passing out in the guest suite with Hector snoring in her ear and Georgiana's feet in her face.

Sebastian, who had been off the booze for so long that his tolerance levels had dropped dramatically, had face-planted on the sofa and woken up with a dreadful crick in his neck.

Congregating in the kitchen the next morning, Hattie had stumbled around making eggs and bacon, while Georgiana lay with her head on the table, be-moaning her over-indulgence. Olivia had hidden her self-inflicted pain behind a newspaper and some dark glasses and Sebastian had been the only one remotely on form, still high from his Spanish victory.

After eating every scrap that Hattie had put before them, Sebastian and Olivia had taken the dogs for a walk around the estate and Georgiana had taken to her bed.

They had walked silently and companionably, arms occasionally brushing together, until they had reached the far side of the lake and, eventually, Sebastian found the courage to ask her about Saul.

"Are you ever going to tell me about Saul?" he asked her gently.

"Saul? What about him?" Olivia was startled that he had mentioned him.

"Well, from what I saw you two looked very cosy. I was expecting to see a ring on your finger when I got back."

"What?" She was dumbfounded.

"I saw him, down on one knee, through your window." Sebastian croaked, his composure failing him.

"Bloody hell, don't you know me at all?" She was astounded. "He nearly killed me, do you really think I'd let him back into my life? When I saw him that day I honestly felt nothing for him at all. It was quite liberating, actually."

"What was he doing there then?" he was surprised.

"Attempting to apologise," Olivia rolled her eyes.

"Just attempting?"

"I think the baseball bat and Hector put him off, somewhat," she grinned.

Sebastian laughed, "That's my girl, I always knew you could look after yourself." He paused, then frowned, "Although I'd prefer it if you didn't have to."

Seeing the relief on his face, she picked up his hand. "Did it bother you that much, seeing me with him, I mean?"

"I wanted to fucking kill him." He couldn't hide his contempt.

"So why's it taken you so long to ask me?"

"Because clearly, I'm an idiot," he grinned.

"Clearly," she laughed. "So now we've cleared that up can we get back to normal please?"

It had been a lovely morning, and Olivia had felt that they had broken down some of the barriers that continued to separate them. She had discovered more about Sebastian's emotions, in those few short hours, than she had in all the time she had been in the village.

He seemed at peace, like he was no longer fighting with himself all the time, and it was both refreshing and compelling to be around.

Olivia stood in the centre of the crowd that had gathered to gawp at Appleton Vale's resident celebrity, and watched in amusement as ladies from far and wide strained to get a better look at Sebastian.

'He's drop dead gorgeous, isn't he?" came a voice from behind her.

"Tell me about it. Surely, it's time he got himself a new girlfriend," came the reply.

"I'd love to get my hands on him, and his money."

Olivia was shocked and couldn't help but turn around to see who was talking - she didn't recognise either voice. Standing just behind her were two incredibly young, and very inappropriately dressed girls who appeared as if they'd just come off the nightshift at Fiddlebury's seedy lap-dancing club, The Doll's House.

They glared at her and carried on discussing Sebastian as if he were a prize bull up for grabs.

Does he have that effect on everyone? She wondered.

Casually dressed in Damian de Landre jeans and sports jacket, Sebastian looked every inch the heartthrob that the media portrayed him to be. He declared the village fête open, and posed for photographs in the local newspaper, *The Fiddlebury, Appleton Vale and Bears Bridge Chronicle*, known locally as *The FAB*. A mish-mash of bad reporting, atrocious spelling and general misinformation, *The FAB* was a compelling read.

Olivia observed Sebastian charming his hosts and flirting outrageously with the buxom Mayor of Fiddlebury, Marjorie Masterson, who was putty in his hands. She thought how little the general public really knew about Sebastian, other than what they read in the newspapers.

Sebastian was cornered by the bumbling Brian Bedlam, editor of *The FAB*, just as he was trying to make a discreet exit. Small, fat and balding, Brian had a stutter and severe halitosis, and was known locally as 'bomb scare' - he had the ability to clear a room within seconds of entering it. He was woefully unprepared for each and every interview he did and, more often than not, ruffled a few feathers along the way.

Realising Sebastian was going to be tied up for some time, Olivia wandered through the thinning crowd in search of Susie. She passed a tent where giggling children were queuing up for face painting and henna tattoos, their parents keeping watch from the beer tent next door. She was astonished when she found out what a five-pound ticket could get you in the raffle, with prizes ranging from a Charles Harkley original of the village green, to a week's skiing in the Walton-Smythe's lodge in Gstaad.

"Completely bonkers," she muttered. She delved into her pocket, pulled out a twenty-pound note, and bought four tickets.

She eventually found Susie sampling the tasty treats on offer in the tented village. The vast, open-sided white tents were where the real action was taking place, and they were a hive of activity. The Bears Bridge WI was deliberating the winners of both the *'create a cake'* and *'best in show jam'* competitions, pursing their lips in distain at the multitude of sticky jam jars in front of them, the contents of which were varying greatly in both taste and consistency.

"This is the highlight of the year to some of these people. They take it very seriously indeed," Susie whispered. "I made some jam the first year we were here, it was a complete disaster, and Tom tried to grow some marrows but failed miserably, he was most put out. Oh look, here's Sebastian."

Sebastian arrived looking a little harassed. "Christ Almighty, how that man's still the editor I have no idea." He rolled his eyes and flashed his megawatt smile at them both. "Susie you're positively blooming, you look gorgeous, impending motherhood clearly suits you." He bent to kiss her on the cheek.

"And Olivia, how are you finding our little jamboree?" Sebastian's lips lingered as he kissed the corner of her mouth.

"I'm enjoying myself so much I'm considering joining the WI," she laughed. "Actually, I've never been to a proper village fête before, it's amazing."

Leaning in towards her Sebastian whispered in her ear: "No, you're amazing."

Her stomach lurched and she flushed pink, hoping Susie had not heard him.

"And now for something truly spectacular," Sebastian grinned, making Susie giggle.

"What?" Olivia asked.

"Purrs and Paws. You've got to see this, it's the highlight of my year." He draped his arm lazily around her shoulder and led her outside, into the blazing sunshine, to watch the hilarious antics of the village pets.

She liked how Sebastian's arm felt around her. He was relaxed and happy and it radiated out of him, it was infectious.

"Ah, my personal favourite," Sebastian pointed to the table where Billy Bradshaw, from Bears Bridge, was showing the judges how his hamster, Tyrion Lannister, could Moonwalk to Michael Jackson's Thriller.

Susie was giggling: "He's entered that bloody hamster the last three years. Surely they've got to give it to him this time?"

"At least before it dies," Sebastian laughed. "Short lifespan," he said when Olivia raised her eyebrows.

"How do we know it's the same hamster?" Olivia asked, trying to keep a straight face.

"Good point. This could get rather exciting," Sebastian grinned. "I reckon the serious money's on the flea circus."

Susie snorted with laughter. "Stop it Sebastian, every time I laugh a bit of wee comes out. This baby has a lot to answer for."

"Christ Susie, I really didn't need to know that!" Sebastian screwed up his face in mock disgust, and Olivia laughed.

"Ah, the obligatory dog on the loose." Sebastian pointed at Evie and Teddy Jenner chasing Woody as he ran riot in the show ring. "See, I told you this was going to be fun."

"Ladies and gentlemen, boys and girls, may I have your attention please?" Tom's voice crackled over the loudspeaker. "I'm pleased to announce that the winner of this year's Purrs and Paws, by an overwhelming majority, is Tommy Robert's flea circus. Come on up and get your prize Tommy."

"I bloody told you that's where the smart money was." Sebastian was jubilant and started hollering and whooping, much to the amusement of those around him.

"I feel a bit sorry for Tyrion Lannister," Olivia giggled.

"There's bound to be a steward's enquiry," said Susie. "Happens every year."

"Seriously?" asked Olivia.

"Seriously," Susie and Sebastian replied.

The major event of the day, the tug of war, was due to be held at six o'clock, but had been delayed thanks to the steward's enquiry that Susie had foreseen. Disgruntled parents and devastated children tried to overturn the result, but the judges' decision was upheld, and Tommy Robert's flea circus was crowned Best in Show.

The rivalry between the tug of war teams was stuff of legends, and many friends and neighbours had fallen out, albeit temporarily, when a result had not gone their way. It was the absolute highlight of the fête, and the crowd swelled as the start time drew near.

Appleton Vale and Bears Bridge, both small villages, joined forces against the team from the much larger town of Fiddlebury, and there was much at stake – mostly pride, and bragging rights for the next twelve months.

Susie had gone to check on Tom and, as she waddled back towards them, Sebastian took one look at her face and shook his head. "Oh, no you don't," he laughed. "There's no bloody way I'm getting involved. What happened to Tom?"

Olivia pointed at the beer tent where Tom, decidedly worse for wear, was serving one hundred and fifty different kinds of real ale to his customers.

"I'm fairly certain he's tried them all," Olivia laughed.

"Sebastian Bloom, you can't refuse a pregnant woman. I absolutely insist you take Tom's place on the team." Susie poked him in the ribs.

"Ouch! Do I really have a choice?" Sebastian grinned and walked off to join his team, rolling his sleeves up as he went.

His arrival generated a huge cheer from the watching crowd, and a few sighs of relief from his teammates.

"Thank God it's you," Peter grinned and slapped his back. "Susie was frantically looking for Tom's replacement and we'd laid bets that she'd come back with old Mrs Banks."

"She'd probably do a better job than me," Sebastian joked. "Where do you want me?"

"I think we're just making it up as we go along, there doesn't seem to be a game plan as such, or at all if I'm honest! I'd say nearer the back, given your height."

Kev the Rev was in charge of proceedings and he blew the whistle to get everyone's attention.

"Line up teams," he shouted. "I want to see fair play. Now, let us pray."

Sebastian snorted and received an elbow in his ribs from old Mrs Banks who had suddenly appeared behind him.

"Ouch! You don't half pack a punch Mrs B," he called, as she disappeared into the crowd.

"Lord, grant us thy wisdom to set aside our differences. Look after these brave men in their time of need, and bless the rope that shall be tugged, as it is a symbol of the eternal battle between good and evil. Amen."

"Is it?" Olivia sniggered.

"I'd say it was more a symbol of beer-fuelled, testosterone-filled fun," Andrea's voice came from just behind Olivia.

"Where've you been all day?" Olivia hugged her.

"In charge of the bloody hog roast, that's where. I've seen enough pork to last a lifetime. Wasn't going to miss this, though."

"Is that because a certain someone is in the team?" Olivia winked at Andrea.

Andrea blushed crimson. "Shit, is it that obvious?"

"Only to me, and only because I know you like him," Olivia put a reassuring arm around her friend's shoulder.

"Mad, isn't it? I mean, I know I can't have him but it doesn't stop me fantasising, does it?"

"It's not mad, and who says you can't have him? He needs some time, I'll give you that, but one day, not too far from now, who knows what'll happen?"

Andrea beamed at Olivia: "You always say the right thing at the right time, don't you?"

"I aim to please," Olivia joked. "I think they're starting."

Kev the Rev blew the whistle again and shouted, "Take up the slack. On your marks, get set, TUG!"

The hotly-contested duel was underway, and the air was thick with roars of support for both teams.

"Who's the incredible hulk at the back?" Olivia pointed to a huge man who looked as if he could single-handedly take on Sebastian's team, and win.

"That's big Trev, he's an accountant from Fiddlebury, lovely man," Susie replied.

"An accountant? I thought you were going to tell me he's some sort of world wrestling star," Olivia laughed. "He looks unbreakable."

"He's the reason we've not won this thing in five years. He moved down here from London, joined the team and they've dominated ever since."

"Come on Daddy, pull, pull!" Evie and Teddy were jumping up and down with excitement.

"Let's do this," yelled Sebastian through gritted teeth - it was an effort just to talk.

"Come on Peter, you can do it," shouted Andrea, who then looked around furtively to see if anyone had heard her.

Just three minutes later it was all over and big Trev had tugged his men to victory in record time. He let go of the rope and sent Sebastian's team tumbling backwards.

Sebastian dusted himself down. "Right. That's it. I've got twelve months to come up with a win strategy. Do you think I can persuade big Trev to move to Bears Bridge?"

"Either that or we all decamp to Fiddlebury," Peter joked.

"Who's for a beer?" Sebastian shouted over to the rest of the tuggers. "On me." His generosity was met with the biggest cheer of the day.

An hour later, Susie wanted to put her feet up and Olivia and Sebastian offered to escort her back to the pub. Tom was fast asleep on the floor of the beer tent and Peter promised to get him home as soon as he was able.

They were half way back to the village when Susie grabbed her swollen belly and doubled over in pain.

"Oh my God, there's something wrong with the baby," she cried out.

Sebastian immediately got his mobile out and dialled for an ambulance. "We're not taking any chances, we're both over the limit."

Olivia helped Susie lower herself down on a mound of grass by the side of the road, and held her hand. "I'm sure it's nothing. You've had a long and exciting day. You just need a hot bath and a good rest and you'll be fine."

"We've waited so long for a baby, I can't lose it now," Susie sobbed, and grimaced as another pain shot across her belly.

"The ambulance is on its way and I've just called Peter to rouse Tom and meet us at the hospital." Sebastian was masterful when he was in control.

He walked over to Susie, crouched down in front of her and lifted her chin with his hand so she was looking directly at him.

"Don't panic, lovely, it'll most likely be something simple. I know you want Tom, but Peter's going to get him to the hospital, come hell or high water."

In the distance, the muffled sound of sirens carried across the valley and Sebastian smiled. "See, what did I tell you, we'll have that ultrasound on you in a flash."

Tom arrived at the hospital just as Susie was being wheeled in for her scan.

"Thanks for being with her. I'm a bloody fool, got carried away with the real ales." He was anxious, scared for his wife.

"You're here now. Go with Susie, we'll wait," Olivia said. "And don't beat yourself up about it."

To Olivia it seemed an eternity until they got some news, but in fact it had only been an hour when Tom came bouncing into the relatives' room.

Sebastian stopped pacing up and down and looked at him: "Well?"

"Wind! It was just wind," he said gleefully. "God knows what she's been eating, but the doctor said it's quite common and can cause terrible pains." His relief was evident. "She's mortified though. Feels like she's wasted everyone's time."

Olivia let out a huge sigh: "Oh, thank God."

"Do you think she'll take offence if we call her farty Feltham from now on?" said Peter as he walked over and engulfed Tom in a hug.

"I wouldn't try it," Tom laughed. "You can go and see her if you like. They want to keep her here for a couple of hours to monitor things, and then I can take her home."

They stayed for another half an hour, chatting with Susie, relieved to see that she was back to her old self, before Sebastian looked at his watch. "It's gone ten o'clock, let's go home."

"My dad's waiting outside," said Peter. "He was the only one who hasn't been drinking today, and drove me and Tom here earlier."

Twenty minutes later they pulled up outside Appleton Manor and Sebastian groaned under his breath. He took Olivia's hand, leaned over and whispered in her ear.

"I had plans for us tonight, but it's late now. Plus, we've all had a bit of a scare and I'm leaving at the crack of dawn.

"Oh." Olivia was disappointed.

Sebastian kissed her neck, sending shivers down her spine. "I want it to be special, not rushed like Christmas."

He jumped out of the car, thanking Peter and James for their help, and bounded up the steps, taking them two at a time, turning when he reached the front door to blow Olivia a kiss before disappearing inside.

Olivia sighed, part of her delighted that Sebastian had been so wonderful and considerate, and the other part of her frustrated. He had re-awoken in her the sexual needs and desires she had lost after Saul, and she wanted him, badly.

Peter turned around, grinning. "You and Sebastian, eh? It's about time someone made him happy again." He winked, and James beamed at her through the rear-view mirror.

She was about to open her mouth to protest, but decided it was safest to say nothing, just smile.

A few minutes later they were at Brook Cottage and Olivia climbed out of the car.

"Thanks so much, James, it would've been hell trying to get a taxi on a Saturday night."

"A pleasure, my dear," he replied, and then turned to Peter. "I'll take you home, son, you look done in. The children can stay with us tonight."

"Ok, thanks Dad, if you're sure?"

"Course I am, your mother would have them all the time if you let her."

Peter turned back to Olivia: "'Night Liv, what a relief eh? See you soon."

"Bye, and thanks again." She walked up the path-way to the front door where Hector, who had been waiting with his nose pressed up against the lounge window for her to return, was barking manically.

Chapter 40

There were two different routes that Andrea could take to work, both on foot, and both of equal distance. Lately she had found herself walking straight past Blossom Hill in the hope she would get a glimpse of Peter.

Since the night of his first pub quiz they had become friends, although Andrea hankered after more than that. She had fallen for him and it was tortuous, knowing she could never tell him, and that he could never feel the same.

The day after their first meeting at the quiz he had popped into the farm shop to grab some supplies, and they had chatted for a few minutes until she had been called away.

Andrea admired his tall, slender physique and his salt and pepper hair that was always a little unkempt. She loved to debate, particularly about history and politics, and Peter was well versed in both, as they had found out over the course of their friendship so far.

Every morning since, she had taken much more care with her appearance than usual in the hope that she would bump into him. Even though she knew it was futile, she still wanted to look her best for him. To give him his due, Peter had never once hinted at anything more than friendship, and Andrea had never expected him to.

Unrequited love's a bitch, she thought as she examined her face in the mirror that morning. She was not completely offended by what stared back at her, because for all the hell her red curls had put her through, she was now thankful for the complexion that went with it. Her pale, freckled skin was smooth and line free, and at forty-two she didn't look a day over thirty-five.

She stood up straight, thrust her shoulders back and sucked in her tummy, regretting the extra cupcake she had eaten the previous day. Finishing the last sips of her coffee, she stroked Cleopatra and headed for the door. Turning right out of her house she drifted towards Blossom Hill with her head full of what ifs.

The Jenner's sitting room was located at the front of the house, looking out on to Blossom Hill and the valley beyond. Peter was staring out of the window, lost in thought, whilst waiting for the children to finish breakfast and get ready for school.

Hearing giggles and shouting from the kitchen, he knew he should be supervising but was rooted to the spot, waiting for his daily dose of Andrea. He had been silently watching her for a few months. Twice a day she would float by his house to and from work, and he had begun to hate the days where bad weather forced her into her car.

She was a breath of fresh air and held a certain appeal for him that he could not quite put his finger on. She was funny, full of life and caring. She had patiently and quietly listened as he had opened up to her over the course of their blossoming friendship, finally confiding in her about Sarah and how wracked with guilt he was.

Completely oblivious to Andrea's growing feelings for him, Peter was fighting his own emotions. He could offer her nothing but pain. He was still a married man with no way out of a desperate situation.

She deserves better, someone who can give her the world, he thought.

His heart skipped a beat when she came into view, a vision of beauty amongst the blossom trees. He inhaled sharply, *wow, she looks stunning.*

Wearing a 50s-style tea dress that made the most of her curves, in an electric blue fabric that was stunning against her alabaster skin and vibrant red hair, she looked incredibly sexy and Peter felt a stirring in his jeans.

As if sensing she was being watched, Andrea paused, looked around, and then carried on as normal. Peter shrank back from the window, hoping that she had not seen him.

He loved the time that they spent together. There had been many hours walking in the meadows, drinking coffee in the tearooms and having one too many tipples at the weekly pub quiz, and he knew so much about her life. He envied the way she was able to express and share her emotions. His own had been boxed up and packed away a long time ago, and he had become an impenetrable force, until now.

He was summoned out of his trance by a crash from the kitchen.

"Daaaaaaad," Evie shouted. "Piglet's escaped again."

Making his way into the kitchen, he found Teddy giggling uncontrollably, holding an open cage in his hands, and Evie on the floor in a futile pursuit of Piglet the mouse.

"Teddy, how many times have I asked you not to let Piglet out?"

"Four," he replied, giggling like a machine gun.

"Now I think you'll find it's more than that, you cheeky little monkey." Picking Teddy up in his arms, he swung him around the room until he begged him to stop.

"Got him!" Evie was jubilant. "Quick, Dad, get the cage."

She bundled Piglet back into the safety of his home and ran off to get her school bag. Peter helped Teddy with his shoes - he was just learning to tie his laces

- and then it was time to leave for St. Augustine's Preparatory, in Bears Bridge.

As Peter started up the car he began planning that night's dinner in his head, and decided a trip to Church Farm Food Barn was required.

Chapter 41

Sebastian had finished in the top five in Asia and his confidence was growing with the knowledge that he had finally perfected his new swing.

He had gone straight from the tournament to meet with his new sponsors, Hiro and Akio Iwakura, in Tokyo. As promised, he had been treated like a king. He had enjoyed the few days in their company, meeting staff and playing golf, but he was itching to get home, back to what he had started with Olivia.

As his plane touched down at Heathrow, his thoughts turned to the PGA European Tour annual players' gala dinner later that evening. Olivia had agreed to be his 'plus one' and he was, for the first time in years, looking forward to it.

The BMW PGA Championship was the Tour's flagship event, and took place at Wentworth Golf Club in Surrey every May. The tournament attracted a top-class field, and was also a huge draw for celebrity golfers who loved to play in the pro-am every year. It was a real opportunity for the spectators to do some star-spotting.

"I'm back," he called as he walked through the front door of the manor.

Ace came bounding into the hall and skidded to a halt at Sebastian's feet. He was quivering with joy that his master had returned once more.

"Where's everyone gone?" he asked Ace, who responded with one raised eyebrow, and an expression that said *fucked if I know*.

A moment later Hattie came bustling out of the kitchen, her apron covered in flour, some of which had made its way into her hair.

"Welcome home," she smiled and engulfed him in a cloud of dust.

"Hey, Hatts." He kissed her cheek. "Where's Georgie?"

"She went up to London on the early train this morning and said she'd be back tomorrow."

"Didn't you ask why, and with whom?" Sebastian didn't like her disappearing, especially when he didn't know who she was with.

"I'm not her keeper Sebastian, she's a grown woman. I didn't keep tabs on you at that age, and believe me when I say I know exactly what you were getting up to."

"I just don't like it, she's my responsibility. And come on, let's face it, she's got pretty rotten taste in men, judging by what's crawled through these doors thus far."

"Let her make her own mistakes. She's not stupid, and with all those self-defence classes and kick-boxing you made her do, she can take care of herself." Hattie patted his arm and steered him in the direction of the kitchen. "Come and get a drink. Your dinner suit is pressed and ready for tonight, before you ask."

"Wasn't going to," he grinned.

"Yes, you were. It's an important night, you'll want to look your best." Hattie knew him well.

"It's no big deal." He rolled his eyes. "It's only the Tour dinner, I've been to a million of them,"

"Not with Olivia you haven't," she replied.

Olivia heard the car pull up outside the cottage and took a deep breath. Grabbing her Dior dress and other essential items for the dinner that evening, she made her way down the hallway and stepped out into the brilliant sunshine.

She hadn't seen Sebastian since the night of Susie's hospital drama, and she was both nervous and ex-cited. Taking her bags, the chauffeur opened the door and motioned for her to climb in next to Sebastian.

"Hey," she said in a small voice, grateful her eyes were covered by her sunglasses. She knew they would betray her feelings, should he have the opportunity to look into them.

"Hey yourself," he replied, his voice positively dripping with sexual intention.

She slid across the leather seat towards him and leant over to kiss his cheek. He quickly turned his head, at the last second, and their lips met briefly, making Olivia jump as if she'd been tasered.

"Am I making you jumpy, Ms Carmichael?" Sebastian laughed. "I do hope so."

Taking a moment to regain her composure, Olivia replied: "I believe you're fully aware of what you're doing, Mr Bloom."

"I am," he grinned. "Have you got everything? Where's the mutt?"

"Susie's having him until tomorrow. So, tell me about tonight? What kind of dinner is it? Raucous or a total bore? "

"Usually a total bore, but I have a feeling it's going to be a fun night tonight."

Ninety minutes later, the car swung into the grand stone pillar entrance to the Wentworth Estate, home to celebrities, Russian Oligarchs and the well-to-do.

They wound up the leafy, rhododendron-lined, drive where Olivia glimpsed a good number of gated mansions - some tasteful, some absolutely hideous — all surrounded by lush fairways and perfectly-manicured greens.

As they reached their destination Olivia was greeted with one of the most celebrated and best-known sights in golf, the opening hole on the legendary West Course overlooked by the famous, turreted clubhouse.

Sebastian was in a hurry to get out and practice, having missed a day coming back from Tokyo. He grabbed his clubs from the chauffeur and turned to Olivia.

"I'll catch up with you later," he said, then whispered in her ear: "I trust you've got an amazing dress, one that I'd very much like to take off."

Before she could respond he was gone.

"Olivia, bonjour!" A familiar voice came from behind her.

She turned around and was delighted to see Angelica de Silva. They had really hit it off in Abu Dhabi and had met a few times since for lunch.

"Where's Sebastian?" Angelica asked.

"He's dashed off to get a practice round in. He only flew back from Tokyo this morning. Have you got time for a coffee?"

"Of course, chérie." Angelica linked arms with Olivia and guided her in through the clubhouse entrance, towards the oak-panelled Burma Bar. The doors to the terrace were wide open, taking advantage of the beautiful May morning, so they decided to take coffee out there amongst the honeysuckle and roses that smelled heavenly.

"So chérie, what do you have to tell me?" Angelica smiled knowingly at Olivia.

"Nothing! What? Don't look at me like that, there's nothing going on," Olivia spluttered.

"I've seen the way he looks at you and I've listened to the way you talk about him. It is amour chérie, even if you deny it." Her laugh was infectious, and Olivia couldn't help but join in.

"Nothing's happened since Christmas, well not really. On one or two occasions I thought it would, but something has always got in the way. Bad timing, maybe? Or someone's trying to tell us something."

"Believe me, you are not alone in this. Sebastian has changed since he met you. I know he isn't perfect, but you weren't here over the last two years and he is much improved. No drink, no women, no scandal, so what does that tell you?" Angelica was firmly in Sebastian's corner.

"I'm going to stop obsessing about it all and try to have a good time tonight. Just don't let me drink too much. I've got a meeting with my editor tomorrow and need to be on form."

Just around the corner from Olivia and Angelica, close enough to hear their conversation but not be seen, Poppy Jones was sitting alone, plotting her next move.

She had worked for Richie as Sebastian's PA long enough and it was time to move on to something, or someone, bigger and with better prospects.

She came from a working-class family in Walthamstow, where her father had laboured himself into an early grave. Her mother, who regularly worked three jobs just to keep a roof over their heads, had led a miserable life. Poppy had, from a very young age, planned on getting out and getting rich, as soon as was humanly possible.

With no formal qualifications, and in a bid to kick-start her social climb, she had enrolled in a secre-tarial college alongside the slightly dim, but gloriously wealthy daughters of some of London's finest families.

The first victim of her social ascent was a plain and dumpy girl who was crying out to be befriended. The Honorable Charlotte Penry-Taylor was the daughter of the fifth Earl of Stranmount, who owned half of London's premier real estate. As an only child, she would one day inherit a vast fortune and was, in Poppy's eyes, the perfect stepping stone in her quest for fame and fortune.

In the end, it was Charlotte's father who had set Poppy on the road paved with gold. She had been staying with the Penry-Taylors for the weekend and, finding herself alone in the library with the Earl, she had taken him by surprise, unzipping his trousers, and giving him a blow-job that had been the undoing of him.

For the next two years, she had willingly been tied up, whipped and spanked, and taken part in several orgies at his behest – he preferred to watch when she was indulging in some girl-on-girl action.

Her reward was a swanky serviced apartment in Knightsbridge, unlimited spending at Harrods, and a job at the top sport and talent agency in the world.

"My dear, you can't just go in at the top," he had told her. "This will put you in direct sight of some very rich men. Use it well, just as you've used me."

Olivia and Angelica's conversation had moved on to children, so Poppy switched off. She made a mental note to bump into Troy McLoud later on, Sebastian hated him and she was sure that, between them, they could stir up some trouble that would be of mutual benefit.

She was hell bent on becoming the next Mrs Sebastian Bloom, and the only fly in the ointment was the one person she hadn't factored into her plans, Olivia Carmichael.

Chapter 42

"Now that's some dress." Sebastian inhaled sharply, looking Olivia up and down, slowly and precisely, drinking her in. "You're breathtaking."

Olivia smiled nervously and turned around so Sebastian could take in the full effect of her incredible dress. He watched in delight as the tiny, hand-sewn Swarovski crystals, interwoven with swathes of satin and lace, shimmered in the lights. The vintage Dior draped luxuriously over her frame and lingered on every curve, with just the right balance of sexy and sophisticated.

She had fashioned her hair back in a French chignon, placing tiny diamante pins throughout to keep it in place. At her neck was a teardrop diamond in a platinum setting that her parents had given her for her twenty-first birthday - it was classic and understated, as were the matching earrings. To complete the look, Olivia was wearing silver

Jimmy Choo's that perfectly complimented the Dior number.

"Do you like it?" she asked Sebastian, tentatively. "It's not too much?"

"Olivia, you look stunning. I'll be the envy of every man in that room tonight." Sebastian grinned, and offered her a glass of champagne.

"You don't look so bad yourself," she laughed, delighted that her appearance had had the desired effect. She was nervous and excited at the same time, and couldn't decide if it was the bubbles or the undeniable sexual tension between them that was making her giddy.

Sebastian was wearing a Damian de Landre dinner suit that had been handmade to perfection. As she regarded him, Olivia felt the now-familiar jolt of electricity to the core of her very being, and she knew Angelica was right, she was falling in love with him.

"Shall we go?" Sebastian drained the contents of his champagne flute in one gulp. He took Olivia's hand and led her downstairs towards the ballroom.

"Wow," Olivia gasped as they entered the room. "Look at all those diamonds."

Everywhere she looked there was a breathtaking amount of bling on show.

"Do you like diamonds?" Sebastian was eager to know more about her.

"Find me a woman who doesn't," she grinned. "But I'm a little more understated, and on a budget."

"You're beautiful, you don't need anything else to make you sparkle. Let's find our table, we're sitting with José and Angelica, that much I know."

As he led her across the ballroom, Olivia looked around, taking in the fabulous dresses and jewels of the wives and girlfriends of the world's best golfers. It suddenly occurred to her that everyone was staring at them.

She gripped Sebastian's hand for reassurance. "Why's everyone looking at us?" she whispered.

Sebastian shrugged his shoulders and replied: "They're probably waiting for me to fall down drunk. That's what I did last year."

"Well I won't let that happen tonight, you can use me as a prop," Olivia laughed. She was beginning to relax and wanted to enjoy herself.

"There's a lot of things I'd like to use you for Olivia, but that's not one of them." He flashed his movie-star smile.

"Oh," she gulped, and once again felt the butterflies in her stomach doing summersaults.

They reached their table, where the De Silva's were already deep in conversation with the Spanish golfer, Javier Manuel Busso and his stunning wife Marta, who was as funny as he was droll.

"Sebastian!" Marta jumped up and kissed him on both cheeks. "It's nice to see you sober."

He laughed. "Marta, you look lovely as always. May I introduce Olivia Carmichael?"

She immediately pulled Olivia into a warm embrace, and then turned to her husband, saying:

"Javier, I told you there was a reason he stopped drinking," smug that she'd been proven right.

Olivia laughed. "Nobody can stop Sebastian doing anything. It's nice to meet you both."

"And this is Wilfred," Sebastian continued, turning to the blond, lanky, German golfer, who stood up and offered a rigid hand to Olivia.

"Wilfred von Adleman," he said in a clipped voice.

Olivia shook his hand and turned to his partner - a bottle-blonde, pneumatically-enhanced glamour model - who ignored her, instead turning her attention to Sebastian.

"I've been looking forward to meeting you," she purred. "I'm Krista, but you already know zat." She ran her hand up his arm.

"Should I?" he replied. "I'm afraid I'm not familiar with your work." He gave Olivia a look of mock desperation and stepped out of Krista's advancing grasp.

Trying not to laugh, Olivia put herself between the German supermodel and Sebastian, forcing her to acknowledge her presence. Krista looked her up and down and greeted her with disdain.

"You work for Sebastian?"

"Err no," Olivia laughed - nothing was going to ruin her good mood. "I'm helping him write his book."

"Let's sit," Sebastian interrupted. He took Olivia's hand once again, much to the annoyance of Krista, and crossed to the other side of the table.

"What a bitch," Angelica whispered to Olivia when Krista was out of earshot.

"She's got some front," Olivia laughed and reached up to accept a glass of champagne from the passing waiter. "She's not his type anyway, he hates plastic surgery and thinks all models are vacuous."

"So you have nothing to worry about then."

"Who said I was worried," Olivia grinned and relaxed back in to her chair.

Sebastian slipped into the seat next to her and continued to caress her hand, turning it over and running his thumb across her palm.

"You're going to have to let go of my hand at some point you know," she laughed.

"Why? I like it," he murmured in her ear.

"And so do I, but it could get a little awkward when it comes to eating."

Sebastian laughed and licked his lips: "I'm pretty sure nothing on that menu is going to taste as good as you."

Olivia gasped and furtively looked around to see if anyone had heard him. She was momentarily lost for words.

Shit, this is really happening, she thought.

She had no response for Sebastian, who was grinning at her, knowing full well that he had temporarily floored her. She was saved by the arrival of Gregor and Elena Balatov, a Russian couple who made their table complete.

Sebastian introduced Olivia to the Balatovs and then it was time for the entrée. The noise in the room abated as the guests settled down for dinner, eagerly anticipating a sumptuous feast that was, this year, being created by Michelin-starred Italian chef, Paulo Rammilo, whose services had been employed at great expense.

"I've been dreaming about this for weeks." Elena studied the menu in detail. "Roman and Dasha hired him for a party last year and said he was spectacular."

"Roman Abramovich?" Krista's interest suddenly spiked. "Are they friends of yours?"

"Gregor and Roman go back a long way," said Elena dismissively. "You know Roman don't you Olivia?"

Olivia laughed, "Well I wouldn't say I know him but, yes, I did interview him a few years back when he first bought Chelsea. He was a tough nut to crack, but I think I got there in the end. I actually found him quite charming. Ouch!" Sebastian tightened his grip on her hand, clearly put out with her admiration of Abramovich.

"Is he happy wiz Dasha?" Krista butted in.

"And what business is that of yours?" Elena could hardly contain her disdain for such a blatant fishing expedition.

"He's hosting a charity event I'm modelling at next month. I vud go for him if I thought he vas awailable," said Krista, unabashedly.

"And Wilfred?" Marta was shocked.

"Vot about him?" Krista replied.

"Ya, vot about me?" said Wilfred, who'd been listening intently to the conversation and had not liked what he had heard.

"Is zat what you vant? Money?" Wilfred was crestfallen.

"No darling, zis is vat I vant." Krista put her hand under the table and grabbed at his groin. Wilfred inhaled sharply, and was quickly mollified when she whispered, "You can fifty shades me zis evening, big boy."

Angelica and Olivia burst out laughing - Marta and Elena were less amused.

"Tramp!" spat Elena.

"Whore," Marta muttered under her breath.

"Now, now ladies, let's be nice to each other." Sebastian was laughing.

He bent and nuzzled Olivia's neck, whispering "Fifty shades, eh?"

"Have you even read it?" she wriggled away from him.

"Don't want to, don't need to. Let's just say I've never been lacking in imagination in that department," he grinned, and Olivia felt her stomach lurch once more.

By the time the first course arrived, Wilfred and Krista were engaged in some heavy petting that was quickly getting out of hand. She was straddling him, and groaned loudly every time he tilted his hips towards hers.

"For fuck's sake, Wilfred," Sebastian finally exploded. "Would you just go and get a fucking room, the rest of us are trying to eat, you moron."

"Ya, I sink zat is best." Wilfred stood up, grabbed Krista's hand out of his trousers, and dragged her away from the table without a backwards glance.

"Wow!" Angelica laughed.

"Wow, indeed." Olivia was stunned.

José, Gregor and Sebastian were giggling like schoolboys, and it was infectious. Both Marta and Elena had finally seen the funny side of it and joined in with the rest of them.

"Looking at him, I'd never have thought he'd have it in him," Olivia giggled. "He looks so stern and, well, German."

"Wilfred's a legend with the women. They fall over themselves to get to him, can't see it myself though," said Sebastian.

Halfway through the second course Olivia decided she could not eat another thing. Delicious as the food was, her mouth was dry with anticipation of what would come later, and it didn't help matters that Sebastian's hand was caressing her thigh under the table.

"And who's the unlucky lady who gets to spend a night in hell with you, Bloom?" The unmistakable Southern drawl put Sebastian immediately on edge, and he dug his fingernails into Olivia's thigh.

"Ouch," she yelped. Looking over her shoulder, she saw Troy McLoud with his perma-tan and movie-star teeth glistening under the twinkling lights of the ballroom's chandeliers.

"Fuck off McLoud. I'm not interested in anything you have to say, just piss off back to your table."

Sebastian remained composed, but Olivia knew he could explode at any minute.

She felt his good mood evaporate in a split second, and her heart sank. She looked over at Angelica who was hiding behind the menu, and then made eye contact with José, urging him to step in.

"Come on Bloom, don'tcha wanna introduce me to your girl, or are you scared she'll prefer me, like they all do?" Troy continued to goad him.

Sebastian banged his fists on the table. Jumping to his feet, he was nose to nose with Troy and, for a moment, Olivia was terrified he was going to punch him. Instead, he turned and stalked out of the room, leaving Olivia and the rest of their party open-mouthed.

Silence had descended on the ballroom as the other guests watched the ugly scene unfold, anticipating an explosive fight that would give them something to gossip about for the next few months.

"Always cause trouble, no?" José's fists were clenched, and he was ready to fight for his friend until Angelica put a calming hand on his arm and turned to address Troy herself.

"You should be ashamed of yourself." She jabbed her finger in his direction. "I don't know why you absolutely insist on upsetting Sebastian at every opportunity. You're a horrible man and nobody wants you here."

"Aww, come on honey, I was just trying to spice up the evening." He wasn't embarrassed in the slightest.

"You Europeans don't know how to have a good time. How about I show you?"

"How about you don't." Angelica stood up and emptied the contents of Olivia's uneaten dinner over his head.

Riotous applause rang out across the ballroom as Troy, humiliated, fled towards the exit, and Angelica bowed to her audience.

"Incredible!" José was delighted with his wife's ability to punch above her weight. "You were amazing, no?"

Angelica let out a nervous laugh and tried to hide her shaking hands.

"I'm so sorry everyone, I don't know what came over me," she said, mortified.

"Who needs entertainment when we've got Angelica de Silva?" Gregor was delighted. "They should book you for next year. Always hated him."

Waiters sprang into action, cleaning up the mess that Angelica had made, and they settled back to finish their meals.

"Go after him," Angelica whispered to Olivia. "He needs you. You can talk to him, I know it."

"I've never seen him that angry." Olivia was worried. "I'll give him a minute to calm down."

Across the room, Troy was being cleaned up by a vision of loveliness in a show-stopping Valentino dress.

She leant towards Angelica. "Is that Poppy Jones? Troy isn't a client of Richie's, why's she with him?"

Angelica wrinkled her nose in disgust. "She's a gold-digger and a whore, and Troy's available. I always thought she'd go after Sebastian though."

Olivia cringed - she couldn't bear to think of Sebastian with anyone else. "She's beautiful, I can see how it would be hard to turn her down."

"Go to him," Angelica begged. "Please. Don't leave him on his own."

"Ok. Although I'm not sure what I can do." Olivia turned and addressed the rest of her table, "And we were having such a lovely evening. Sorry to have to go everyone, it was great to meet you all."

She followed the route that Sebastian had taken out of the ballroom, hoping to find him in the Burma bar where she could make an attempt at calming him down.

The bar was empty, aside from a few members enjoying a quiet drink.

"Have you seen Mr Bloom?" she asked the barman.

"He did come in madam, but he didn't stay. He asked for a bottle of malt whiskey and left."

"Oh, ok, thank you."

"Would you like a drink?"

"No thanks. Actually yes, I would. May I have a large G&T please?"

She sank into a leather armchair in the corner of the dimly-lit room and sipped her gin and tonic, contemplating her next move. She was torn between feeling terrible for Sebastian and angry that he had walked out on her without a second thought. She procrastinated for almost half an hour, and was just about to leave when a large shadow loomed over her.

"Hey baby, left you has he?"

She looked up in horror as Troy McLoud positioned himself between her and the exit.

"He's an ass and you're beautiful. How about you and me grab a drink and get to know each other better?" He lurched towards her, reeking of brandy.

"You're joking, right?" She was stunned at his audacity, but remained composed. "Excuse me, I need to find Sebastian and you're in my way," she was polite, but firm.

"You won't find him here honey, he went home with my date, so it's just you and me babe." His eyes glinted at the possibility of getting another one over on his rival.

Sebastian and Poppy? No!

Olivia could not believe it, she didn't want to believe it and, for a moment, felt completely hopeless. She mustered up every last bit of strength she had and looked him straight in the eye.

"Troy, please believe me when I say if you were the last man on earth, I wouldn't touch you with a barge pole. Now, if you'll excuse me, I need to get back to my friends."

She steadied herself, and walked slowly out of the bar with her head held high, leaving Troy in her wake.

Chapter 43

Sebastian was caught somewhere between desperation and fury. He knew he shouldn't have stormed out and left Olivia, but he was completely irrational when it came to Troy McLoud.

He thought back to his first meeting with Troy, when they'd battled against each other in the Walker Cup. Troy was a cocky teenager from South Carolina who had been brought up to believe that, like all American children, he would be the best. They had had some intense and exciting on-course encounters, and Sebastian had wiped the floor with him every time.

Troy couldn't stand Sebastian, calling him 'a fucking stuck up Limey', and had vowed to not only beat him at golf, but also destroy him personally. He played most of his golf on the lucrative USPGA Tour for the money, fame and world-ranking points, and was universally adored by American golf fans - something he revelled in.

Over the years their rivalry had intensified each time they met on the course and their mutual hatred had grown with every moment they were in one another's company.

For Troy, the bitter rivalry was born from the loathing he felt towards Sebastian, based purely on the fact that he would never be as naturally gifted. He hated his impeccable British manners and his superior attitude, as if being English upper class gave him some God-given right to look down on others.

Sebastian was the first to win a Major, and he had done it in some style. At just twenty-three years old he had led the field at Augusta, wire to wire, and had stormed to a four-shot victory to take the US Masters title.

The following year, he had returned to Augusta as defending champion with his new wife, Ellie, on his arm. He had hoped for a wonderful week and had been excited to show Ellie off to the world, but it had been the exact opposite, and they had rowed almost from the start.

He remembered the shocking argument they had had that first night in Georgia, and also what followed.

"You're neglecting me," Ellie pouted and slammed her glass of wine down on the table.

"Darling, you know my schedule is packed this week, that's the price one pays for being a champion," Sebastian tried to placate her.

"So why the fuck did you bring me, then?"

"You're my wife and, let's not forget, you wanted to be here," he sighed, and crossed the room to take her in his arms. She pushed him away and walked to the fridge to refill her glass.

"Do you even love me, Sebastian?" she pouted.

"What? Don't be bloody ridiculous, of course I do, you're my whole life, Ellie." He was stunned.

"You see, that's where you're wrong. I'm not your whole life, I have to share it with your bloody career."

"Christ, you knew what I did when you met me, you married me knowing what I did so you can't start complaining now."

"I'm starting to think that was a mistake, you don't give a shit about what I want."

Sebastian lost his temper and rounded on her. "And what is it exactly that you do want?" he spat.

"Tonight, it's anyone but you." Ellie shot him a pitiful look.

He was stunned. "God, you can be a real bitch sometimes. I haven't got time for this, I'm going to dinner."

He had slammed out of the house and spent a thoroughly miserable evening with his sponsors, brooding on their argument. He had left dinner early, determined to restore harmony to his marriage, but when he had returned the house was empty.

She had stumbled through the door a few hours later in a drunken stupor, and Sebastian had been waiting for her.

"Where the fuck have you been? I was worried sick."

"Out having fun, wass it to you anyway?"

"And may I ask with whom?" He could see she was drunk, and spoiling for a fight.

"Troy," she slurred, and gave him a maniacal smile.

"What? How?" Sebastian was floored.

"He noticed you were alone at the party, so left and called to see if I wanted entertaining. I said yes, of course. Why wouldn't I?" She was goading him.

"Wow you really are a piece of work. You know full well that I hate that man, yet you still went ahead and did it." He was distraught. "Why Ellie?"

Before she had been able to respond, she turned a sickly puce colour and Sebastian quickly ushered her to the bathroom. She spent the next twenty minutes vomiting, before allowing Sebastian to gently undress and wash her before putting her to bed.

The next morning she had appeared at breakfast, full of remorse for her behaviour and the terrible things she had said to him.

"Did you fuck him?" Sebastian asked with his back to her, staring out of the window, unable to meet her eyes.

"What? No, of course not," she stuttered.

Blinded with love, he had chosen to believe her, and she spent the next few hours making it up to him in the bedroom, putting on a performance worthy of an Oscar.

Sebastian turned his thoughts back to Olivia. He had been gone from the dinner table over an hour, hiding out in one of the oak-panelled meeting rooms that were dotted around the clubhouse, slowly working his way through the bottle of single malt procured from the bar.

He stumbled towards the ballroom and bumped into Poppy at the entrance.

"Sebastian," she purred. "I've been looking for you."

"Seen Olivia?" he slurred, looking straight through Poppy, scanning the room ahead of him.

"She isn't here, left about ten minutes ago with Troy," she sneered. "They were all over each other, it was a bit embarrassing really."

She smirked as Sebastian's face fell. He was so clearly distressed by what she had told him - exactly the result she and Troy had hoped for. If she couldn't have him, she was damn sure that no one else would either.

She moved in for the kill. "Why don't you have a drink with me? I'm sure I can make all your problems go away." She pressed the palm of her hand against his groin and reached for his zip.

Sebastian sobered up in an instant, springing back and pushing her away.

"What the fuck do you think you're doing?" he snarled.

"Only what you want, what you've always wanted. I know you want to sleep with me, and I'm saying yes." She was daring him.

"Then you're very much mistaken," he was disgusted. "You're just a cheap, common little gold-digger who gets her leg over anyone who'll give her a leg up. Girls like you repulse me."

Poppy was stunned. She had gambled and lost, and now she knew her job was on the line, she went on the attack.

"And you're a pathetic old has-been who couldn't even hold onto his wife and child," she said, going for the low blow. "I suggest you take a fucking good look in the mirror before you start doling out judgment on me, you wanker."

Sebastian gave her a withering look. "I may be many things, but at least I'm not a jobless whore. Consider yourself fired, you'll never work in this industry again."

He left her standing, open-mouthed, and walked unsteadily towards the exit, still clutching the half empty bottle of scotch.

He was relieved when the chauffeur pulled up outside Appleton Manor, it was his sanctuary, he could lock himself away to lick his wounds. He imagined, and believed, that the worst had happened, that Troy had got his hands on Olivia, just has he had done with Ellie, all those years ago.

Chapter 44

Olivia had spent the night in turmoil, unable to understand why Sebastian had left with Poppy. She needed to clear her head, get some perspective, and taking Hector for a walk in the fresh morning air would do just that.

As she walked through the wildflower meadow - a riot of reds, purples and blues swaying in the gentle breeze - Olivia resolved to stay away from Sebastian, where possible, and complete his autobiography quickly, without further drama.

She followed Hector down to the river, and sat on the grass as he splashed around in the cooling water.

"How did I get it so wrong, Hec?" she sighed.

He gave her a goofy smile, and stuck his head under the water in search of fish.

The thought of Sebastian with Poppy, with anyone, made her feel sick. Checking the time, she decided it was a reasonable hour to call on Susie, she really needed a shoulder to cry on. She dropped Hector back to the cottage and wandered to the pub.

I really do love this village, she thought. *But how can I stay now there's nothing here for me?*

She let herself in through the back gate, where she found Susie hanging out some washing. Having promised herself that she would be stoical, she immediately burst into tears.

"Oh shit, Liv, what's wrong?" Susie waddled over to her as fast as her huge baby bump would allow, and engulfed her in a comforting hug.

It was a few moments before Susie could interpret Olivia's sobs.

"He did what? Are you sure? Did you see him leave with her?" Susie was shocked.

"You didn't see the way he reacted when Troy came over. It was awful, I've never seen him so angry." She sobbed, and a fresh river of tears began to fall.

"Oh Liv, darling." Susie stroked her head and waited for Olivia to talk again.

Tom appeared from the kitchen, looking apologetic. "Sorry Liv, couldn't help but overhear. You look dreadful. Here, drink this. It'll make you feel better." He thrust a large glass of brandy into her hand.

Smiling through her tears, Olivia accepted it willingly. "Bit early for the hard stuff isn't it Tom?"

"Just drink it! In Sebastian's defence, may I say that we men are strange creatures, everything for us is black and white, no grey areas, and the poor man's been mostly stuck in the black for the past few years." Tom was standing by his friend.

"He left me alone and walked out of there, with Poppy, and that's unforgivable, no matter how many excuses you make for him. He made me believe there was something between us." Olivia sniffed.

"But there is!" Susie exclaimed. "He's in love with you, everyone but you two can see it. Give him the benefit of the doubt."

"No. Not this time," Olivia was insistent. "I've only just recovered from Saul, and I'm not letting another man treat me badly ever again."

"Oh darling, I know you're hurting but you need to talk to him, find out what really went on. Did you even stop to think for a minute that Troy may not have Sebastian's best interests at heart?

"What? You think he was lying?" Olivia was astonished.

"You'll never know if you don't ask," Tom chipped in, rather unhelpfully.

"I'm not putting myself out there again just to get shot down." Olivia shook her head. "I really thought I could make this place my home, I love it here, but I can't stay, not now." She was unable to hold back her tears.

Susie and Tom exchanged worried glances, struggling to find the right words.

Olivia gave them a watery smile. "Thank you, you've been great. And I'm sorry you had to see me like this."

"Don't be silly, you know we're always here for you darling, but you don't have to go." Susie hugged her again. "At least pop in tonight for supper, and if you can't face it just text me and I'll send Tom over with meals on wheels."

Olivia was grateful for the support of her friends. "I'm really going to miss you both when I go, you've been so good to me."

"Think it over, don't make any rash decisions, Liv. We don't want you to go, and I'm damn sure Sebastian won't either." Tom was adamant.

"Oh Tom," Olivia sighed. "You're such a lovely man. Why can't I find one like you?"

Tom smiled. "You have found one, he's just a little more complicated than me, but deep down he's got a heart of gold."

Chapter 45

"I'm not going to disagree with you," Peter laughed as he walked side by side with Andrea from Church Farm back to the village. "I know when I'm beaten."

"Ha! I knew you'd have to back down when the evidence was in front of you," Andrea was delighted that she'd finally come up with a fascinating fact that Peter didn't already have the answer for.

"I'm still finding it hard to believe that Hippo's milk is pink, but a fact is a fact, well done you," he smiled and linked arms with her.

It was a glorious Sunday afternoon and Peter had walked up to the farm just before closing time under the guise of urgently needing lettuce, and in the hope that he would be able to walk home with Andrea. He had started doing his food shopping just before closing time so he had an excuse and it had become a very enjoyable routine.

They had grown close, much closer than either of them thought they should be, but neither could take a step back from their burgeoning friendship. She knew that he visited Sarah in the nursing home on Saturday mornings, when Evie was riding and Teddy was learning to swim with his grandmother, but it was still something they didn't discuss. It was the one subject they skirted around, and Andrea knew it wasn't for her to bring up. She had to wait for him to be ready to talk about it, and that didn't look like happening any time soon.

He was distracted, and she knew it had something to do with his visit to his wife the previous day. What she did not know was that Sarah's health had been going downhill over the last few months, and now her heart was failing. The doctors could not tell Peter how long she would last, or if she would need a transplant, or even be eligible for one. He was in the dark and hanging on by a thread.

Seeing Andrea soothed him, she was an escape from the pain, and she understood him. He was still completely wracked with guilt whenever he thought about her in various states of undress, but she was never far from his thoughts these days. He hated himself for what he called his 'emotional cheating' on Sarah, and had finally broken down and poured his heart out to his sister late one evening.

Annabelle had sat across from her brother in the kitchen, listening in silence as the words tripped out of his mouth.

"How did I let this happen? I feel so guilty, but I can't stop thinking about Andrea," Peter said, tormented.

"Stop beating yourself up." Annabelle was desperate for her brother to find peace and happiness. "It's time to let Sarah go and move on. All this living in the past, and putting your lives on hold, is doing you no good. Think about the kids and what they're missing out on."

"I can't." He could not contain his anguish any longer, the tears started falling. "I can't pretend I'm not married and carry on with another woman, Andrea deserves so much more, and I don't want her to be the centre of a village scandal, what'll people think?"

"Bugger what anyone thinks," Annabelle replied. "And don't you think it's time you told the kids about Sarah - Evie at least? She's eight Peter, she's not a baby anymore, and you can't lie to them forever."

"I wish I'd never told them she was dead, truly I do," Peter whispered. "It just seemed like the right thing to do at the time. They were so young, too young to cope with that, it would've destroyed us all."

Annabelle's eyes welled up, she felt desperately sorry for her brother. "You have our support, they know we love them, and they can come to us for a hug any time they need to," she said. "Mum and I are so proud of you for holding things together for so long, but it's time. You're making a good life here for them, they're thriving, they're strong enough, I promise you that."

He had taken heart from Annabelle's words, and when he sat Evie down and explained that her mother was alive, but very, very ill, it had not been quite as devastating as he had imagined.

Evie's initial shock had soon turned to tears, and Peter had held her quietly in his arms, waiting for her pain to subside. He tried, but failed, to hold himself together for her.

After what seemed like an eternity, she had looked up at him and began asking questions.

"Why did you lie to me Daddy?"

"I thought it was the right thing to do at the time, darling," Peter replied, wiping away her tears with his thumb. "I now know that it wasn't, and I'm so dreadfully sorry, adults make mistakes too. I wanted to shield you from the pain."

"Can I see her?" Evie was hopeful.

"She's very sick Evie, she won't know who you are. Do you understand that?" Peter stroked her hair.

"I think so, but wouldn't it make her better seeing us?"

"No darling, she isn't going to get better. She's confused and has no memories of us, but that doesn't mean she didn't love you and Teddy because she did, so very much. You were everything to her and made her incredibly happy."

"I'd like to see her Daddy, if it doesn't hurt you."

Peter had been devastated. This was the last thing he had wanted her to experience, but he was determined to let her navigate her own way through what was to come with his unwavering support and guidance.

He suggested: "We can go after I pick you up from the stables on Saturday morning if you like? I'll see if Granny can keep Ted for the whole day."

"Thank you, Daddy." She smiled weakly, then she reached up, putting her hands on either side of his face and whispered: "Are you ok Daddy? Does it still hurt you too?"

"I'm fine sweetie, thank you for asking. Yes, it still hurts, but every day it gets a little bit easier, and I've got you two little rascals to keep me busy, haven't I?"

He had put her to bed not long after, and only then had he allowed himself to break down. He wept for his own pain, and for the woman he had loved and lost and for the little girl whose innocent childhood had just been ripped apart by his foolish lies.

A week later, he had taken Evie to see her mother and it had not gone at all well. Evie, for all her bravery, had been distressed that Sarah hadn't know who she was, and Sarah had been confused and angry at strangers asking her questions she had no answers for. He had spent the rest of the day and night consoling his daughter in his arms as she sobbed her heart out, before eventually falling asleep from exhaustion.

The next day when she had come downstairs, Peter had been bracing himself for more tears. Instead, she threw herself into his arms, and whispered: "I love you Daddy, you're the best Daddy in the whole wide world." His relief had been immense.

Feeling a nudge in his side, he realised he had been daydreaming, ignoring Andrea's anecdote about a customer who had come in with a very strange request, only that morning.

"Nice to know I can hold your attention," she joked.

"Sorry. I was just thinking about Evie. I told her about Sarah."

Andrea was stunned. He didn't talk about his wife, ever. She composed herself and replied, "Oh Peter, you poor thing. How did she take it?"

"Better than I thought to be honest. I tried to explain everything to her in a way she would understand and I think she took it all in. I can't say I'm proud of myself for lying to them in the first place."

Andrea turned to face him and said: "You did what you thought was right at the time, and no-one can blame you for that. You were just trying to protect her and Teddy from more pain, and they'll both understand that when they're a little older."

Peter sighed: "Christ I hope so, really I do."

They continued on in companionable silence until they reached the bottom of Blossom Hill and Peter's house.

"Same time next week?" She asked tentatively.

"I'm sure I'll be needing to restock the fridge again by then," Peter grinned. "Thanks for listening, you've a very comfortable shoulder to cry on, but I promise I won't make a habit of it."

He watched as she walked home, until she disappeared from view into the village. He suddenly realised he felt better than he had done for a long time - a big weight had finally been lifted from his shoulders.

Later that evening, after the kids were in bed, the phone rang and he received the news he had been dreading - his beloved Sarah had died peacefully in her sleep. Her heart had given out and she had finally left him for good.

Chapter 46

A few days after the Sebastian and Poppy debacle at Wentworth, Olivia started making plans to leave Appleton Vale. Susie and Tom had tried to talk her out of it several times, but she remained resolute.

She had exchanged several curt emails with Sebastian, in which they had agreed to finish the last chapters of the book without meeting up. She was glad he felt the same way, it made things easier, although no less painful, for her. When it came to Sebastian Bloom, she knew everything that she needed to, and an awful lot she did not.

She was woken from her daydream by her phone ringing, and picked it up without checking the caller ID.

"You're leaving?" Georgiana squeaked.

"I am." Olivia had wanted to avoid Georgiana, knowing she would try to persuade her to stay.

"Why? What did he do?" Georgiana sounded panicked. "Tell me, you can't just run away."

"You don't want to know." She couldn't tell her what Sebastian had done, she knew she would not be able to hold it together. "It's time I got back to reality, this has been a nice break but that's all it was ever supposed to be."

There was an uncomfortable silence for a moment, before Georgiana spoke. "Will you come to dinner tonight?" she pleaded. "Don't worry, he's in London until tomorrow. At least give me a chance to change your mind."

Olivia sighed in resignation. She owed Georgiana that much, they had become so close. "You won't change it, but ok, I'll come for dinner as long as you're sure Sebastian won't be around. I don't want to see him."

"Please tell me what happened?" Georgiana begged. "I need to know."

"Later, maybe." Olivia changed the subject. 'What time?"

"Sevenish, and Hattie's cooking coq au vin. I know it's one of your favourites." She was pulling out all the stops to influence Olivia's decision.

Olivia laughed. "If you think Hattie's cooking is going to sway me to stay, then you could be right."

"Good, ok, gotta go. See you later, Liv." Georgiana hung up the phone before Olivia could change her mind.

She spent the rest of the day hiding away, packing up the beautiful cottage she'd been so happy in, and preparing herself for re-entry into her old life.

At precisely seven o'clock, she pulled up outside the manor and walked around the side of the building to the kitchen door, with Hector by her side.

"Olivia dear, come on in." Hattie was delighted to see her. "I hope you're hungry. Georgiana absolutely insisted on coq au vin, no idea why."

"I think it's for my benefit. It smells amazing." She walked over to Hattie and pulled her into a hug. "I'm going to miss you, and your cooking."

Hattie stepped back: "Yes, Georgiana told me you were thinking of leaving. What a lot of nonsense." She was disapproving.

"It's not nonsense. I can't stay forever. I have a life in London and I need to get back to it," Olivia replied. "Please try and understand."

"And what about Sebastian?" Georgiana's voice came from the doorway behind her.

"What about him?" Olivia tried her best to appear nonchalant.

"If you leave him now he'll never recover from it. You must know how he feels about you?" Georgiana's attempt at emotional blackmail didn't go unnoticed.

"Stop it. Don't try to make me feel worse than I already do. I don't know how he feels about me, he's never told me, and quite frankly, I don't care. Can we please just have a nice meal and some conversation that doesn't involve your brother?" She was becoming irritated.

Not wanting to risk upsetting her further, Georgiana quickly changed the subject, and silently vowed not to mention Sebastian again for at least an hour.

"Have you got somewhere to live yet? Didn't you give up your flat when you moved here?" Georgiana pushed her for information.

"I was living with Saul so technically it was his place, not mine. I'm going to stay with Emily for a while, just till I know what I'm doing with work." Olivia glanced at Georgiana and realised she was genuinely upset.

She walked across the kitchen and put her arm around her friend's shoulder.

"You, I like. Your brother, not so much," she joked, in an attempt to lighten the mood. "Your friendship means a lot to me, and I hope we'll stay in touch when I'm gone."

"Come on now you two, you'll have me weeping at this rate." Hattie bustled around the kitchen, laying the table for their meal. "Let's have a nice glass of wine and enjoy our last night together, for a while at least." She took three glasses from the cupboard and began pouring the wine. "I do hope you won't be a stranger Olivia, you're always welcome here."

They were halfway through supper when they heard a car roll up outside. Georgiana went pale and Olivia's stomach lurched, she was suddenly gripped with panic.

"It can't be him, he said he was staying in London. I'll go and see who it is." Georgiana fled the table and made her way down the hall just as Sebastian crashed through the front door and fell in a heap at her feet.

"You're not supposed to be here," she said, horrified.

Sebastian clung onto the fireplace in a bid to get
himself upright. "I fucking live here, can come and
go as I please." He was drunk, and Georgiana could
sense he was spoiling for a fight.

"Go to bed Sebastian," she pleaded with him.

"Where is she?" he looked around for Olivia. "I
know she's here."

"She doesn't want to see you, please just go to bed,
you're really drunk." She tried to steer him towards
the stairs, but he refused to move.

"Why's she here anyway?" He had one eye closed,
trying to focus as the room started to spin.

"I asked her to supper, you weren't supposed to be
here." Georgiana was apologetic, knowing she was
about to bear the brunt of his temper.

"Where the fuck is she? Hiding? Too embarrassed
to face me?" he sneered.

"I'm here Sebastian," Olivia walked towards him,
and nodded at Georgiana to leave them alone. "Let's
take this to your study." She walked off down the
corridor and he stumbled behind her, bouncing off
the walls as he went.

"Thought you couldn't bear to be around me?" His
words were laced with venom.

"I came to have supper with Georgiana. Had I
known you'd be here I'd have stayed well away, believe me." She knew she couldn't reason with him in
this state, she had to be cruel and make it clear that
it – whatever it was – was over.

His face fell fleetingly, as if her words had cut right through him, and then his eyes darkened.

"Did you fuck him, Olivia?" he slurred.

"I beg your pardon?" She was shocked.

"McLoud. Did you fuck him?"

The menace in his voice set of warning bells in her head.

"How dare you. I'm not going to justify that with an answer, and I hardly think you're in a position to be asking that question anyway."

She turned to leave, tears stinging her eyes and lead in her heart. She had been desperate for him to come to her, begging for forgiveness, or at least admitting he had slept with Poppy, but astonishingly, he was accusing her of the very same thing with Troy McLoud.

Sebastian grabbed at her shoulder and spun her around. They were now face-to-face, and she was intoxicated by the stench of scotch on his breath. As she looked into his eyes she was overwhelmed by the desperation she saw, and she knew she had to try to help him.

"Sebastian this is ridiculous," she said gently. "Why don't you sober up and we can have an adult conversation about this tomorrow."

"What makes you think I want to have an adult conversation about it?" He pulled her towards him and began to kiss her, forcing his tongue in her mouth, and pulling at her hair. The more she fought him, the more aggressive he became.

Suddenly she was terrified. She had seen that same look in Saul's eyes, right before he attacked her. She tried again to push him away, screaming silently for Georgiana or Hattie to help, but his strength was overpowering. He forced her back against the wall and grabbed her leg, lifting it up his side, and started to unzip her jeans with his other hand.

"You know what you are? A fucking tease," he whispered menacingly. "You've been playing with me for months, and yet just one wink from McLoud and your knickers are down faster than lightening. If you think for one minute that I actually cared about you, then you're sadly mistaken."

He had her arms pinned up against the wall and was fumbling with her belt. She was rooted to the spot, gripped with fear, unable to speak. Tears began to escape her closed eyes, and she knew she had to muster every little bit of strength she had left to get him away from her.

She opened her eyes and found Sebastian staring at her. He blinked, as if he'd been in a trance, and suddenly jumped backwards, freeing her from his clutches. She leapt away from the wall and moved towards the door, gripping its handle for support.

"How could you?" Her voice was trembling. "How could you do that to me?" She was distraught. "Don't ever come near me again."

Sebastian sobered up in five seconds flat, but he was lost for words, there was nothing he could say or do that could excuse his behaviour. All he could do was watch as history repeated itself and she walked out of the door without a backwards glance, just as Ellie had done that fateful night.

Chapter 47

Rosie Feltham was born at exactly midday on the twenty sixth of June. She arrived with a shock of bright red hair and announced herself to the world with a set of lungs to rival Pavarotti's. Tom and Susie were ecstatic, Rosie was their little miracle, and they delighted in showing her off at every opportunity.

The week before Rosie's birth, Susie had been in the post office and had seen Sebastian striding across the village green. Wanting to speak to him, she extricated herself from the clutches of Marjorie Rose – who had been showing her the photographs of her Saga mini-break to Reykjavik - and went out to confront him.

"Hi, you look well," he said when Susie waddled across the green towards him.

"Why did you do it?" She demanded to know why he had behaved so badly.

"What did she tell you?" He was surprised at her tone.

"Enough to piece together at least part of the story. So why did you do it?" She narrowed her eyes and stared at him, willing him to offer up answers that her friend had refused to give her.

"Well if she won't tell you, then I really don't think it's my place to say anything," he said, dismissively.

"You know what? Maybe everyone else is right and I'm wrong. I championed you right from the start, and God knows you didn't deserve it, not after the way you've behaved since Ellie and Lizzie died. I convinced Liv that you were worth the effort, and now she's gone and she's never coming back."

Sebastian was dumbstruck. Susie had hit a raw nerve and kept on prodding it.

Her anger turned to tears, and she stood in front of him red-faced and shaking. "I'll never forgive you for this Sebastian, you've probably destroyed the last ounce of self-worth she had left. I should've kept her well away from you."

Unable to muster a response, Sebastian turned and walked in the opposite direction, leaving Susie sobbing into a handkerchief.

Within seconds Dee Dee was by her side. She had been tending to her window boxes and witnessed the whole encounter.

"There, there dear, don't cry." She pulled Susie into a motherly hug, wiping away her tears with a tea towel she pulled from her pocket. "Why are you fighting with Sebastian? Is it anything to do with Olivia leaving?" She was fishing for information.

Susie sniffed: "Oh it's nothing, you know how in-furiating Sebastian can be, I swear he winds me up on purpose sometimes." She gave Dee Dee a weak smile. She was purposely vague.

"Everything alright?" Devon popped his head out of the surgery door. He had been watching the exchange between her and Sebastian with interest, and also wanted to know why Olivia had left so suddenly.

"Sebastian's upset her," Dee Dee offered by way of explanation.

"He's been doing a lot of that lately, it would seem," Devon wasn't impressed. "You'd think he'd know better than to pick on a pregnant woman. You sure you're ok?"

"I am, thank you both. It's probably just the pregnancy hormones on overdrive." Susie gave them a weak smile.

Dee Dee patted her arm. "Why don't you go and have a nice little lie down and relax, not long till this little one pops out, make the most of the time you have left."

"Yes, I think I will," she smiled at Dee Dee. "And please don't say anything to Tom, it really was much ado about nothing and I don't want him blowing a gasket."

"Your secret's safe with us dear," Dee Dee winked.

Susie knew that it was anything but safe in Dee Dee's hands.

A week later she had given birth to Rosie and, amid all of her joy, she was saddened that Olivia had not been there.

Olivia was devastated she had missed Rosie's birth and was yet to meet her, but wasn't ready to return to the village with the possibility of bumping into Sebastian at every turn. She had refused all contact with him since walking away from the Manor over a month ago, and had avoided speaking to Georgiana, who had been hounding her night and day for answers.

On that disastrous night, she had left her bag in the kitchen at the Manor and stumbled home in the dark. She had to climb into her cottage through the utility room window that she had luckily left on the latch.

She had sat on the kitchen floor with Hector soaking up her tears until the early hours, and had then fallen into an exhausted yet fitful sleep. She had fully expected Sebastian to follow her home, but thankfully he hadn't. He had scared her, and she wasn't going to allow him to do that twice.

The next morning, she had packed up the remainder of her belongings, said her goodbyes to Tom, Susie, Dee Dee and Jane, and had driven out of Appleton Vale for the last time.

Being back in the city was suffocating. She had grown used to the rolling fields and lush green valleys of Appleton Vale, and felt trapped. Her only saving grace, making London just about bearable, was her best friend Emily who hadn't judged or admonished her in any way, just welcomed her into her home with open arms and an unending supply of gin.

That first night, they had sat on the floor in the living room of Emily's tiny house in Chelsea and drowned Olivia's sorrows together.

"Darling, you know the only way of getting over him is by getting under someone else. I insist you get laid as quickly as possible. You haven't had sex since Christmas! How on earth are you still sane?"

"But I'm not, am I?" Olivia hiccoughed and fell about laughing.

"Let's find the positive in all this, shall we darling?" Emily poured them both another drink.

"Wass that then?" she slurred.

"At least you're not crying about Saul the Shit anymore."

They had exploded into a fit of giggles and, for a brief moment, Olivia had been transported back to a time when they were much younger, and with much less baggage.

A week later, Olivia had moved into a pretty Victorian terrace house close to Wimbledon Common and had settled into a simple, quiet routine of early morning dog walks, followed by days of writing and nights of crying. She had never shed so many tears, not even after Saul, and she was beginning to wonder if somewhere inside her a dam had burst.

Despite Emily's insistence, she just wasn't interested in meeting anyone else. Her heart was well and truly broken, and she doubted it would ever fully heal.

Chapter 48

Sarah Jenner was laid to rest at St Saviour's church on a wet and warm morning, in a private service given by Kev the Rev and attended only by close family.

News of her death had spread rapidly through the village and there were outpourings of sympathy for Peter and his children, having been through so much already.

Peter stood by the graveside after the simple ceremony and silently cried for the loss of his beautiful, talented and loving wife. He had spent the week since her death with the children, consoling them and trying to deal with his own grief.

When the call had come through that night he had been thinking about Andrea, and was immediately wracked with guilt when he heard the voice of the care home's manager.

"Mr Jenner. I'm dreadfully sorry to inform you that your wife passed away a half an hour ago. It was very peaceful, she went in her sleep and we doubt she felt any pain. We've already set in motion the plans she made for her funeral."

Peter had sat at his desk for some time, before he found the strength to call his sister and break the news to her. Twenty minutes later his parents were on the doorstep, and his mother had held him in her arms as he mourned the loss of his wife.

Breaking the news to Evie and Ted had been incredibly difficult, but Annabelle had been there to help. Evie was remarkably stoical in her grief, as if she had been preparing for it since she visited Sarah. Teddy was less upset about the mother he had never known, and his smiling face and constant chatter kept Peter going in those first dark days.

He also felt a certain sense of relief, like a weight had been lifted from his shoulders, and the burden of pain had now moved into their past.

They had gone back to Blossom Hill after the funeral and then Evie and Ted had stayed with their grandparents for the night, to give Peter some time alone.

He stood in the bay window, looking out onto the deserted street, and watched the sun set on the worst day of his life. His thoughts turned to Andrea. He hadn't seen her since Sarah had died, but she had sent a beautiful card and her words had moved him to tears. He had been touched by her kindness, but still couldn't face her, or his growing feelings, whilst his grief was so raw.

Over the next few weeks he moped about the house when the children were not there. He made a monumental effort to keep things normal for them, but when he was alone he disappeared into his misery.

After a month had gone by, Annabelle took the no-nonsense approach with him.

"Pete, you need to get out of the house," she urged. "You can't hide away here forever. She's gone and there's nothing you can do about it. I don't want to be harsh, but I can't bear to see you in such turmoil when a simple visit to a certain farm shop manager would solve at least one of your problems."

Peter shook his head. "And why would she want a wreck like me? Besides I don't even know if she likes me like that."

"Of course she does, I've seen the way she looks at you," Annabelle smiled and patted his hand.

"Don't you think it's too soon? What about the kids?" He was still so tormented.

"They'll be fine, they like her, don't they?" Annabelle knew they did. "You deserve some happiness after everything you've been through. Let it happen, don't fight it, please."

Andrea stood at the bottom of Blossom Hill, deciding which route to take to work. She had deliberately stopped going past Peter's house in an attempt to avoid him, instead cutting through the woods and across Church Farm's paddocks. She didn't know what to say to him, and felt an invisible gulf between them that had not been there before Sarah had died.

"What ARE you doing, my dear?" Dee Dee tapped Andrea on the shoulder. "You've been standing here for ages, I've been watching you from the tearoom."

"Oh, Dee Dee, hi. You made me jump. I'm deciding on the best route to work."

"Well it's quicker to go up Blossom Hill, but you already know that. Why don't you just go and see him?"

"Who?" Andrea feigned ignorance.

"Peter!" Dee Dee cried. "What's wrong with all you youngsters? Why can't you just talk to each other instead of playing games? It wasn't like this in my day."

"He's not ready," Andrea replied, looking over to Peter's house.

"How do you know that if you don't go and see him?"

"It's too soon, his wife's still fresh in the ground. I think I'm going to have a wander through the woods." She cut Dee Dee off before she could say another word and walked in the opposite direction, away from Blossom Hill.

She arrived at Church Farm fifteen minutes later, and pulled the keys out of her bag to open up. Inside, brilliant sunshine was beaming through the glass doors and windows, filling the room with warmth, and bouncing light off the carefully-arranged displays. She was just about to throw her bag into the staff room and switch on the kettle when a voice made her jump.

"Hello Andrea." Peter was standing in front of her, looking wretched.

"Peter," she exclaimed. "How are you? Oh, that was a silly question to ask, of course you're not ok. What have you been up to? Sorry, that's another ridiculous question." She was babbling nervously.

He stood silently in front of her, tears welling up in his eyes.

"What do you need Peter?" She reached out and took his hand.

"I'm so sorry, I didn't mean to come here, I just wanted to see you."

"Don't apologise, you have nothing to say sorry for. It must've been so hard for you and the children, I can't imagine what you've been going through."

"Would you be shocked if I told you that Sarah dying was a relief? Does that make me a bad person?" He looked ashamed.

"Nothing you say will shock me," Andrea reassured him.

"She was my life for so long, and I was holding on to the old Sarah without allowing myself to believe she was gone. The essence of what made her wonderful died years ago, and I've been trapped in this circle of pain. She would never have wanted me to live like this, and it took Annabelle to point that out. Sarah knew how to live and how to love, and expressed it vigorously. I know she would want me to be happy, and for Evie and Teddy to grow up in a home full of joy, not pain, like it has been for years."

Andrea was dumbstruck. She was vaguely aware of her staff arriving, followed by one or two early bird customers, but she was transfixed on Peter.

"I'm not expecting you to say anything," he said, aware she was slightly stunned by his revelation. "I needed to get that off my chest, and you were the one person I knew who'd listen and not judge me."

"I just want to help you get through this." She squeezed his hand.

"Seeing you has helped immensely, thank you. Do you think you might like to join me for a walk in the meadows at some point this week? I've missed you."

Andrea gulped. *He missed me*, she thought gleefully.

"I'd love to," she breathed. "I've missed our jaunts too. Just let me know when's good for you."

"Tomorrow afternoon? You're on a half day aren't you, so I'll meet you here at twelve thirty, if that's ok?"

"It's a date," she blurted out and then realised what she'd said. "Well no, not a date, well you know what I mean." Her face was as red as her corkscrew hair.

Peter smiled, "Actually, it would be nice if it was." He kissed her hand and turned to leave, "Until tomorrow Ms Hartley."

Chapter 49

Sebastian woke up full of self-loathing. What he had done to Olivia was unforgivable and he had no idea how to make it right. He had fallen into a drunken stupor a few hours after she had left, and was still in a heap on the floor in his study when Georgiana found him.

"What did you do?" she yelled. "I've been calling Olivia, I even went over to the cottage this morning, but she doesn't want to talk. She left without saying goodbye, so what did you do?"

"Don't yell at me," Sebastian pleaded with his sister. "My head's banging, and I feel like shit."

"I'll yell all I want, you fucking idiot. What the hell happened last night?"

"I scared the shit out of her, that's what." Sebastian was horrified at his actions the previous night.

"What? How?" Georgiana was shocked. "Please don't tell me you hurt her, physically I mean?"

"I was a bit rough with her," he confessed. "And I said some pretty shit things. I even accused her of fucking Troy when I know she wouldn't do that."

"Oh my God, what the fuck were you thinking? How could you do that? You know what she went through with Saul," Georgiana screamed at him. "God Sebastian, you disgust me." She shook her head and turned to leave, stopping dead in her in her tracks when she heard him whisper just two words.

"Help me."

The next morning, he joined her in the kitchen for breakfast.

"You look better," Georgiana said, sliding the coffee pot across the table. "Although, to be fair, you looked like total shit yesterday, so this is an improvement at least," she grinned.

"I'm going up to London," he replied, averting her eyes.

"Don't be bloody ridiculous, she won't see you, and we don't even know where she is anyway," she was desperate to talk him out of it. "What did we talk about yesterday? Baby steps. If you go bowling in straight away you'll never get near her."

"Well, what do you suggest? I can't sit here and do nothing, not when she hates me and thinks I don't care about her." He was becoming frantic.

Georgiana reached over and touched his arm. "I don't know. Christ, send her a letter or something that doesn't involve her seeing you in the flesh. If it were me, I'd run a mile if you turned up, but a letter is much less threatening."

"When did you get so wise?" Sebastian smiled and ruffled her hair.

"About the same time you went off the rails," she grinned. "Well, someone had to keep it together, didn't they?"

Sebastian laughed and relaxed for the first time in days. "So where am I going to send this letter then?"

"What about Liv's editor? We know who she is, and you could ask her to pass it on."

"See, I knew you were more than just a pretty face." He jumped up and headed for the door. "I've got a letter to write."

He remained in his study for the rest of the morning, emerging at lunchtime looking grim.

Georgiana was heading out for a ride when he appeared in the hallway.

"Well?"

He sighed and handed her an envelope. "It's the best I can do, but I'm not convinced it'll be enough to get her to talk to me. Can you stick it in the post box? I'm scared I won't be able to do it."

"Consider it done, bro." She grabbed the letter out of his hand and skipped through the door, before he could change his mind.

"There's a letter here for you," Stella passed the envelope across her desk as soon as Olivia arrived for their meeting.

She looked at the handwriting and gasped. Shakily she handed it back to her editor. "I don't want it; can you send it back?"

"Who's it from?" Stella was concerned, she wasn't used to seeing her so distressed. "Liv, honey, what's been going on? You're normally so together, and right now you're a mess, if you don't mind me saying?"

"I don't want to talk about it. Just return it to sender and that'll be the end of it."

She was adamant, and Stella didn't question her further.

Chapter 50

"If she won't even read my letter what chance do I have of seeing her." Sebastian was pacing back and forth across the living room.

"Try again, you idiot." Georgiana was lying on the sofa trying to watch television, and he was annoying her. "Did you really think it was going to be that easy?"

"I thought she'd at least be curious enough to open it." He folded it into his back pocket and looked at Georgiana.

"What's this crap you're watching?" He waved his hand at the television.

"Real Housewives of Cheshire, it's awesome," she laughed. "It's my guilty pleasure."

"You really do watch some rubbish." He rolled his eyes. "Whatever happened to a good book?"

"When was the last time you read a book?" Georgiana looked at him quizzically.

"I'm writing one," he smirked.

"Liv was doing all the hard work, you just had to talk." Seeing his face fall when she mentioned Olivia, she quickly sat up and clapped her hands.

"Ok, plan B."

"There's a plan B?" He was surprised. Her determination to get Olivia back almost matched his own.

"And a plan C," she grinned.

Sebastian stopped pacing and slumped into an armchair. "Come on then, let's have it.'

"B is for bombardment. You have to send her flowers every single day until she breaks. If nothing else, she'll get in touch to tell you to stop, and then you can pounce."

"And plan C?" he asked, not entirely confident that showering Olivia with dazzling bouquets was the way forward. Georgiana grinned with a wicked glint in her eye. "You know how you've always turned down the chat shows? Well how about you use one to talk to her? If you're looking for a grand gesture, then you can't do much better than prime time TV."

Sebastian looked pained. "I turn then down because they're utter crap."

"So what if they are? I happen to like Graham Norton, actually."

"Graham bloody Norton?" he scoffed. "Not a chance Georgie."

"I didn't mean you go on his show, I was only saying I found him amusing. I know exactly who you should be talking to but you're not going to like it." She was apprehensive.

"Who?" He was curious, although still sceptical.

"Piers Morgan," she cringed, and waited for Sebastian to explode.

"Ok. I'll do it, what have I got to lose?" He was prepared to do anything to get her back.

Georgiana was shocked. "WHAT?" she squeaked. "Christ, you really must love her if you're agreeing to Piers Morgan. Aren't you going to sit here ranting about why you hate him so much?"

"I think you're right, as much as it pains me to say it. I'll do whatever it takes to get through to Liv, and if that means pouring my heart out to that tosser, then so be it."

Georgiana fizzed with excitement. "This is so cool, it's definitely going to work."

"It's on you if it doesn't." He ruffled her hair affectionately. "I'll get Richie to sort it."

Sebastian grabbed his mobile and quickly punched in Richie's number, while Georgiana pressed pause on the remote control so she could listen in.

"It's me...yeah fine....Can you get me on Piers Morgan's show?...I know what you think, you've told me enough times....Don't question me Rich, just make it bloody happen...because I'm sick of being the bad guy, it's time everyone knew the truth...Yes, it's got everything to do with Olivia....I want it aired the week of The Open...For Christ's sake Rich, stop bleating and get it done...good...ok....bye."

Georgiana's eyes were almost popping out of her head. "The whole truth? Are you bonkers?"

"It's got to be a clean slate, no more secrets and lies," said Sebastian. "I want to be free of the past and move on, hopefully with Liv, if I ever see her again."

"What did Richie say?"

"He thinks I'm losing it, but he's talking to the PR team now."

"This is so cool," Georgiana repeated, grinning from ear to ear.

Richie picked up the phone on his desk and dialled up to the press office. Vanessa Cartwright, head of PR, answered on the second ring and was down in Richie's office within ten minutes.

"Well, that was the easiest sell ever," she joked. "I called Becky on my way down here, she's the celebrity booker for the show, and she's delighted. It's a real coup for her and for ITV, they've wanted Sebastian on for ages."

"And they agreed to air it during Open week?"

"They did indeed, but I suppose it makes sense timing-wise, especially as they'll get one over on the BBC," she said.

"Great work, thanks," Richie smiled and got out his phone to text Sebastian. "When's it being recorded?"

Vanessa checked her phone. "It's a pre-record on the fifth of July, with the promise of a prime-time slot."

"I can't say I'm all that happy about it," Richie frowned. "Did he really have to choose Piers bloody Morgan's Life Stories for his first major chat show?"

Vanessa rolled her eyes. "I know, Piers is a total Rottweiler, we'll have to coach Sebastian, give him some pointers, find a way to keep some of those skeletons in the closet."

"I think that's the point," Richie sighed. "He wants to wipe the slate clean, and be remembered for the great player that he was, and still is, not for all the shit that rained down on him in the last few years."

"What aren't you telling me?" Vanessa looked worried.

"For once you'll have to remain in the dark, sorry." Richie wasn't giving anything away. "Don't look so worried, he'll handle Morgan. This is Sebastian we're talking about, he'll hold his own."

"Yeah, if he holds it together long enough," she was concerned. "Get some time booked in with him as soon as he's available and I'll put him through his paces. Let's touch base later to confirm things."

"Thanks Vanessa, I owe you one."

"Yes you bloody well do, and one day I'll be calling it in," Vanessa laughed and headed out of Richie's office, leaving him to contemplate his star client's foolish move.

The letter from Sebastian had completely thrown Olivia. Her immediate reaction had been the right one, which is exactly what she kept telling herself when she felt her resolve weakening.

The day after 'letter-gate,' she received a text from Stella with an attached photograph of her office packed to the rafters with flowers.

That's a hell of an apology, they're all for you honey. Stella x

She had told Stella to distribute them amongst the staff, who each went home that evening with a beautiful, hand-tied bouquet. This carried on for two weeks, before Stella sent Olivia another text, begging her to put Sebastian out of his misery.

Please, please make it stop, there are only so many flowers a girl can reject. Stella x

She had sent a message to Georgiana, through Susie, to tell Sebastian to stop wasting his time and money, and it seemed to have worked. The flowers stopped, but three days' later the cards started arriving.

Stella had eventually, and very deliberately, stopped mentioning the daily offerings from Sebastian. She'd thought it best to let Olivia assume that he'd backed off.

Olivia dedicated herself to finishing Sebastian's book, so she could move onto her next project and forget all about him. The more she thought about how he had treated her, the angrier she became, and she resolved to cut him out of her life entirely.

On the first of July, she handed the finished manuscript to Stella, and she was finally free of Sebastian Bloom.

Chapter 51

"Are you ready?" Richie asked when he called Sebastian on the morning of the big interview.

"I'm about to air my dirty linen in front of the nation, how does one prepare for that?" His laugh was hollow. "I'm really fucking nervous Rich, I kind of wish you were coming with me."

"You'll be great, call me after."

Sebastian knew he could hold his own with any journalist, but his strength was with quick, funny quips that always seemed to disarm the most hardened hack. This time he had to offer up the keys to his closet and let Piers Morgan unleash the skeletons.

The car sent to collect him arrived at ten o'clock, and he was soon being whisked through the unusually quiet streets of London towards the ITV studio.

On arrival, he was met by the show's producer, Mark Jobson, and taken straight into make-up. He sat down in one of the leather chairs and squinted in the spot-lit mirror. Looking back at him was a wretched, tired face he no longer recognised.

A petite redhead entered the room and sashayed towards Sebastian. "Hello, I'm Chantal, my dad's a huge fan," she giggled.

Sebastian suddenly felt as old as he thought he looked.

"Sebastian Bloom, delighted to meet you." He thrust a hand in her direction. "Now let's see what magic you can work on this battered old face."

Still giggling, Chantal set about getting Sebastian stage-ready.

"You've got a lovely bone structure, and look at your eyes, they're so dramatic." She smoothed on a layer of foundation and topped it with powder and some bronzer. She then turned her attention to perfecting his hair, and fifteen minutes later she stood back and smiled.

"There, don't you look gorgeous?" She was proud of her efforts.

"I doubt it," he grinned at Chantal, "But thank you, you've taken years off me."

"Yeah, I bet you were a right looker in your day," she giggled, and dashed off to see to her next celebrity client.

He was shown to the green room, where he helped himself to a revolting coffee and began pacing the room.

"Sebastian!" Piers popped his head in the door. "Sorry, I meant to get here earlier but I've been held up in a production meeting. We don't have time for a chat now, so let's just get on with it, and I promise not to be too intrusive."

The audience was in place and Sebastian heard a ripple of applause echoing around the studio. A wave of nausea hit him, and the next thing he knew he was being ushered onto the set and into the wolf-like clutches of Piers Morgan.

Chapter 52

Olivia's phone had been buzzing constantly for the last ten minutes and she couldn't ignore it any longer. Reaching across the table she grabbed it and saw, amongst others, eight missed calls from Angelica, two from Emily and one from the gossip columnist at The Sun whom she loathed with a passion.

She decided to ignore everyone when Angelica's name flashed up again.

"What's with all the calls, Angie?" she sighed. "I just want to be left alone to wallow in my misery."

"Oh my God Liv, where are you? Are you at home? Turn on the television right now. NOW," she shouted.

"Why?"

"Sebastian's on."

"I know he's on, it's the bloody Open Championship, why do you think I'm not watching it," she snapped.

"No! He's not playing, he's doing an interview with that horrible man."

"What horrible man?" Olivia was confused.

"Piers Morgan," Angelica replied.

"What?" She gasped and fumbled for the remote control, scrolling through the channels until she found Piers Morgan's Life Stories. Suddenly her living room was filled with Sebastian, larger than life and looking decidedly uncomfortable.

"What the hell is he doing?" she asked Angelica, as her heart thumped so hard she thought it would burst through her chest. "He swore he'd never do a chat show, let alone with Piers, he hates him."

"Chérie, he has tried many ways to talk to you, he is desperate, and desperate men do silly things."

"But he doesn't need to wash his dirty linen in public like this, especially not with that loathsome man and certainly not during the most important Major of the year. Angie I have to go, I need to watch this, I'll call you back later."

She switched off her mobile, pulled her legs up under her on the sofa and waited, holding her breath as he was introduced to the audience. He looked utterly wretched and her heart broke all over again.

Piers Morgan had not been true to his word, and had taken a hard line from the start. Luckily for Sebastian, the work he had done with Vanessa had paid off and he had managed to answer every question thus far calmly and honestly.

After a few minutes, he began to settle into the interview and found the audience responding warmly to him. He had thought he was entering hostile territory but had, instead, found it filled with allies, apart from the ghastly Piers Morgan.

"Well I was expecting that question Piers, so no, you've not offended me. There's a lot that nobody knows about what went on before Ellie died. All I wanted to do was protect her memory, and that of my beautiful little girl Lizzie.

"After the accident, I swore that I'd never talk about what happened that night and I've lived the last few years completely and utterly wracked with shame and guilt.

"So, to answer your question, yes, I did hit Ellie. Only the once, not that that excuses my appalling behaviour. I did have a ferocious temper, still do really, but that was the only time in my entire life I've ever struck a woman."

Piers leaned forward in his leather chair, looked directly into Sebastian's eyes and, after a dramatic pause for effect, asked, "What was it that drove you to hit her that Christmas Eve night? What was going through your mind?"

Sebastian shifted uncomfortably in his seat. "I don't know, I guess I saw red. We'd had such a wonderful family day, decorating the tree and preparing to spend the day with friends and family. Lizzie, who always got herself into a complete state around Christmas, had fallen asleep on the sofa, so I carried her upstairs and put her to bed."

Sebastian looked pained at having to re-live that dreadful day, but carried on talking in a calm and measured voice.

"When I came back downstairs, Ellie was standing in the doorway to the library and told me she'd something to say that I wasn't going to like. It was then that she informed me she'd been having an affair with Troy McLoud." Sebastian paused as an audible gasp rippled through the audience. He almost lost his nerve.

He gripped the arms of his chair, straightened his back and continued. "She said it had been going on for years and that she was leaving me for him, that night, on Christmas Eve. I was blindsided, I never saw it coming. I was arrogant enough to ignore the cracks that had been appearing in our marriage."

Piers leaned in again. "And what happened then?" He urged Sebastian to continue, knowing the audience was gripped.

"Well let's face it, there's never been any love lost between myself and McLoud, she couldn't have picked a worse man to leave me for. At the time, it felt like she'd chosen him deliberately, to inflict maximum pain. I now believe that he was every bit to blame for their deaths as I felt I was."

The audience gasped in union.

"But I guess the killer blow was when she said that she was taking Lizzie to live in America with Troy. I was shell-shocked. I threatened to take her to court to stop her taking my daughter out of the country, and that's when the bottom fell out of my world." Sebastian paused, remembering how he felt on that fateful evening. "She said that Lizzie wasn't mine:

that Troy was the father, and I had no legal ties to my own daughter."

There was another collective gasp from the audience, some of whom were openly sobbing. There was an outpouring of sympathy for a man they were growing to like more and more, as the interview went on. The studio fell into silence once more, save the rustling of tissue packets, and waited for Sebastian to continue.

He looked Piers directly in the eye and said: "And that's when I hit her. I'm ashamed of what I did, and I'm certainly not condoning it, but she had just snatched away the most important thing in my life. It was a moment of madness I will regret forever." Anguish was etched into his face.

"My actions caused her to drag Lizzie out of bed and into the car that night. She couldn't bear to be anywhere near me for a moment longer than she had to. I drove them to their deaths."

Sebastian dropped his head and closed his eyes, as he recalled that very worst of nights when the police turned up at Appleton Manor to break the news to him.

"Well, Sebastian, I think I can speak for everyone in this room when I say how shocked I am at your revelations," said Piers. "You allowed yourself to be turned into a villain, and allowed the media to vilify you for all your wrongdoings, when in fact your conscience is clear. Quite astonishing, wouldn't you agree ladies and gentlemen?"

The audience burst into applause, and started shouting out words of encouragement to the man who had just, very publicly, opened his heart.

"We love you Sebastian," a woman shouted from the seats at the back.

"Don't let the bastards get you down," another voice bellowed out of the crowd.

A gentleman called out, "Get in the hole" which was received with laughter, and rewarded with a dazzling smile from Sebastian.

"I see we've got at least one golf fan in here," he laughed, and the audience burst into applause once more.

Suddenly, the heavy atmosphere that had hung so densely in the room at the beginning of the interview had lifted.

The producer signalled for a break and Sebastian breathed a sigh of relief. He knew that nothing else Piers could throw at him would be as horrendous as what he had just been through.

Chantal appeared by his side, fluffed a few brushes over his face and smoothed his hair back into position. Then they were ready to resume.

Piers pushed him further. "Talk of threesomes, gang bangs and other indiscretions have littered the press for the past couple of years, and there were a few sleazy kiss and tell stories along the way, so what's true and what's a lie, Sebastian?"

Sebastian grinned, slightly embarrassed. "Talks of my sexual exploits have been wildly exaggerated, but yes, there were a few women I turned to in the beginning to ease my pain, but it never really went away. Apparently, you can't shag your way out of grief, no matter how hard you try, Piers.

"My biggest downfall was the booze. The more I drank the more trouble I found myself in. I didn't care about anything, not my career or reputation, and my game completely fell apart. There were times, in the days immediately after the accident, that I felt I couldn't go on." Sebastian could feel the sympathy pouring out of the audience and enveloping him in an enormous hug.

"Ellie was dead and I felt I was to blame," he continued. "I didn't want to tarnish the memory of her with the truth, so I buried it."

Piers leaned in once more. "And what of Troy?"

"He never stepped forward to take the blame for his part in two beautiful lives being lost. He never said a thing, and just carried on like it had never happened."

"Did you ever confront him about Ellie?" asked Piers, sensing that there was another juicy account to come.

"Yes, of course I wanted to, who wouldn't? He was in America at the time of the accident, and he couldn't even find it in himself to come to the funeral to say goodbye to the woman, and daughter, he supposedly loved."

Gasps echoed around the studio.

"Against my better judgment, and believe me I was drowning in a never-ending bottle of scotch, I got on a plane the day after the funeral and went to have it out with him," said Sebastian. "I was in no fit state to travel, but I guess that's where it helps being a celebrity. I was poured on and off the plane by a very accommodating British Airways flight crew."

"And what were you thinking at this point? What were you planning to say to Troy?" Piers probed further.

"I wasn't thinking, Piers, that's the point. I was blinded by grief and drowning in guilt. God knows what I would have done had I actually fronted it out with him. Fortunately my sister, Georgiana, had called Richie and he met me off the plane."

"Richie Rogers, your long-time manager," Piers informed the audience.

"Yes, and I'm eternally grateful to him for stopping me from doing something I seriously doubt I'd have been able to come back from."

"But you must have spoken to him Sebastian. You've met on the course several times over the last few years. So if you haven't talked about Ellie and Lizzie, what is it that you do talk about? How is it that you haven't punched him square in the face?" Piers asked.

"After Richie sobered me up and got me back home, I locked it all away in my head. It wasn't up for discussion, and nobody dared ask me. That's just how it was." He shrugged his shoulders and stared at the floor. "I didn't feel anything, I was completely numb, and when I finally came face to face with Troy, I'd lost the will to fight. He was laughing in my face and I did nothing about it."

"At that stage I assume you felt that you were protecting Ellie and Lizzie," said Piers.

"Well, I suppose if I'd launched myself at him and wrapped a nine iron around his head on the first tee, it would have raised suspicion," Sebastian laughed and looked up from the floor.

"I managed to avoid him. It's amazing how many strings you can pull with three Major titles behind you. Let's just say that the Tour was very accommodating, and since then we've never been paired together. And seeing as I forgot how to play golf for a while, I didn't have to worry about meeting Troy in the closing stages of a tournament."

"So are you saying that you asked the Tour to fix the draw whenever you were playing together?" Piers sensed another scandalous admission.

"Yes, Piers, that's exactly what I'm saying," Sebastian grinned. "I said I'd be honest with you, didn't I?" Piers nodded and he continued.

"Look, it's no big deal in the grand scheme of things, and there's nothing in the rule book that says you can't do it. Let's move onto your next question before we bore this audience to death with the rules of golf. God knows, I make a living out of the game and they bore me senseless." Sebastian leant forward to take a sip of water and waited for the probing to continue.

Almost half an hour later, Sebastian was exhausted but still holding his own. He'd confessed his sins and asked for forgiveness on prime-time national television, and it was almost over.

Piers sat back in his chair and asked his final question.

"Finally, Sebastian, what stopped the drinking? What was it that pulled you out of your depression? What was it that made you want to get control of your life again?"

"Piers, it's not a question of what, but who," Sebastian corrected him.

"Ok then, who? asked Piers earnestly.

Sebastian paused and took a deep breath.

"This is the question I wanted you to ask. I knew talking about the past would be painful, but my future rests on what I'm going to say next."

The audience crackled with excitement, sensing they were about to hear yet another revelation, and Piers knew he'd lost the battle to keep them on his side, they were putty in Sebastian's hands.

"I'd pretty much hit rock bottom when I had to fulfil the commitment I'd made to write my autobi-ography. I tried to back out of it, fought tooth and nail with Richie to get it canned, tried to give back the advance I'd taken from the publisher. You name it, I did it, but in the end, as I sit here now, I can say that I'm so very glad that it went ahead as planned."

Piers smiled knowingly at the audience: "Olivia Carmichael, I presume?"

"Good God, does nothing escape your beady eyes, Piers?" Sebastian joked. "Once a tabloid hack always a tabloid hack, eh? And there's me thinking you were too highbrow for the gossip magazines these days."

The audience, sensing an upwards shift in Sebastian's mood, were delighted that he seemed to be in control of his host.

"Well Sebastian, there've been some photographs of you both making the rounds, and she's been on your arm at most of the major events in the last year, so it isn't hard to put two and two together." He turned to the audience: "And for the benefit of our viewers, if you don't know, Olivia Carmichael is an award-winning sports journalist who was commissioned to help write Sebastian's life story."

"Yes, Olivia's been instrumental in my recovery, she made me want to get better, and that's what helped me find form on the golf course again. My game has always been linked to my emotions. If I'm happy I play well, if I'm not, well we all know what happens. My freefall from the world golf rankings is testament to that."

"So how did she get through to you when your close friends and family couldn't?" asked Piers.

"She didn't put up with any of my crap from day one," Sebastian explained. "She took me on and came out on top, and made me see how badly I'd been behaving. She made me want to be a better person, and I hadn't felt like that for a very long time. Look Piers, I'm not going to go into detail and tell you the how and the why. I know you want me to, but let's just say that this extraordinary woman saved me."

"And where is she now? Are you together?" Piers was on the edge of his seat, almost as excited as his audience.

"I never told her how I really felt about her. In fact I did the opposite, I told her I didn't love her and that I didn't care about her. I accused her of sleeping with Troy, when I knew deep down that she hadn't. It was my own paranoia that kept eating away at me, I couldn't bear for history to repeat itself, and I behaved very badly."

Sebastian looked directly into the camera and spoke to Olivia, hoping she was watching, not caring that the rest of the world was witnessing his very public declaration of love.

"Livy, my darling, I've been stupid, stubborn and insensitive. I've been a fool, and pushed you away when all you did was give me my life back. I behaved like a monster. If you can find it in your heart to forgive me, I promise to spend the rest of our lives making it up to you. Since the day we met there's been no one else, no other woman, you need to believe this is the truth. It's over to you now, you know where I'll be."

"Wow, that certainly was unexpected, it's not often we have a Romeo and Juliet moment on my show," Piers exclaimed. "That was a brave thing to do, don't you agree ladies and gentlemen?" He almost burst with joy. He knew this would be front-page news, and he had the exclusive.

"So, Sebastian, don't keep us in suspense, where will you be if Olivia comes calling?"

"Piers, even you know where I'll be," he replied. "At The Open Championship in the home of golf, St Andrews, taking on the world and hoping to bring home the Claret Jug. It's the one I've always wanted to win and this is my year. I feel good about my game. Hell, I feel great about it. I can't wait."

"And in taking on the world you're also taking on Troy McLoud, who is, in fact, the defending champion."

"Yes, and I'm going to beat him," Sebastian grinned.

The audience was on its feet, cheering and whooping, willing their new favourite golfer to succeed. It took a full minute for Piers to restore peace.

"Well, I think we can safely say you've won over our audience, and I'm certain the viewers at home too. You've gained some new fans today, Sebastian. You've given us an unusually open and honest insight into your life. You've been weighed and measured, and let me tell you, you've not been found wanting. I think I can speak for everyone when I say that I wish you the very best of luck, both on and off the golf course."

Sebastian ginned. "Piers, I'd like to say it's been a blast, but that would be my first lie of the night. Thank you for giving me the stage to set the record straight. The time to move on is now, and I'm grasping it with both hands."

Piers had the last word. "It's been a real pleasure having you on, and thank you for your genuinely honest answers to some tough questions. Ladies and gentlemen, Sebastian Bloom."

The room erupted once more and Sebastian felt the weight of the world lifting from his shoulders. All he had to do now was win The Open Championship and convince Olivia to come back to him.

Chapter 53

The practice ground was packed full of spectators watching the world's best golfers going through their warm-up routines, smartphones capturing every swing and close-up encounter.

A huge cheer erupted when Sebastian walked in with Hugh by his side for his first practice of the week. The British public was extremely patriotic and loved to support homegrown stars.

"Fickle bunch, aren't they?" he muttered. "I was persona non grata a few months ago, and now look at them." He turned to the crowd and waved, before walking over to the far end of the range where Aiden was waiting.

"Morning boss." Aiden was cheery. "Beautiful day for it."

"Sunshine in Scotland, who'd have thought?" Hugh, a Glaswegian by birth, joked.

Sebastian was excited by golf again, and was confident that he could compete against anyone. Hugh had high hopes after the work they had put in since January.

He looked at Sebastian. "How do you feel?"

"Ready, and I'm in a pretty good place mentally, other than the obvious." It was painful to think about Olivia. "I can't worry about things that are out of my control."

Hugh slapped him on the back: "Good man, great focus. Your ball striking's better than it's ever been, the putter's hot, and you know the plan. No distractions, no arguments, play it safe."

Sebastian snorted: "Play it safe? When have I ever done that? The course wants me to take it on, and I'm going to do exactly that. I know it like the back of my hand, I love it here, don't worry."

Hugh's response was measured: "Just remember what we worked on."

Sebastian was suddenly aware of chatter amongst the spectators, and a presence behind him.

"Well, well, well." Troy looked him up and down with disdain. "I guess you got a flight booked for Friday night already, huh?"

Sebastian stiffened, gripping his club with murderous force, but was resolute in his refusal to rise to Troy's goading. Looking straight past him, as if he were invisible, he turned and started pounding balls down the range.

All around, eyes were firmly fixed on their encounter. The other golfers on the range had stopped their practice, eager to get a front row seat at what could be the fight of the century. Spectators were nudging each other and pointing at them, and Troy continued to provoke him.

"I wanna thank you for that awesome night with Olivia. She was a real peach."

Sebastian was shaking, his rage barely contained. Hugh and Aiden stepped between him and Troy, expecting fireworks, but Sebastian continued to ignore the man who had caused him so much pain. He knew Troy was lying. Olivia hadn't been anywhere near him, but it still hurt like hell to hear it, and he badly wanted to defend her honour.

"Ignore him," Hugh said, under his breath. Sebastian had filled him in on the Piers Morgan interview over breakfast, and he was determined to keep him focused. "He's of no consequence to you, nothing he can do or say can touch you."

Sebastian nodded. "If he wants to do battle then it can be on the golf course. I'm fairly certain he'll be laughing on the other side of his face in a few days anyway." Sebastian grinned, his anger dissipated, as he imagined the fall-out for Troy when the interview was aired.

"What's going on boss?" Aiden's curiosity got the better of him. "Anything I need to know, just so I can keep you focused out there, like."

"There's going to be a shit storm, and you need to be prepared," Sebastian said in a low voice. "But not here, let's get out on the course, less chance of being overheard."

Aiden threw the Tour bag on his shoulder and headed towards the exit in double quick time. "Come on then, no time like the present," he grinned at his boss.

Sebastian turned towards the stands and waved at the spectators again, before leaving the range. He was milking it, making sure he had them on side to guarantee their support when he would need it the most.

"Let battle commence," he muttered as he walked past Troy.

Chapter 54

The Open Championship was in full swing, and Sebastian was on a mission. His immediate priority had been to make the cut and get into a good position high up the leaderboard for the weekend, and he'd managed that in some style.

His first two rounds had been resplendent with birdies and eagles and he had yet to drop a shot for the tournament. He had been long and accurate off the tee, coupled with superb iron play, and the few times he ventured too far from his target, he had dazzled with his short game.

"I told you so," said Hugh when Sebastian came off the 18th green after the completion of his second round on Friday afternoon. "You just needed to focus. I'm concerned about this interview tonight though, you've got to keep up this level of concentration. I don't like it."

"I'll be fine." Sebastian's smile lacked confidence. "I know what I'm doing."

His *Piers Morgan Life Stories* interview was being broadcast that evening and, although he knew it was going to cause an uproar, he didn't care. Getting the truth out in the open had been cathartic, and he wouldn't apologise for it, to anyone.

"I'm having room service and an early night, and switching everything off. I'll let the front desk know to put Olivia through to my room when she calls." He was certain that his interview would have the desired effect.

He spent the evening in his suite with a dossier that Richie had collated for him of everything that Olivia had ever written, and reading it somehow made him feel closer to her. He fell into a deep sleep just before midnight, blissfully unaware of the pandemonium he had unleashed.

Olivia was sitting open-mouthed, reeling from what she had just seen. Anger erupted inside her, and she hurled the remote control at the television.

"You absolute bastard," she screamed at the top of her voice.

Her phone started ringing, and Angelica's number popped up on the display.

"Bastard," Olivia yelled down the phone. "He fucking lied to me. I've wasted months, working my arse off, writing his fucking autobiography, and now it's fucking redundant. Just wait till I get my fucking hands on him." She was apoplectic.

"Well that's not the reaction I expected," Angelica said, taken aback.

"What did you expect then? For me to be taken in by his little-boy-lost routine and go running into his arms?" she snapped at Angelica.

"Olivia, calm down. Why are you so angry, didn't you listen to what he said?"

She continued to rant. "He was going to let my book be published knowing it was all lies. How do you expect me to feel?"

"Sebastian said he loved you, and this is what you do? I will never understand your English ways. Why can't you just be happy, in love?"

"Do me a favour," Olivia asked her. "If you see that bastard tell him I'm coming for him, all guns blazing. He isn't getting away with this. He might fool everyone else but not me."

"Liv, chérie, don't you think you're taking this a little too far? Be reasonable." Angelica tried to make her see sense.

"Don't tell me to be fucking reasonable," Olivia yelled. "Put yourself in my shoes, how would you feel?"

"Ok, I can see you're angry, perhaps we should talk later?"

"No. Oh shit, I'm sorry. You're the first person I've spoken to so you're getting it with both barrels. I really am sorry."

"I know you don't mean it, I'd be in shock too. Look, I'm going up to St Andrews tomorrow now the kids are better. I didn't want José to catch anything this week of all weeks. Do you want to come?"

"I'm not sure I trust myself not to kill him," her laugh was hollow. "I've got to have it out with him though, I won't rest till I do."

"So come. We're leaving at one o'clock from Farnborough Airport."

"Farnborough? I thought you'd gone home this week?"

"No, we decided to stay and go straight to Scotland, I don't like travelling with sick children. So you'll come with us?"

"I don't know, I'll text you later, is that ok?"

Olivia finished talking with Angelica and switched her phone off. She didn't want to talk to anyone tonight, let alone Sebastian if he attempted to make contact. She walked into the kitchen and retrieved a half-drunk bottle of wine from the fridge. Pouring herself a large glass, she sat on the floor with Hector and downed it in one.

"Fuck him," she muttered. "Fuck, fuck, fuck him."

Hector raised an eyebrow, then wagged his tail in agreement.

Chapter 55

Sebastian was severely disappointed when he woke to find that Olivia had not called. He checked with the front desk twice, and the receptionist informed him, on both occasions, that he had had several dozen calls from various people, but none from Olivia Carmichael.

He switched on his phone and started trawling through the hundreds of missed calls, texts and voice-mails that had been left overnight, looking for one from Olivia.

It started ringing and Richie's number appeared on the display.

"Jesus, Sebastian, you've created the biggest shit-storm going. I told you, time and time again, this would happen. It is fucking huge news, and your timing is awful. You've hijacked the headlines and the R&A is pretty pissed off at you."

Sebastian took a deep breath: "How bad is it?"

"Bad for McLoud. He couldn't have been in a worse place for this to happen. The press is destroying him. You've been praised for your chivalry, of all things."

"Good, he deserves what's coming to him." Sebastian was unrepentant. "We always knew today was going to be rough, but for all the right reasons. I've nothing to be ashamed of."

"Have you heard from Olivia? Did you think for one minute what all this press intrusion would do to her? She isn't used to being on the receiving end of it, and I'm damn sure she won't like it."

"She didn't call," he admitted, feeling hopeless.

"Maybe she didn't see it," Richie offered reassuringly. "Maybe she had better things to do on a Friday night than watch that prick."

Sebastian glared at him: "And that makes me feel so much better, imaging her out with someone else."

"Christ, get a grip. Get her out of your head and get in the game," Richie was exasperated. "I'm downstairs with Aiden. You're going to need us to get out of here safely, it's like a fucking mad-house, bloody press everywhere."

An hour later, Sebastian ventured out of his suite for the first time since the interview had aired, and was met by Richie and Aiden in reception. The security team at The Old Course Hotel had done a stellar job keeping the press out of the foyer, penning them into a makeshift enclosure in the car park.

"It's mental out there, boss." Aiden looked slightly alarmed. "But we can handle it, eh? You were fantastic with your man, Piers, just fantastic."

"You dumb fuck." Richie slapped him on the back and laughed. "But when have you ever listened to me? Aiden's right though, you were excellent. I'd hate to be McLoud right now."

"Best get it over with, then." Sebastian readied himself for what was to come. "There's a car waiting, right?"

"Yep, just outside and I've told the driver to make a quick get-away," Aiden grinned. "Walking to the course isn't really an option, you'd be mobbed."

Sebastian slipped his sunglasses on and headed for the exit, with Richie and Aiden flanking him for protection. Taking a deep breath, he stepped outside - and into the lions' den.

"Heard from Troy?" David Duncan from The Times shouted, jostling for position with the other drooling press-hounds.

"Nope, don't expect to either," Sebastian replied.

"Where's Olivia?" came another voice from the crowd.

"No comment." Sebastian wasn't going to be drawn into speaking about her until he had managed to talk to her directly. He didn't have a clue what she would do in response to his revelations.

"She ain't at home, not been there all night, do you think she's on her way?" The reporter from The Sun was under orders to find Olivia and get her side of the story, if he could make her talk.

"What made you do it now, this week?" yelled Anthony Curtis, the Chief Sports Editor of the Daily

Mail, furious he'd been rammed into the pen with the other reporters.

"It's time to set the record straight, that's all." Sebastian ducked into the waiting car, followed by Richie and Aiden who were desperate to get him away from the hotel.

"Let's go," Richie instructed the driver. "And give it some welly."

The car sped away from the hotel, and Sebastian breathed a sigh of relief, "Wasn't that bad."

"It's going to be hellish at the course, so keep your head down, and for Christ's sake, avoid any confrontation with McLoud." Richie wanted to eliminate any possible distractions.

They arrived outside the clubhouse a few minutes later, only to be met by another mob of reporters, photographers and television crews that surged as one towards the car. Richie and Aiden jumped out and tried to clear a path for Sebastian.

"How do you think Troy's feeling this morning, Sebastian?" Kyle Beaumont, from the American station NBC asked, thrusting a camera and microphone in his face.

"I have absolutely no idea," he batted off the question, and allowed Richie and Aiden to guide him into the clubhouse as cameras clicked from every direction.

They eventually made it through the doors of the clubhouse, where the R&A Captain, Hamish McDougal, was waiting for them, his face thunderous. "A word, please, Sebastian."

"Before you say anything," Sebastian stopped him in his tracks. "I know I shouldn't have done it, it wasn't my intention to detract press coverage from the tournament, I was only thinking of myself, and I'm dreadfully sorry." He shot Hamish a disarming smile.

The Captain was stunned, the last thing he had expected from Sebastian was an apology, and a seemingly genuine one at that.

"Right," he stuttered. "Let's say no more about it. Good luck out there today old boy, we could do with a British win, it has been too long."

"Jaysus," Aiden grinned. "Thought you were going to get bollocked."

"Me, too!" Sebastian was surprised, but relieved. He didn't need any more trouble right now, especially not with golf's governing body.

"You're an arse." Richie was less amused. Turning to Aiden, he said, "Keep him focused, don't let him make any dodgy club choices."

"I'll do my best," Aiden promised, and walked off towards the locker room.

"So," Richie put his arm round his friend's shoulder. "Two more rounds to glory. You've got this."

"Do you think he'll show his face?" Sebastian wondered how Troy was going to react. "Fight or flight?"

"Fight. He's fucking brazen enough." Richie hated him too. "Forget about Troy, forget about Olivia. This is what counts, this tournament, the Claret Jug, the title."

Sebastian grinned. "Don't worry, like you said, I've got this." He followed Aiden into the locker room and left Richie to handle the ever-increasing throng of journalists and photographers that had gathered outside.

Aiden would usually have gone ahead of Sebastian and set up his pitch on the practice range, but today he knew his boss needed his support, and there was no way he was going to let him face it alone.

"Ready boss?" He slung Sebastian's bag across his shoulders, and waited for him to change into his golf shoes.

They left the locker room together and jumped on a buggy to go to the practice ground of The Old Course. It was just a few minutes' drive away from the clubhouse, and Sebastian wished the buggy was capable of doing more than five miles per hour. They were chased the entire way by photographers snapping their cameras furiously and by one or two of the more tenacious, and physically fitter, journalists.

The buggy stopped at the entrance to the range and he was immediately surrounded by a team of security guards that escorted him in. "This'll be interesting." Sebastian was anxious as to how the spectators, and his fellow pros, would react.

He need not have worried. The second he came into view, the crowd went wild. Cheering, clapping and stamping feet, they welcomed him with a warmth he had not felt since before Ellie and Lizzie had died.

He waved, and flashed a brilliant smile at the spectators. "Not too bad then," he muttered to Aiden.

"Sure, why wouldn't they love you?" he grinned. "Shame Troy's out later than us, I'd pay good money to see the reception he'll get."

"Knowing the great British public as I do, it isn't going to be pretty. Let's hit some balls and get out of here."

Other golfers started approaching him as he warmed up.

"Great interview, man," Tiger shook his hand and didn't wait for a response.

"Zat voz brave, I vish you zee best old friend," Wildfred von Adleman pulled Sebastian into an uncharacteristic embrace.

"Hell man, you don't hold no punches, do ya?" Ory Hazard was back to challenge for another Major after his meltdown at Augusta, and didn't much care for his fellow countryman. "He ain't gonna get outta this one too easy," he grinned.

Sebastian saw José heading his way and waved him over. Seeing his face, he said, "I know, before you get mad I didn't tell anyone I was doing the interview other than Georgie and Richie."

"Why you no tell me?" José was most put out. "We're friends, no?"

"Yes," Sebastian smiled at his friend.

"So why?" he pouted.

"Because it was hard enough doing it, let alone telling anyone."

"Where ees Troy?" José wanted to know the very latest. This was the most explosive story to hit the golf scene in many years.

"Don't know, don't care. Can we just stop talking about him please?" Sebastian was starting to get irritated.

"Angelica and me, we think you did great job. Ees Olivia coming?"

Sebastian frowned: "Doesn't look like it. You can't say I didn't try though." Inside he was dying. Every minute of every hour she was on his mind, but he was doing a decent job of convincing everyone he was fine.

"Angelica spoke with her last night."

"Really?" Sebastian's eyes lit up. "What did she say?"

José slung an arm round his friend's shoulder. "She no tell me, she say I'd tell you. Sorry, my friend."

"Christ, I can't stand this. I just want to know one way or another." Sebastian was in danger of letting his frustrations boil over.

Aiden quickly checked his watch, and caught Sebastian's eye.

"Time to go boss, on the tee in twenty."

"Shit!" José was panicked. "I'm late." He sprinted across the range, jumped into the waiting buggy and just made his start time with seconds to spare.

Sebastian received rapturous applause as he made his way towards the exit. He waved his thanks at the crowd again and stopped to sign a few autographs before Aiden steered him into the buggy.

"Let's go get 'em boss," he grinned, and jumped on the back while Sebastian slid into the seat next to the driver.

The way to the first tee was lined with well-wishing spectators, and Sebastian was happy to acknowledge their support, nodding and smiling as they drove by. As they pulled up just behind the clubhouse he took a breath, straightened his shoulders and prepared to face the world.

He strode past the throng of photographers and cameramen that had gathered for his tee time, and as he stepped onto the first tee, the crowd went wild. The sound of stomping feet echoed through the grandstands and the deafening roar of approval from the crowds gave Sebastian a surge of confidence. "Forgiving lot, aren't they?" he murmured to Aiden.

Stepping forward, he reached for the hand of his playing partner, Avery Kendrick – they had made the cut on the same two under par score. The young Canadian looked like a rabbit caught in headlights. He had never played with Sebastian before, and the media attention he was generating was unfamiliar and unnerving.

"This is gonna be interesting," he smiled weakly as he shook Sebastian's hand.

"Yeah, sorry about that, looks like we'll have a bit of a following today," Sebastian apologised, and offered some advice. "Just play your own game, you're good, you'll be fine."

Sebastian bent down and placed his ball on the tee, pulled out his driver, and smashed it down the fairway. His third round was underway.

Chapter 56

"Are you going to stay glued to the television all day Georgie?" Hattie wandered into the lounge, where she found her lying on the sofa.

"Yep," she replied without looking up.

"You could've at least changed out of those filthy breeches before you smeared mud everywhere." She crinkled her nose in disapproval, and stood with her hands on her hips, waiting for Georgiana to move.

"Aw, come on Hatts," she moaned. "Sebastian's teeing off in a minute, we can't miss it."

"Gosh, is that the time?" Hattie glanced at the clock on the mantelpiece. "Have you spoken with him today at all?"

"He texted this morning and no, Liv hasn't been in touch. I can't believe she didn't see the interview. He was so good, wasn't he?" She was proud of her brother's handling of Piers Morgan.

"He was, I'm so pleased," Hattie beamed. "And you, young lady, I'd be proud of you too if you hadn't left a trail of mud and destruction through the house. I suppose you'll be wanting lunch in here, too?"

"Might as well, 'cos I've no intention of moving till this is over, and you wouldn't want me to starve, would you?"

"You're a cheeky little madam, it's a good job I love you, isn't it?" Hattie picked up a newspaper and threw it at Georgiana. "Get it under those boots, NOW."

"Hey!" The newspaper landed on her head and she repositioned it underneath her feet. "There. Happy now?"

Eddie Franklin's voice boomed out of the television, making them both jump.

"*Sebastian Bloom has arrived on the first tee, ready to start his third round, just two shots off the lead. I wonder what's going on in his head right now? We'll soon find out if he's in the game, or if his focus is elsewhere, and who could blame him after that astonishing interview with Pier Morgan last night. For those of you who didn't see it, you can watch it on catch-up TV, quite remarkable, I wouldn't want to be Troy McLoud today.*"

"Shut up, you fucking arse-wipe." Georgiana hurled a cushion at the television. She was excited and nervous at the same time, desperate for Sebastian to do well and get himself into the final pairing on Sunday.

"Your language is appalling." Hattie shook her head and walked towards the door. "I'll be back in a minute, don't want to miss anything."

"Ok, hurry up though, he's about to tee off," Georgiana called after her.

Hattie walked towards the kitchen and paused by the telephone on the hallway table, wondering if it was safe to put it back on the hook. It had rung constantly for an hour after Sebastian's interview was broadcast and they had got fed up with it. There were journalists camped outside the gates, hoping for a comment from Georgiana or for Olivia to arrive, and they showed no sign of leaving any time soon.

Her mobile sprang into action. She fished it out of her apron pocket and saw it was Tom.

"Christ, Hattie, it's bedlam in the village. The press is everywhere, asking questions about Sebastian and the whole Ellie, Troy, Olivia thing."

"Sorry Tom, we should've warned you. Did you see it?" she referred to the interview.

"Did we see it? Bloody right we did, and wasn't he marvellous?" Tom was proud of his friend. "Did Olivia turn up?"

"Not as far as we know. Sebastian sent Georgiana a text this morning. Has Susie heard from her?"

"Nothing at all, she's quite upset if I'm honest, they'd grown so close."

"I'm sure she has her reasons, don't take it personally. How's Rosie?" asked Hattie.

"Marvellous, she's amazing, just like her mother" he replied.

"Why don't you come up here and watch it with us? Although you'll have to excuse Georgiana, she's refusing to move off the sofa and stinks to high heaven of horse manure."

Tom laughed. "Nothing changes. Let me check with Susie but I'm sure it'll be fine. Can we bring anything?"

"Just that gorgeous little girl of yours, I want to make a fuss of her. Oh, and a battering ram to get past the television crews camped outside."

Tom laughed. "Ok, we'll be there in thirty minutes, hopefully we'll only miss one or two holes. And don't worry, everyone in the village is keeping quiet, we're all like one giant clam."

Tom rang off, and Hattie busied herself getting salads and cold cuts of meat ready for lunch.

"Nooooooo," she heard Georgiana yell from the lounge and went running back in.

"What? What's happened?" she cried.

"He's made a bloody bogey on the first. I hope he's not falling apart. Maybe we should have gone up there to support him?"

"It's only one hole, seventeen more to go, don't worry darling." Hattie patted Georgiana's head, went back to the kitchen and prayed for Sebastian.

Chapter 57

By the time Sebastian had reached the third hole, the wind had started to get up and was whipping across the course with a ferocity that started to affect play. He had made a bogey on the first and had only just managed to par the second, and now he was struggling with the weather.

At the start of his third round, he was lying in seventh place on the leaderboard at two under par, four shots off the lead that was held by the Korean, Sung Nah Po. Troy was at three under par, and was, despite everything, playing incredibly well.

Sebastian somehow managed to par the next six holes, but he was barely holding it together. Aiden was growing increasingly worried, aware his boss was losing focus.

"Hey boss, you ok?" he asked. He didn't often intervene, but this was different: they were in contention for a Major title.

"Why wouldn't I be?" Sebastian bit his head off.

"Let's take it down a notch or two, you're trying too hard against the wind." Aiden's advice was solid and he hoped Sebastian would take heed.

"I'll play golf, you carry the bag," he snapped.

For the next four holes he played like an amateur, spraying his iron shots and misjudging putts. Nothing was going right, and the rot was starting to set in.

He stood on the thirteenth tee, and pulled his cap down over his face to hide his anguish from the watching media and spectators.

Aiden stood immediately in front of him, to shield him from the intrusive cameras, and let his boss have a few moments of privacy.

"Come on boss, you've got this," he tried to get him up. "Troy's making a move, you've got to get it together or he'll win." He braced himself for Sebastian's reply.

"Don't you ever fucking mention that man's name again," he snarled. "And I'm doing my fucking best."

"Do better," Aiden muttered.

He somehow made par on the next four holes, mostly thanks to his short game that hadn't completely deserted him. He had another wobble on the seventeenth, driving his ball into the infamous Road Hole bunker where many a player had come unstuck over the years. By some miracle, he played his way beautifully out of the sand trap, and made bogey again, although it could have been much worse.

The eighteenth green of the Old Course was just about reachable in one shot. Sebastian hit his drive straight for the Martyrs' Monument, toward the Valley of Sin, which was the final hazard on the course. His tee shot found the ridge at the top of the green, where the ball faltered, before rolling back into the Valley of Sin.

He received rapturous applause on his walk up the eighteenth fairway, which grew even louder as he reached the green. The crowd was willing him on, wanting him to do well, and collectively groaned when he three-putted, chalking up his final bogey of the day.

Shaking Avery's hand at the end of the round, he apologised: "I'm sorry, I know it was tough out there, you played really well."

"Never played in front of that kind of crowd before, I kinda liked it man," Avery laughed. He'd played a decent round of golf, despite all the distractions.

Sebastian walked off the green shaking his head. It was his own fault he had dropped away from the rest of the field. There were still two pairings out on the course, and the only golfer who was making any headway was Troy McLoud.

"Fuck me boss," Aiden grinned. "Look at the leaderboard. We're second. Jaysus, how did that happen?"

Sebastian did not care, he was desperate to get away from the fans and, with the media waiting to pounce on him, he refused to do a post-round press conference, much to the displeasure of R&A Captain, Hamish McDougal.

Aiden got him into the car and back to the hotel in record time, avoiding the waiting media by depositing him at the kitchen doors.

"Looks like we're paired with Troy tomorrow, boss." He winced as he said it. "Final round, final pairing, you and him. Let's take him down."

"That isn't going to happen if I'm playing this badly." Sebastian was distraught. "What the fuck happened out there? I was feeling great." He couldn't understand what had gone wrong. "Maybe the pressure's getting to me".

"Forget about it. Move on. Tomorrow's a new day, and we've the chance to win and beat that bastard, once and for all." Aiden was fired up.

"I'm six shots back, I'll need a miracle to overturn that." Sebastian was feeling utterly wretched.

"Ah, six shots is nothing," Aiden replied. "We've done it before, and we'll do it tomorrow. Sure, it'll be grand."

"Your confidence in my abilities is misguided Aiden." He could not see a way back.

"Nah, I'm bang on and you know it. I'm going to meet some of the lads at the Jigger for a beer - you're welcome to join us."

"Thanks, but I'm not leaving my room until I've sorted myself out. Plus, I don't think anyone wants me around with all this shit going on." Sebastian shook his head. "You go, just don't overdo it, I'm going to need you tomorrow more than ever."

He sat on the bed with his head in his hands, knowing a six shot lead in the Open Championship was pretty much unassailable unless Troy had a meltdown and he played like a god. And quite frankly, he just couldn't see that happening.

He needed to get some sleep. He needed Olivia. He got neither that night.

Chapter 58

Olivia had spent another sleepless night in London. The press had been camped outside her door since Friday night and she hadn't dared go out and face them. She cowered behind closed curtains and hadn't even ventured into the garden for fear of being 'papped' with long lens cameras.

Emily arrived early on Saturday morning with supplies of food, gin, and a welcome shoulder to cry on. She barged through the paparazzi and let herself in.

"Right you, go and shower, you look dreadful," she said as she wrapped her arms around Olivia. "I'll take Hector for a quick spin while you sort yourself out."

Forty minutes later she returned and Olivia could hear her batting off questions from outside the front door.

"Why's she not coming out?" asked one of the photographers.

"None of your business," Emily snapped.

"Is she going to Scotland?" asked another.

"What's it to you," she replied angrily.

"What's the dog called?"

"Fuck off," she snapped again.

"Strange name for a dog," the same journalist replied, much to the amusement of the rest of the pack.

She ushered Hector into the house and slammed the door.

"Jesus Christ," She was a little overwhelmed.

"Why do you think I've not been out. Now I know what it's like being on the other side," Olivia sighed, and walked into the kitchen to start breakfast.

"Well, your taste in men is questionable at best," Emily said, as she poured some coffee. "Although he did pour his heart out, and I reckon he meant it too. What are you going to do?"

Olivia slipped into a chair and pondered Emily's question.

"I don't know." She shrugged her shoulders. "What I do know is that I'm not going up there. It's not the place to have it out with him, and I'm still so angry."

"Let it go Liv, it's just a book, it's not life and death. And seriously, if I had a man as great as him declaring his undying love for me on national television, I think I'd be swayed. How do you feel about him, besides wanting to commit murder?"

"He scared me, I mean really scared me. I though he was going to hit me so I ran. I'm getting quite good at this running lark." She felt wretched. "If I'm honest I probably over-reacted, he was drunk and seriously pissed off. He really believed I'd gone off with Troy that night - what does that say about his lack of trust in me?"

Emily replied: "He's clearly not rational at all when it comes to that man, but if you want my honest opinion, I think you're crazy to let him go. Apart from being seriously gorgeous and a real catch, with an amazing house, it's obvious he loves you and you're in love with him."

Olivia shook her head, she was in denial.

"For fuck's sake Liv." Emily was getting frustrated. "How long have we been friends? I know you better than you know yourself. You love him, just admit it. You can't hide away forever, what Saul did was unforgivable but Sebastian isn't like him, you said it yourself enough times. You've changed since you left London, for the better in my opinion, and some of that has to be down to him."

Olivia pushed her uneaten breakfast away and looked at Emily, tears welling up in her eyes. "Please Em, just let it go."

Emily knew she had pushed her friend too far. "Ok, fine. But if you change your mind and want to go, just call me, I'll get you out of here incognito. There's no way I'll let the bastard paparazzi corner you."

Olivia laughed for the first time in days: "And just how to you propose we do that?"

"Subterfuge. Don't worry, I'll find a way to get them off your back, I promise."

"You don't know them, they'll stop at nothing to get the story, but thank you, it's good to know I've got you in my corner." She leaned over and hugged her friend.

Emily returned the hug. "We've been fighting each other's corner for almost thirty years, there's no way I'm going to stop now. Whatever you decide, I'll back you one hundred per cent. Always have, always will."

Olivia changed her mind over and over again after Emily left, weighing up the pros and cons and coming up with the same result every time, she had to stay away from Sebastian. She slumped on the sofa, with Hector lying across her feet, and tried to bury herself in a book, but she couldn't concentrate. Eventually, she grabbed the iPad, launched The Open app, and waited for the scores to appear - she needed to know how he was getting on.

She gasped when she saw that he was lying in second place, but a massive six shots behind the leader, and gasped again when she realised the leader was Troy.

"It would have to be him, wouldn't it?" she said to Hector who raised an eyebrow and snorted.

Sebastian drew back the curtains, slid the balcony doors open and stepped out into the morning air. His room overlooked the eighteenth fairway and below him was a hive of activity, with the green-keeping staff hard at work getting the course in pristine condition for the day's play.

Dark clouds lined the horizon and the air was thick and damp. The rain that had been threatening all week was rearing its ugly head and it was set to be a blustery day.

He dialled down for room service to bring him breakfast and sat down at the table to scan the morning newspapers, his curiosity getting the better of him. He needed to find out what the great British media had written about Troy.

Much to his satisfaction, he'd been crucified, vilified, belittled and pulled to pieces, not only by the British press, but also by the American press which had turned on its own golden boy.

"No less than you deserve you bastard," he muttered, as he skimmed through the many articles.

Up at the five star St Andrews Bay hotel, on the outskirts of town, Troy was reeling as he watched the morning news. He had made it through the previous day by playing great golf, keeping his head down and avoiding the paparazzi.

Even though every single newspaper and television channel had come down firmly on Sebastian's side, his ego was such that he still believed he could play his way out of it.

"Fuck you, Bloom," he screamed at the television. "No-one will give a shit about you when I win today. I'm gonna cream you out there."

Chapter 59

There was a tangible air of excitement coursing through St Andrews, with golf fans arriving early to get the best vantage point, jostling for seats in the huge grandstands that surrounded each green and fighting for space behind the ropes on the fairways and at the tee boxes.

The crowd was standing ten-deep by nine o'clock, desperate to get close to the action, admiring and acknowledging good shots from the early starters, before moving onto the next hole.

The tented village, where the public congregated to eat, drink and be merry, was a hive of activity, with throngs of people queuing for artisan coffee, pulled pork rolls, fish and chips and pints of lager. Plastic tables and chairs were dotted all over, and there wasn't a spare seat in sight. Even the red and white candy-striped Bollinger tent was heaving with the more sophisticated spectators, enjoying a Buck's Fizz or two before heading out onto the course.

Giant television screens were dotted in prime viewing locations throughout the village for those who preferred to watch the live action without fighting for space out on the course, and groups of spectators were soaking up the atmosphere without missing a shot.

Eddie Franklin's dulcet tones boomed out from every television and loudspeaker in the grounds.

"We're all set for a superb finale to what has been a tremendous tournament, and I for one can't wait for the leaders to get out on the course. And what a final pairing we have. With all the incredible off-course action between our very own Sebastian Bloom, and current world number one Troy McLoud, it's set to be an explosive afternoon of golf. DO NOT GO ANYWHERE, we'll bring you all the action which will, with any luck, include some heated exchanges between the two sworn enemies.

"Can we really believe that Sebastian can come out today and play the kind of golf he used to? Even at his best, is it possible that he can make up the six shots he needs just to draw level with McLoud, let alone go on and win?

"Well, ladies and gentlemen, you'll just have to stay glued to your television sets to find out. To be honest, your guess is as good as mine. Now we're going to take a short break to bring you the weather, and then we'll return with a very special guest joining us in the studio. Ellen-Sue, may I say how lovely you look today, what does the weather have in store for us here at St Andrews?"

"Fucking imbecile," Sebastian yelled at the television as he changed into his golf clothes. He listened intently to Ellen-Sue giving her run-down of the weather, cringing when she, somewhat gleefully, announced that a storm was on the horizon. She ended her segment and handed back to Eddie Franklin in the studio.

"So viewers, there we have it. There's a storm coming, and it's not just in the skies. Now, while Sebastian Bloom and Troy McLoud prepare to face each other on the course for the very first time in years, and indeed for the first time since Sebastian's incredible revelations, let's take you back to some of their past encounters."

Sebastian switched off the television, gathered his belongings, and made his way down to the lobby where Aiden and Richie were waiting to escort him to the course.

"All set?" Richie asked, fizzing with excitement that Sebastian was back in the running for another Major title.

Sebastian nodded but didn't reply - he was too hyped for small talk.

Aiden, who knew his boss better than most, said nothing and headed towards the exit, and into the waiting car. They pulled up in front of the clubhouse, and there was an explosion of flashbulbs from the hordes of photographers awaiting his arrival. Sebastian climbed out of the car with a forced smiled on his face and waved at the spectators who had gathered for a glimpse of the man who was dominating the front and back pages of the newspapers.

"Well Ade, this is it." He looked at Aiden and smiled. They'd been through so much together, over the last ten years.

"Yes, boss, it is," he grinned. "I've got a good feeling in my bones, and you know they're never wrong."

Sebastian raised an eyebrow, "That remains to be seen. Let's go and hit some balls, and get this show on the road."

Their way to the practice range was packed with well-wishers, all of whom were staunchly supporting Sebastian, and he suddenly felt a huge responsibility to deliver the title for them, as well as for himself and Aiden.

"Christ, I've never felt this kind of pressure," he said. "And yes, I know it's all my own doing, before you say anything."

"Wasn't going to say a word, boss." Aiden wasn't going to disagree with him when he was in this kind of mood.

The spectators in the grandstand at the range, sensing his arrival, started chanting his name before he had even got out of the buggy.

Hugh was waiting to bolster his protégé. "Well Sebastian, are you ready? Listen to that, they're all behind you, that's got to be worth a shot or two."

He felt tight, he needed to relax or he would be misjudging yardages and angles right from the start. "I'm ready."

"Your swing is solid and fluid, your putter's hot and, bar a few bad holes yesterday, you've played great all week. This is your time Sebastian, seize it with both hands and don't let that bastard live in your head." Hugh was fired up.

The mood in the crowd changed in an instant as Troy arrived to warm up. He was being booed and jeered by the incredibly partisan crowd and he looked like it was starting to get to him.

They didn't acknowledge each other, and started practicing at either end of the range, as far from one another as was possible. In contrast to the beginning of the week, the practice range was almost deserted of players, and it only served to emphasise the gulf between the two men.

Over in the tented village, Eddie Franklin's voice was roaring out of the speakers once more.

"*Just thirty minutes to go before the final pairing gets underway, and I for one can't wait. This has classic written all over it.*"

Sebastian went through his usual warm-up routine, with Hugh and Aiden by his side, and then spent a few minutes signing autographs, thanking the spectators for their support.

"Go get him, Sebastian," a woman shouted from high up in the stands.

"Take the bastard down," came another voice.

"Troy's a wanker," another yelled, and the crowd rippled with laughter.

Eddie Franklin's commentary continued to reverberate around the tented village and Sebastian caught some of it as he made his way back to the clubhouse.

"*These two have some serious beef, would it be wrong to say I'm wishing for some fireworks? We're minutes away from the most anticipated final round in recent Open Championship history, so get your bums on seats and get ready for what I'm sure will be an explosive round of golf."*

"Jesus, somebody shoot that man," Sebastian said, irritated.

"Relax, boss." Aiden was determined to get him focused on the task ahead. "You've got this, you've always had it. One hole at a time, that's how we'll take it."

He arrived on the tee to deafening applause that carried on for a full minute until Troy appeared, when it fell deathly silent. He was public enemy number one. Sebastian extended his hand to Troy, as was the custom at the start and end of a match, but he was left hanging.

"Ladies and gentlemen, this is the final game of the one hundred and forty first Open Championship. On the tee from England, Sebastian Bloom." The unmistakable voice of Ivor Robson, the official starter of the Championship for the past thirty-eight years, rang through the speakers surrounding the tee box.

Sebastian acknowledged the crowd, pulled out an iron and took a few practice swings, steadying his nerves. He looked straight down the widest fairway in golf, trying to visualise the shot he wanted to make. Addressing the ball, he took a deep breath, and hit it pure and straight, about as perfect as it could be. The crowd erupted and he was on his way.

When Ivor Robson's singsong voice announced Troy on the tee, there were boos and jeers aplenty.

Sebastian felt a certain amount of satisfaction that the spectators were firmly on side. It gave him some encouragement, which he badly needed.

Troy bombed a three wood dead straight, and stalked off after it before it even landed.

Sebastian's second shot was a full wedge that stopped just short of the pin on the manicured first green. It should have been a tap in for a birdie — three shots on this par four hole - but he putted left and missed the hole, walking off with a par four. He was frustrated and angry that he had missed a certain birdie.

Luckily, Troy fared no better with a two putt for par four that he made by the skin of his teeth. Sebastian knew he was rattled. Troy was one of the best putters in the game, and he rarely had a bad day on the greens.

They played the next four holes as though they were involved in a very public game of cat and mouse, each trying to predict the other's shot and club choice, each wanting to outdo the other. The gamesmanship seemed to work for Troy as he made birdie on the second and laughed as Sebastian missed another chance to make up a shot on the third hole. Troy's lead was now seven shots.

Aiden intervened on the walk to the sixth tee. "What are you doing boss? Play your own game, forget him, you can't win like this."

Sebastian was about to bite his head off, before realising he was right. "Thanks Ade, that's why you're here."

Troy made a bogey - one shot more than par - on the next hole after struggling to get out of the rough, and they were back to where they started, with six shots between them.

Sebastian desperately needed something to kick-start his round, but he had no idea where the inspiration was going to come from.

"You're playing solid golf, boss," Aiden reassured him. "Keep on doing what you're doing and they'll drop."

"Easy for you to say," Sebastian grumbled. "He's playing too well. We need a miracle."

As if by magic, he felt a drop of rain, and the wind started to whip up around them. There was a dull rumble of thunder in the distance, and thirty seconds later the claxon sounded, indicating that the final round of The Open Championship was suspended, due to the impending electrical storm.

"Jaysus, I think he heard you." Aiden looked up to the skies and thanked God for their good fortune.

Chapter 60

"It's me, I need you." Olivia rang Emily.

"Are you going up there?"

"Yes, but I need to get out of here undetected."
She peered through a crack in the curtains from the
bedroom at the front of the house and looked down
on the ever-present paparazzi.

"I'm so glad. Good decision. Give me half an hour
and I'll have a way out for you." Emily sounded
delighted that she had decided to go up to Scotland.

"I've got to have it out with him, I can't just sit
here like a prisoner in my own home. Will you have
Hector?"

"Of course, as long as you need. What made you
change your mind?"

Olivia sighed: "You were right, I do love him, and I
got an email from Stella saying *Fuck the book, go get
your man,* so at least she's on side."

"Ha! She's bang on, I'll call you in a bit." Emily rang
off and Olivia started throwing some clothes in a bag.

"Don't look at me like that," she said as Hector raised an eyebrow, putting on his best hangdog expression. "I'll be back tomorrow."

Half an hour later, true to her word, Emily turned up on the doorstep, having secured a corporate jet that was fuelled and ready to go from London City airport.

"I just talked to your neighbours and we're going to be doing some fence-hopping. Ready to go?" Emily was fired up.

"Christ, I thought you'd come up with a better plan than climbing into people's gardens at this time of the morning," she grumbled.

"Best I could do. Come on, there's a bike waiting to get you to the airport in double quick time." Emily started ushering her towards the door.

They headed outside where Bill and Kate Fasset, her immediate neighbours, were waiting with a stepladder into their garden.

Olivia started giggling as she climbed over the fence, so much so she almost fell into their rose bed.

"Get a bloody grip." Emily was trying not to laugh. "This is no time to be having hysterics."

Bill helped her down and Emily chucked her overnight bag into Kate's hands.

"Go," Emily whispered. "And you'd better bloody text me when you've seen him. Don't be too hard on him, Liv, I know what you're like when you get the bit between your teeth."

"Thanks Em, you're bloody brilliant. Love you." She ran across the lawn and Bill helped her over the fence into the next garden.

"Won't be sorry to see the back of those pesky journalists," Bill said as he handed her bag over.

"I'm so sorry, I really didn't mean for all this to happen. Emily will make sure they know I'm not here, and hopefully they'll disappear quickly."

"It's actually quite exciting," he grinned. "We've been following it on the news and we wish you well."

Olivia shot them a grateful smile and hot-footed it across the next garden, aided by the teenage grand-son of Mr Bailey from number twelve. She continued to fence-hop, and finally made it to the end of the street, gasping for breath. Waiting for her, as Emily had promised, was the motorbike, ready to whisk her away.

Twenty minutes later they arrived at City airport, having breezed through the light Sunday morning traffic. The driver deposited her at the plane, and they were airborne in no time.

"May I get you a drink, Ms Carmichael," the flight attendant asked her once they had reached altitude.

"Could I have a tomato juice please?"

"Coming right up. Can I just say how wonderful it is that you're going. We all saw Mr Bloom's interview on Friday and were hoping you'd turn up. It's like a fairy tale."

Olivia was embarrassed, "It's been touch and go, but I can hardly bail out now, unless you've got a parachute somewhere in here."

The flight attendant laughed and placed her drink on the table in front of her.

"We'll be there in a flash. We're landing at Leuchars in about forty-five minutes, and there's a car waiting to take you the rest of the way."

"Thank you," Olivia smiled at the attendant.

"No, thank you, this is the most exciting thing to happen to me in a long time," she replied. "Let me know if you'd like anything else."

Olivia leaned back in the leather seat and stared out of the window, thinking about how she was going to handle Sebastian when she finally saw him.

"You'd better know what you're doing," she muttered, and then closed her eyes and tried to relax.

Chapter 61

The rain was falling so hard by the time Sebastian and Aiden reached the clubhouse that the officials announced play would be suspended until two o'clock.

"I'm going back to the hotel, stay here and keep an eye on things," he told Aiden. "Call me if anything changes."

He was only five minutes from the course and knew he was safe to go. Aiden wouldn't let him be late once they had confirmed when play would resume.

He sat down on the bed and closed his eyes, breathing deeply, in an attempt to transport his mind to a place where he was at peace. This kind of meditation had helped him in the past when he suffered panic attacks, in the immediate aftermath of the accident.

A knock on the door snapped him out of his trance.

"Since when does do not disturb mean you can disturb me, just fuck off," he yelled.

The knocking became more insistent and he wearily got off the bed and walked over to the door, ready to jump down the throat of the chambermaid he assumed was on the other side. He gasped when he looked through the spy-hole and saw Olivia standing there.

He flung open the door.

"You came." He was overcome with emotion.

"I did." She was trembling.

"Why now?" He took her hand and led her into the room.

"I was so angry with you. All my hard work went down the drain and I wanted to murder you. I had to give myself time to calm down. Emily talked me round."

Sebastian grinned: "Thank the Lord for Emily Delevigne, I really must meet her soon."

Olivia let go of his hand and walked across to the balcony. The rain was pouring down the window and thunder continued to rumble in the distance.

"I'm still mad at you." She stared at the floor. "You lied to me, and you scared the shit out of me, too."

His face turned crimson, still mortified by his actions, "I'm so fucking sorry. I couldn't tell you the truth about Lizzie not being mine, I was so messed up about it, so I buried it. No one knew, aside from Georgie, Hattie, José and Rich, and I thought it was best left that way. It was just too damn painful."

"You could've told me. I thought we were being honest with each other." She couldn't bring herself to look at him.

He reached out and touched her face, tilting her chin up so their eyes met.

"I know it was wrong but hell, I told the world, didn't I?" he smiled and reached for her hands. "I'll never forgive myself for hurting you, especially after everything you went through with that bastard. Please give me the opportunity to make it up to you. I know I can make you happy."

When she didn't respond, he pulled her towards him and held her close to his chest.

"I've been such a fool Liv. You're the love of my life and I need you never to leave me again. You've brought me back to life and I don't want to be without you." Sebastian's emotions exploded with as much force as the storm that was raging down on St Andrews.

"Do you feel anything for me, or have I just imagined it?" He was suddenly terrified of what her answer would be. "Tell me Liv, I need to know how you feel."

Tears welled up in her eyes, and she whispered: "I love you."

"Thank Christ for that." He bent to kiss her and she melted into his arms.

Her response to his lips on hers was so intensely passionate that he lost all self-control. "I've been waiting to do this since Christmas," he purred in her ear.

Olivia gasped as he ran his hands over her body and kissed her neck, and she was overcome with longing as his passion grew deeper. Sebastian started peeling her clothes off, and once she was naked he stepped back and stared at her.

"You're so damn beautiful," he whispered in awe.

He pulled her towards the bed, lowered her onto the crisp white sheets and kissed her again. She fumbled to undo his belt such was her haste to feel his skin on hers. He quickly intervened and stripped naked in seconds.

"I need to make love to you right now." His voice was hoarse with longing. "I wanted to wait and explore every inch of you but I can't, I'm sorry."

"I want you too," she groaned, and arched her back pressing against him, craving his touch.

He parted her legs and thrust himself inside her with such passion that she cried out in rapturous pleasure. They moved together as one, frantic in their mutual desire.

Sebastian felt her shudder and let out a long, quiet moan, and he knew she had reached the dizzy heights of orgasm. She clung to him and moments later he groaned, "Oh Liv, I can't hold back."

"Then don't," she whispered.

Afterwards they lay together, legs entwined, and Sebastian kissed her gently. "Now that was worth the wait," he grinned. "You're an incredible woman."

"You're not so bad yourself, when you're not being all moody," she joked.

"I'm so happy right now, I don't want to go anywhere," he sighed. "I think I'm going to need to keep you in my bed for a very long time, until I've satisfied both our needs."

"As much as I'd love that, don't you have a golf tournament to win?" she laughed.

"Christ, I'd almost forgotten, but first I'm going to have my wicked way with you again."

He rolled over on top of her, and had just started nuzzling her neck when his phone rang.

"Ignore it," he said gruffly, his face buried deep in her cleavage.

"Answer the bloody phone," she laughed and swatted him off.

Groaning, he stretched over and picked it up.

"Aiden, your timing as always is impeccable. What's the latest?" He was running his hands up and down Olivia's thigh.

"Ok, yep got it, see you at the clubhouse then."

Olivia assumed Aiden was calling to get him back to the course for the restart. She reached over and pulled Sebastian towards her and kissed him lightly on the lips.

"You'd better get in that shower then, we can't have you going back out there looking like you've been up to no good."

"Who said anything about getting back out there? We've at least an hour before the restart, they've pushed back to three o'clock, and I can do an awful lot to you in that time. But now you come to mention it, a shower would be good, as long as you're in it with me."

Chapter 62

An hour later Sebastian returned to the course a changed man. The wind had dropped and the sun was pushing through the dark clouds, signalling the storm had passed.

Restarting on the seventh hole, Sebastian knew he had serious work to do. The green was reachable in two shots, so he hit his fairway wood dead straight off the tee and played his wedge to within two feet of the hole, tapping in for birdie.

"One down, five to go, boss," Aiden grinned.

Over in the commentary box, Eddie Franklin was screaming into the microphone. *"I'm sensing a shift in power ladies and gentlemen. Sebastian Bloom had come back from the enforced break like a man possessed. I think he's going after the win. Glory or bust, do or die, go on Sebastian, go for it."*

"Everything ok, boss?" Aiden had also sensed a changed in his mood.

"Couldn't be better," he replied, and flashed a mega-watt grin. "Olivia's here."

"Well that's just grand." Aiden was relieved. "We're going after the win, right?"

"Damn straight, just make sure I don't do anything stupid."

Aiden had never seen Sebastian so animated or buoyed up on the golf course, not even when he'd won his other three Majors.

"Ok boss, let's do this." He picked up the bag and walked ahead with a definite spring in his step.

Troy, aware that Sebastian had come back rejuvenated, started to fall apart. Spectators were pointing at him and laughing, cheering as he made enforced errors, and vocalising their support for his opponent forcefully. He made double bogey on the next hole, where Sebastian tapped in for a par, and now there were just four shots between them.

For the following few holes, Sebastian played like a God, using every shot in his arsenal to great effect. He finished the thirteenth hole with another birdie, while Troy struggle to get out of Hell Bunker.

"*Class, pure class,*" Eddie Franklin bellowed across the airwaves to the millions of fans watching across the globe.

"*This is exciting stuff. We haven't seen a collapse like this since Norman rolled over and had his tummy tickled by Faldo at The Masters back in '96. Troy's falling apart, and our very own Sebastian Bloom is picking him off hole by hole. He's playing some remarkable golf, so talented. It really is compelling viewing.*"

Troy made a shocking mess of the next two holes, and suddenly Sebastian was out on his own, two shots clear of the rest of the field.

Stepping onto the sixteenth tee box, Sebastian had a sudden attack of nerves. Adrenalin was driving through his veins and he was feeling the pressure, he wanted to win more than anything. This was the one tournament he knew would give him legendary status, for the rest of his career and beyond. He closed his eyes and breathed deeply, knowing that being this pumped would transfer into his play.

When he opened them, he was firmly in the zone. It was just him against the course he knew so well, and he could visualise every shot he needed to take him to victory.

"Let's have a word with our on-course reporter," Eddie screamed from the commentary box. *"Jim Morgan, what's the atmosphere like out there?"*

"Well Eddie," Jim whispered into his microphone as he stood inside the ropes, close to Sebastian and Troy. *"It's incredibly exciting out here. There's a ripple of anticipation running through the crowd, and the expectation is that, barring any madness, it's in Sebastian's hands to win or lose. Never in my career have I seen such determination from an individual who, let's face it, was down and out at the start of the day. He's the most talented golfer of his generation, and where better to come back to form than here? Never in my wildest dreams did I imagine this happening."*

"Thrilling, isn't it?" Eddie replied. *"What's going through Troy's mind right now?"*

"*I hardly think it's the time to ask him,*" Jim shot back.

"*Yes well, good point,*" Eddie was miffed. "*Back to the action, ladies and gentlemen. I think we're witnessing one of the greatest comebacks in sporting history. Let's see how it plays out.*"

The noise levels had increased ten-fold as they neared the end of the course. The cheers from the spectators were ear-splitting, and every shot Sebastian made was met with rapturous applause, whooping and hollering.

After each tee shot there were calls of "Get in the hole," something Sebastian normally despised, but today it just served to encourage him further. He looked over at Troy, who was white-faced and visibly shaking. His was the kind of round that could ruin confidence and, with any luck, kill a career.

"We've got him on the ropes, boss," Aiden grinned.

The next two holes went by in a flash. Sebastian turned to Aiden for advice on seventeen, after the bogey he had made there the previous day. Calmly, Aiden gave him the yardage, pointed out his line, and stepped back behind the bag.

"You have this shot, boss, just hit it, don't think about it."

Between shots the noise was deafening, with huge crowds packing out the grandstands around the green and hanging out of every window and balcony of the buildings that lined the walk from the seventeenth fairway, right up to the eighteenth green.

His tee shot was perfect, soaring over the railway sheds and landing in the middle of the fairway. His second shot came up just short of the green, leaving him with a sixty-foot putt for birdie. His ball grazed the hole, missing just a fraction left, and he tapped in for par.

He remained two shots clear of the field with only the eighteenth left to play. He felt himself getting tight.

"Don't fuck it up now," he muttered. "Focus, don't fuck it up, don't fuck it up, don't fuck it up."

He hit iron off the tee, laying up before the Valley of Sin and hit a glorious wedge stone dead at the pin. It was one of the easiest putts of his career but one that meant the most. He walked over to the hole and marked his ball, his hands shaking, feeling the weight of expectation from the thousands of spectators watching his every move.

It was the honour of the leader to make the final putt of the competition, and Sebastian stood back and watched as Troy missed his by some way, making another bogey. The crowd went wild, stomping its feet on the wooden floors of the grandstands, cheering and chanting Sebastian's name.

Aiden cleaned the ball and handed it back to him to place on his marker, just inches from the hole. He had a tap in for birdie, and The Open Championship title.

"*Well I've never seen such a majestic display of golf in my life,*" Eddie was screaming at the top of his lungs in the commentary box. "*This is it ladies and*

*gentlemen, a tap in for The Open Championship title
and eternal glory."*

Back in Appleton Vale, the entire village had
crammed into the pub to watch the final round and
they were all going crazy. Drinks had been free-
flowing since the morning and the atmosphere was
super-charged. Susie and Old Mrs Banks were crying openly, Andrea was doing a jig on the bar with
Evie and Teddy, and Tom and Peter were popping
open champagne bottles in celebration. Georgiana
and Hattie were nowhere to be seen.

"This is it, quiet everyone," Tom yelled across the
pub. Silence fell immediately, and they all focused on
the television.

Sebastian lined up his putt and tapped the ball into
the hole. He fell to his knees, tears pouring down his
face, and was swept into an embrace by Aiden, who
had run across the green and hauled him to his feet.

"We've done it!" he cried, bouncing around Sebastian. "You were fucking amazing, boss. If we never
win anything again it doesn't matter one jot, it
doesn't come any better than this."

They hugged each other and turned to soak up the
adulation of the crowd as they chanted Sebastian's
name, clearly delighted to finally have a British winner after so many years of American dominance. He
was dizzy with relief and fizzing with excitement, but
only had one thing on his mind - Olivia.

"*He's looking for someone,*" Eddie shrieked from the
floor of his commentary box, where he had collapsed

in excitement. *"Someone special. perhaps? This is too much, I can't cope."*

Sebastian picked his ball out of the hole and launched it into the crowd, almost causing a stampede from spectators desperate to take home a souvenir from the best final round of golf they had ever witnessed. Turning to face Troy, he held out his hand, expecting him to shake it, but was refused. Troy, stony-faced, walked off the green, breaking with etiquette and infuriating the crowd even further.

"Did he really just do that?" Sebastian asked Aiden.

"He's finished, boss," Aiden grinned. "No one's going to touch him with a barge pole now. Couldn't happen to a nastier man."

It wasn't official until he'd signed his scorecard and Sebastian was keen to get it done. He waved at the crowd once more, and walked off the green towards the scorers' hut where his card would be verified. As he reached the edge of the green, Georgiana and Hattie, who had secretly flown up the previous night to support him, pounced. Richie was also waiting for him, sobbing openly.

"Oh my God," Georgiana screamed. "That was amazing, you were awesome. I'm so proud of you." She threw herself into his arms with such ferocity she almost knocked him off his feet.

"Oh Sebastian, oh, oh, I don't know what to say. You were wonderful." Hattie reached up and touched his face fondly, tears pouring down her cheeks. "Your mother would be so proud."

Sebastian grinned: "Yeah, that wasn't too bad, was it?" He looked over Georgiana's shoulder, his eyes scanning for Olivia amongst the pandemonium.

"She's over there." Richie pointed at Olivia, who was standing watching him. He quickly ran to her side, swept her into his arms and started spinning her around. They were oblivious to the television cameras and mass of photographers clamouring around them, desperate to capture their intimate embrace.

"Sebastian, stop, you'll make me sick," she laughed. He put her down but held her tightly in his arms, savouring the moment.

"I knew you could do it, I never had any doubts. You were incredible out there," she grinned, and reached up to kiss him again.

"It was because of you that I came through," he replied. "You gave me the strength to fight for it. I love you."

"I love you too you great oaf, now go and sign your card and let's get this party started."

Chapter 63

"Congratulations, Sebastian. Your fourth Major, that puts you up there with the likes of Raymond Floyd, Bobby Locke and Ernie Els," The excitable Eddie Franklin was in front of him: his microphone in Sebastian's face. "How does it feel to have won The Open Championship after all these years of trying, but failing?"

"Nice of you to say that, thanks Eddie," Sebastian laughed - nothing could ruin his mood now. "It feels great. I made no secret of the fact that this is the one I really wanted. To win The Open, at the home of golf, is very special indeed."

Eddie hopped from one foot to the other: "What was going through your head before the storm delay? Things weren't going quite so well those first few holes, were they?"

"Let's just say I got off to a slow start and the delay helped me refocus." Sebastian beamed into the camera. "I could bore you with a hole-by-hole analysis, but I think I'll leave that to the pundits. I played really well all day. Even when things weren't going quite so well at the start, it wasn't because I was playing badly, I just needed a bit more luck."

"And how have you been coping with everything that's been going on in your life, off the course?"

"Now Eddie, I'm sure the viewers want to hear about golf, not my personal life," Sebastian grinned again.

Eddie ignored him. "Tell me about Olivia Carmichael?"

"Nothing to tell," he grinned.

"Did she come?" Eddie was a little slow off the mark.

Sebastian didn't want Olivia to be swept up in the media frenzy, but neither did he want to hide her away from the world. He was in love and he wanted to shout it from the rooftops.

"Who on earth do you think I was kissing Eddie?" He raised an eyebrow.

"Almost every email, text and call into the studio the past few days has been about THAT interview, so you have to give the viewers something more than that."

Sebastian was laughing his head off and pulled Olivia into camera shot: "We're both very happy."

Richie caught his eye, motioning it was time to wind up the interview and move on to the trophy presentation.

When Sebastian stepped out onto the green, with the iconic Royal and Ancient clubhouse in the background, the crowd had another opportunity to celebrate with their hero. He was joined by the leading amateur, Elliot McBride, who was an incredibly talented seventeen-year-old who had announced himself to the world in some style.

The Korean, Seung Nah Po, had stolen second place from Troy McLoud and couldn't contain his delight when he was called up to receive his runner-up prize, the Silver Salver. If he hadn't known better, Sebastian would have thought that the small, stocky man from the Far East had actually taken the title, such was his joy.

Finally, it was his turn. The microphone crackled and the voice of the R&A captain echoed across the green: "Ladies and gentlemen, I give you the Open Champion of 2016, Sebastian Bloom."

It had been a very long time since an Englishman had won The Open, and Sebastian had done it under incredibly difficult circumstances, which made the victory all the more poignant. He had faced disaster, been down and almost out, and had fought his way back to the top again.

When he was handed the Claret Jug he almost crumbled. It was the moment he had dreamt of his entire life, the moment he had re-enacted on the final hole of the Riverside Golf & Country Club, over and over again as a teenager. He had won The Open Championship.

He took the microphone and began his speech.

"It's been a rollercoaster of a ride to get to this point, but I couldn't be happier. I would like to thank the R&A, the Championship committee, and all the incredibly hard-working greens staff who kept the course in top condition when the weather was against them. Thank you to the sponsors, and each and every volunteer who willingly gave their time to make this tournament such a success.

"On a more personal note, thank you to my caddy Aiden: without him there is no way I would be standing here now. He's been with me for a long time and he deserves this victory. To my coach Hugh, thank you for guiding me back to the light, and my manager Richie, who's unwavering belief in me was clearly not misplaced. To my family who've put up with an awful lot the past few years, and stood shoulder to shoulder with me throughout. And to my darling Olivia, who's timing was impeccable. She was, and will always be, my inspiration.

"Last, but by no means least, a heartfelt thank you to all the golf fans out there who literally carried me around this course today. This is for you. I'm humbled and honoured to be in your company." He held the trophy aloft and an explosion of flashbulbs went off in his face.

Dictating Sebastian's every move, Richie dragged him to his press conference in the media centre. As he walked in, he was both surprised and delighted when the hardened hacks all got to their feet to applaud him. He sat down at the table, adjusted the microphone and looked out at the packed room.

"Let's keep this brief boys and girls. I've somewhere I need to be."

"And where would that be Sebastian? With a particular colleague of ours I presume?" came a voice from the back of the room.

"Correct and right, Paul," he replied to the man from the Daily Express.

"Do you care to elaborate?" he continued.

"No, and while we're at it I've nothing else to say about Troy McLoud, so don't bother asking."

The questions came thick and fast, mostly off topic and on Troy, and Sebastian handled them with grace and aplomb, all with a beaming smile on his face.

Finally, they reached the end of their allotted half hour slot. "Let's make this the last question please," said the Tour press officer, Murray Evans.

Hands shot up in every direction, and Sebastian nodded at John Jones, from The Daily Telegraph.

"Sebastian, are you back?"

Sebastian paused, and then replied with a grin, "I never left."

Chapter 64

They celebrated long into the night after his win, inviting a select few to his hotel suite to share in his success. Sebastian had not let go of Olivia's hand since he had exited the press conference and she stayed firmly by his side, basking in his love and sharing in his glory.

Angelica, Georgiana and Aiden danced around the room, spilling champagne and infecting everyone with their gaiety, while José, Richie and Hugh continually toasted the sweet victory.

In the early hours of Monday morning Sebastian asked everyone to leave. He was desperate to be alone with Olivia and they fell into each other's arms as soon as the door had closed.

Exploring every inch of her glorious body, he made love to her slowly and tenderly, taking her pleasure to a whole new level, and she gave herself to him willingly. As they lay in the dark afterwards, he said,

"You won't leave me, will you? You're coming home with me?"

"If you'll have me, I can't think of anywhere I'd rather be," she grinned. "My life is with you now, but I need to go and get Hector. Emily's not the most dog-friendly person in the world, and he'll be pining for me."

"If I'll have you?" he was incredulous. "It's me who should be asking you that. And I'll send a car for Hector, he can travel back to Appleton Vale in style."

Olivia burst out laughing, "He'll love that, and he loves you too, maybe not as much as I do, but it's a close-run thing."

By midday on Monday, they were on their way back to the village to a hero's welcome. Angelica and José had left earlier that day with the promise they would come to Appleton Vale for the celebrations later that evening. José was emotional when they parted.

"So my friend, you're The Open champion. Eees good, no?"

Sebastian threw his arms around him and smiled fondly: "It's your turn next, I promise you that."

Aiden, Hugh, Richie, Hattie and Georgiana joined them on the jet and the champagne flowed from take-off to landing - they were all slightly inebriated when they touched down at the airport. They travelled in convoy back to the village and arrived to find bunting hanging from every door, window and tree, and the church bells ringing out in joyous celebration.

Tom and Susie had hastily thrown together a party, laying on a sumptuous feast of hog roast, barbecue and huge bowls of salads, dips and breads, along with what seemed like the entire contents of their cellar. The drinks had been flowing since Sebastian's final putt, and everyone was in high spirits, including old Mrs Banks, who was a little unsteady on her already frail legs.

Susie was still crying. "It's the post-baby hormones," Tom told Sebastian, rolling his eyes. "She's been at it since you won, we've taken out shares in Kleenex."

Sebastian was overwhelmed by the support and warmth he was receiving, and realised how incredibly lucky he was to have such good friends surrounding him. One by one, they congratulated him, and said how pleased they were that he and Olivia had finally seen sense.

"Didn't I tell you?" Dee Dee cried when she saw Olivia. "I knew from the moment you walked into my tearoom that you were the one for him."

Jane took her drink out of her hand. "I think you've had enough dear, leave the poor girl alone."

Olivia laughed and hugged Dee Dee. "Yes, you were right," she whispered, and Dee Dee beamed.

"Olivia!" Georgiana called her over to where she was sitting with Susie and Andrea on the bench by the duck pond. She went over to join them and Susie thrust another glass of champagne in her hand.

"If I have any more of this I'll drown," she joked, and took a huge gulp, only to spit it out laughing as old Mrs Banks tumbled into the pond. Sebastian fished her out, and sent her off with Jane to find a towel and a change of clothes.

Georgiana stumbled toward Sebastian and grabbed his arm for support. "I need to talk to you and don't look like that, it's nothing bad."

"You can't burst my bubble." He slung an arm around her shoulder. "I haven't been this happy for a long time, if ever, really. And how pissed are you? You can't even see straight," he laughed.

"I can shee juss fine thank you," she hiccupped. "I'm moving into the lodge house and Hattie's doing a runner too."

"So you're all deserting me?"

"You have Liv, you don't need us getting in your way," she grinned. "I don't want to hear you two going at it like rabbits all night long. Don't try to talk me out of it, I'm old enough to live on my own."

"Do you hear me protesting?" Sebastian grinned, and ruffled her hair. "You've turned out ok little sis, I'm proud of you."

"You're the best brother ever," she giggled and promptly fell on the floor. Hattie came running over and scooped her up. "No more champagne for you darling, why don't you go and lie down in the pub, I'm sure Susie won't mind."

Sebastian looked towards the bench where Olivia was sitting with Andrea and Susie.

"Am I the only one who's not pissed?" he grinned. "May I please steal Olivia for a moment?"

Taking her hand, he led her away from the celebrations.

"Georgie's moving out," he told her.

"Yes, she told me. Don't look so sad, she's only on the other side of the estate." Olivia reached up and caressed his cheek. "She's planning on getting the business off the ground in the next month or so. I said I'd help. Perhaps I could even get a horse now I'm staying here?" She looked hopeful.

Sebastian pulled her towards him and planted a kiss on her lips "The only thing you'll be riding in the foreseeable future, my darling, is me. Now can we go home? I want to be alone with you."

Olivia laughed, and gazed up at him with a twinkle in her eyes, "I thought you'd never ask, just don't tell anyone we're going otherwise we'll never get out of here."

Hand in hand, they slowly made their way into the shadows, and wandered back to the manor.

Susie looked at Andrea once they were alone and, fuelled by alcohol, decided it was the right time to broach the subject of Peter.

"So what's the latest with a certain single father-of-two?" She pressed her for information.

"You know we're just friends, stop pushing me." Andrea glared at Susie.

"Bollocks," she snorted. "Friends my arse. He's bonkers about you, and you're madly in love with him, so what's the problem?"

"He just lost his wife."

"Oh, darling." Susie reached out and took her hand. "He didn't just lose his wife, he lost her years ago, really. No one would begrudge either of you some happiness, and if you can find that together, then all the better."

Andrea buckled, she couldn't keep it in any longer. "Of course I love him, how could I not? He's a wonderful man and an even better father, but he needs time. I couldn't make a move, I wouldn't dare. I don't want to rock the boat when we're such good friends. It might ruin everything and I'd rather have him in my life like this than not at all."

"Oh, stop being so obtuse." Susie was exasperated. "What are you waiting for?"

"I'm terrified he'll reject me." Andrea was downcast. "How could I possibly match up to Sarah? Everyone says how wonderful, and fun, and beautiful she was. I'm just a lumpy short-arse, with ridiculous hair."

Susie stared at her in amazement. "You're gorgeous. You've curves in all the right places and a pair of boobs any hot-blooded man would kill to get his hands on, and as for the hair, it's stunning. Always has been, in my mind."

"Now you're just trying to make me feel better," she sniffed.

"Don't be ridiculous," Susie grinned. "So, what are you going to do? I for one refuse to let this go on much longer, so either you deal with it or I'm going to be forced into doing something drastic."

"Susie, leave it, please," Andrea begged. "Let's just enjoy the evening and forget about all the angst. Top up?" She splashed more bubbles into both of their glasses and deposited the empty bottle by their feet.

A rustling in the bushes behind made them jump.

"Sorry, it's only me, didn't mean to startle you both." Peter was standing behind them, looking sheepish.

Andrea gasped: "Were you listening?"

"I couldn't help but overhear." Peter was embarrassed. "Can we talk?"

Needing no prompting, Susie made her excuses and staggered off to find Tom and baby Rosie.

Andrea patted the bench, inviting him to sit next to her.

Peter took a deep breath. "Look, I'm just going to come out and say it. I'm not much good at this kind of stuff, so please just let me speak before you say anything, ok?"

Andrea nodded her agreement.

"I've been stuck for years, not being able to move forward because of Sarah, and when she died I thought my world would cave in, but it didn't. Ever since I met you I've been beating myself up, wracked with guilt because of how much I felt, and do feel, for you. Losing Sarah the way we did was heartbreaking, but life goes on and I know she'd want me to be happy. I understand if you think it's too soon, but please believe me when I say my feelings are true, I'm not grief-ridden and making bad decisions, life's too short and I want to get on with mine."

Andrea was stunned, and sat opened mouthed for a full minute before she replied. "Oh Peter," she whispered breathlessly. "Are you sure this is what you want? I mean, are you sure I'm what you want?"

Taking her hand in his, he replied: "I've never been so sure in my life about anything. Could it be possible that you love me too?"

"I do," she breathed.

"And will you allow me to kiss you?"

"I will." She readily granted his wish.

Peter pulled her towards him and kissed her with the lightest of touches as she melted into his arms.

"Evie and Teddy are at my sister's tonight." It was a statement that needed no explanation. Holding hands, they stood up and walked away from the duck pond, in the direction of Andrea's cottage. They did not care that the entire village was watching them.

Chapter 65

Five days later, St Saviour's church was packed to the rafters for the christening of Rosie Feltham, where her godparents, Olivia and Sebastian, proudly stood at the font and promised to guide her in her Christian life.

Everyone was delighted to see Peter and the kids arrive at the christening with Andrea. They already looked like a proper little family, and Evie held on tightly to Andrea's hand all through the service with a big grin on her face. Teddy was telling anyone who would listen that he was going to have a new mummy and Peter nodded in agreement. As a couple they looked blissfully happy, and as a family they looked like the perfect unit.

With the service at an end, the guests quickly exited the church and made their way across the green to the Riverside Inn where the party was taking place.

Olivia and Sebastian were among the last to leave and, as they walked hand in hand through the graveyard, he pulled her to one side and whispered in her ear: "I've got something to show you, come with me."

"You're incorrigible," she laughed.

"No, not that," Sebastian grinned. "Come here." He led her over to the 'Lovers' Oak tree that she had so admired when she had first come to the village.

"Look." He took her hand and ran it over the rough bark of the trunk until it reached a fresh set of engravings. "I've been dying to bring you here but I wanted it to be perfect. Today just seemed like the right day for it."

Olivia gasped. There, etched deep into the wood, were the initials O and S intertwined with a B. "When did you do that?"

"Before I left for Scotland. I didn't know if you'd come to me, but I hoped with all my heart that you would. It felt right to wipe out the past and pin my hopes for the future on this old bit of wood, somehow."

Olivia scanned the surface for Sebastian's original carving all those years ago, and found it was nowhere to be seen, just a smooth patch of wood remained, no longer a painful reminder of the past.

"It's beautiful Sebastian, thank you." She threw her arms around him.

"There's one more thing I need from you," he said, staring deep into her eyes with an intensity that rocked her very core.

"Anything," she whispered.

"Will you marry me, Olivia Carmichael?"

The joy in her face, and the depth of her kiss, were all he needed to know that her answer was "yes!".

The End

Dear reader,

We hope you enjoyed reading *The Sweet Spot*. Please take a moment to leave a review, even if it's a short one. Your opinion is important to us.

Discover more books by Anneli Lort at
https://www.nextchapter.pub/authors/anneli-lort

Want to know when one of our books is free or discounted? Join the newsletter at
http://eepurl.com/bqqB3H

Best regards,
Anneli Lort and the Next Chapter Team

The story continues in:

Flowers In Bloom

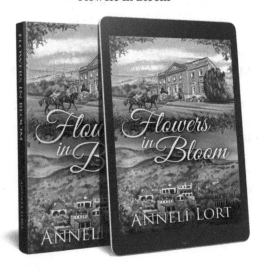

To read the first chapter for free, please head to:
https://www.nextchapter.pub/books/flowers-in-bloom

About the Author

Anneli Lort lived with a charming cast of characters in her head for a number of years before she found the time to sit down and bring them to life in the Appleton Vale series. Once she put pen to paper her imagination was free to create a character driven world of contemporary romance that is both heartwarming and engaging.

In a public relations career that spanned more than two decades Anneli worked for some of the world's biggest sporting companies. With this came an access-all-areas pass to some of the greatest sports events on the planet where she saw for herself the tension, drama and emotions that were played out behind the scenes.

While TV audiences around the world watched the sporting excitement unfold, she was there to witness first-hand what really happened before and afterwards – the untold stories the rest of the world never got to see. Using this unique insight into the tangled lives and loves of professional athletes Anneli developed the idea that eventually became The Sweet Spot.

Anneli lives in a village much like her fictional creation - Appleton Vale - that is nestled against the foothills of the South Downs. She spends her days working in brand communications, writing, walking the dogs – Hector and Milo – and riding her New Forest Pony Henry. The dogs share the house; the horse has his own rather spacious accommodation.

She is currently using her wealth of experience to write the follow-up books to The Sweet Spot.

The Sweet Spot
ISBN: 978-4-86751-737-6 (Mass Market)

Published by
Next Chapter
1-60-20 Minami-Otsuka
170-0005 Toshima-Ku, Tokyo
+818035793528
14th July 2021

Lightning Source UK Ltd.
Milton Keynes UK
UKHW041938010821
388033UK00001B/28